JF V. 2

Justice League adventures

JUSTICE LEAGUE ADVENTURES

FRIENDS AND FOES

Written by:

Michael Bernard

Jason Hall

Matthew Manning

Scott McCloud

Dan Slott

Colored by:

John Kalisz

Illustrated by:

Rick Burchett

John Delaney

Min S. Ku

Mark Propst

John K. Snyder III

Lettered by:

Kurt Hathaway

Bill Oakley

*JUSTICE LEAGUE ADVENTURES VOL. 2:
FRIENDS AND FOES*
Published by DC Comics. Cover and compilation copyright © 2004 DC
Comics. All Rights Reserved. Originally published in single magazine
form as JUSTICE LEAGUE ADVENTURES 13, 14, 16, 19 and 20. Copyright
© 2003 DC Comics. All Rights Reserved. All characters, their distinctive
likenesses and related indicia featured in this publication are trademarks
of DC Comics. The stories, characters and incidents featured in this
publication are entirely fictional. DC Comics does not read or accept
unsolicited submissions of ideas, stories or artwork.

CARTOON NETWORK and its logo are trademarks of Cartoon Network.

DC Comics, 1700 Broadway, New York, NY 10019
A Warner Bros. Entertainment Company.
Printed in Canada. First Printing.
ISBN: 1-4012-0180-6
Cover illustration by Butch Lukic.
Publication design by John J. Hill

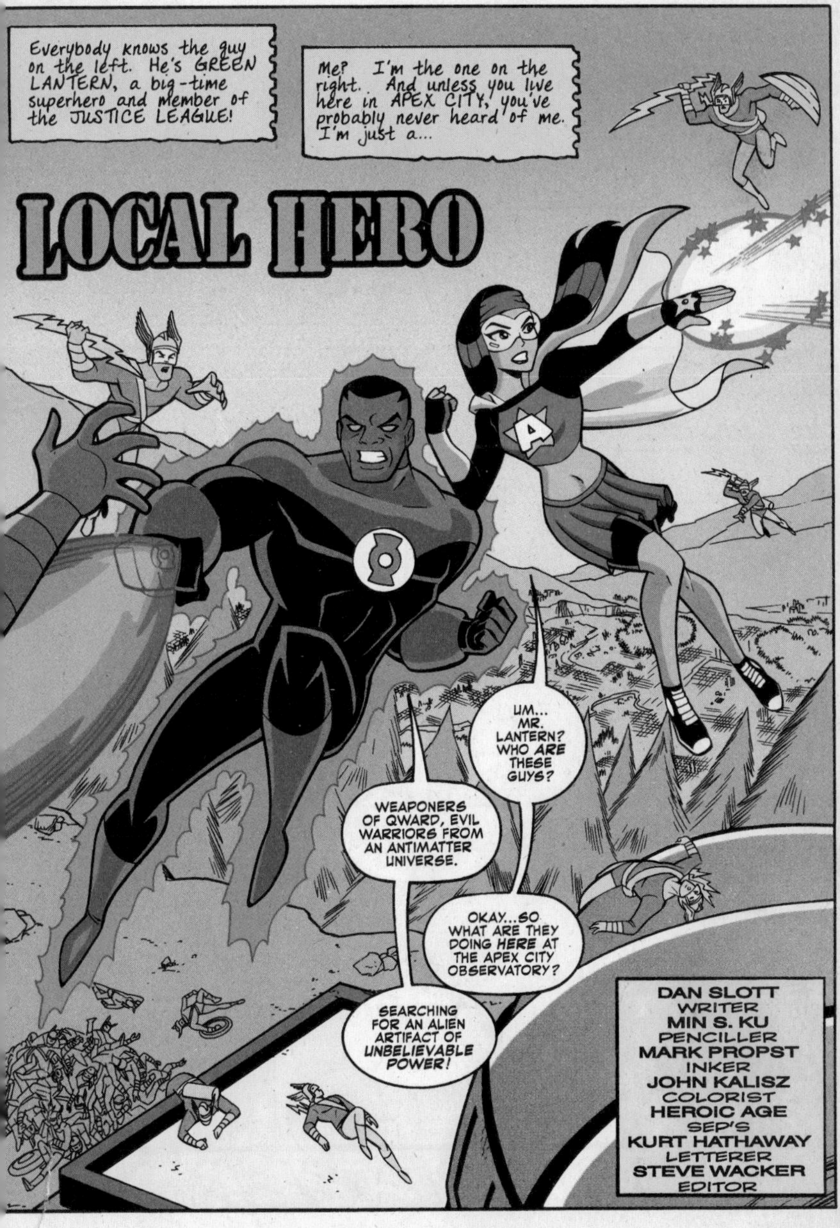
Everybody knows the guy on the left. He's GREEN LANTERN, a big-time superhero and member of the JUSTICE LEAGUE!
Me? I'm the one on the right. And unless you live here in APEX CITY, you've probably never heard of me. I'm just a...
LOCAL HERO
UM... MR. LANTERN? WHO ARE THESE GUYS?
WEAPONERS OF QWARD, EVIL WARRIORS FROM AN ANTIMATTER UNIVERSE.
OKAY...SO WHAT ARE THEY DOING HERE AT THE APEX CITY OBSERVATORY?
SEARCHING FOR AN ALIEN ARTIFACT OF UNBELIEVABLE POWER!
DAN SLOTT WRITER
MIN S. KU PENCILLER
MARK PROPST INKER
JOHN KALISZ COLORIST
HEROIC AGE SEP'S
KURT HATHAWAY LETTERER
STEVE WACKER EDITOR

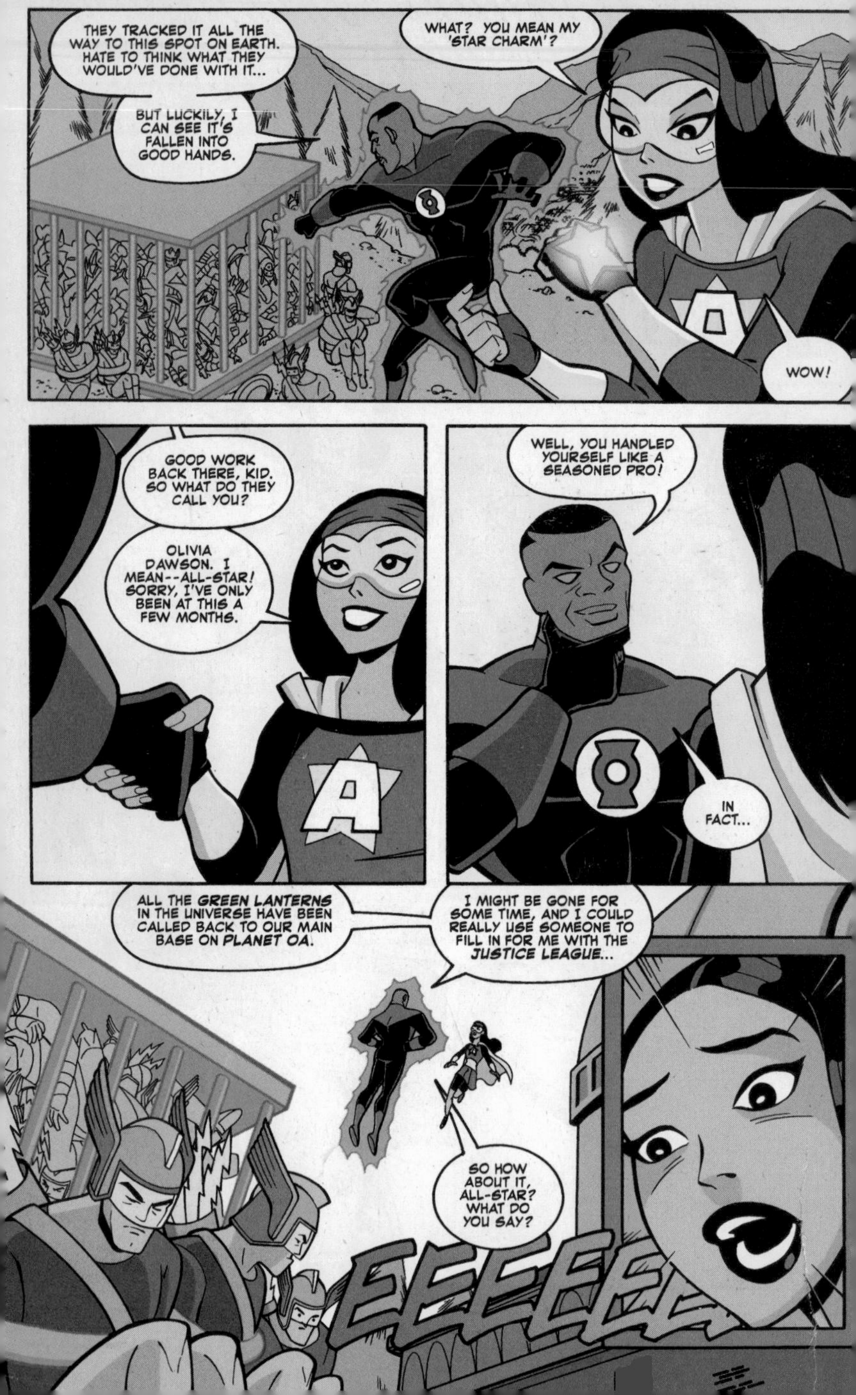
THEY TRACKED IT ALL THE WAY TO THIS SPOT ON EARTH. HATE TO THINK WHAT THEY WOULD'VE DONE WITH IT...
BUT LUCKILY, I CAN SEE IT'S FALLEN INTO GOOD HANDS.
WHAT? YOU MEAN MY 'STAR CHARM'?
WOW!
GOOD WORK BACK THERE, KID. SO WHAT DO THEY CALL YOU?
OLIVIA DAWSON. I MEAN--ALL-STAR! SORRY, I'VE ONLY BEEN AT THIS A FEW MONTHS.
WELL, YOU HANDLED YOURSELF LIKE A SEASONED PRO!
IN FACT...
ALL THE GREEN LANTERNS IN THE UNIVERSE HAVE BEEN CALLED BACK TO OUR MAIN BASE ON PLANET OA.
I MIGHT BE GONE FOR SOME TIME, AND I COULD REALLY USE SOMEONE TO FILL IN FOR ME WITH THE JUSTICE LEAGUE...
SO HOW ABOUT IT, ALL-STAR? WHAT DO YOU SAY?
EEEEEE

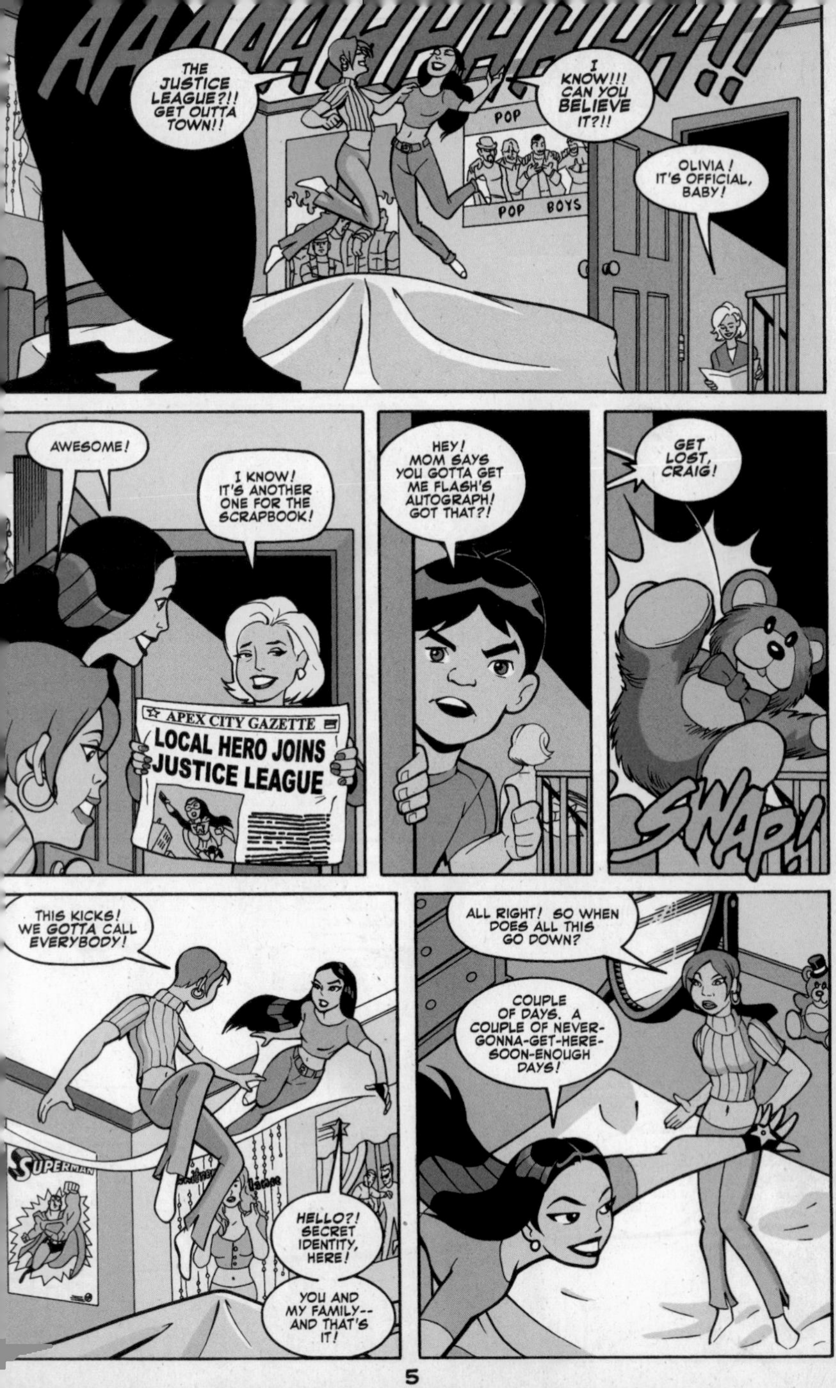
AAAAAHHHHHH!!
THE JUSTICE LEAGUE?!! GET OUTTA TOWN!!
I KNOW!!! CAN YOU BELIEVE IT?!!
POP
POP BOYS
OLIVIA! IT'S OFFICIAL, BABY!
AWESOME!
I KNOW! IT'S ANOTHER ONE FOR THE SCRAPBOOK!
APEX CITY GAZETTE
LOCAL HERO JOINS JUSTICE LEAGUE
HEY! MOM SAYS YOU GOTTA GET ME FLASH'S AUTOGRAPH! GOT THAT?!
GET LOST, CRAIG!
SWAP!
THIS KICKS! WE GOTTA CALL EVERYBODY!
SUPERMAN
HELLO?! SECRET IDENTITY, HERE!
YOU AND MY FAMILY-- AND THAT'S IT!
ALL RIGHT! SO WHEN DOES ALL THIS GO DOWN?
COUPLE OF DAYS. A COUPLE OF NEVER-GONNA-GET-HERE-SOON-ENOUGH DAYS!

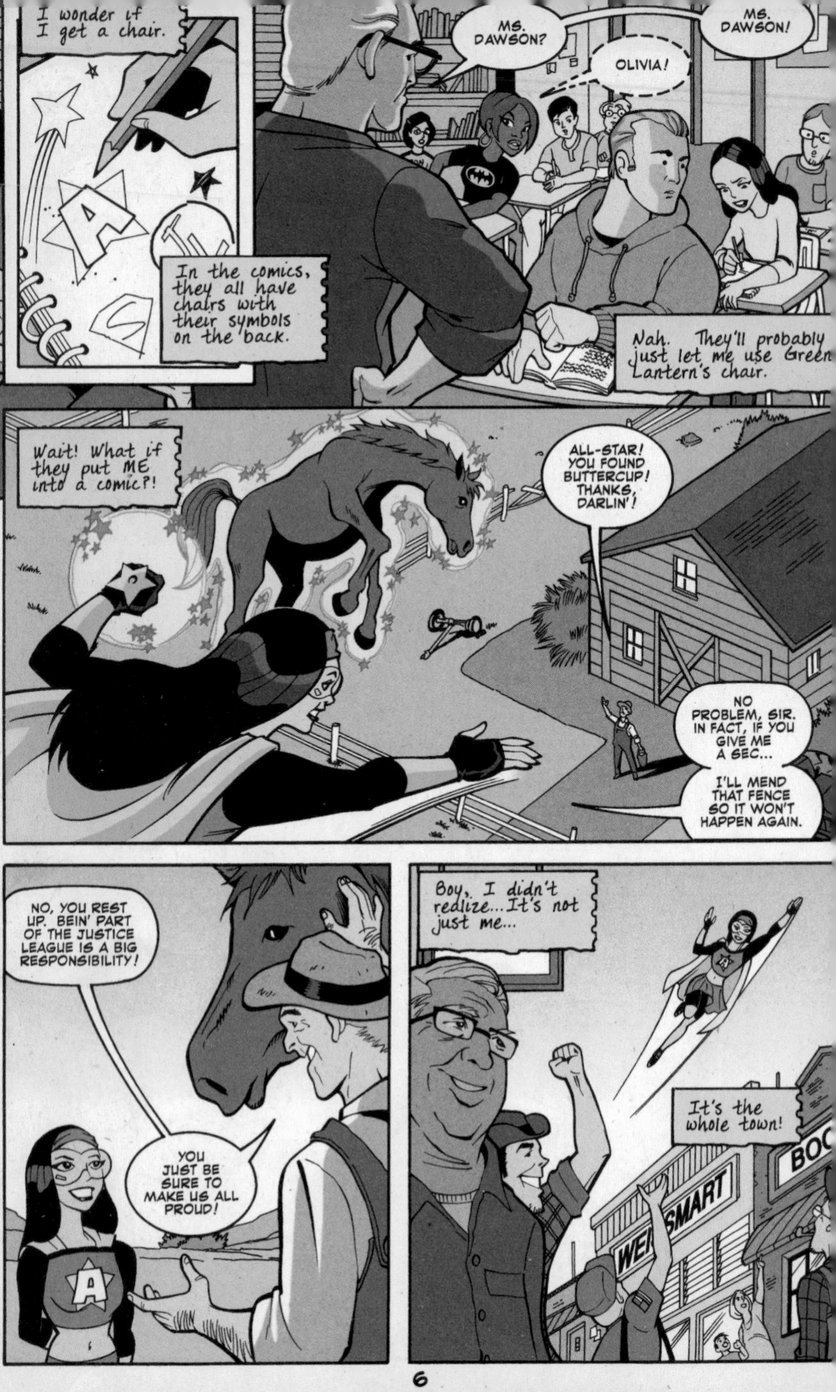

I wonder if I get a chair.
MS. DAWSON?
MS. DAWSON!
OLIVIA!
In the comics, they all have chairs with their symbols on the back.
Nah. They'll probably just let me use Green Lantern's chair.
Wait! What if they put ME into a comic?!
ALL-STAR! YOU FOUND BUTTERCUP! THANKS, DARLIN'!
NO PROBLEM, SIR. IN FACT, IF YOU GIVE ME A SEC...
I'LL MEND THAT FENCE SO IT WON'T HAPPEN AGAIN.
NO, YOU REST UP. BEIN' PART OF THE JUSTICE LEAGUE IS A BIG RESPONSIBILITY!
YOU JUST BE SURE TO MAKE US ALL PROUD!
Boy, I didn't realize... It's not just me...
It's the whole town!

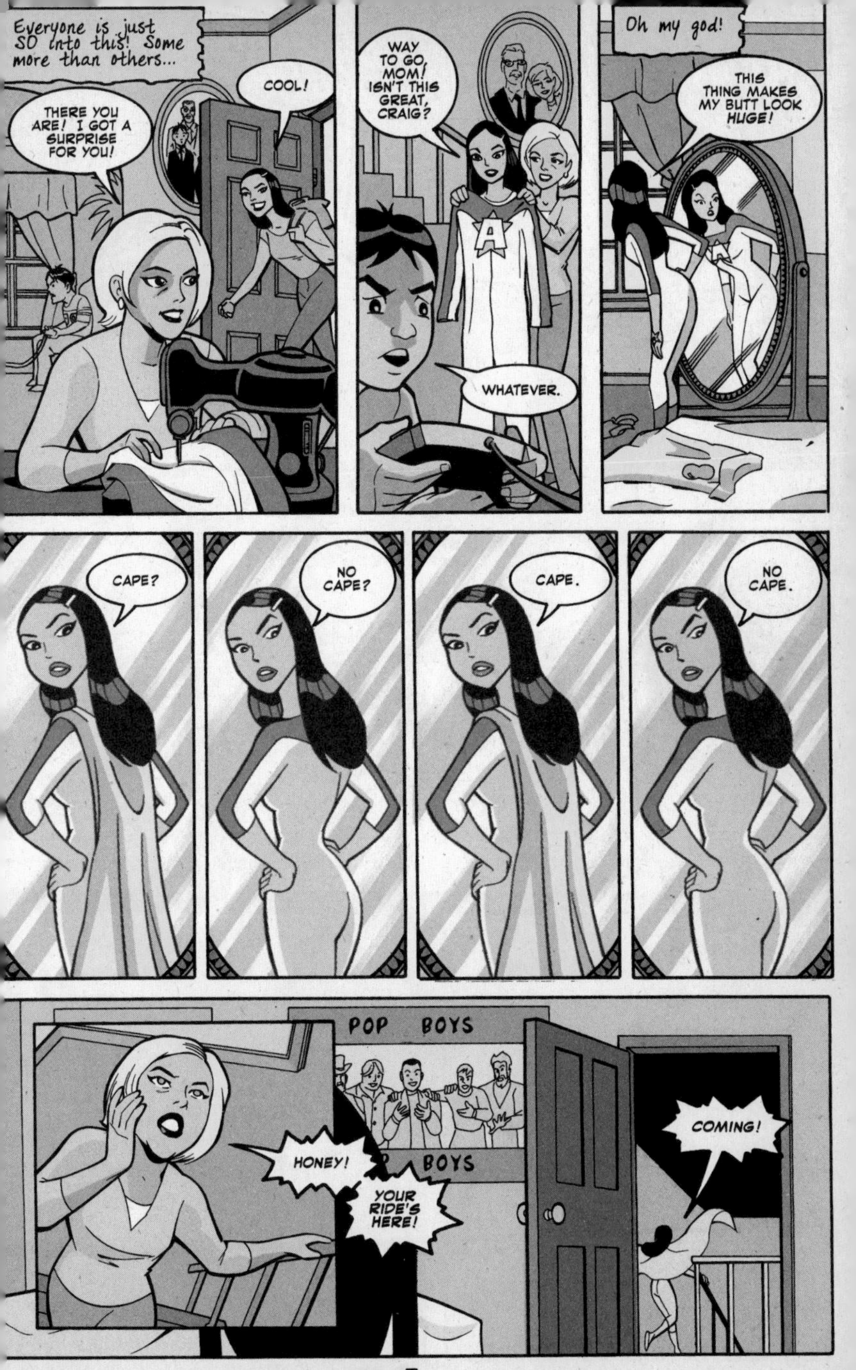

Everyone is just SO into this! Some more than others...
THERE YOU ARE! I GOT A SURPRISE FOR YOU!
COOL!
WAY TO GO, MOM! ISN'T THIS GREAT, CRAIG?
WHATEVER.
Oh my god!
THIS THING MAKES MY BUTT LOOK HUGE!
CAPE?
NO CAPE?
CAPE.
NO CAPE.
POP BOYS
HONEY!
YOUR RIDE'S HERE!
COMING!

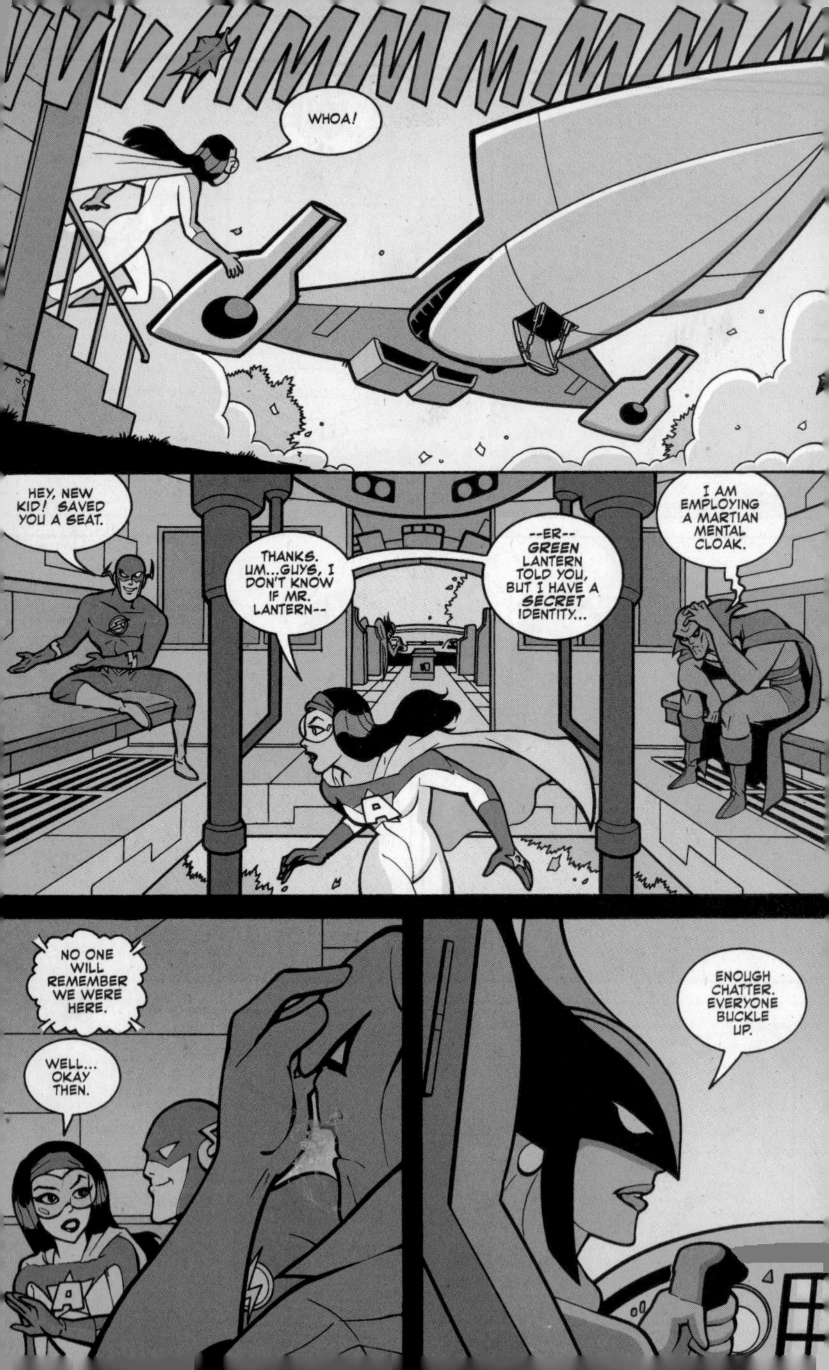
VVVMMMMMMMMMM
WHOA!
HEY, NEW KID! SAVED YOU A SEAT.
THANKS. UM...GUYS, I DON'T KNOW IF MR. LANTERN--
--ER-- GREEN LANTERN TOLD YOU, BUT I HAVE A SECRET IDENTITY...
I AM EMPLOYING A MARTIAN MENTAL CLOAK.
NO ONE WILL REMEMBER WE WERE HERE.
WELL... OKAY THEN.
ENOUGH CHATTER. EVERYONE BUCKLE UP.

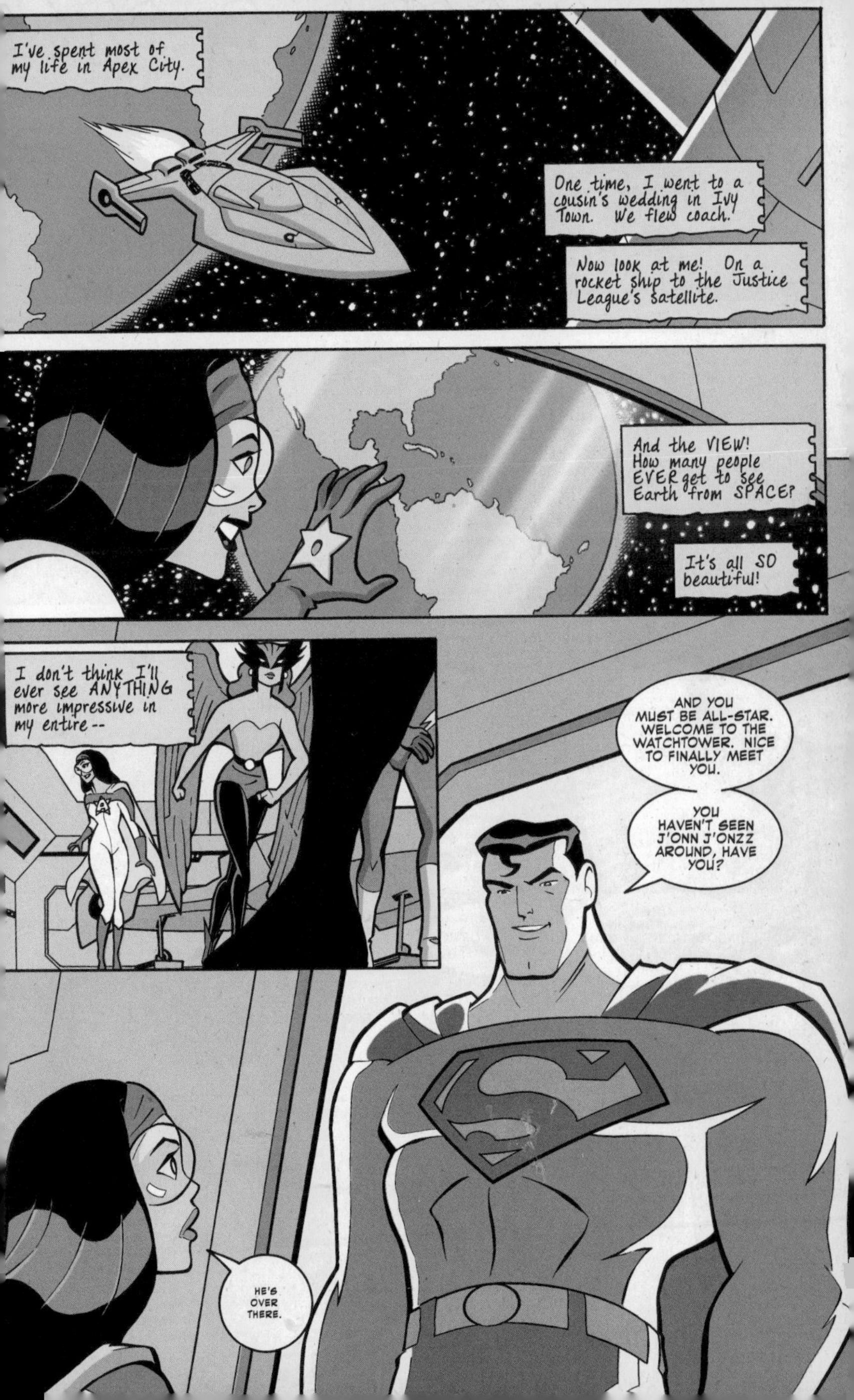
I've spent most of my life in Apex City.
One time, I went to a cousin's wedding in Ivy Town. We flew coach.
Now look at me! On a rocket ship to the Justice League's satellite.
And the VIEW! How many people EVER get to see Earth from SPACE?
It's all SO beautiful!
I don't think I'll ever see ANYTHING more impressive in my entire --
AND YOU MUST BE ALL-STAR. WELCOME TO THE WATCHTOWER. NICE TO FINALLY MEET YOU.
YOU HAVEN'T SEEN J'ONN J'ONZZ AROUND, HAVE YOU?
HE'S OVER THERE.

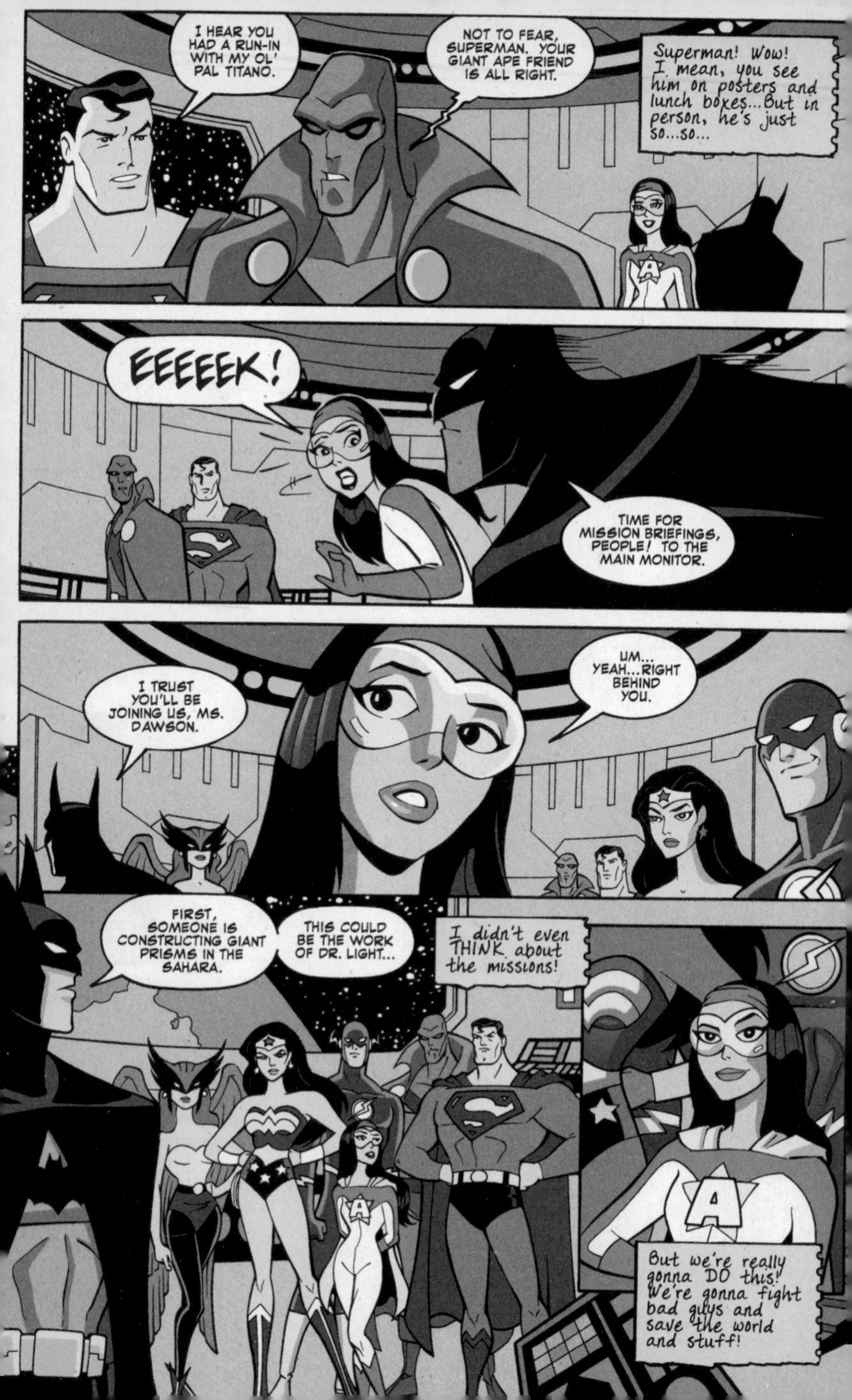

I HEAR YOU HAD A RUN-IN WITH MY OL' PAL TITANO.
NOT TO FEAR, SUPERMAN. YOUR GIANT APE FRIEND IS ALL RIGHT.
Superman! Wow! I mean, you see him on posters and lunch boxes...But in person, he's just so...so...
EEEEEK!
TIME FOR MISSION BRIEFINGS, PEOPLE! TO THE MAIN MONITOR.
I TRUST YOU'LL BE JOINING US, MS. DAWSON.
UM... YEAH...RIGHT BEHIND YOU.
FIRST, SOMEONE IS CONSTRUCTING GIANT PRISMS IN THE SAHARA.
THIS COULD BE THE WORK OF DR. LIGHT...
I didn't even THINK about the missions!
But we're really gonna DO this! We're gonna fight bad guys and save the world and stuff!

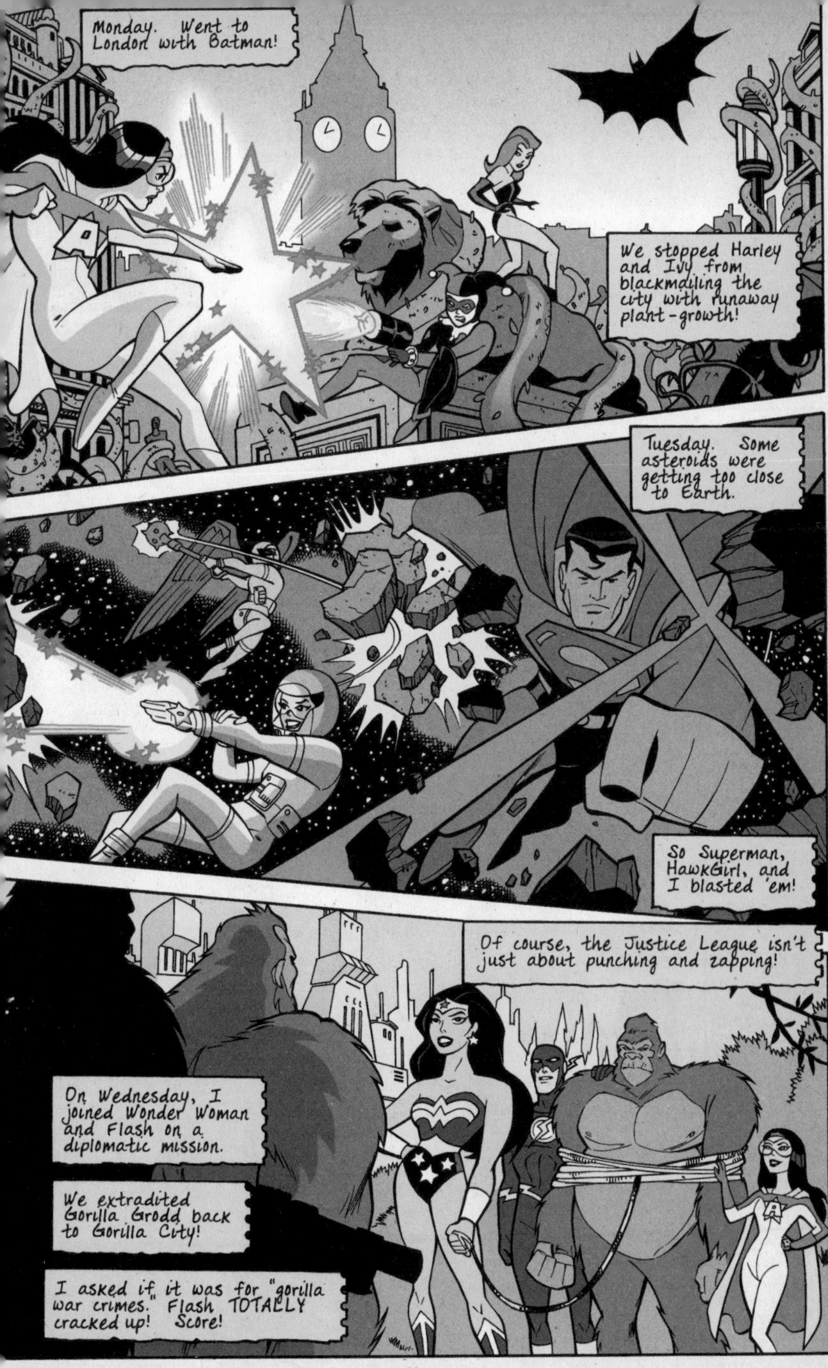

Monday. Went to London with Batman!
We stopped Harley and Ivy from blackmailing the city with runaway plant-growth!
Tuesday. Some asteroids were getting too close to Earth.
So Superman, HawkGirl, and I blasted 'em!
Of course, the Justice League isn't just about punching and zapping!
On Wednesday, I joined Wonder Woman and Flash on a diplomatic mission.
We extradited Gorilla Grodd back to Gorilla City!
I asked if it was for "gorilla war crimes." Flash TOTALLY cracked up! Score!

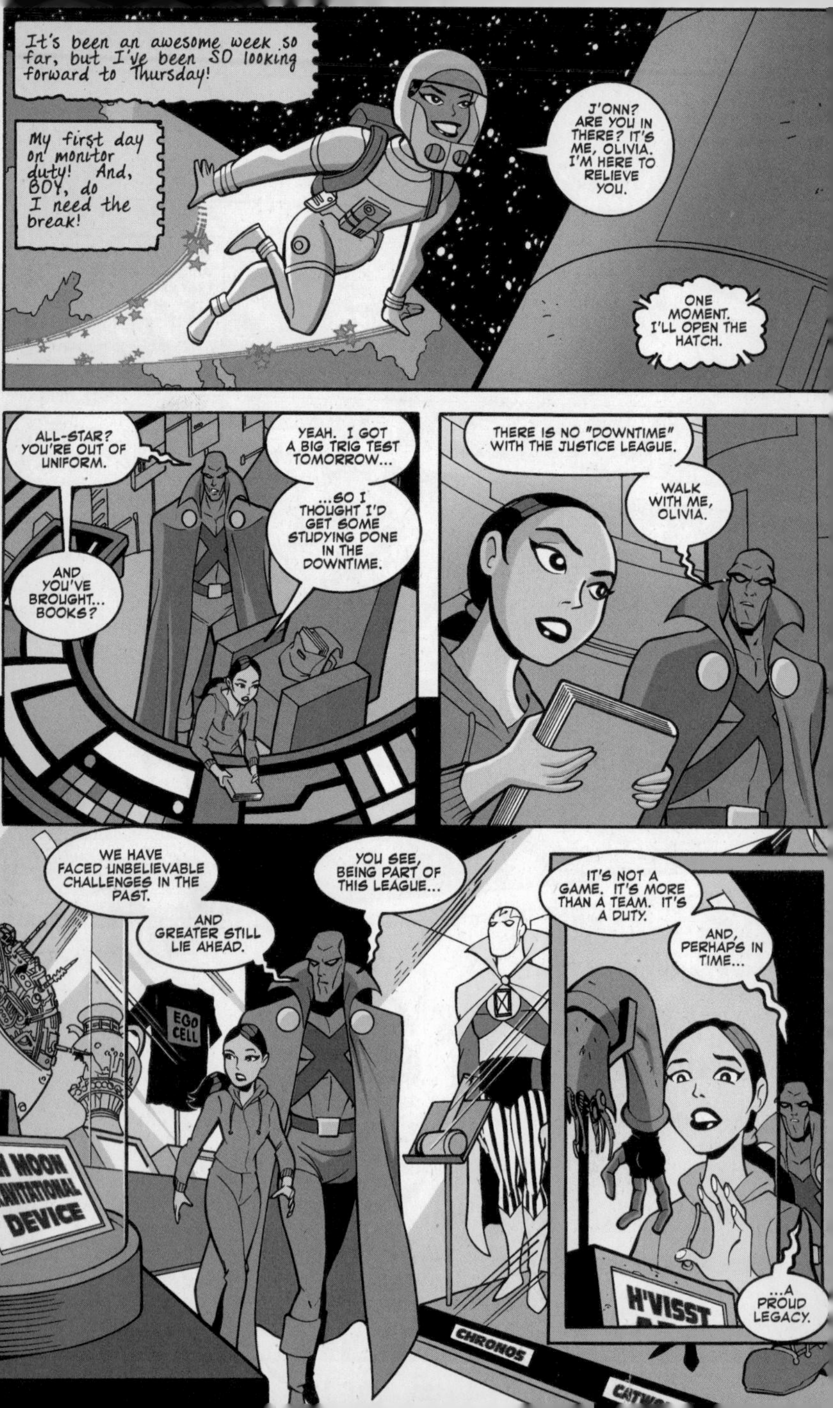
It's been an awesome week so far, but I've been SO looking forward to Thursday!
My first day on monitor duty! And, BOY, do I need the break!
J'ONN? ARE YOU IN THERE? IT'S ME, OLIVIA. I'M HERE TO RELIEVE YOU.
ONE MOMENT. I'LL OPEN THE HATCH.
ALL-STAR? YOU'RE OUT OF UNIFORM.
AND YOU'VE BROUGHT... BOOKS?
YEAH. I GOT A BIG TRIG TEST TOMORROW...
...SO I THOUGHT I'D GET SOME STUDYING DONE IN THE DOWNTIME.
THERE IS NO "DOWNTIME" WITH THE JUSTICE LEAGUE.
WALK WITH ME, OLIVIA.
WE HAVE FACED UNBELIEVABLE CHALLENGES IN THE PAST.
AND GREATER STILL LIE AHEAD.
YOU SEE, BEING PART OF THIS LEAGUE...
IT'S NOT A GAME. IT'S MORE THAN A TEAM. IT'S A DUTY.
AND, PERHAPS IN TIME...
...A PROUD LEGACY.
EGO CELL
CHRONOS
H'VISST

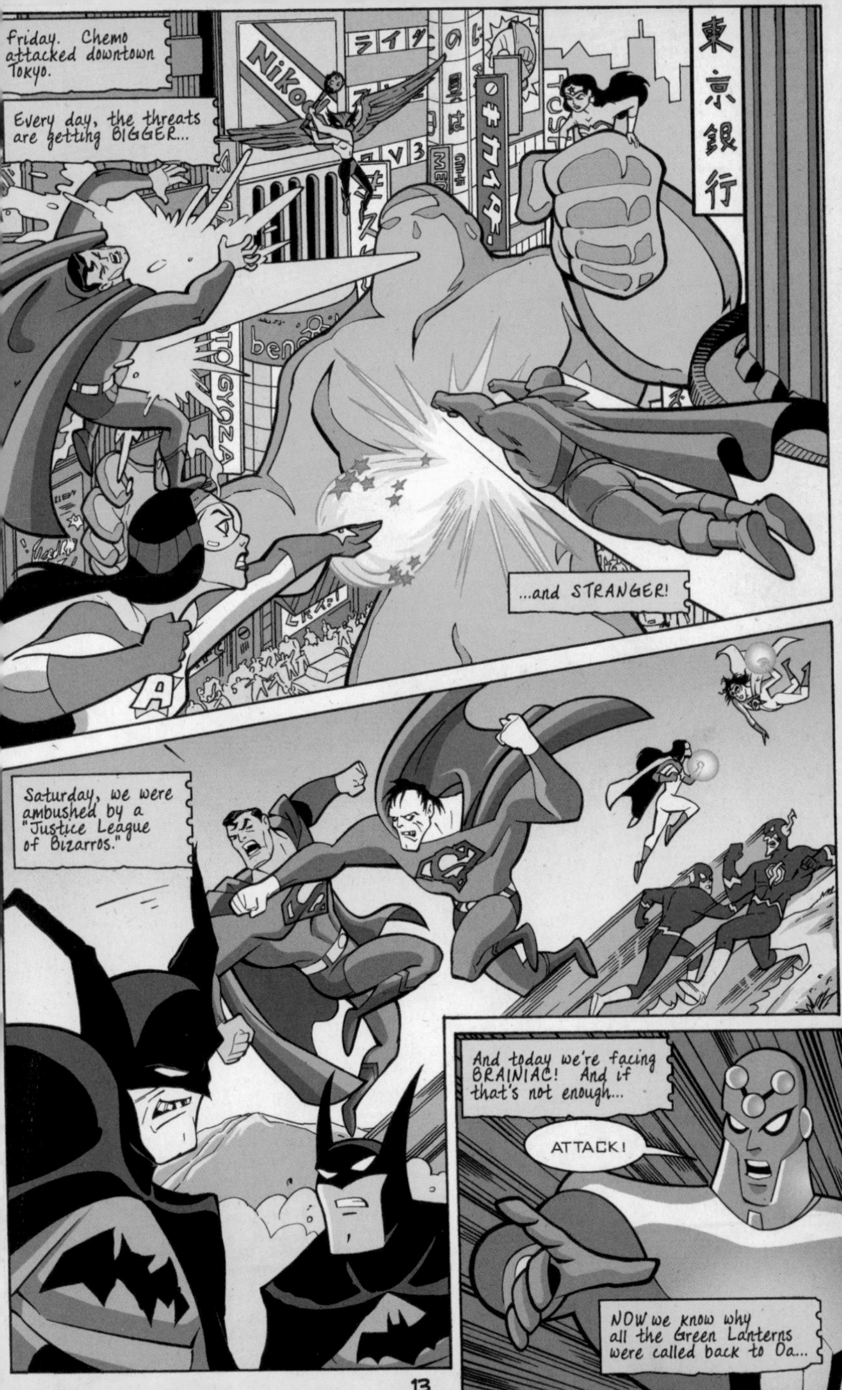
friday. Chemo attacked downtown Tokyo.
Every day, the threats are getting BIGGER...
東京銀行
...and STRANGER!
Saturday, we were ambushed by a "Justice League of Bizarros."
And today we're facing BRAINIAC! And if that's not enough...
ATTACK!
NOW we know why all the Green Lanterns were called back to Oa...

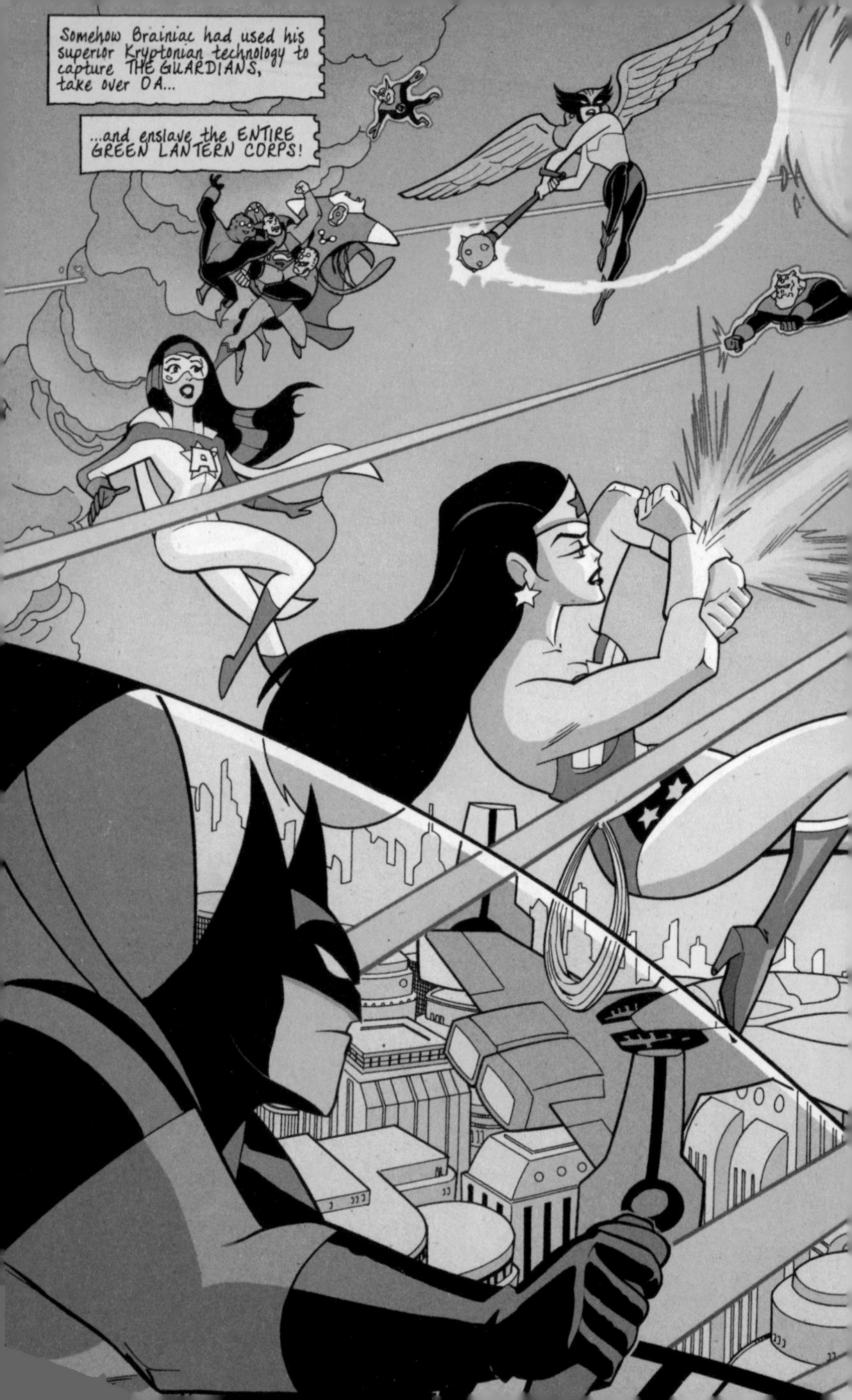
Somehow Brainiac had used his superior Kryptonian technology to capture THE GUARDIANS, take over OA...
...and enslave the ENTIRE GREEN LANTERN CORPS!

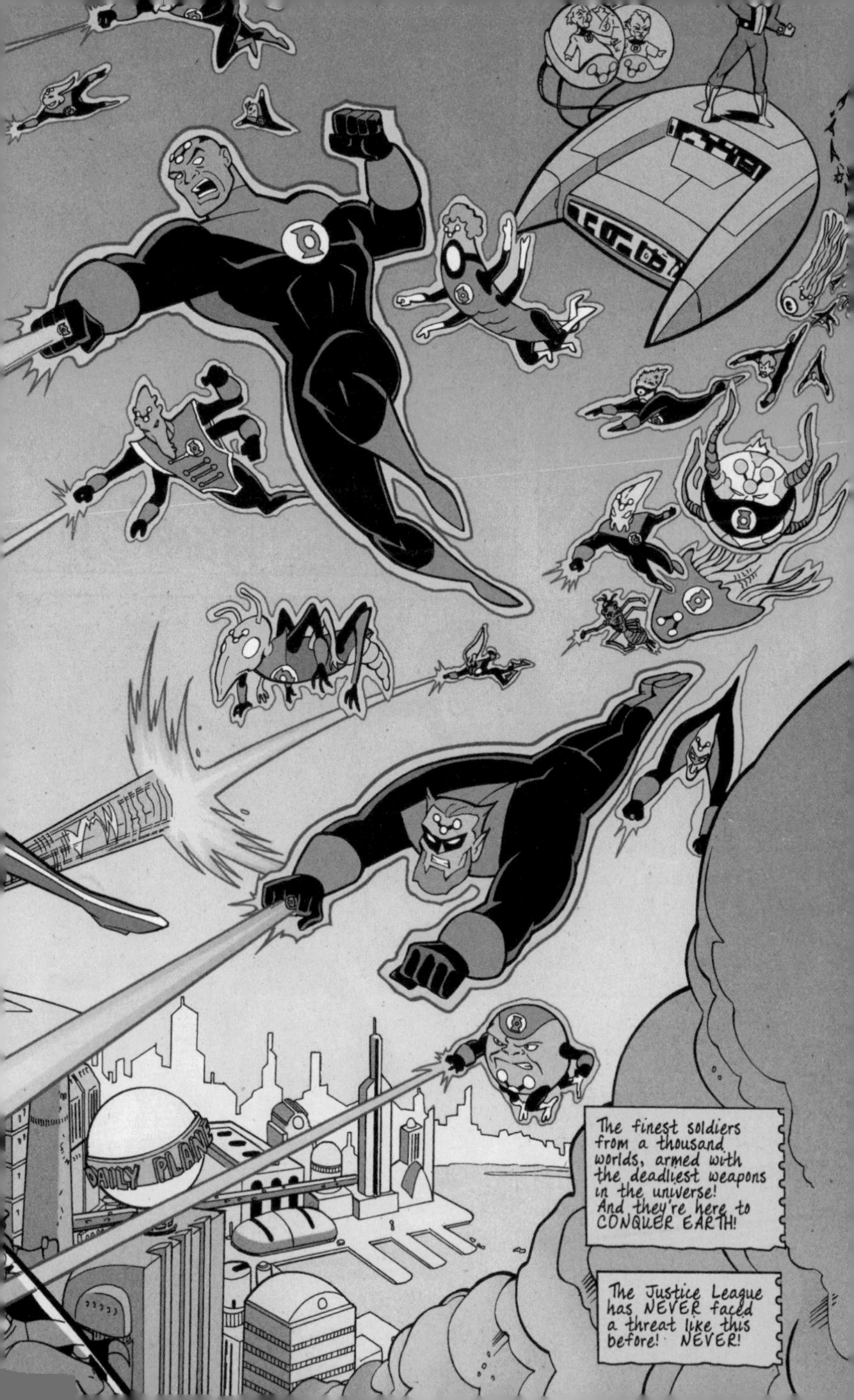

The finest soldiers from a thousand worlds, armed with the deadliest weapons in the universe! And they're here to CONQUER EARTH!
The Justice League has NEVER faced a threat like this before! NEVER!
DAILY PLANET

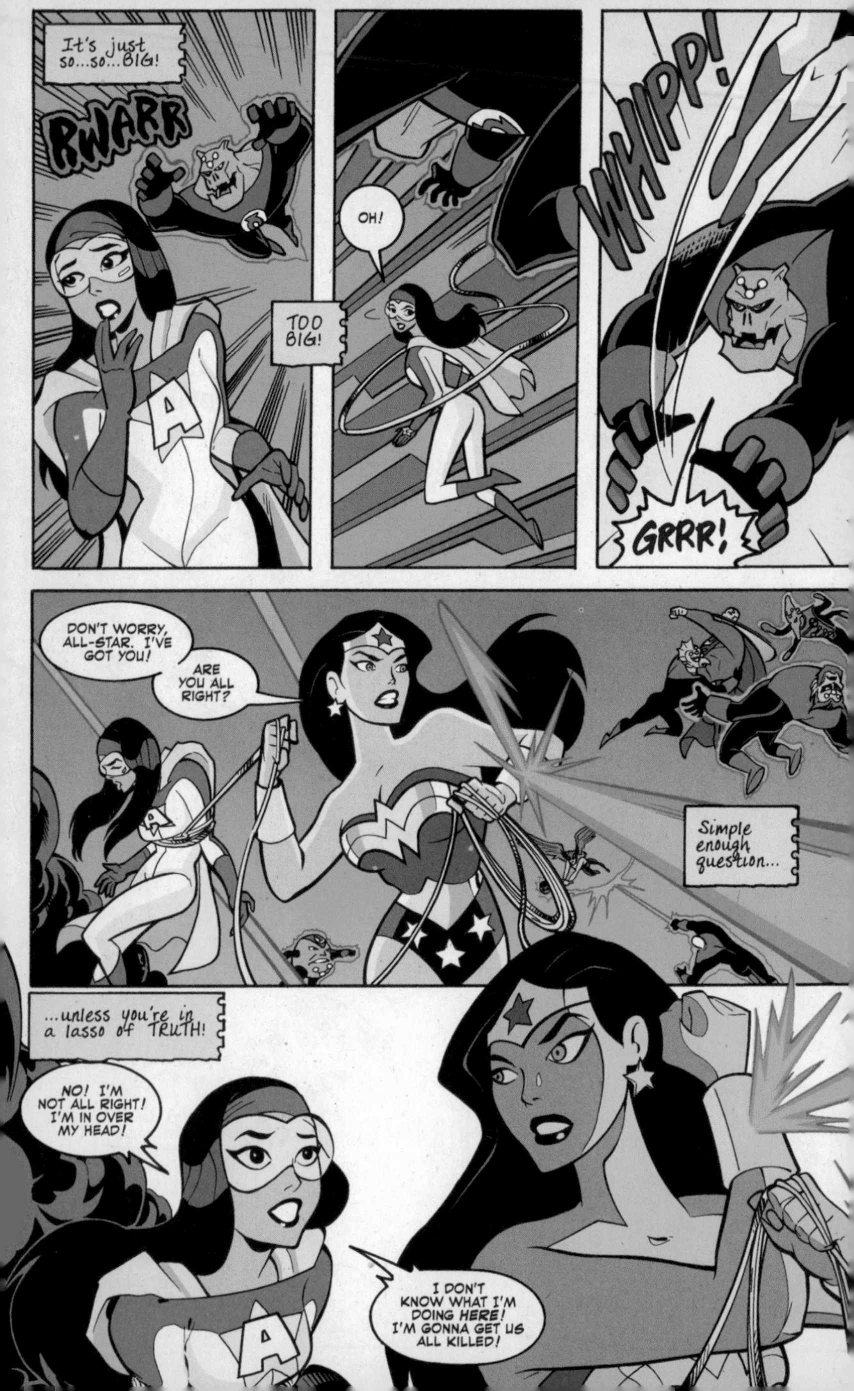
It's just so...so...BIG!
RWARR
OH!
TOO BIG!
WHIPP!
GRRR!
DON'T WORRY, ALL-STAR. I'VE GOT YOU!
ARE YOU ALL RIGHT?
Simple enough question...
...unless you're in a lasso of TRUTH!
NO! I'M NOT ALL RIGHT! I'M IN OVER MY HEAD!
I DON'T KNOW WHAT I'M DOING HERE! I'M GONNA GET US ALL KILLED!

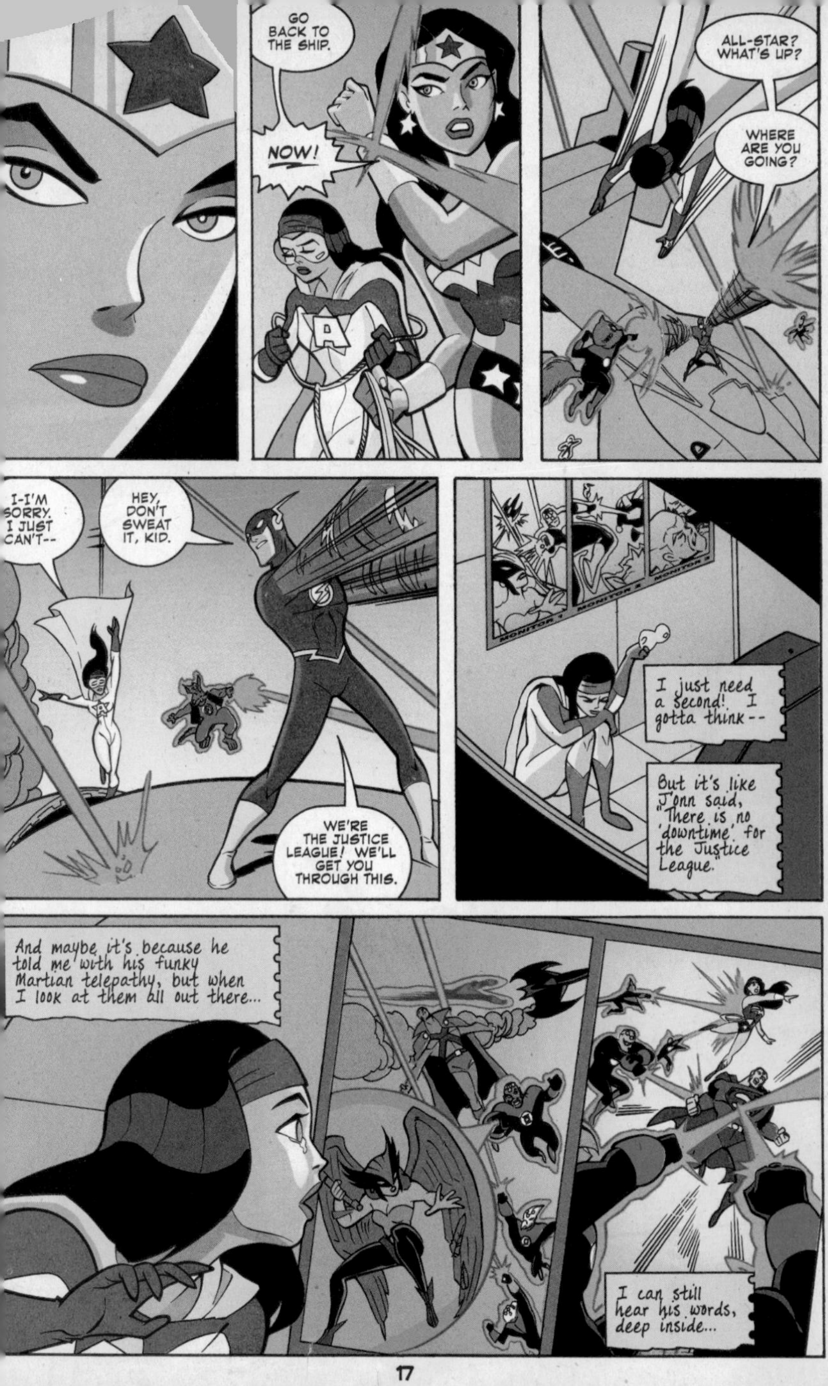
GO BACK TO THE SHIP.
NOW!
ALL-STAR? WHAT'S UP?
WHERE ARE YOU GOING?
I-I'M SORRY. I JUST CAN'T--
HEY, DON'T SWEAT IT, KID.
WE'RE THE JUSTICE LEAGUE! WE'LL GET YOU THROUGH THIS.
MONITOR 1
MONITOR 2
MONITOR 3
I just need a second! I gotta think--
But it's like J'onn said, "There is no 'downtime' for the Justice League."
And maybe it's because he told me with his funky Martian telepathy, but when I look at them all out there...
I can still hear his words, deep inside...

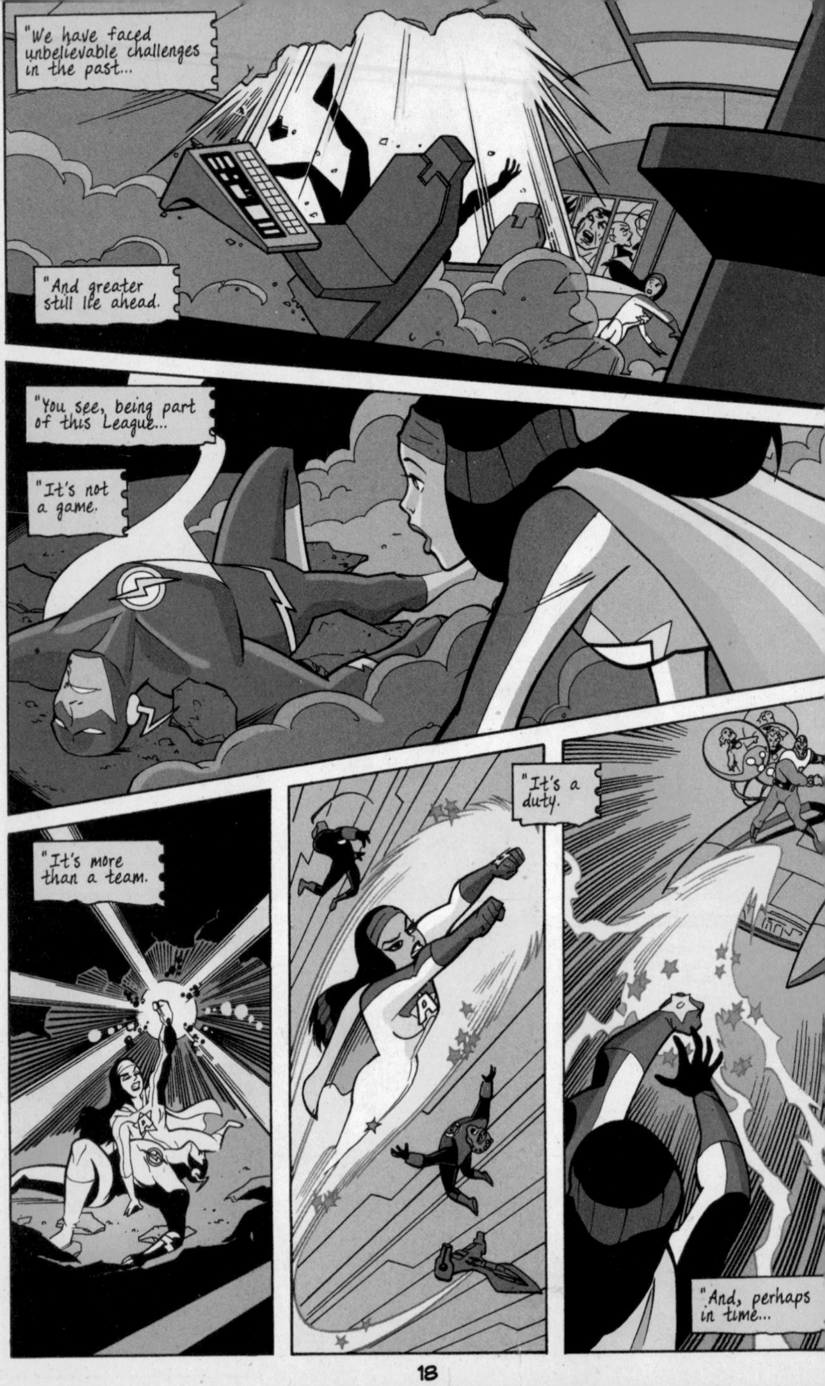
"We have faced unbelievable challenges in the past...
"And greater still lie ahead.
"You see, being part of this League...
"It's not a game.
"It's more than a team.
"It's a duty.
"And, perhaps in time...

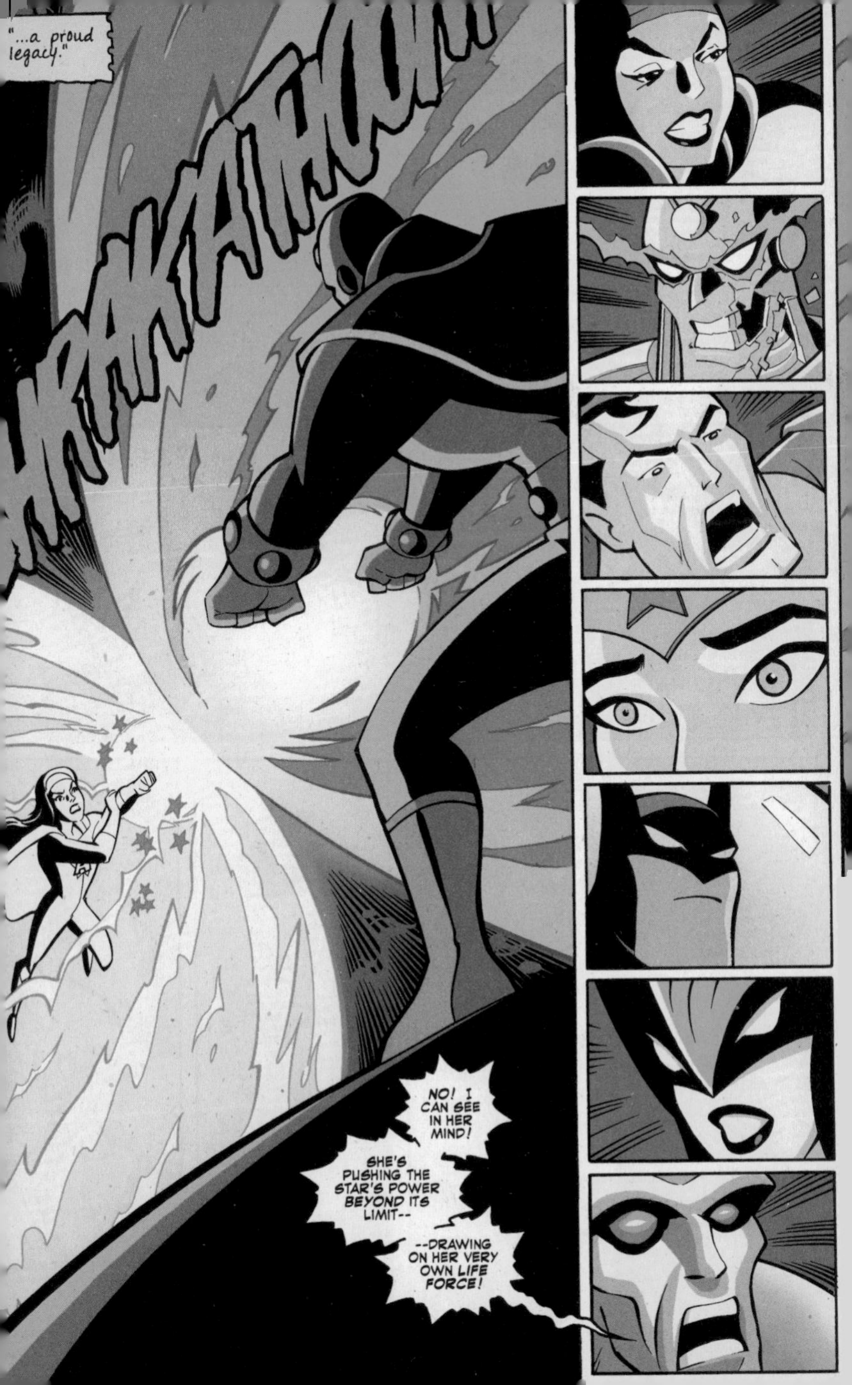
"...a proud legacy."
KRAKATHOOM
NO! I CAN SEE IN HER MIND!
SHE'S PUSHING THE STAR'S POWER BEYOND ITS LIMIT--
--DRAWING ON HER VERY OWN LIFE FORCE!

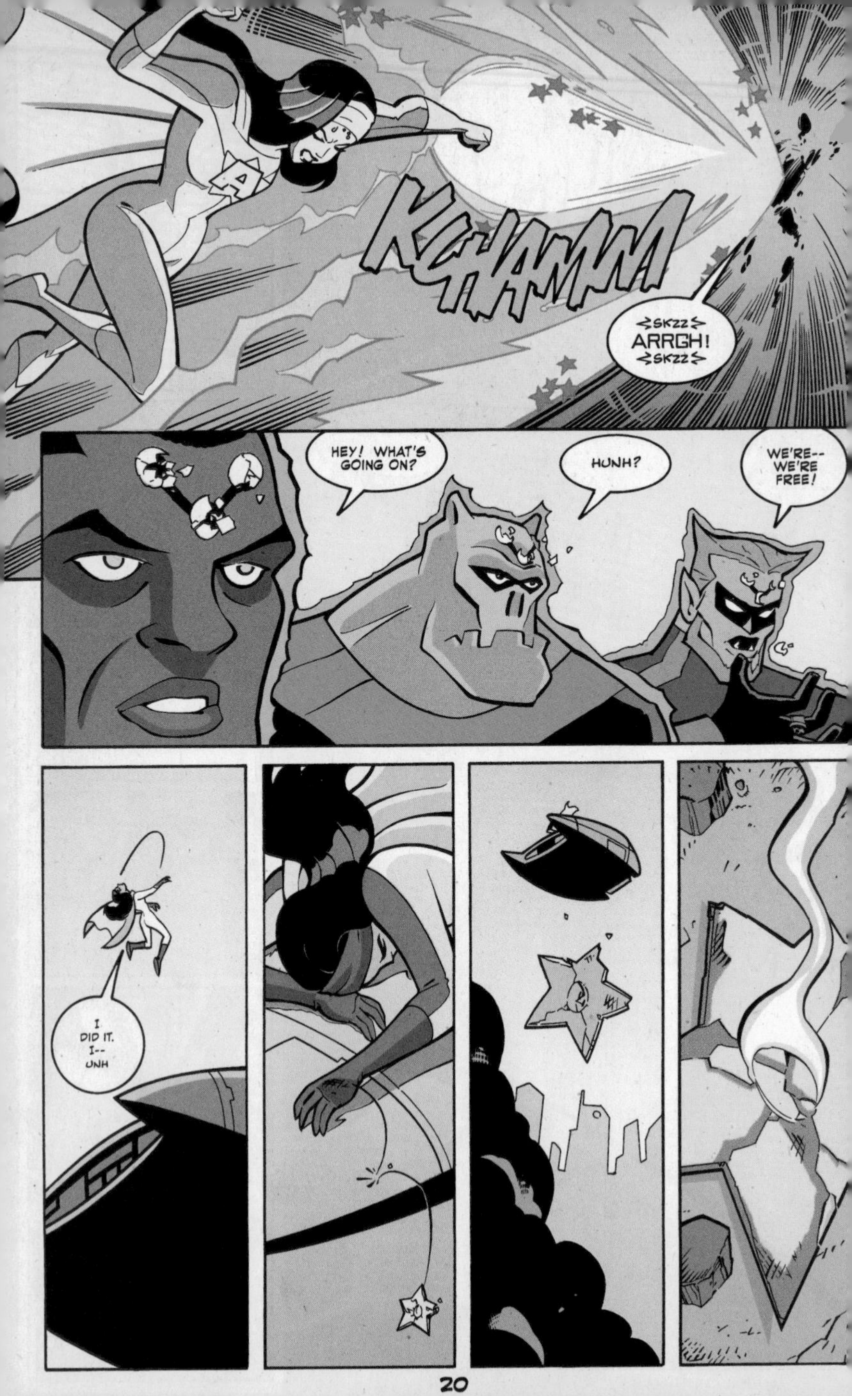
KCHAMMM
≷SKZZ≶ ARRGH! ≷SKZZ≶
HEY! WHAT'S GOING ON?
HUNH?
WE'RE-- WE'RE FREE!
I DID IT. I-- UNH

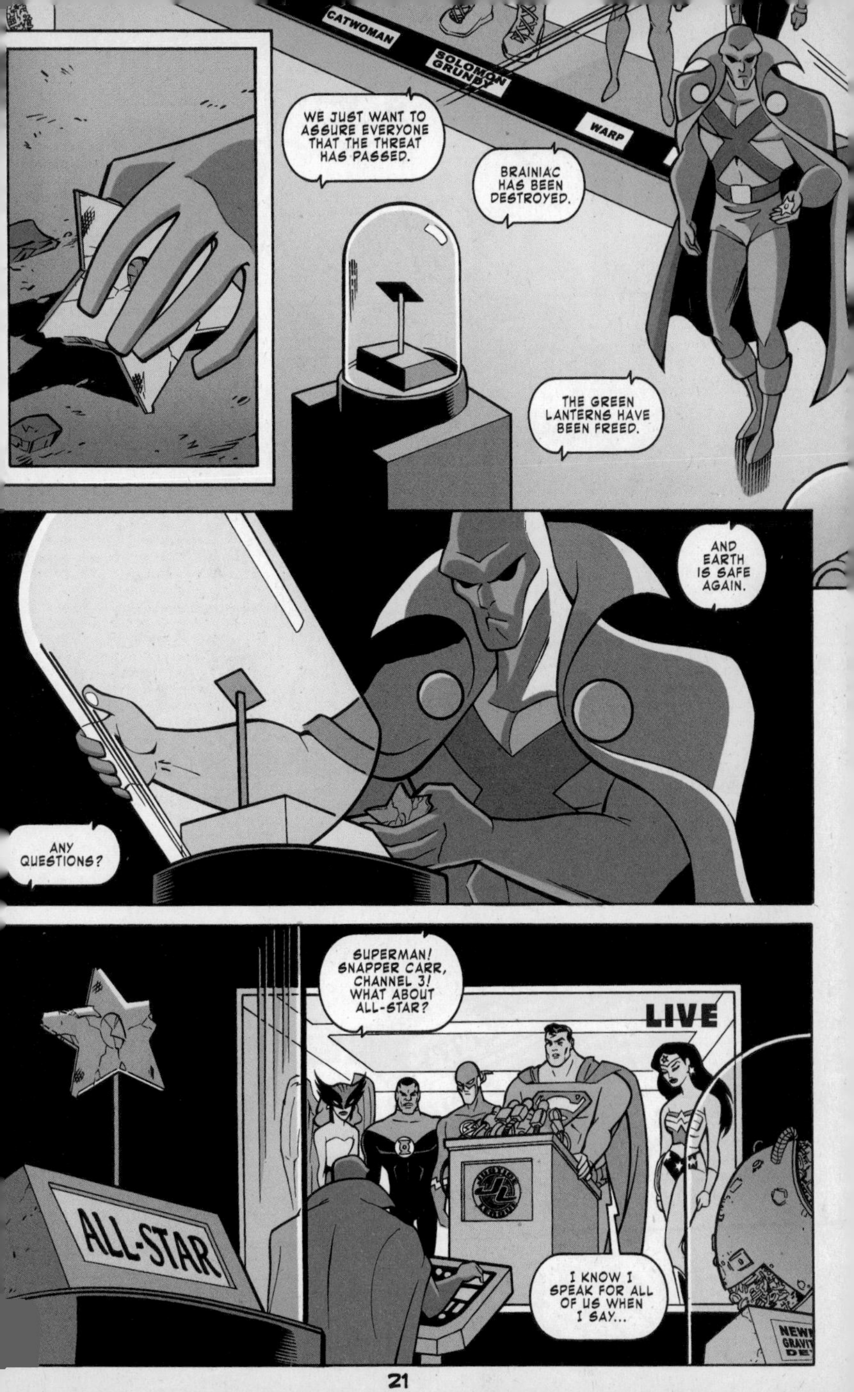
CATWOMAN
SOLOMON GRUNDY
WARP
WE JUST WANT TO ASSURE EVERYONE THAT THE THREAT HAS PASSED.
BRAINIAC HAS BEEN DESTROYED.
THE GREEN LANTERNS HAVE BEEN FREED.
AND EARTH IS SAFE AGAIN.
ANY QUESTIONS?
SUPERMAN! SNAPPER CARR, CHANNEL 3! WHAT ABOUT ALL-STAR?
LIVE
ALL-STAR
I KNOW I SPEAK FOR ALL OF US WHEN I SAY...

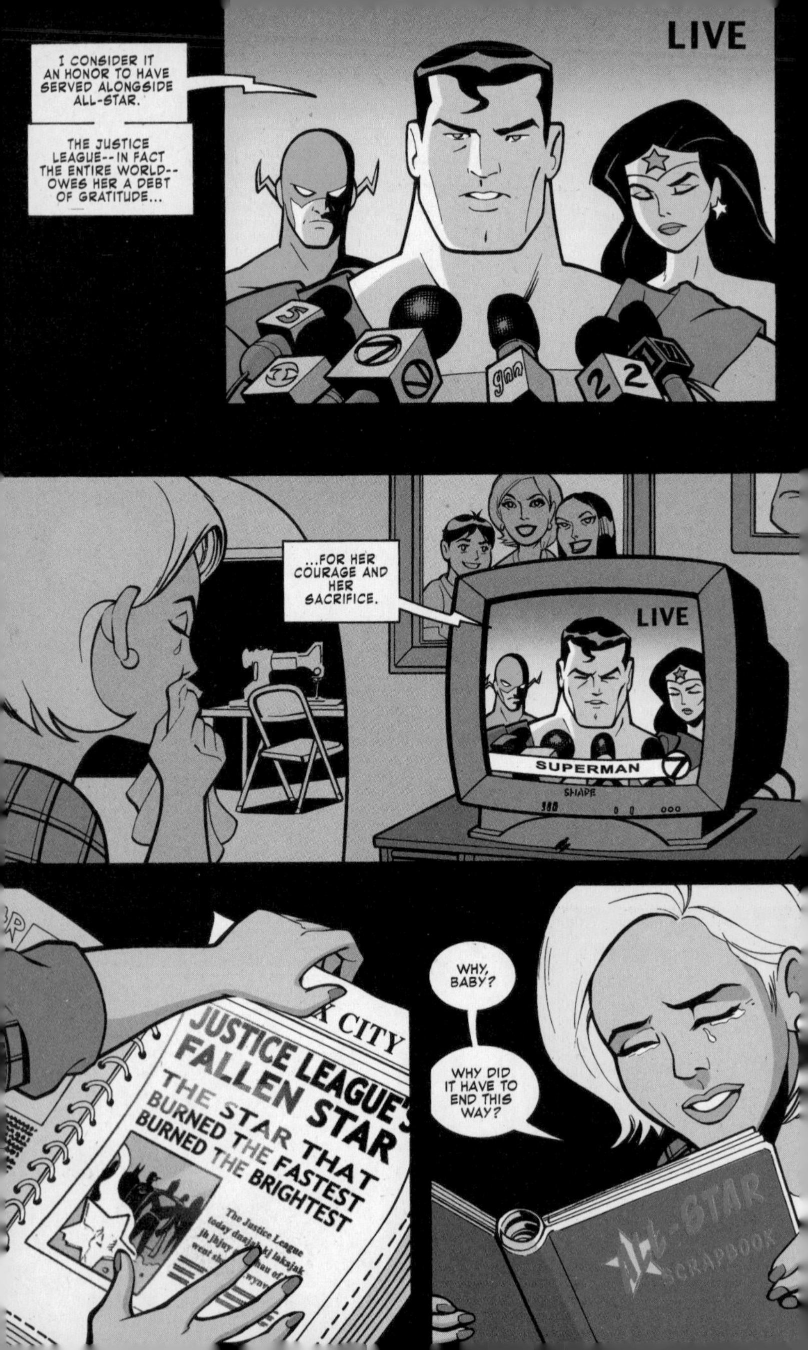
LIVE
I CONSIDER IT AN HONOR TO HAVE SERVED ALONGSIDE ALL-STAR.
THE JUSTICE LEAGUE--IN FACT THE ENTIRE WORLD--OWES HER A DEBT OF GRATITUDE...
...FOR HER COURAGE AND HER SACRIFICE.
LIVE
SUPERMAN
JUSTICE LEAGUE'S FALLEN STAR
THE STAR THAT BURNED THE FASTEST BURNED THE BRIGHTEST
WHY, BABY?
WHY DID IT HAVE TO END THIS WAY?
SCRAPBOOK

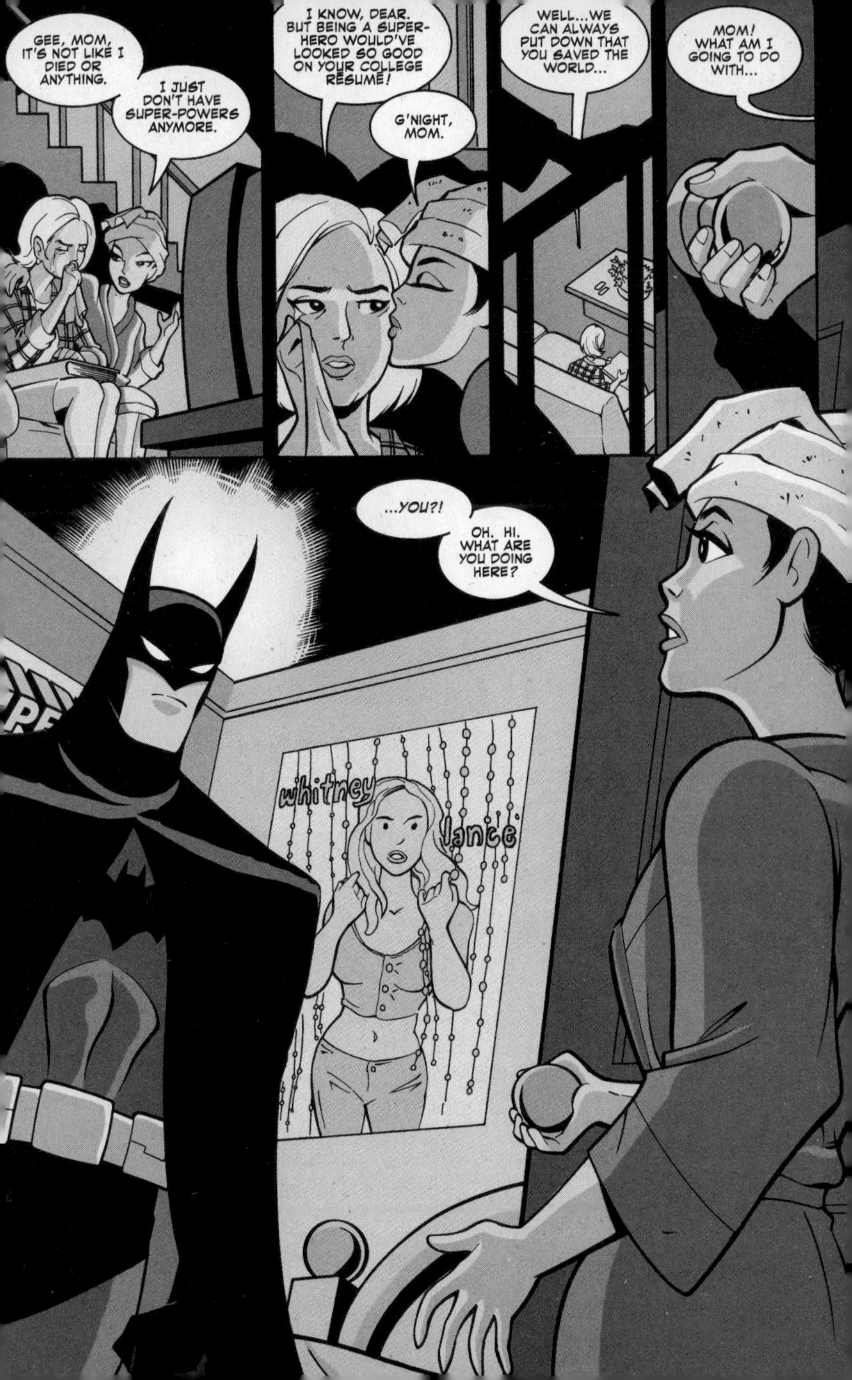
GEE, MOM, IT'S NOT LIKE I DIED OR ANYTHING.
I JUST DON'T HAVE SUPER-POWERS ANYMORE.
I KNOW, DEAR. BUT BEING A SUPER-HERO WOULD'VE LOOKED SO GOOD ON YOUR COLLEGE RESUMÉ!
G'NIGHT, MOM.
WELL...WE CAN ALWAYS PUT DOWN THAT YOU SAVED THE WORLD...
MOM! WHAT AM I GOING TO DO WITH...
...YOU?!
OH. HI. WHAT ARE YOU DOING HERE?
whitney lance

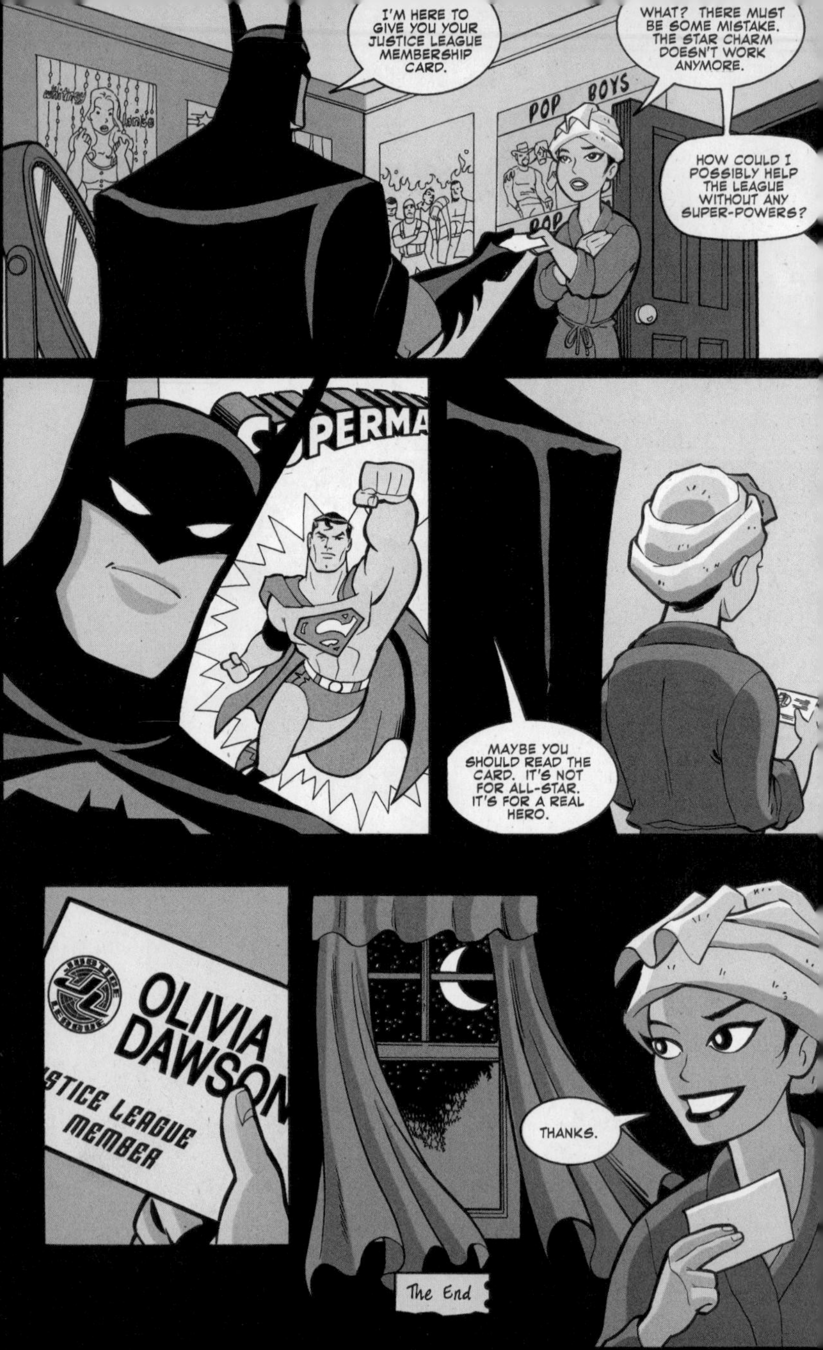
I'M HERE TO GIVE YOU YOUR JUSTICE LEAGUE MEMBERSHIP CARD.
POP BOYS
WHAT? THERE MUST BE SOME MISTAKE. THE STAR CHARM DOESN'T WORK ANYMORE.
HOW COULD I POSSIBLY HELP THE LEAGUE WITHOUT ANY SUPER-POWERS?
SUPERMA
MAYBE YOU SHOULD READ THE CARD. IT'S NOT FOR ALL-STAR. IT'S FOR A REAL HERO.
OLIVIA DAWSON
ISTICE LEAGUE MEMBER
THANKS.
The End

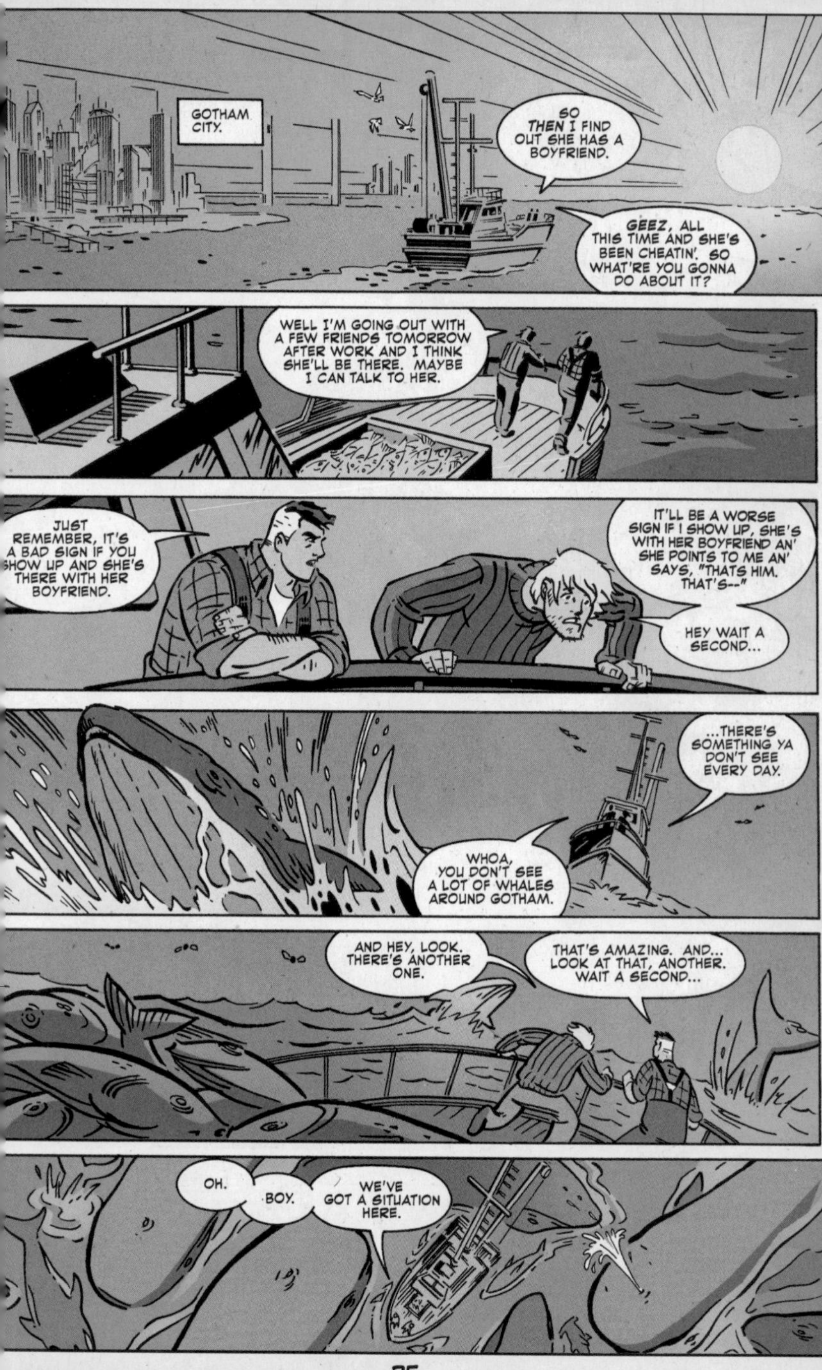
GOTHAM CITY.
SO THEN I FIND OUT SHE HAS A BOYFRIEND.
GEEZ, ALL THIS TIME AND SHE'S BEEN CHEATIN'. SO WHAT'RE YOU GONNA DO ABOUT IT?
WELL I'M GOING OUT WITH A FEW FRIENDS TOMORROW AFTER WORK AND I THINK SHE'LL BE THERE. MAYBE I CAN TALK TO HER.
JUST REMEMBER, IT'S A BAD SIGN IF YOU SHOW UP AND SHE'S THERE WITH HER BOYFRIEND.
IT'LL BE A WORSE SIGN IF I SHOW UP, SHE'S WITH HER BOYFRIEND AN' SHE POINTS TO ME AN' SAYS, "THATS HIM. THAT'S--"
HEY WAIT A SECOND...
...THERE'S SOMETHING YA DON'T SEE EVERY DAY.
WHOA, YOU DON'T SEE A LOT OF WHALES AROUND GOTHAM.
AND HEY, LOOK. THERE'S ANOTHER ONE.
THAT'S AMAZING. AND... LOOK AT THAT, ANOTHER. WAIT A SECOND...
OH.
BOY.
WE'VE GOT A SITUATION HERE.

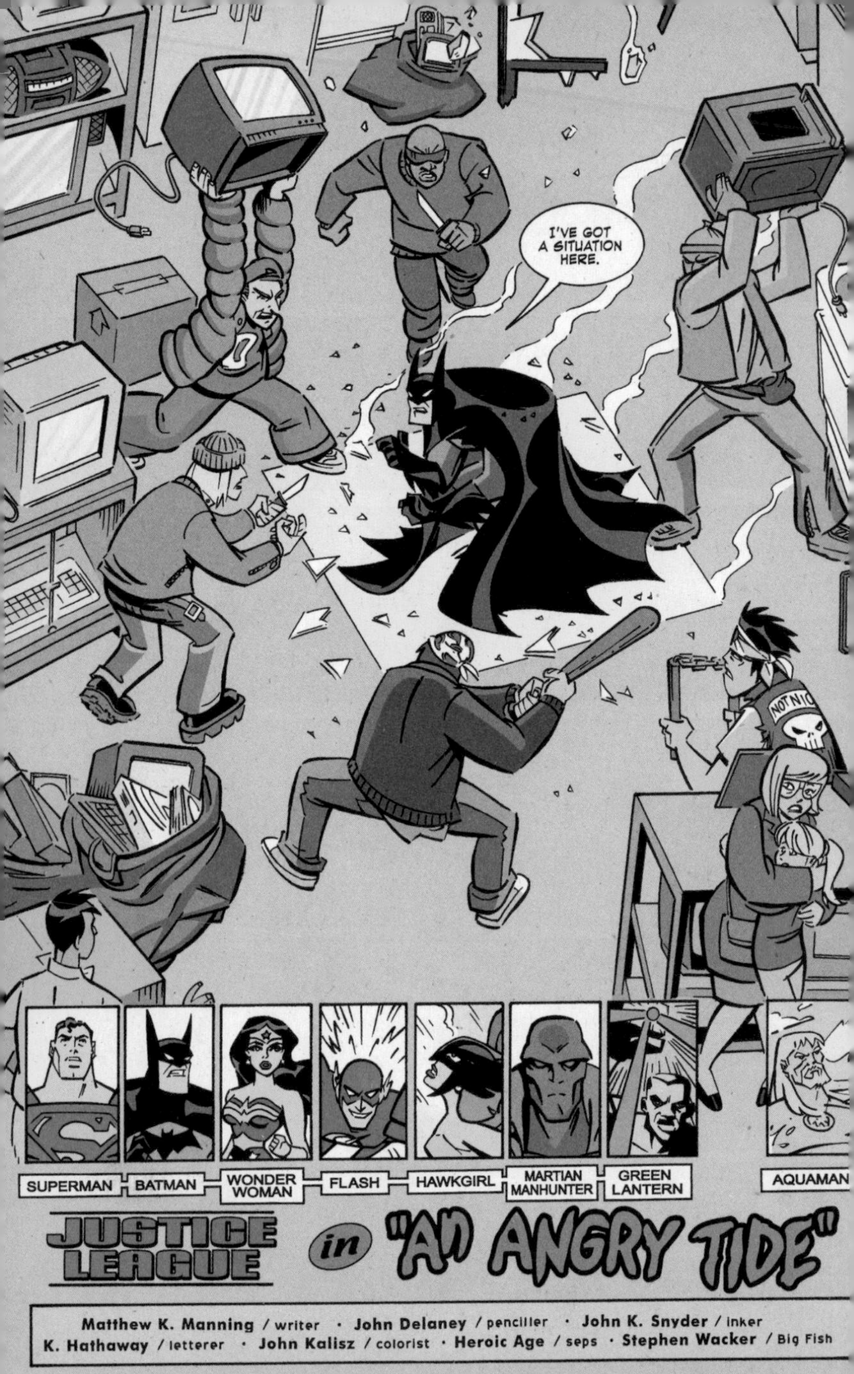
I'VE GOT A SITUATION HERE.
NOT NIC
SUPERMAN
BATMAN
WONDER WOMAN
FLASH
HAWKGIRL
MARTIAN MANHUNTER
GREEN LANTERN
AQUAMAN

JUSTICE LEAGUE in "AN ANGRY TIDE"

Matthew K. Manning / writer · **John Delaney** / penciller · **John K. Snyder** / inker
K. Hathaway / letterer · **John Kalisz** / colorist · **Heroic Age** / seps · **Stephen Wacker** / Big Fish

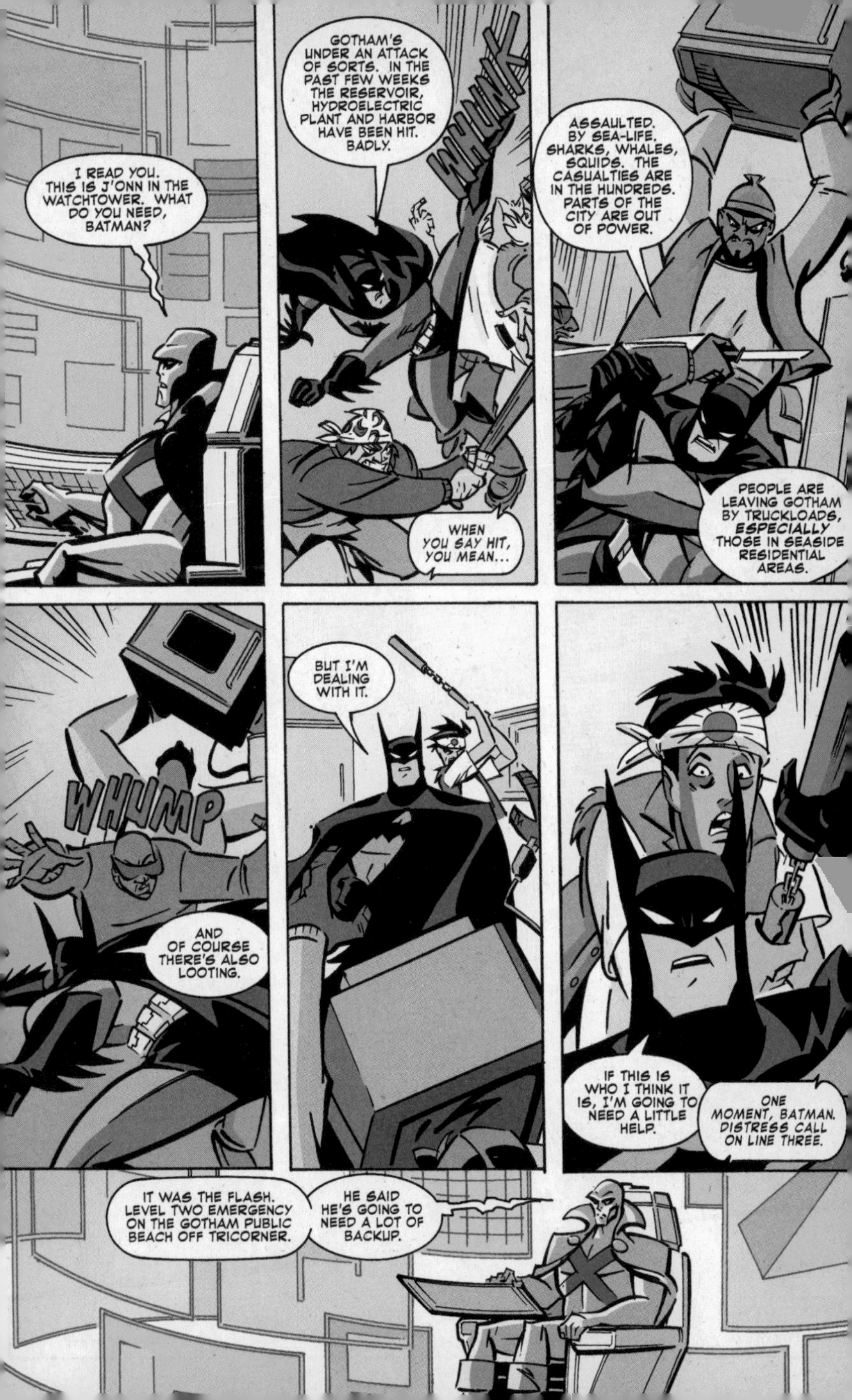

I READ YOU. THIS IS J'ONN IN THE WATCHTOWER. WHAT DO YOU NEED, BATMAN?
GOTHAM'S UNDER AN ATTACK OF SORTS. IN THE PAST FEW WEEKS THE RESERVOIR, HYDROELECTRIC PLANT AND HARBOR HAVE BEEN HIT. BADLY.
WHUNK
WHEN YOU SAY HIT, YOU MEAN...
ASSAULTED. BY SEA-LIFE. SHARKS, WHALES, SQUIDS. THE CASUALTIES ARE IN THE HUNDREDS. PARTS OF THE CITY ARE OUT OF POWER.
PEOPLE ARE LEAVING GOTHAM BY TRUCKLOADS, ESPECIALLY THOSE IN SEASIDE RESIDENTIAL AREAS.
WHUMP
AND OF COURSE THERE'S ALSO LOOTING.
BUT I'M DEALING WITH IT.
IF THIS IS WHO I THINK IT IS, I'M GOING TO NEED A LITTLE HELP.
ONE MOMENT, BATMAN. DISTRESS CALL ON LINE THREE.
IT WAS THE FLASH. LEVEL TWO EMERGENCY ON THE GOTHAM PUBLIC BEACH OFF TRICORNER.
HE SAID HE'S GOING TO NEED A LOT OF BACKUP.

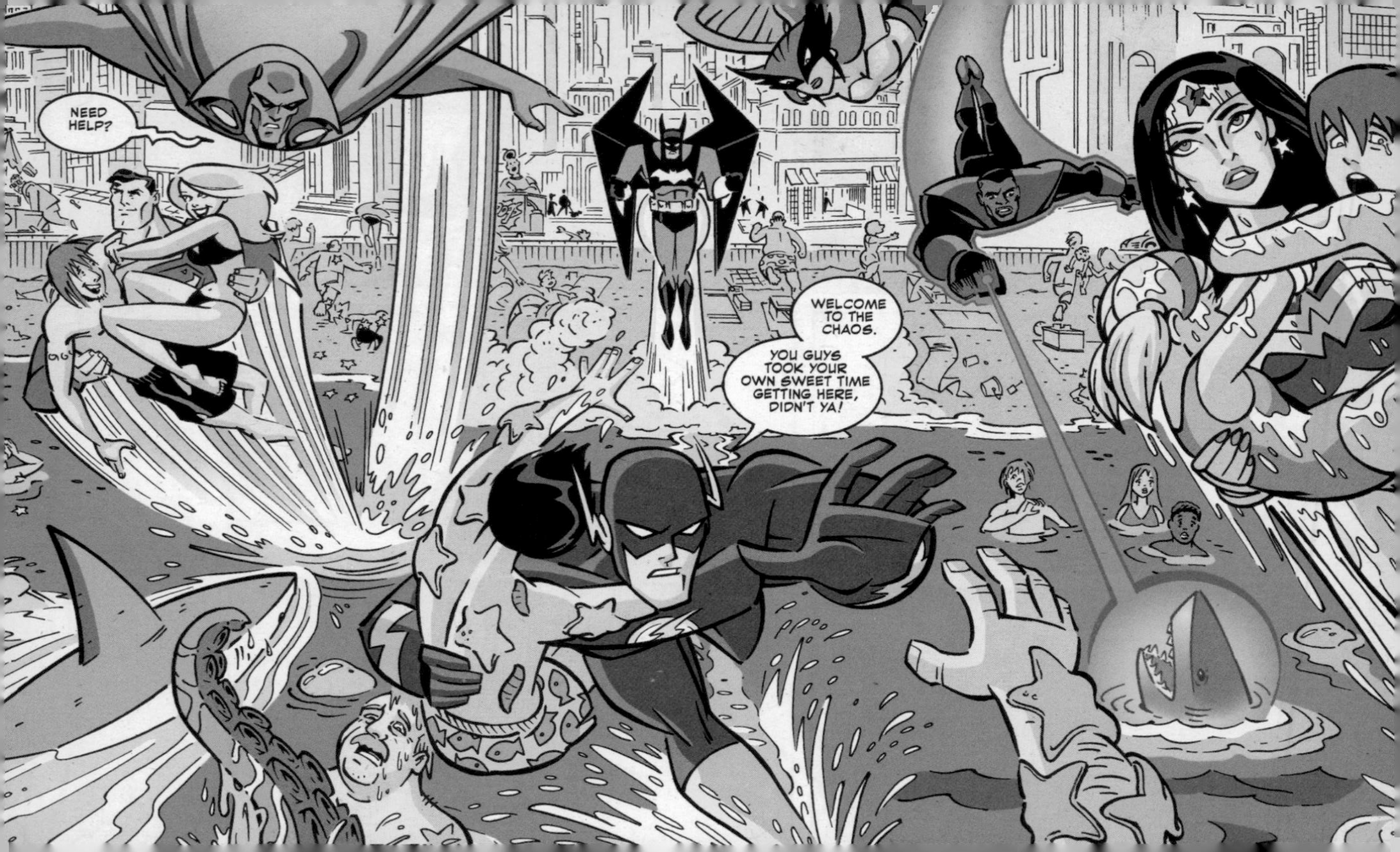
NEED HELP?
WELCOME TO THE CHAOS.
YOU GUYS TOOK YOUR OWN SWEET TIME GETTING HERE, DIDN'T YA!

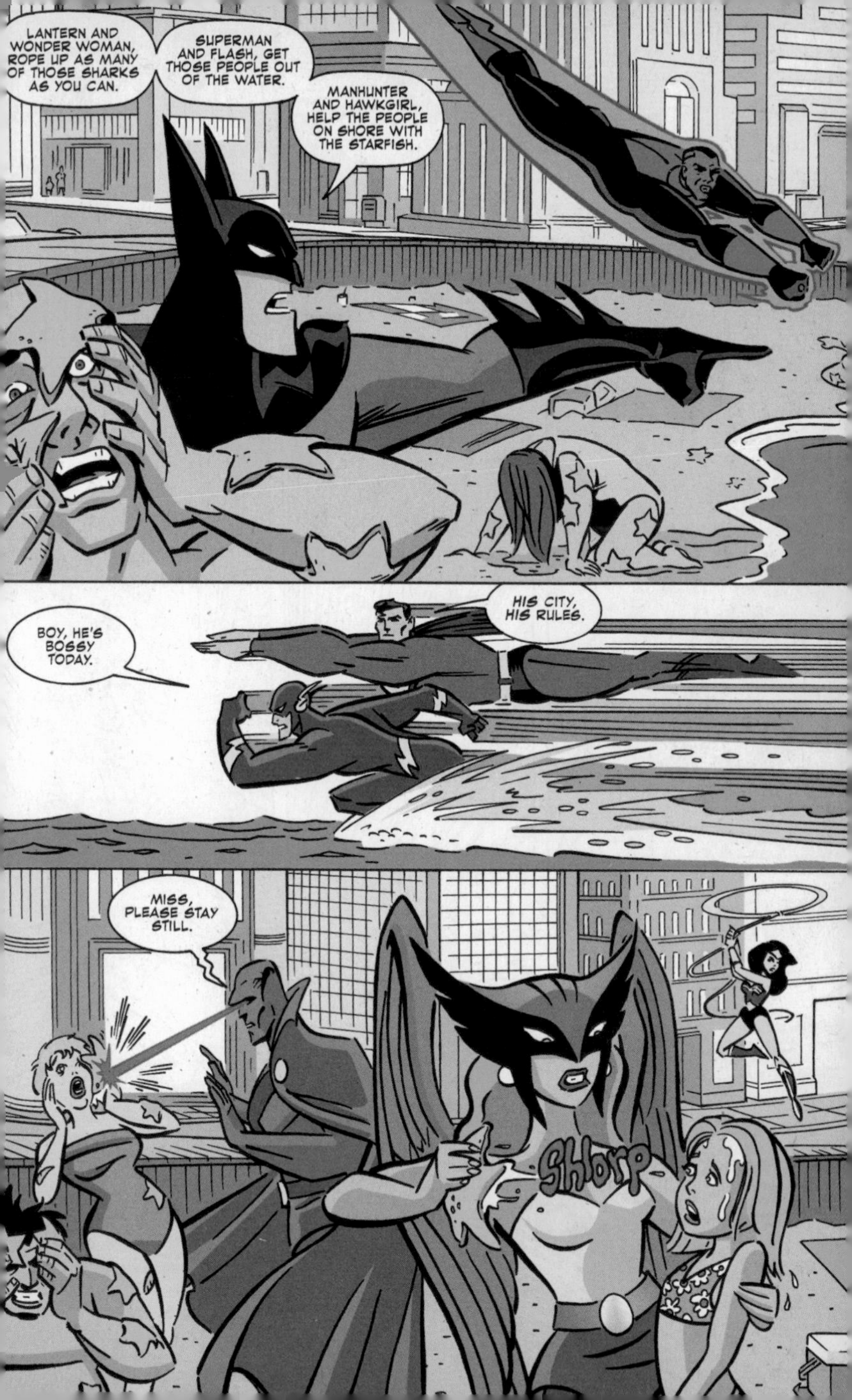
LANTERN AND WONDER WOMAN, ROPE UP AS MANY OF THOSE SHARKS AS YOU CAN.
SUPERMAN AND FLASH, GET THOSE PEOPLE OUT OF THE WATER.
MANHUNTER AND HAWKGIRL, HELP THE PEOPLE ON SHORE WITH THE STARFISH.
HIS CITY, HIS RULES.
BOY, HE'S BOSSY TODAY.
MISS, PLEASE STAY STILL.
SHLORP

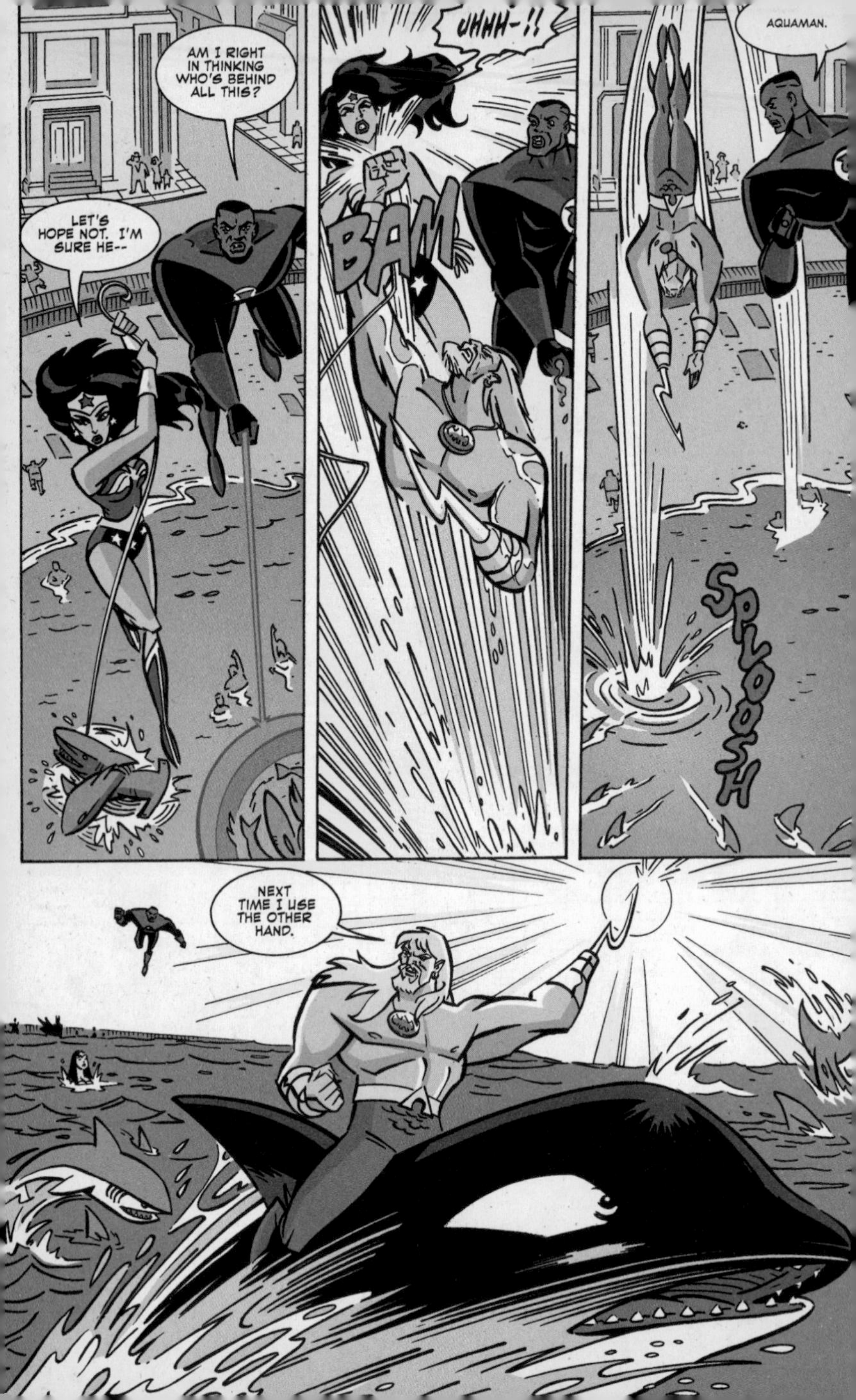

AM I RIGHT IN THINKING WHO'S BEHIND ALL THIS?
LET'S HOPE NOT. I'M SURE HE--
UHHH-!!
BAM
AQUAMAN.
SPLOOSH
NEXT TIME I USE THE OTHER HAND.

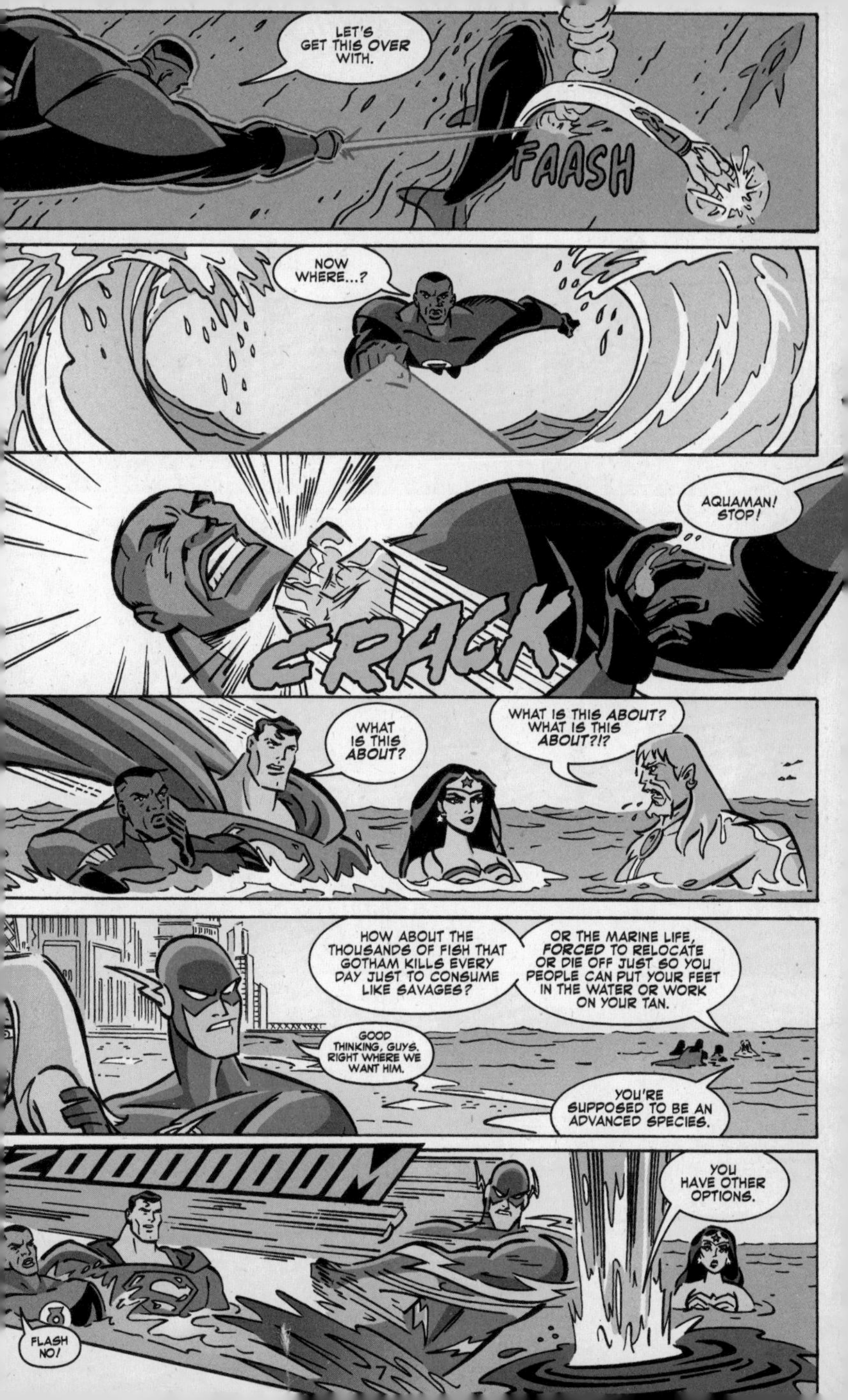

LET'S GET THIS OVER WITH.
FAASH
NOW WHERE...?
AQUAMAN! STOP!
CRACK
WHAT IS THIS ABOUT?
WHAT IS THIS ABOUT? WHAT IS THIS ABOUT?!?
HOW ABOUT THE THOUSANDS OF FISH THAT GOTHAM KILLS EVERY DAY JUST TO CONSUME LIKE SAVAGES?
OR THE MARINE LIFE, FORCED TO RELOCATE OR DIE OFF JUST SO YOU PEOPLE CAN PUT YOUR FEET IN THE WATER OR WORK ON YOUR TAN.
GOOD THINKING, GUYS. RIGHT WHERE WE WANT HIM.
YOU'RE SUPPOSED TO BE AN ADVANCED SPECIES.
ZOOOOOOM
YOU HAVE OTHER OPTIONS.
FLASH NO!

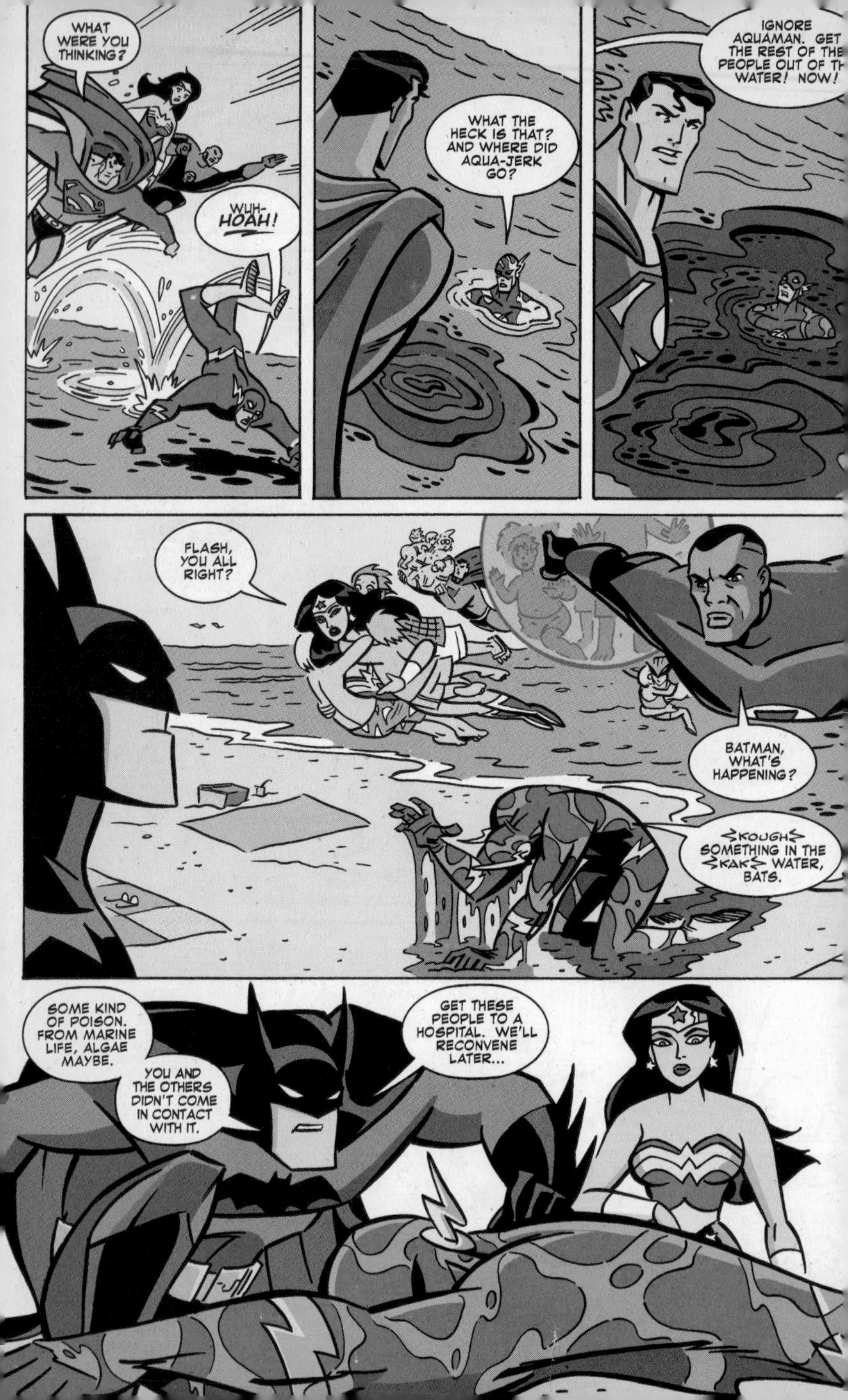
WHAT WERE YOU THINKING?
WUH-HOAH!
WHAT THE HECK IS THAT? AND WHERE DID AQUA-JERK GO?
IGNORE AQUAMAN. GET THE REST OF THE PEOPLE OUT OF TH WATER! NOW!
FLASH, YOU ALL RIGHT?
BATMAN, WHAT'S HAPPENING?
KOUGH SOMETHING IN THE KAK WATER, BATS.
SOME KIND OF POISON. FROM MARINE LIFE, ALGAE MAYBE.
YOU AND THE OTHERS DIDN'T COME IN CONTACT WITH IT.
GET THESE PEOPLE TO A HOSPITAL. WE'LL RECONVENE LATER...

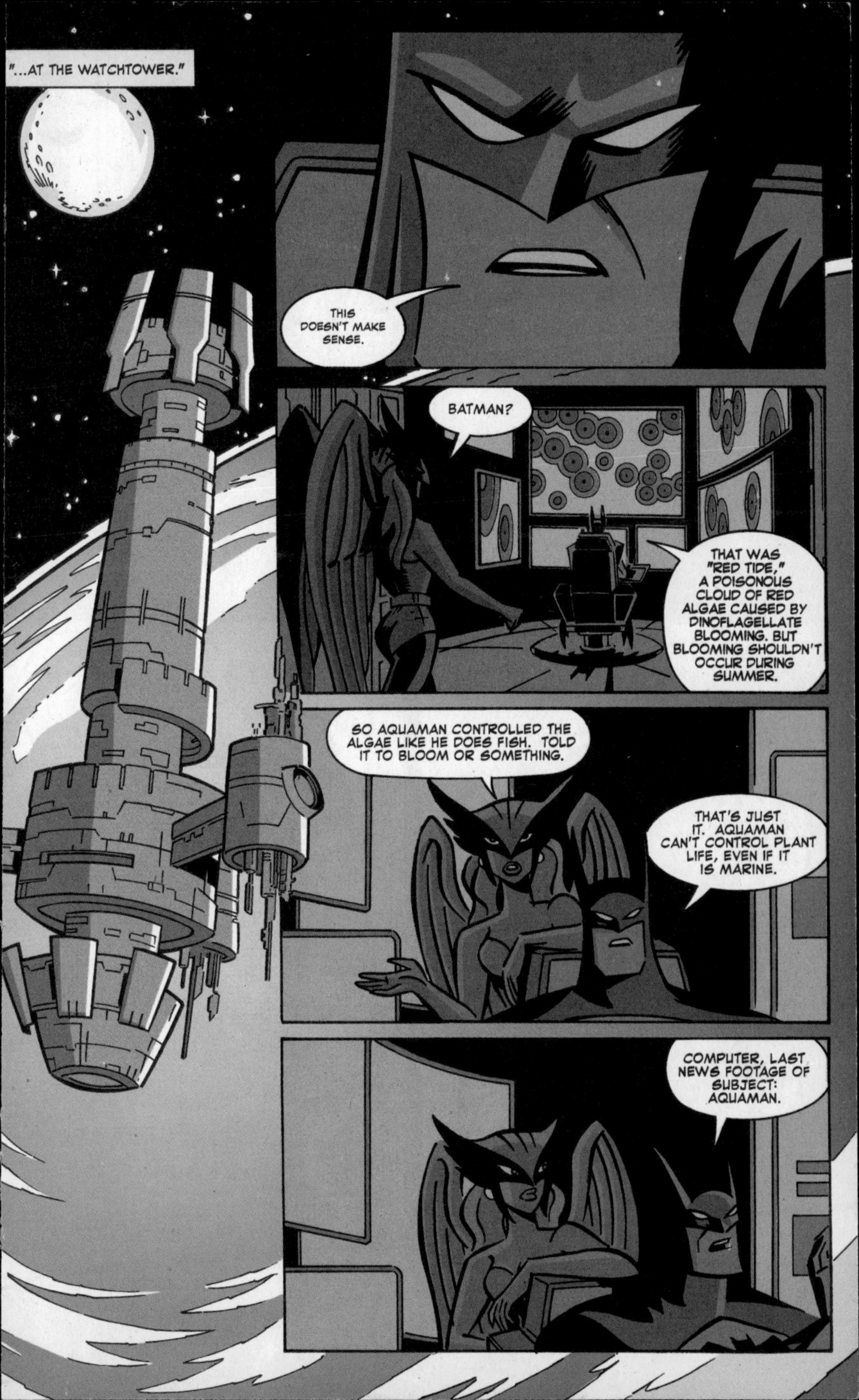
"...AT THE WATCHTOWER."
THIS DOESN'T MAKE SENSE.
BATMAN?
THAT WAS "RED TIDE," A POISONOUS CLOUD OF RED ALGAE CAUSED BY DINOFLAGELLATE BLOOMING. BUT BLOOMING SHOULDN'T OCCUR DURING SUMMER.
SO AQUAMAN CONTROLLED THE ALGAE LIKE HE DOES FISH. TOLD IT TO BLOOM OR SOMETHING.
THAT'S JUST IT. AQUAMAN CAN'T CONTROL PLANT LIFE, EVEN IF IT IS MARINE.
COMPUTER, LAST NEWS FOOTAGE OF SUBJECT: AQUAMAN.

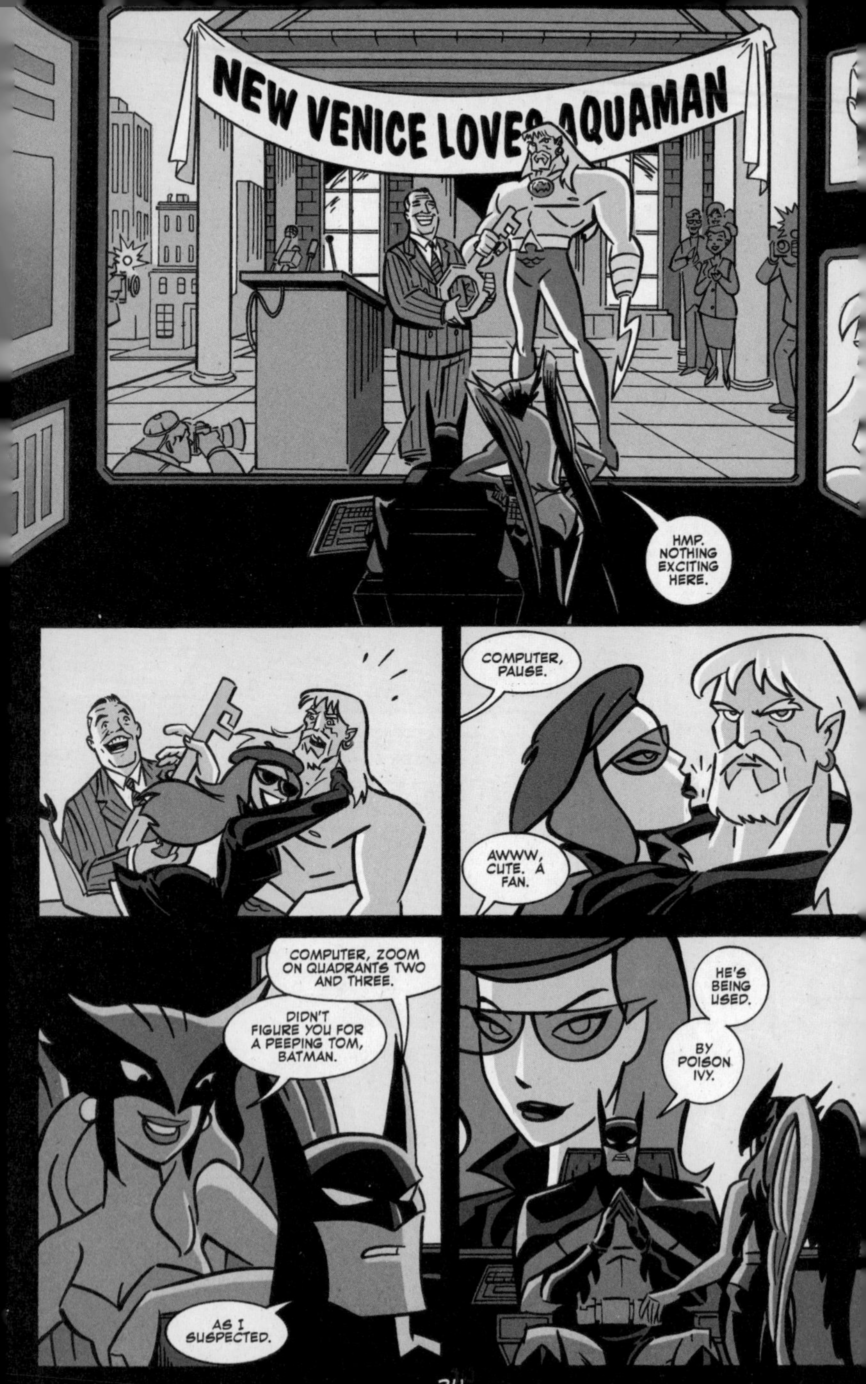
NEW VENICE LOVES AQUAMAN
HMP. NOTHING EXCITING HERE.
COMPUTER, PAUSE.
AWWW, CUTE. A FAN.
COMPUTER, ZOOM ON QUADRANTS TWO AND THREE.
DIDN'T FIGURE YOU FOR A PEEPING TOM, BATMAN.
AS I SUSPECTED.
HE'S BEING USED.
BY POISON IVY.

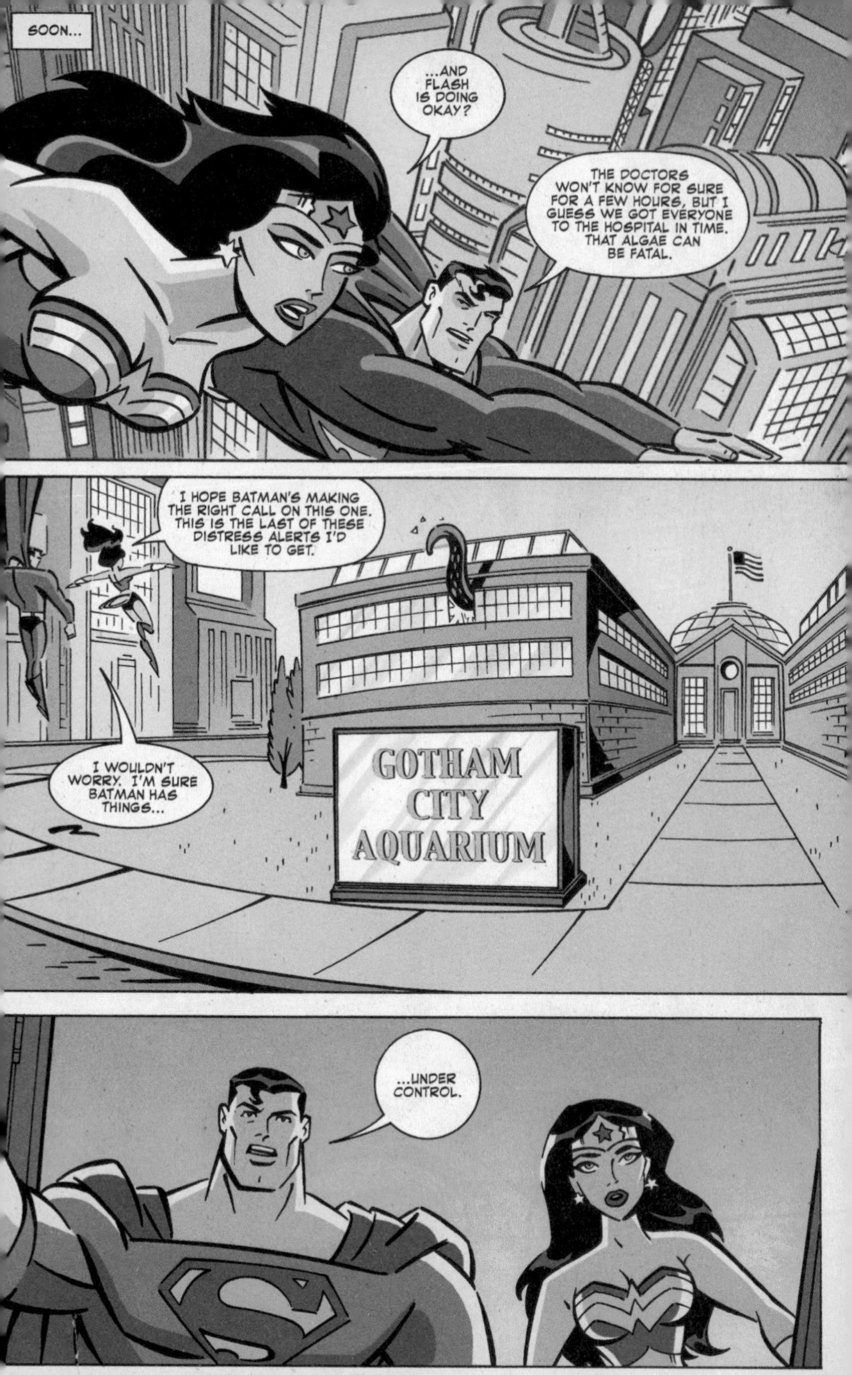
SOON...
...AND FLASH IS DOING OKAY?
THE DOCTORS WON'T KNOW FOR SURE FOR A FEW HOURS, BUT I GUESS WE GOT EVERYONE TO THE HOSPITAL IN TIME. THAT ALGAE CAN BE FATAL.
I HOPE BATMAN'S MAKING THE RIGHT CALL ON THIS ONE. THIS IS THE LAST OF THESE DISTRESS ALERTS I'D LIKE TO GET.
GOTHAM CITY AQUARIUM
I WOULDN'T WORRY. I'M SURE BATMAN HAS THINGS...
...UNDER CONTROL.

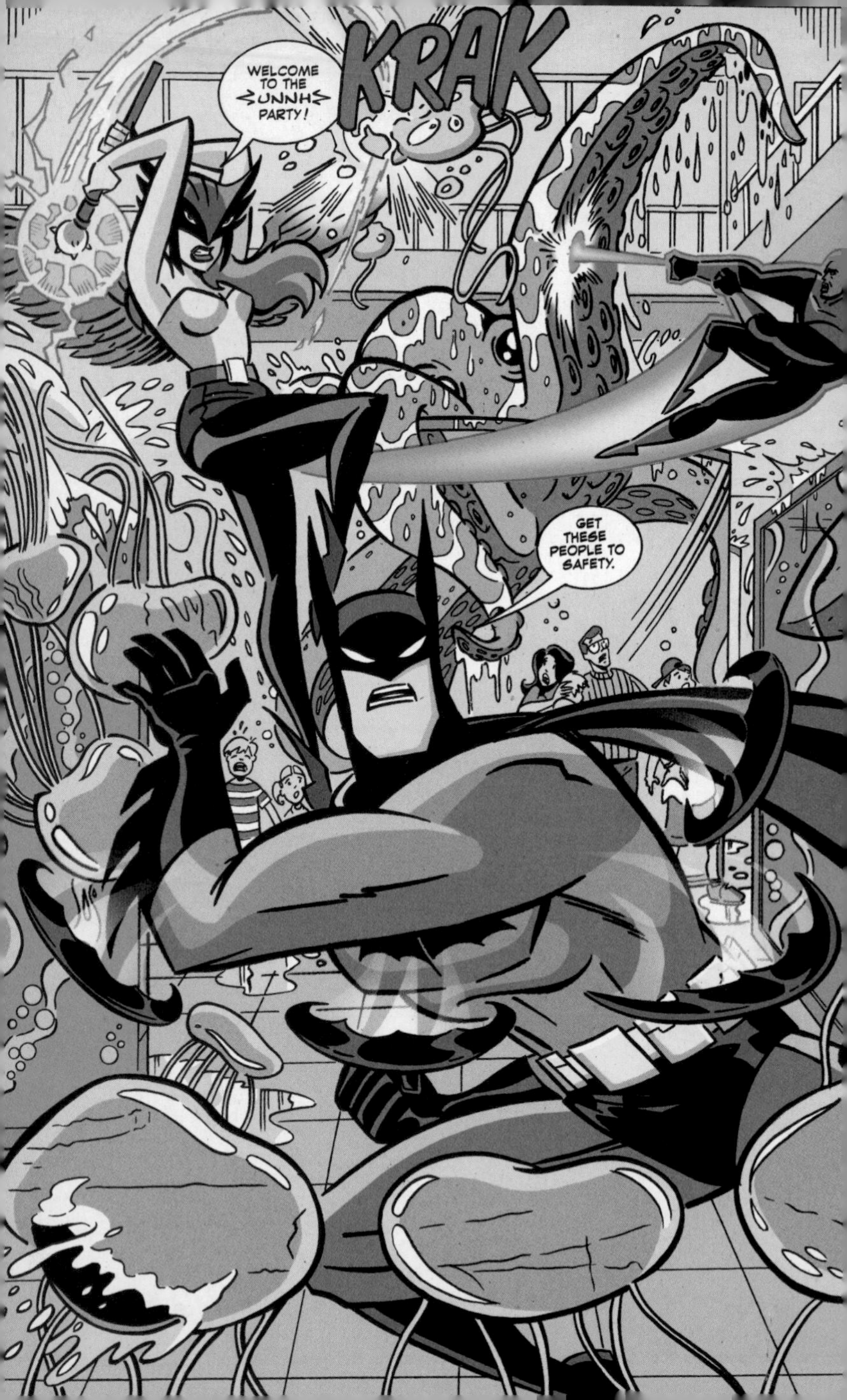
WELCOME TO THE ≤UNNH≥ PARTY!
KRAK
GET THESE PEOPLE TO SAFETY.

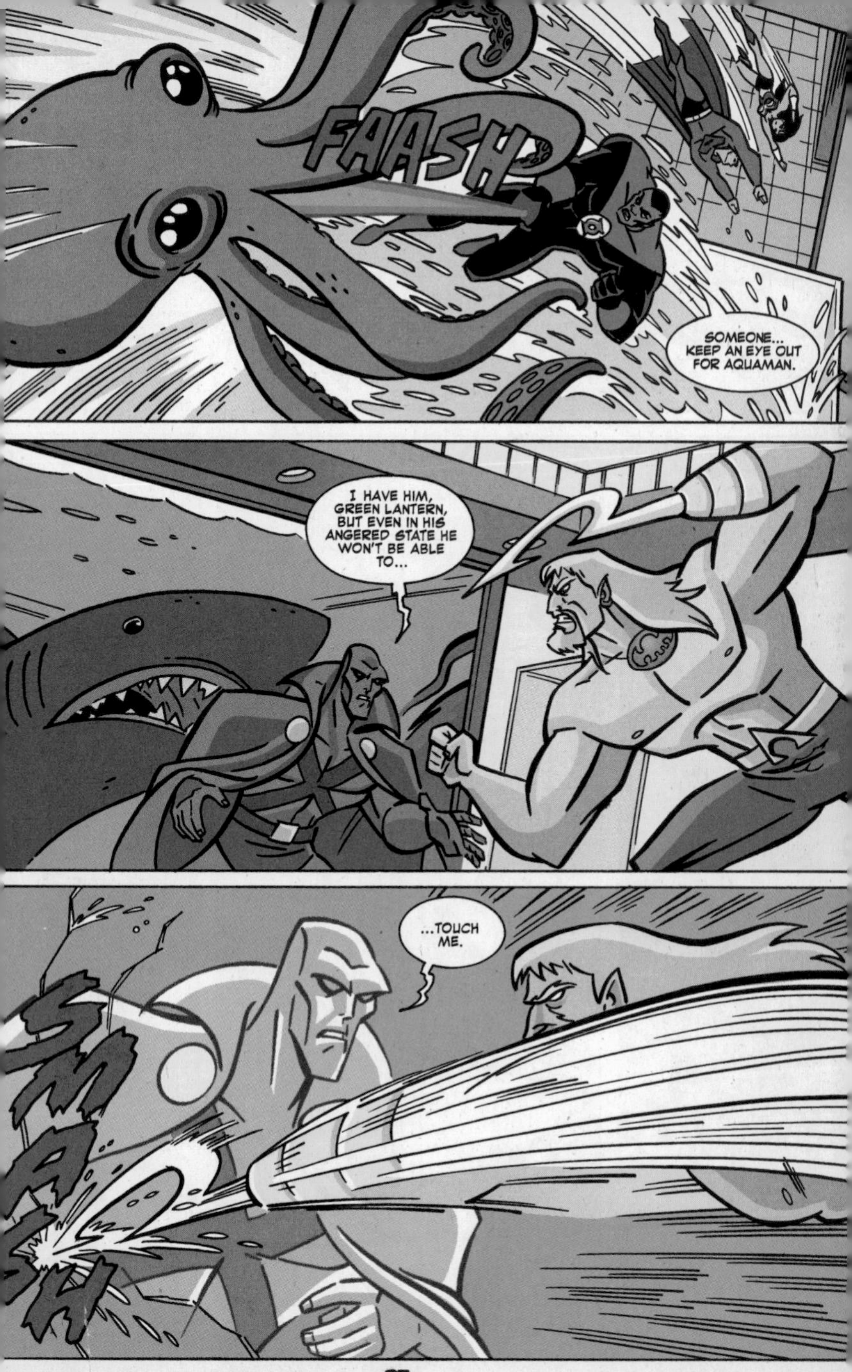
FAASH
SOMEONE... KEEP AN EYE OUT FOR AQUAMAN.
I HAVE HIM, GREEN LANTERN, BUT EVEN IN HIS ANGERED STATE HE WON'T BE ABLE TO...
...TOUCH ME.

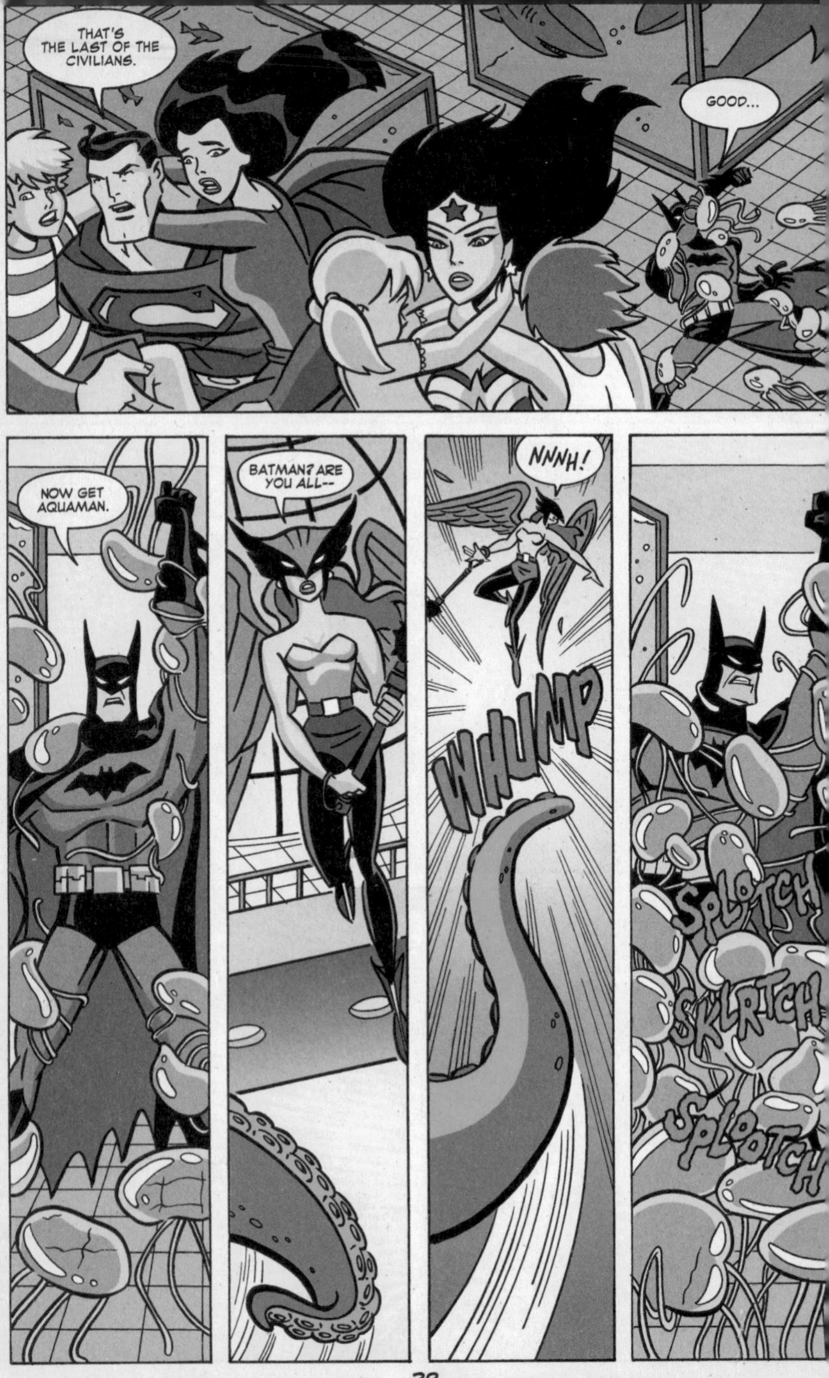
THAT'S THE LAST OF THE CIVILIANS.
GOOD...
NOW GET AQUAMAN.
BATMAN? ARE YOU ALL--
NNNH!
WHUMP
SPLOTCH
SKLRTCH
SPLOTCH

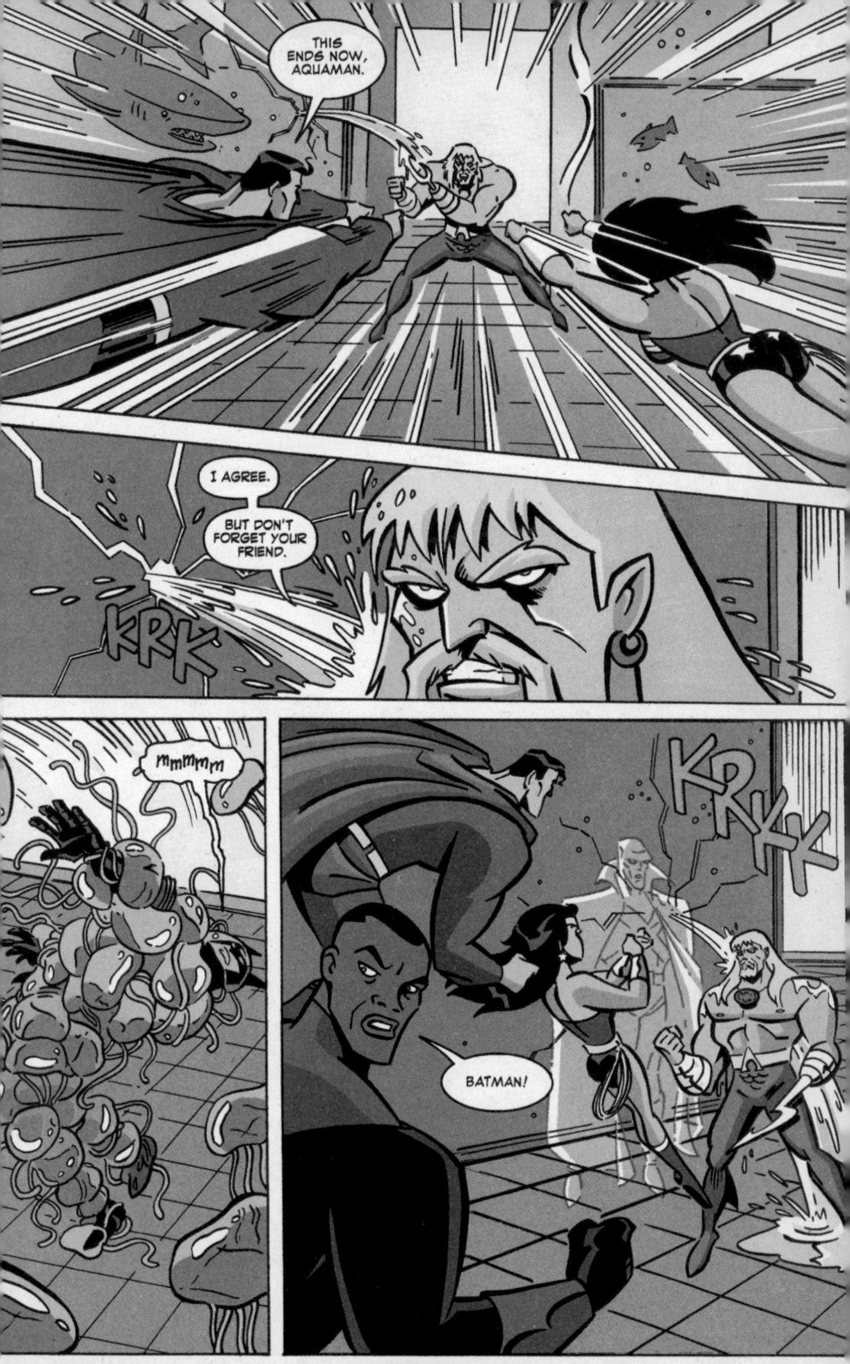
THIS ENDS NOW, AQUAMAN.
I AGREE.
BUT DON'T FORGET YOUR FRIEND.
KRK
mmmmm
KRKK
BATMAN!

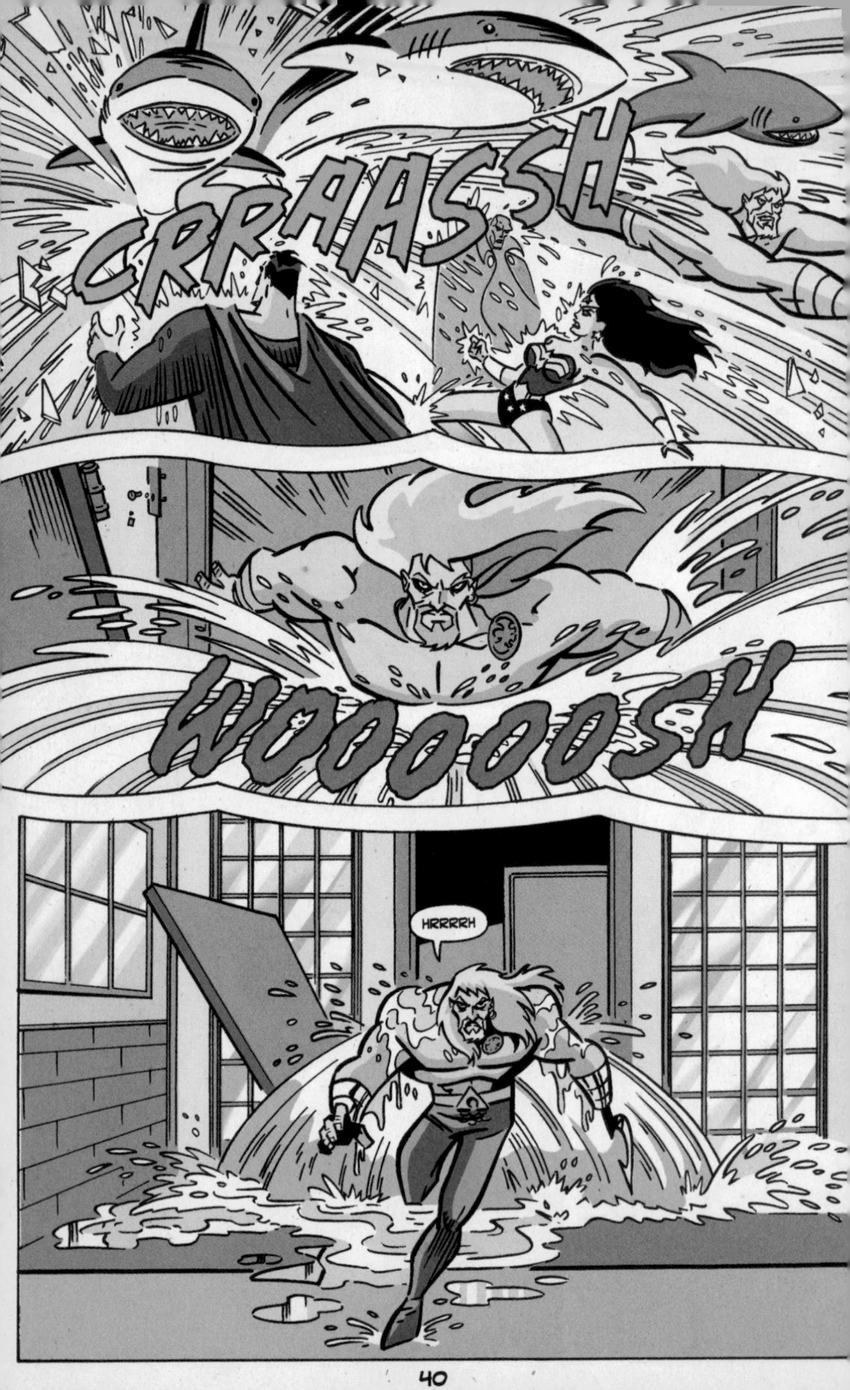
CRRAASSH
WOOOOOOSH
HRRRRH

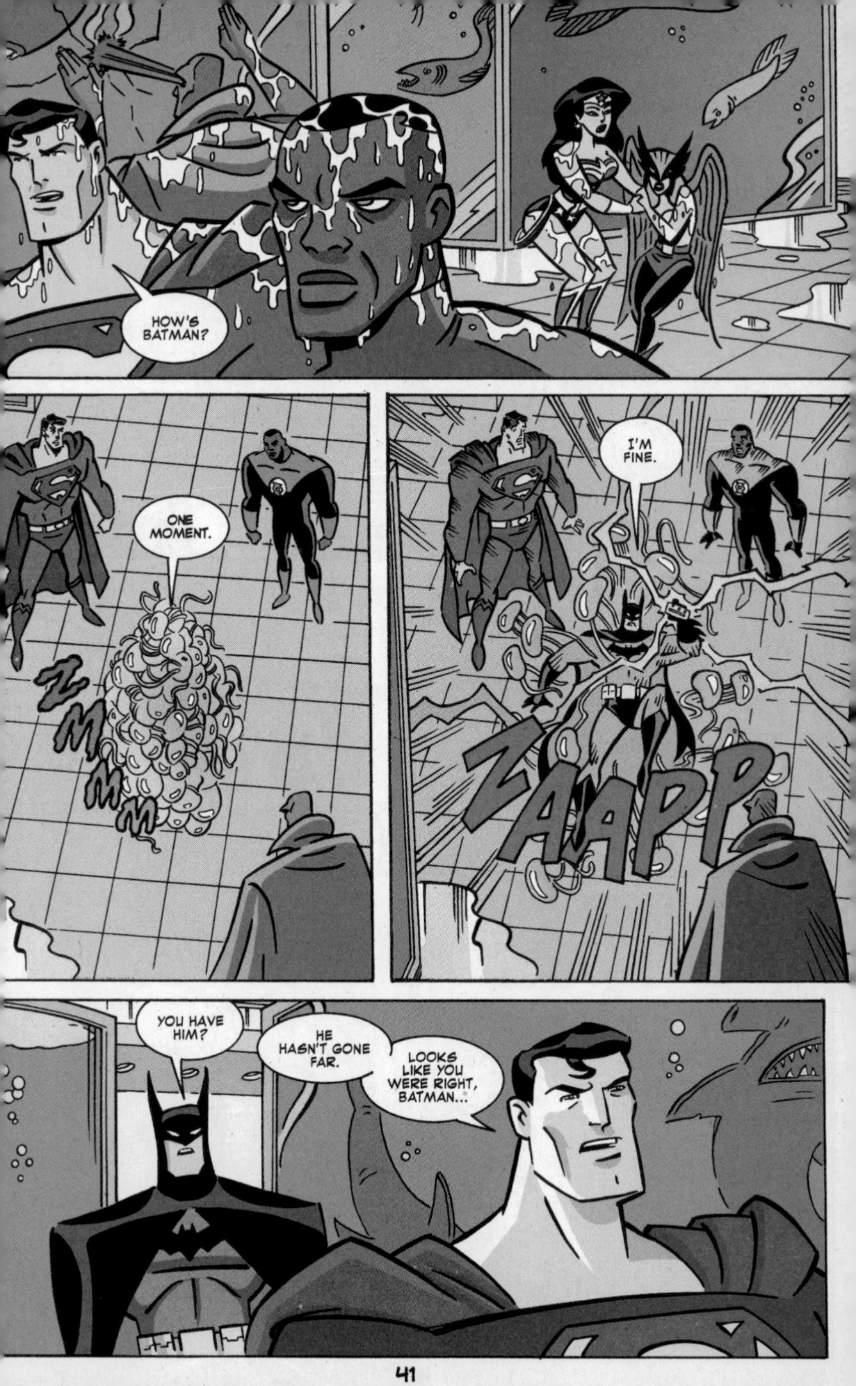
HOW'S BATMAN?
ONE MOMENT.
ZMMM
I'M FINE.
ZAAPP
YOU HAVE HIM?
HE HASN'T GONE FAR.
LOOKS LIKE YOU WERE RIGHT, BATMAN...

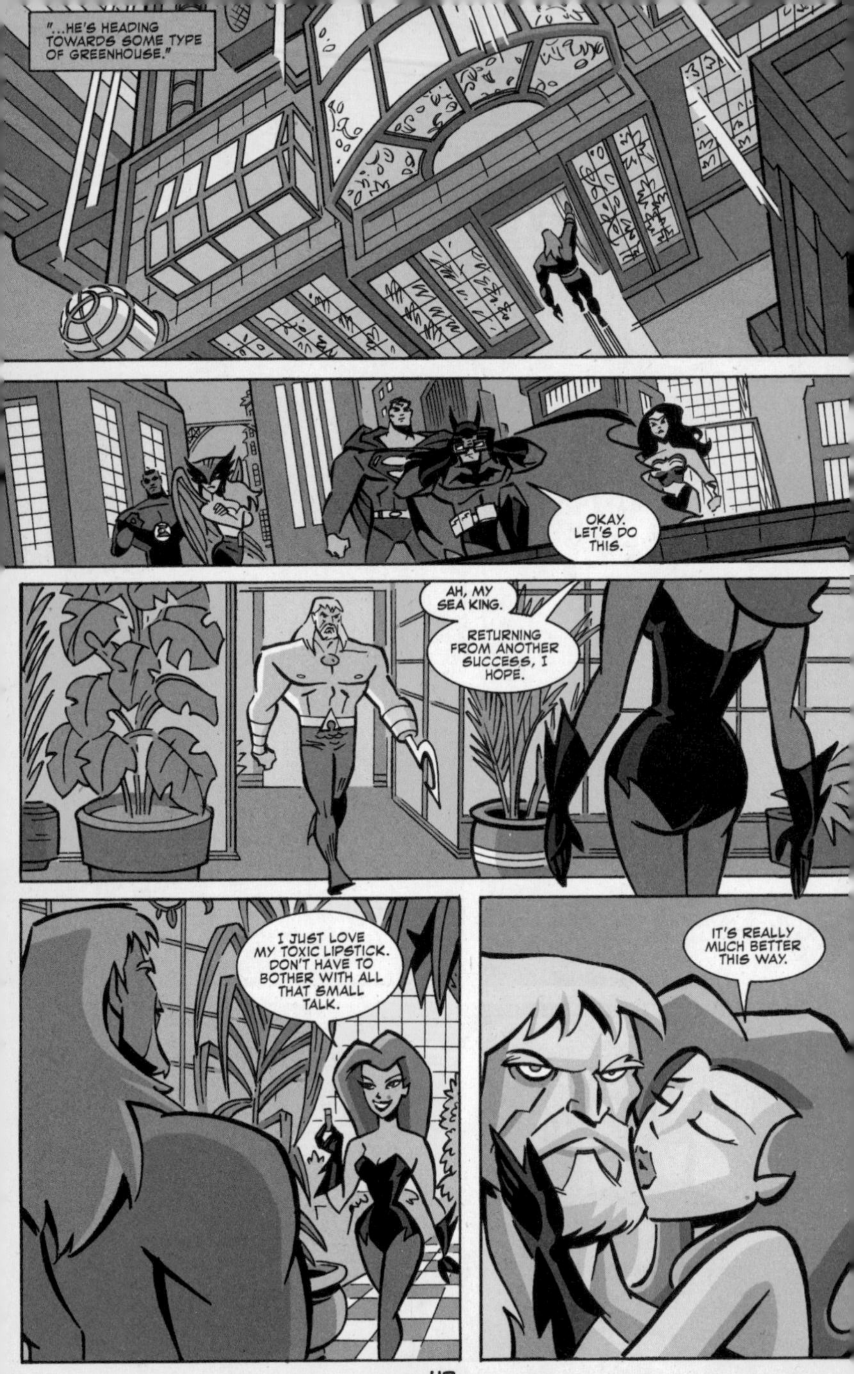
"...HE'S HEADING TOWARDS SOME TYPE OF GREENHOUSE."
OKAY. LET'S DO THIS.
AH, MY SEA KING.
RETURNING FROM ANOTHER SUCCESS, I HOPE.
I JUST LOVE MY TOXIC LIPSTICK. DON'T HAVE TO BOTHER WITH ALL THAT SMALL TALK.
IT'S REALLY MUCH BETTER THIS WAY.

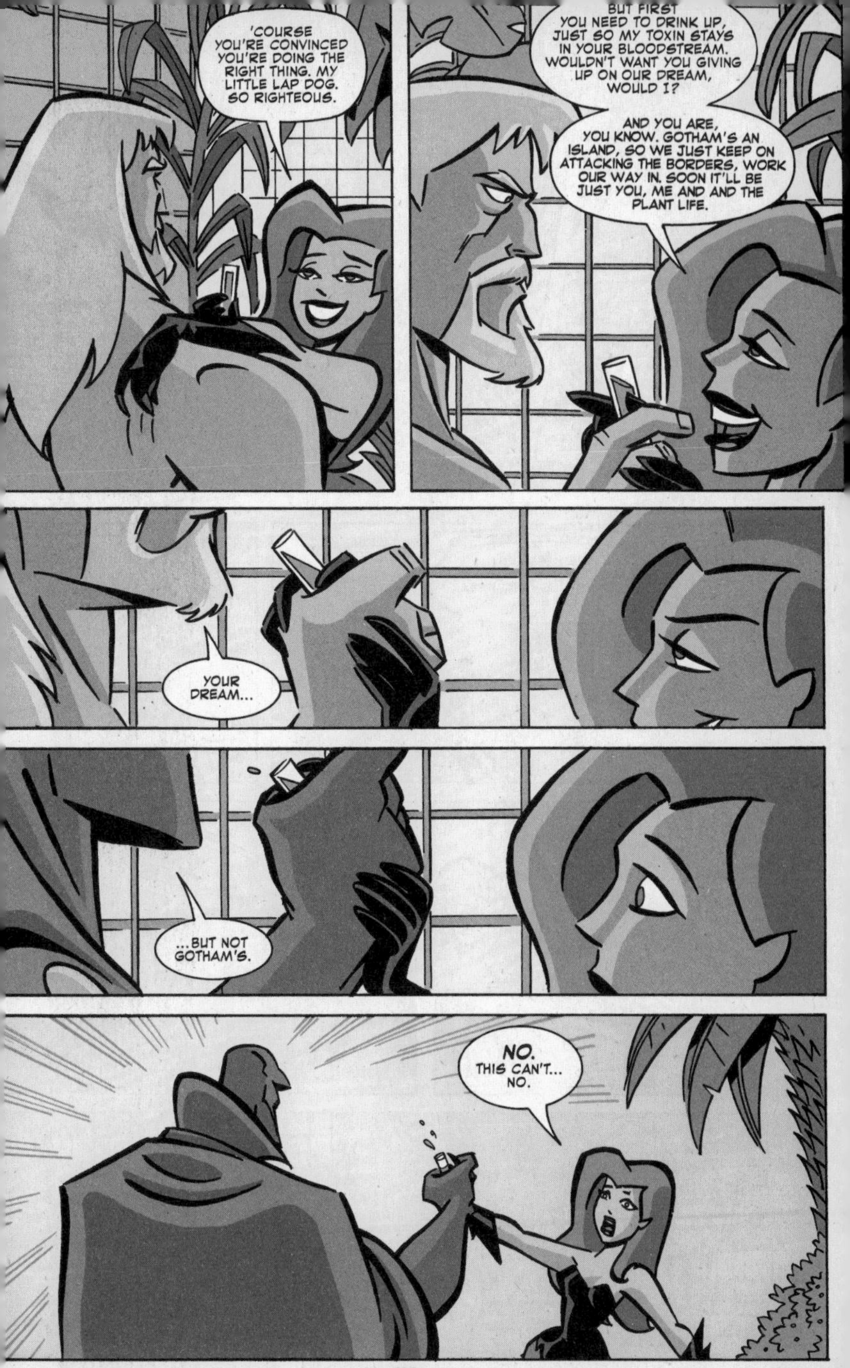
'COURSE YOU'RE CONVINCED YOU'RE DOING THE RIGHT THING. MY LITTLE LAP DOG. SO RIGHTEOUS.
BUT FIRST YOU NEED TO DRINK UP, JUST SO MY TOXIN STAYS IN YOUR BLOODSTREAM. WOULDN'T WANT YOU GIVING UP ON OUR DREAM, WOULD I?
AND YOU ARE, YOU KNOW. GOTHAM'S AN ISLAND, SO WE JUST KEEP ON ATTACKING THE BORDERS, WORK OUR WAY IN. SOON IT'LL BE JUST YOU, ME AND AND THE PLANT LIFE.
YOUR DREAM...
...BUT NOT GOTHAM'S.
NO. THIS CAN'T... NO.

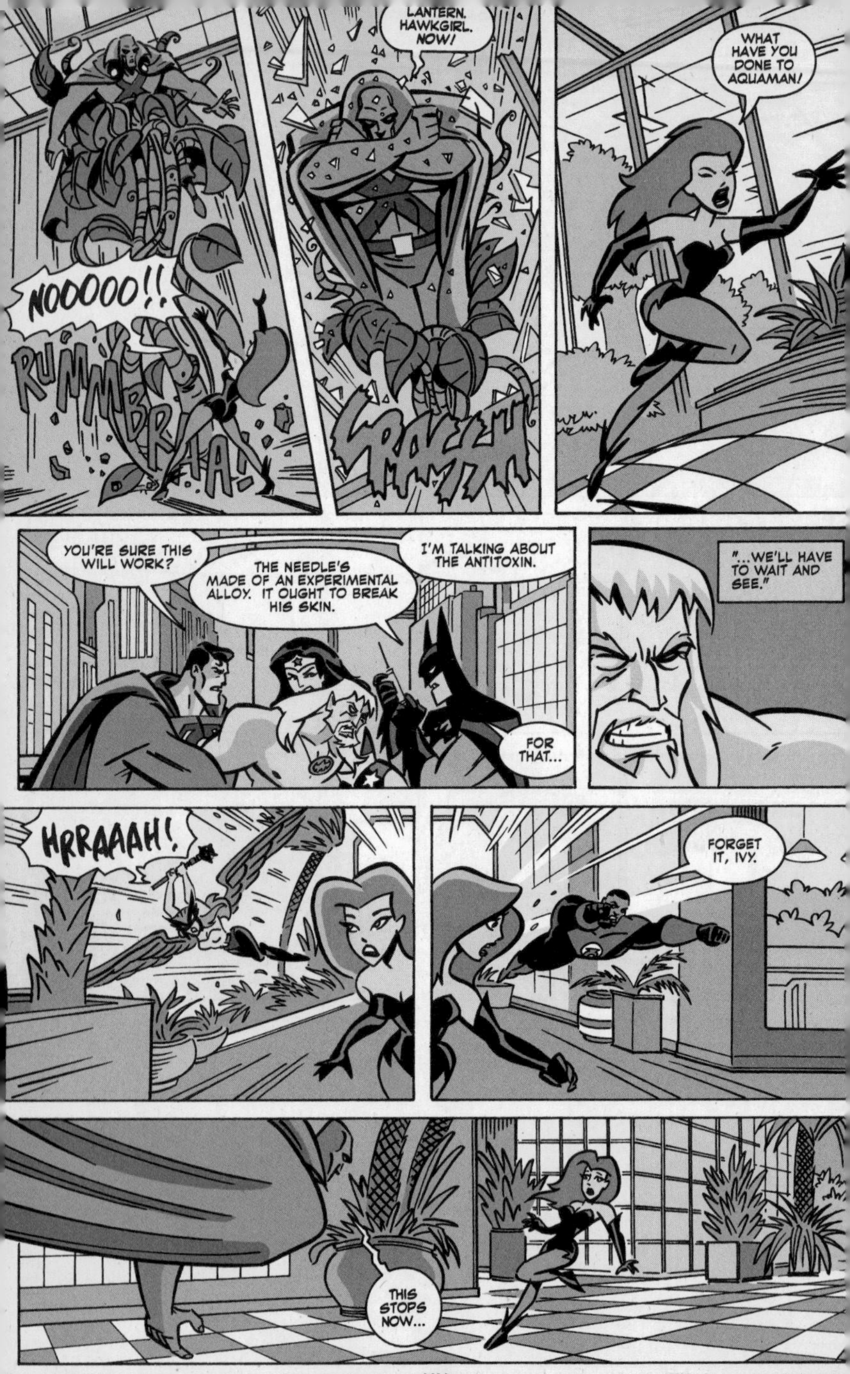
NOOOOO!!
RUMMBRAAA!
LANTERN. HAWKGIRL. NOW!
SPAKSH
WHAT HAVE YOU DONE TO AQUAMAN!
YOU'RE SURE THIS WILL WORK?
THE NEEDLE'S MADE OF AN EXPERIMENTAL ALLOY. IT OUGHT TO BREAK HIS SKIN.
I'M TALKING ABOUT THE ANTITOXIN.
FOR THAT...
"...WE'LL HAVE TO WAIT AND SEE."
HRRAAAH!
FORGET IT, IVY.
THIS STOPS NOW...

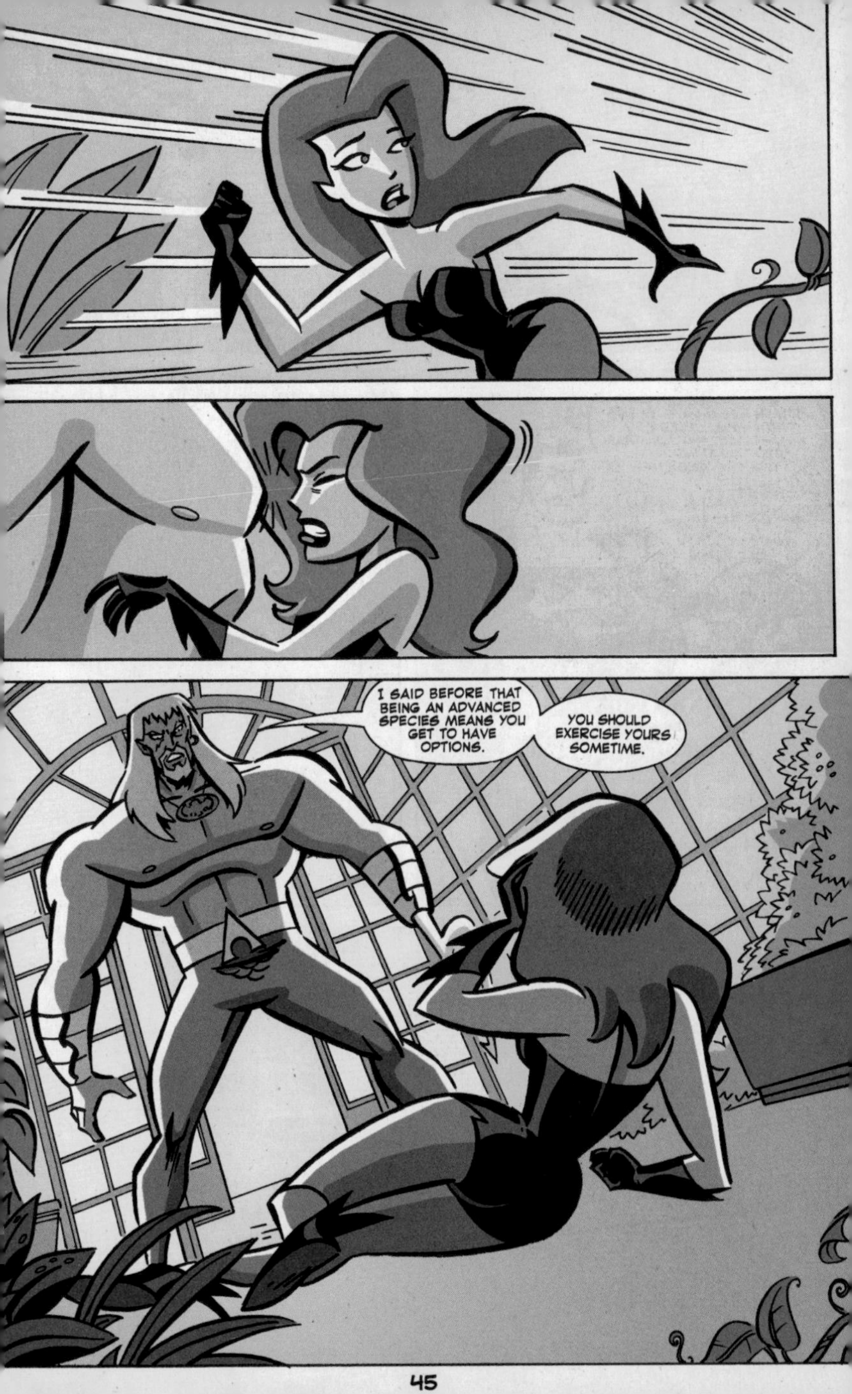
I SAID BEFORE THAT BEING AN ADVANCED SPECIES MEANS YOU GET TO HAVE OPTIONS.
YOU SHOULD EXERCISE YOURS SOMETIME.

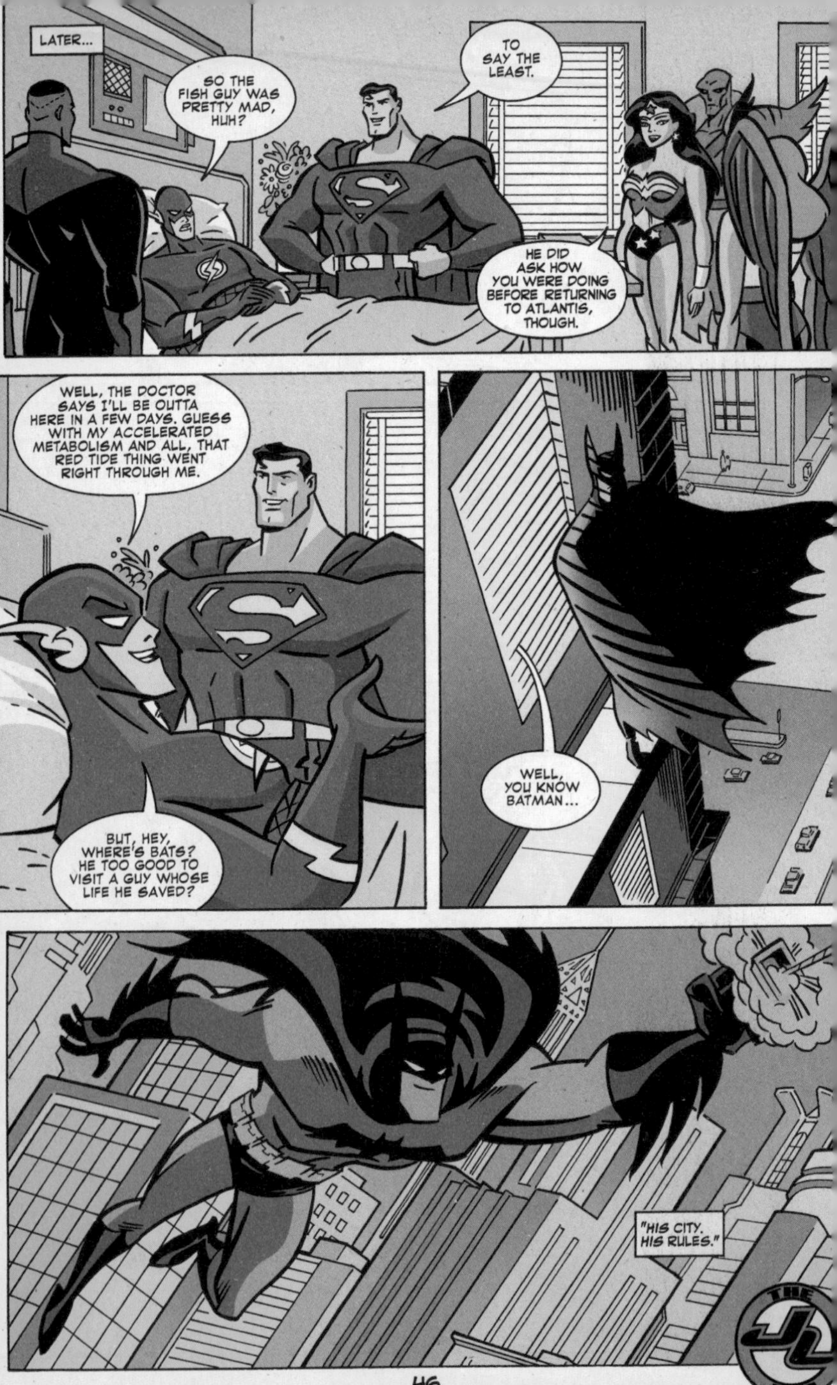
LATER...
SO THE FISH GUY WAS PRETTY MAD, HUH?
TO SAY THE LEAST.
HE DID ASK HOW YOU WERE DOING BEFORE RETURNING TO ATLANTIS, THOUGH.
WELL, THE DOCTOR SAYS I'LL BE OUTTA HERE IN A FEW DAYS. GUESS WITH MY ACCELERATED METABOLISM AND ALL, THAT RED TIDE THING WENT RIGHT THROUGH ME.
BUT, HEY, WHERE'S BATS? HE TOO GOOD TO VISIT A GUY WHOSE LIFE HE SAVED?
WELL, YOU KNOW BATMAN...
"HIS CITY. HIS RULES."

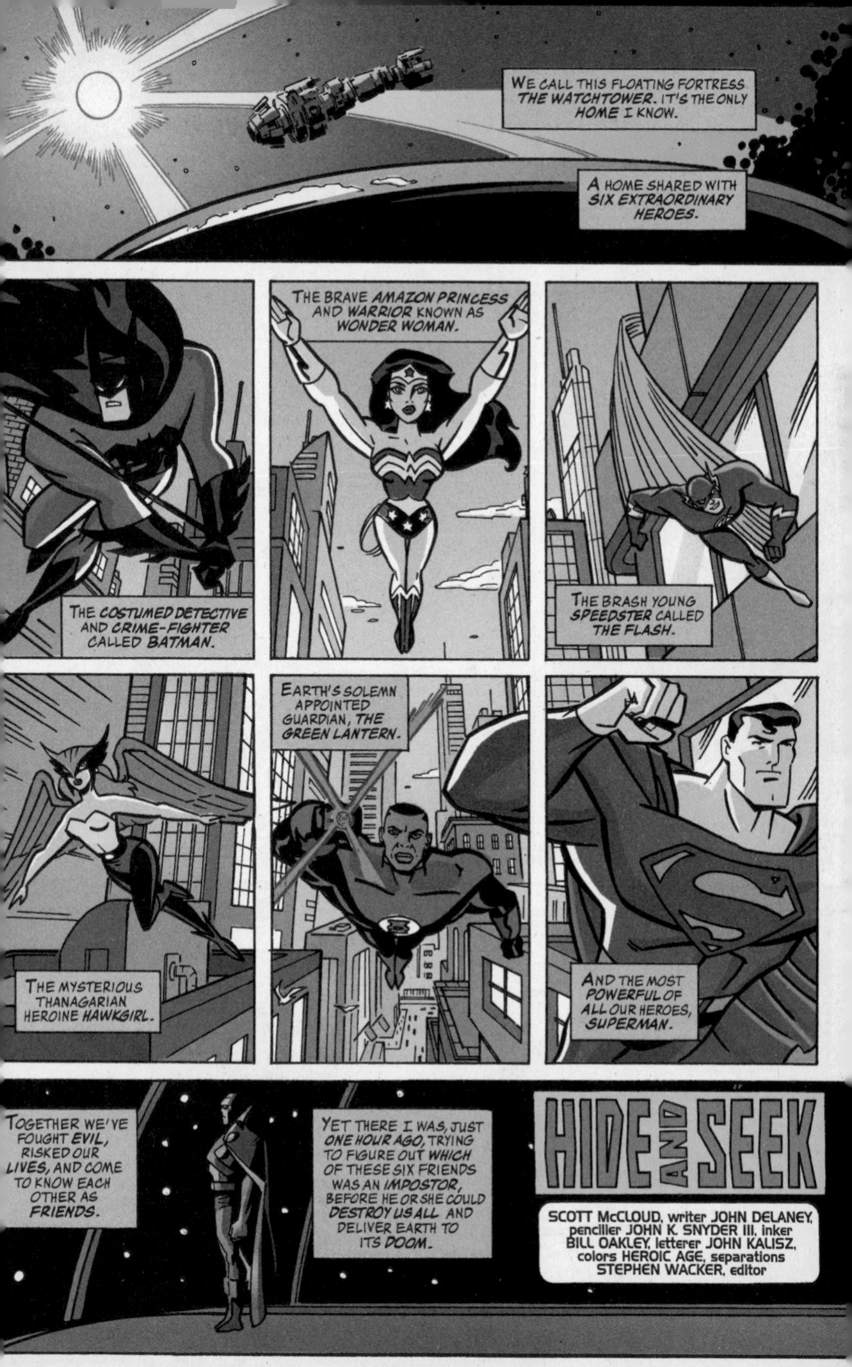

WE CALL THIS FLOATING FORTRESS THE WATCHTOWER. IT'S THE ONLY HOME I KNOW.
A HOME SHARED WITH SIX EXTRAORDINARY HEROES.
THE COSTUMED DETECTIVE AND CRIME-FIGHTER CALLED BATMAN.
THE BRAVE AMAZON PRINCESS AND WARRIOR KNOWN AS WONDER WOMAN.
THE BRASH YOUNG SPEEDSTER CALLED THE FLASH.
THE MYSTERIOUS THANAGARIAN HEROINE HAWKGIRL.
EARTH'S SOLEMN APPOINTED GUARDIAN, THE GREEN LANTERN.
AND THE MOST POWERFUL OF ALL OUR HEROES, SUPERMAN.
TOGETHER WE'VE FOUGHT EVIL, RISKED OUR LIVES, AND COME TO KNOW EACH OTHER AS FRIENDS.
YET THERE I WAS, JUST ONE HOUR AGO, TRYING TO FIGURE OUT WHICH OF THESE SIX FRIENDS WAS AN IMPOSTOR, BEFORE HE OR SHE COULD DESTROY US ALL AND DELIVER EARTH TO ITS DOOM.
HIDE AND SEEK
SCOTT McCLOUD, writer JOHN DELANEY, penciller JOHN K. SNYDER III, inker BILL OAKLEY, letterer JOHN KALISZ, colors HEROIC AGE, separations STEPHEN WACKER, editor

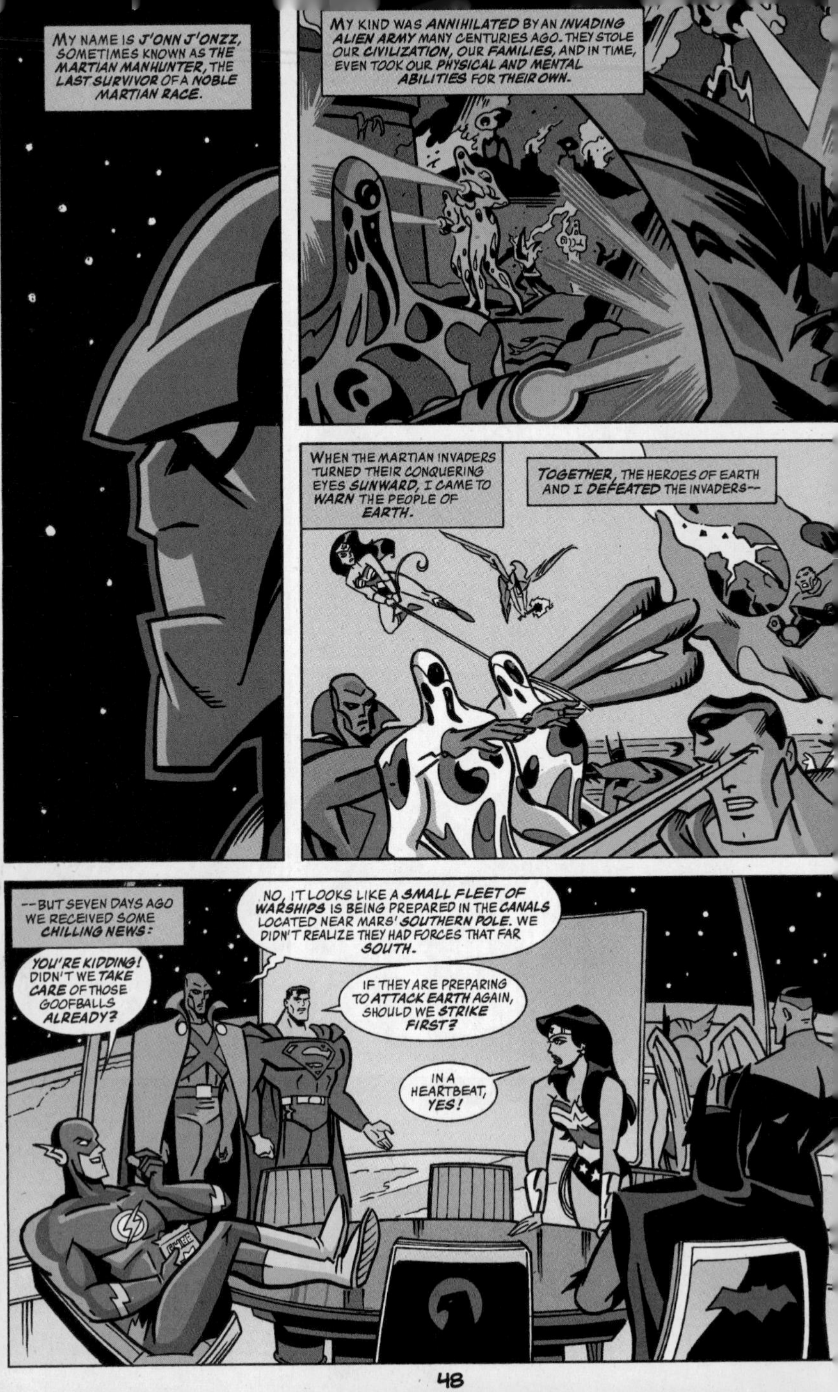
MY NAME IS J'ONN J'ONZZ, SOMETIMES KNOWN AS THE MARTIAN MANHUNTER, THE LAST SURVIVOR OF A NOBLE MARTIAN RACE.
MY KIND WAS ANNIHILATED BY AN INVADING ALIEN ARMY MANY CENTURIES AGO. THEY STOLE OUR CIVILIZATION, OUR FAMILIES, AND IN TIME, EVEN TOOK OUR PHYSICAL AND MENTAL ABILITIES FOR THEIR OWN.
WHEN THE MARTIAN INVADERS TURNED THEIR CONQUERING EYES SUNWARD, I CAME TO WARN THE PEOPLE OF EARTH.
TOGETHER, THE HEROES OF EARTH AND I DEFEATED THE INVADERS--
--BUT SEVEN DAYS AGO WE RECEIVED SOME CHILLING NEWS:
NO, IT LOOKS LIKE A SMALL FLEET OF WARSHIPS IS BEING PREPARED IN THE CANALS LOCATED NEAR MARS' SOUTHERN POLE. WE DIDN'T REALIZE THEY HAD FORCES THAT FAR SOUTH.
YOU'RE KIDDING! DIDN'T WE TAKE CARE OF THOSE GOOFBALLS ALREADY?
IF THEY ARE PREPARING TO ATTACK EARTH AGAIN, SHOULD WE STRIKE FIRST?
IN A HEARTBEAT, YES!

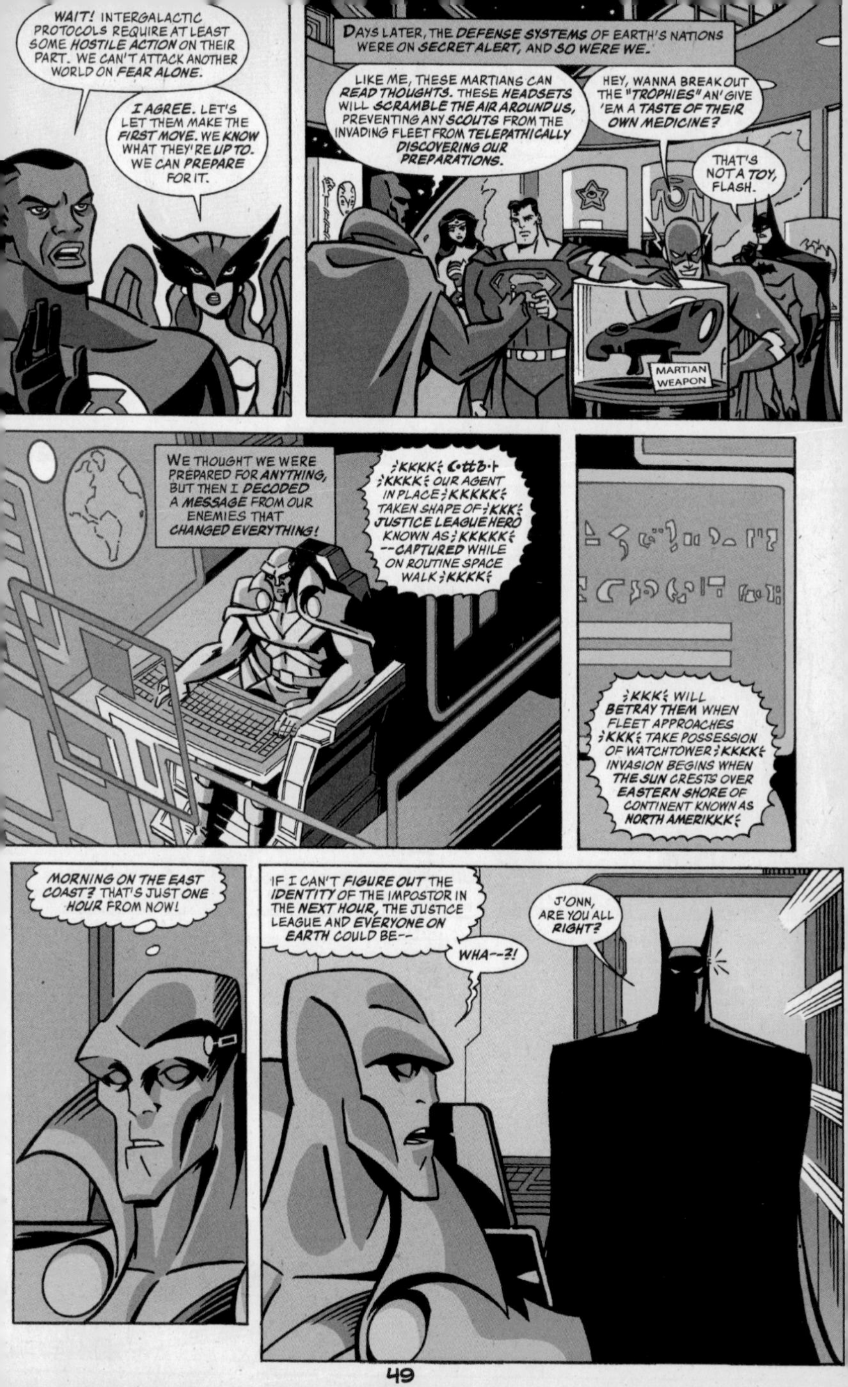

WAIT! INTERGALACTIC PROTOCOLS REQUIRE AT LEAST SOME HOSTILE ACTION ON THEIR PART. WE CAN'T ATTACK ANOTHER WORLD ON FEAR ALONE.
I AGREE. LET'S LET THEM MAKE THE FIRST MOVE. WE KNOW WHAT THEY'RE UP TO. WE CAN PREPARE FOR IT.
DAYS LATER, THE DEFENSE SYSTEMS OF EARTH'S NATIONS WERE ON SECRET ALERT, AND SO WERE WE.
LIKE ME, THESE MARTIANS CAN READ THOUGHTS. THESE HEADSETS WILL SCRAMBLE THE AIR AROUND US, PREVENTING ANY SCOUTS FROM THE INVADING FLEET FROM TELEPATHICALLY DISCOVERING OUR PREPARATIONS.
HEY, WANNA BREAK OUT THE "TROPHIES" AN' GIVE 'EM A TASTE OF THEIR OWN MEDICINE?
THAT'S NOT A TOY, FLASH.
MARTIAN WEAPON
WE THOUGHT WE WERE PREPARED FOR ANYTHING, BUT THEN I DECODED A MESSAGE FROM OUR ENEMIES THAT CHANGED EVERYTHING!
KKKK KKKK OUR AGENT IN PLACE KKKKK TAKEN SHAPE OF KKK JUSTICE LEAGUE HERO KNOWN AS KKKKK --CAPTURED WHILE ON ROUTINE SPACE WALK KKKK
KKK WILL BETRAY THEM WHEN FLEET APPROACHES KKK TAKE POSSESSION OF WATCHTOWER KKKK INVASION BEGINS WHEN THE SUN CRESTS OVER EASTERN SHORE OF CONTINENT KNOWN AS NORTH AMERIKKK
MORNING ON THE EAST COAST? THAT'S JUST ONE HOUR FROM NOW!
IF I CAN'T FIGURE OUT THE IDENTITY OF THE IMPOSTOR IN THE NEXT HOUR, THE JUSTICE LEAGUE AND EVERYONE ON EARTH COULD BE--
WHA--?!
J'ONN, ARE YOU ALL RIGHT?

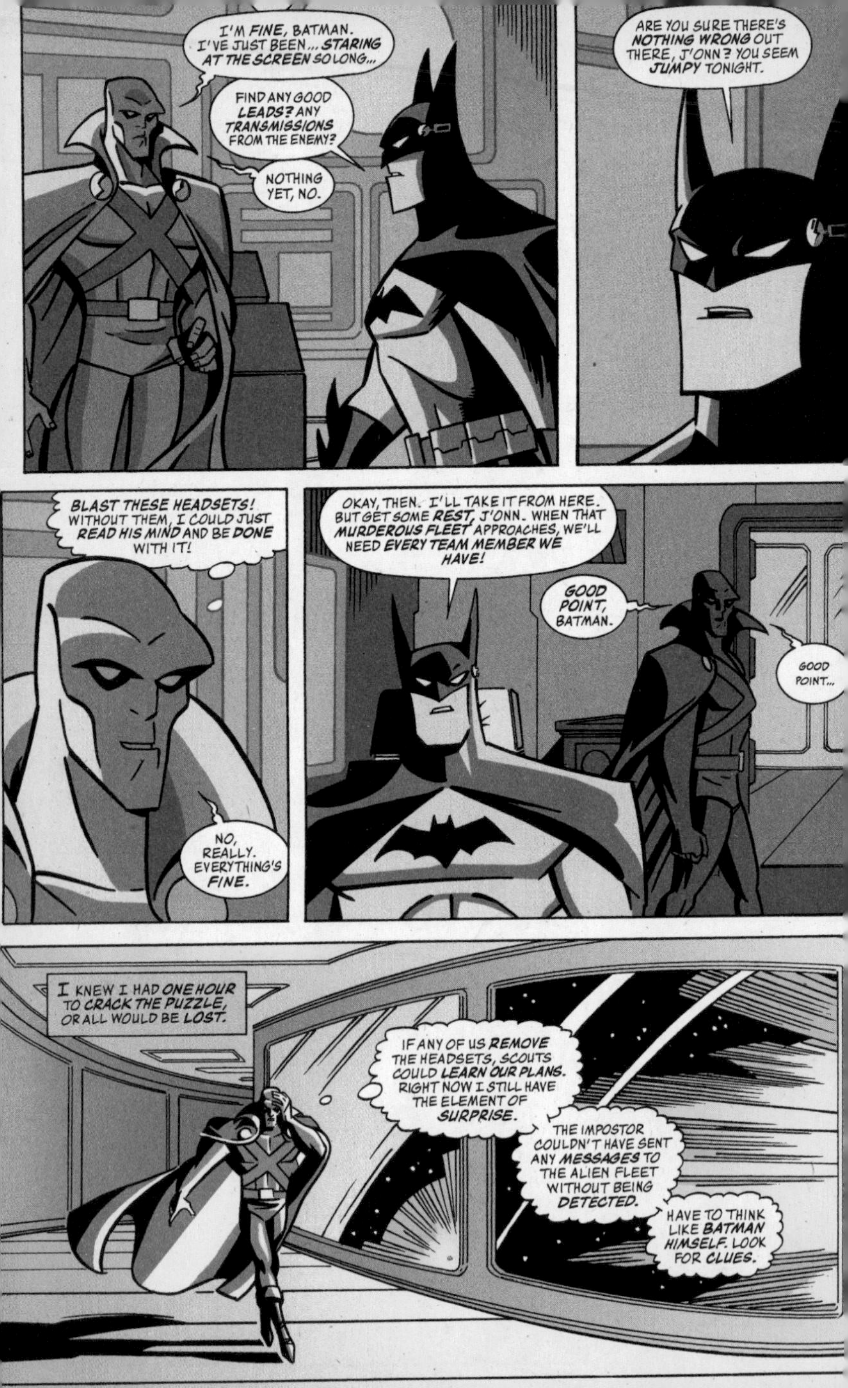
I'M FINE, BATMAN. I'VE JUST BEEN... STARING AT THE SCREEN SO LONG...
FIND ANY GOOD LEADS? ANY TRANSMISSIONS FROM THE ENEMY?
NOTHING YET, NO.
ARE YOU SURE THERE'S NOTHING WRONG OUT THERE, J'ONN? YOU SEEM JUMPY TONIGHT.
BLAST THESE HEADSETS! WITHOUT THEM, I COULD JUST READ HIS MIND AND BE DONE WITH IT!
NO, REALLY. EVERYTHING'S FINE.
OKAY, THEN. I'LL TAKE IT FROM HERE. BUT GET SOME REST, J'ONN. WHEN THAT MURDEROUS FLEET APPROACHES, WE'LL NEED EVERY TEAM MEMBER WE HAVE!
GOOD POINT, BATMAN.
GOOD POINT...
I KNEW I HAD ONE HOUR TO CRACK THE PUZZLE, OR ALL WOULD BE LOST.
IF ANY OF US REMOVE THE HEADSETS, SCOUTS COULD LEARN OUR PLANS. RIGHT NOW I STILL HAVE THE ELEMENT OF SURPRISE.
THE IMPOSTOR COULDN'T HAVE SENT ANY MESSAGES TO THE ALIEN FLEET WITHOUT BEING DETECTED.
HAVE TO THINK LIKE BATMAN HIMSELF. LOOK FOR CLUES.

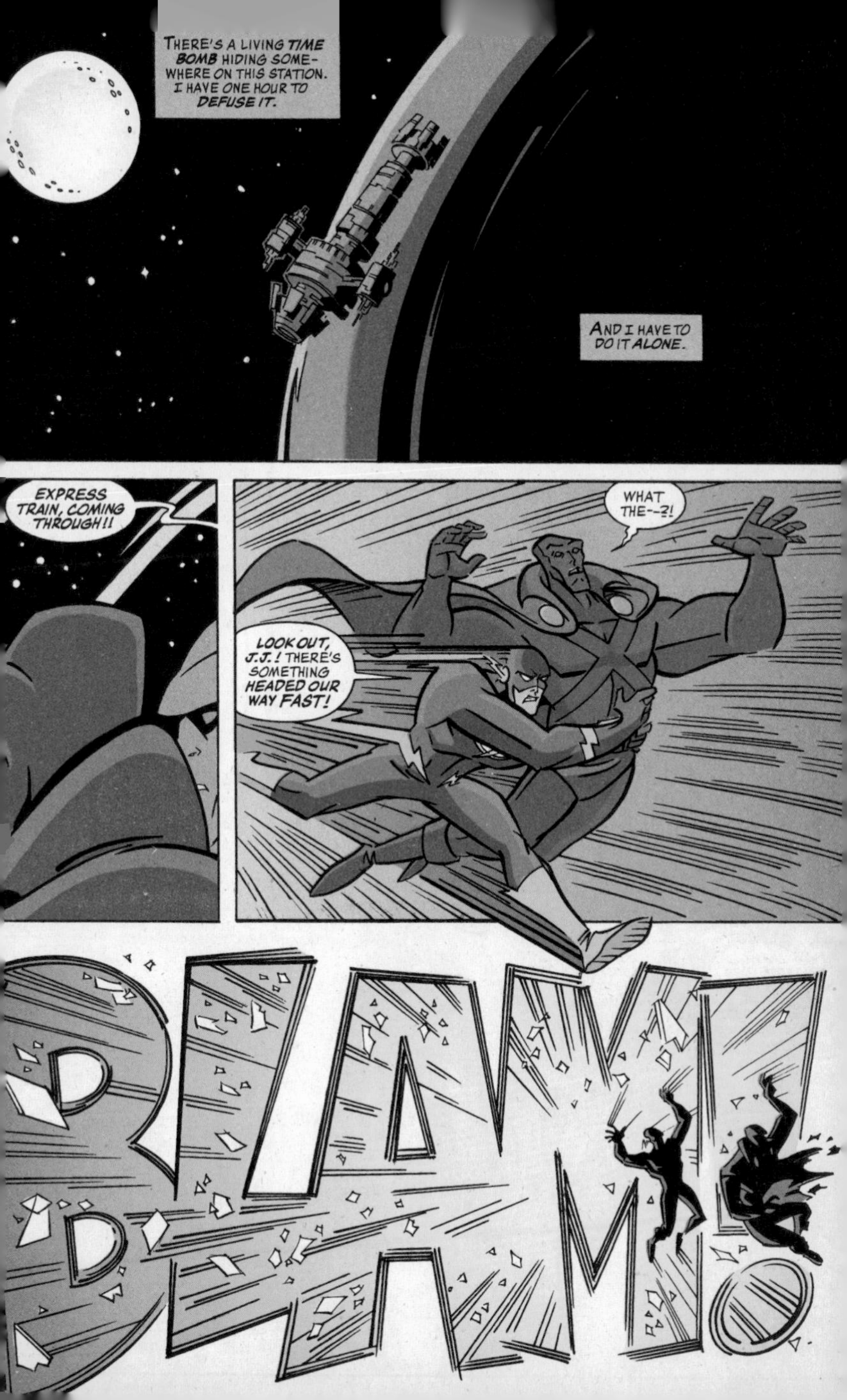
THERE'S A LIVING TIME BOMB HIDING SOMEWHERE ON THIS STATION. I HAVE ONE HOUR TO DEFUSE IT.
AND I HAVE TO DO IT ALONE.
EXPRESS TRAIN, COMING THROUGH!!
WHAT THE--?!
LOOK OUT, J.J.! THERE'S SOMETHING HEADED OUR WAY FAST!
BLAM!
BLAM!

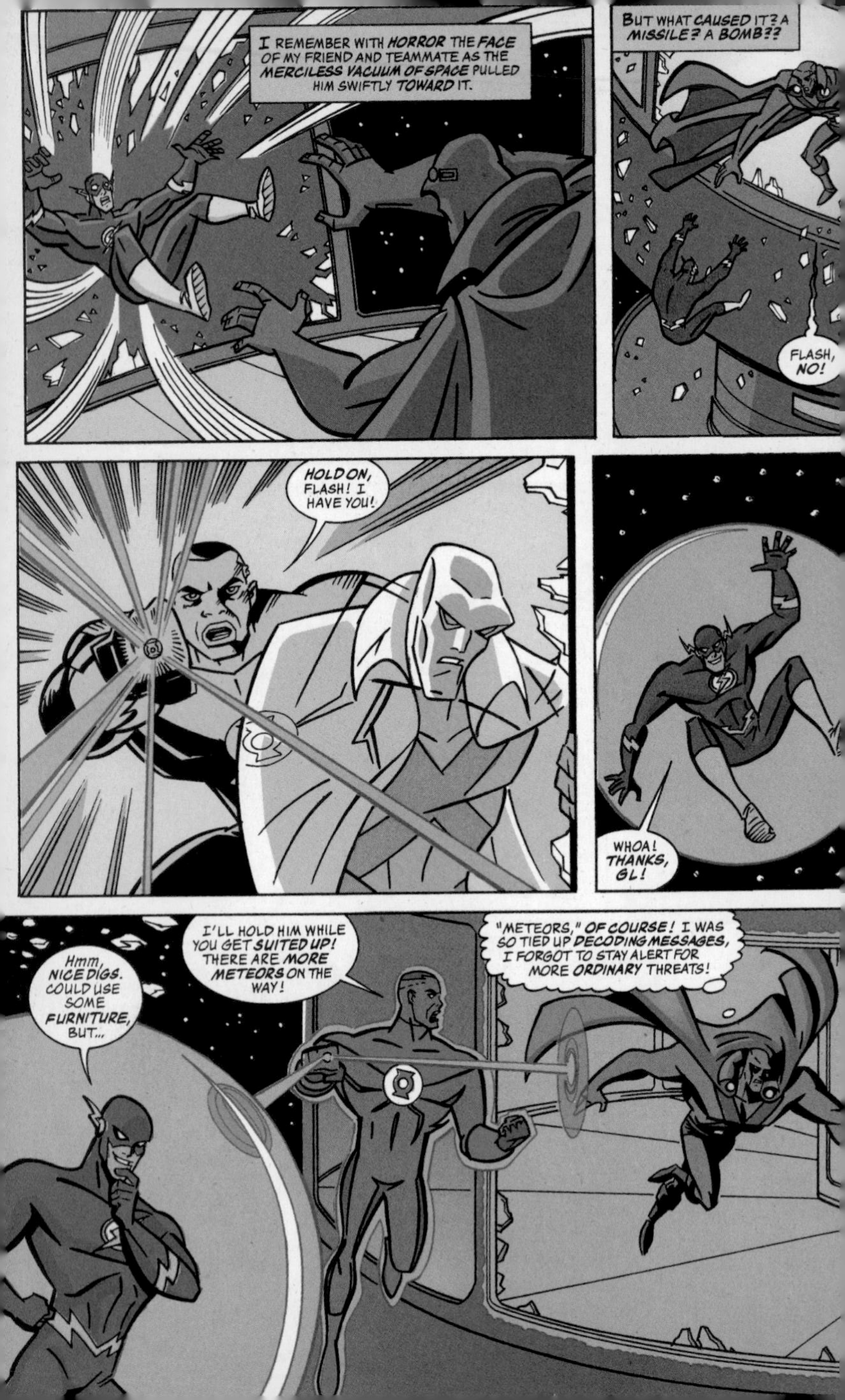
I REMEMBER WITH HORROR THE FACE OF MY FRIEND AND TEAMMATE AS THE MERCILESS VACUUM OF SPACE PULLED HIM SWIFTLY TOWARD IT.
BUT WHAT CAUSED IT? A MISSILE? A BOMB??
FLASH, NO!
HOLD ON, FLASH! I HAVE YOU!
WHOA! THANKS, GL!
Hmm, NICE DIGS. COULD USE SOME FURNITURE, BUT...
I'LL HOLD HIM WHILE YOU GET SUITED UP! THERE ARE MORE METEORS ON THE WAY!
"METEORS," OF COURSE! I WAS SO TIED UP DECODING MESSAGES, I FORGOT TO STAY ALERT FOR MORE ORDINARY THREATS!

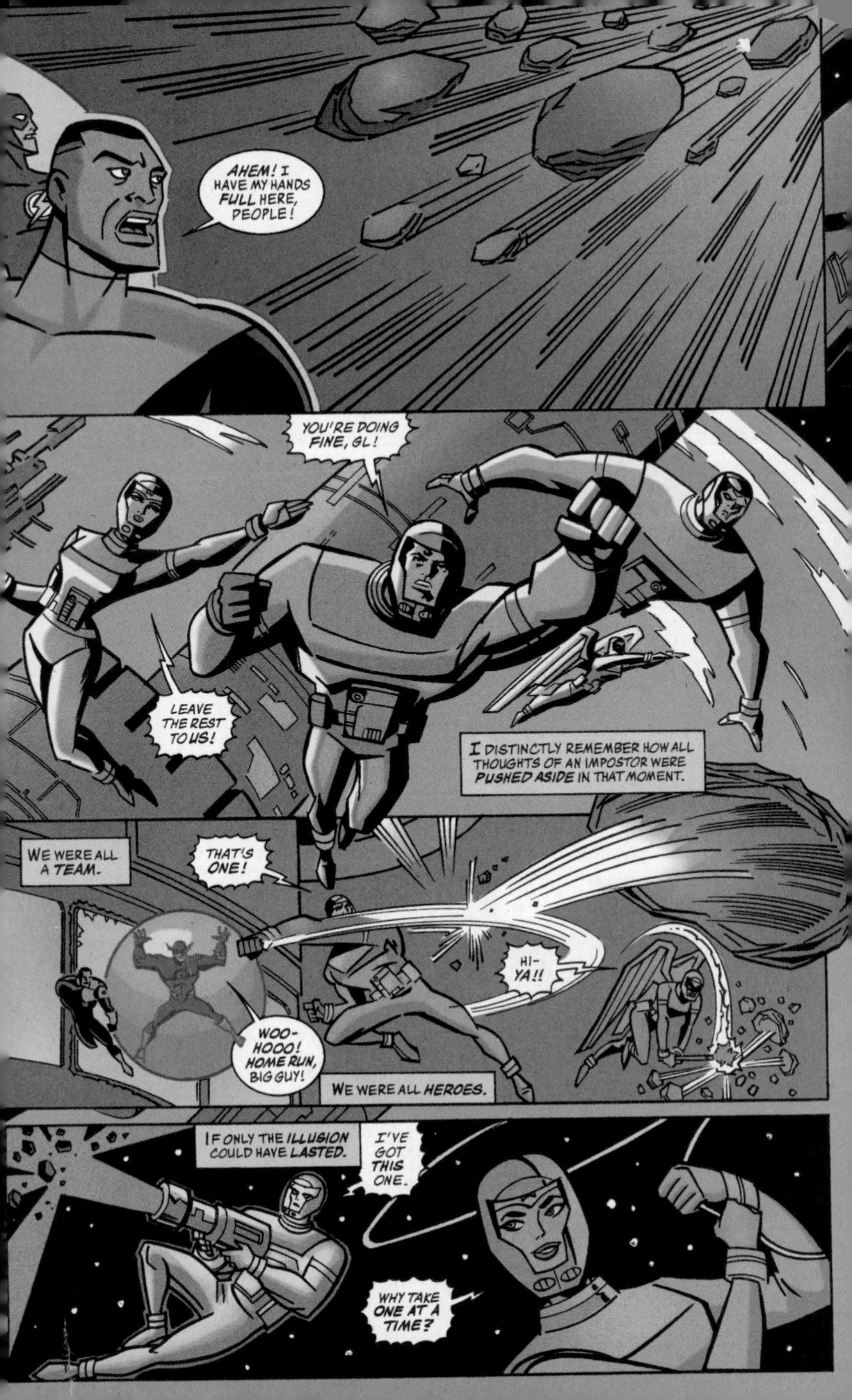
AHEM! I HAVE MY HANDS FULL HERE, PEOPLE!
YOU'RE DOING FINE, GL!
LEAVE THE REST TO US!
I DISTINCTLY REMEMBER HOW ALL THOUGHTS OF AN IMPOSTOR WERE PUSHED ASIDE IN THAT MOMENT.
WE WERE ALL A TEAM.
THAT'S ONE!
HI-YA!!
WOO-HOOO! HOME RUN, BIG GUY!
WE WERE ALL HEROES.
IF ONLY THE ILLUSION COULD HAVE LASTED.
I'VE GOT THIS ONE.
WHY TAKE ONE AT A TIME?

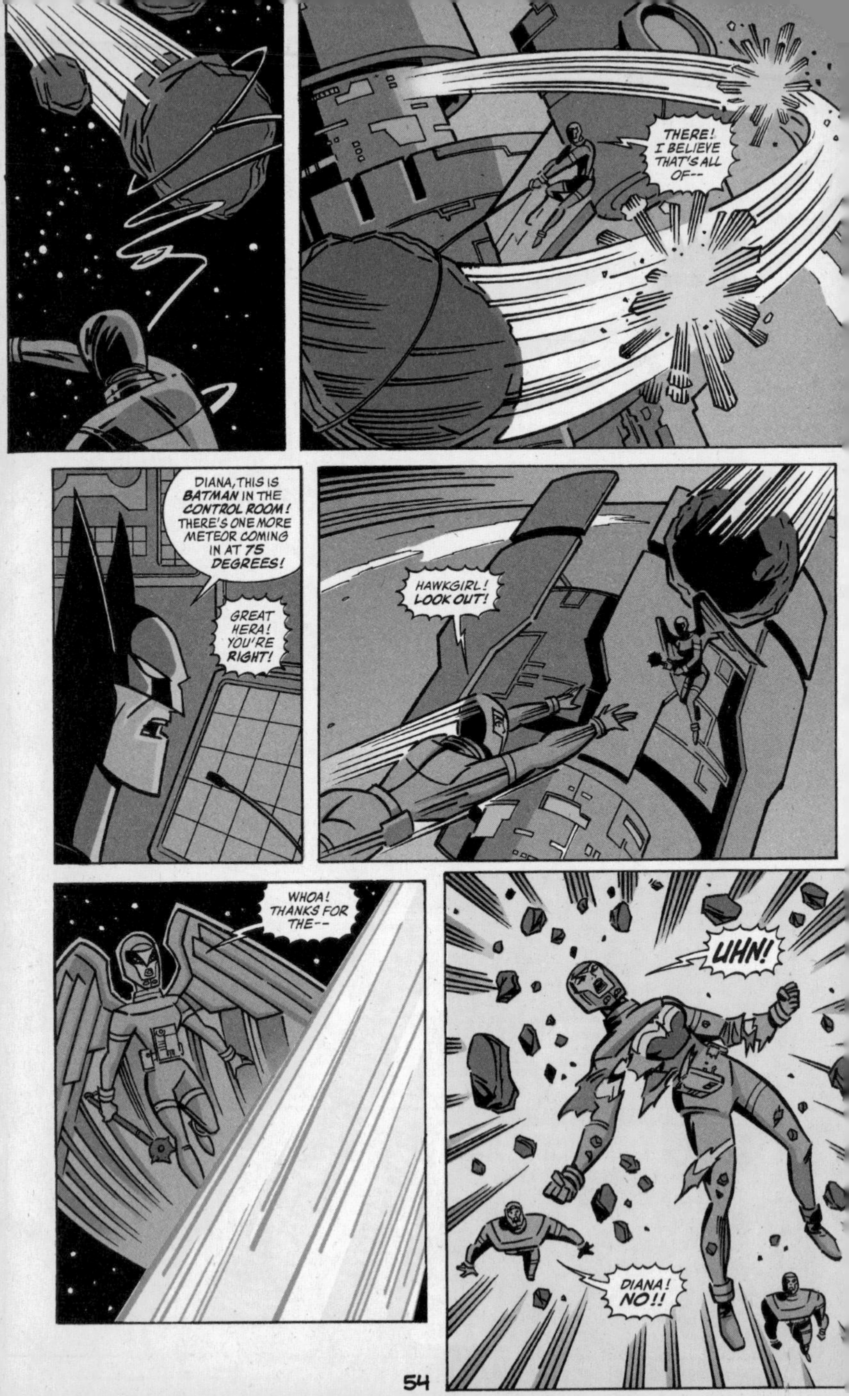
THERE! I BELIEVE THAT'S ALL OF--
DIANA, THIS IS BATMAN IN THE CONTROL ROOM! THERE'S ONE MORE METEOR COMING IN AT 75 DEGREES!
GREAT HERA! YOU'RE RIGHT!
HAWKGIRL! LOOK OUT!
WHOA! THANKS FOR THE--
UHN!
DIANA! NO!!

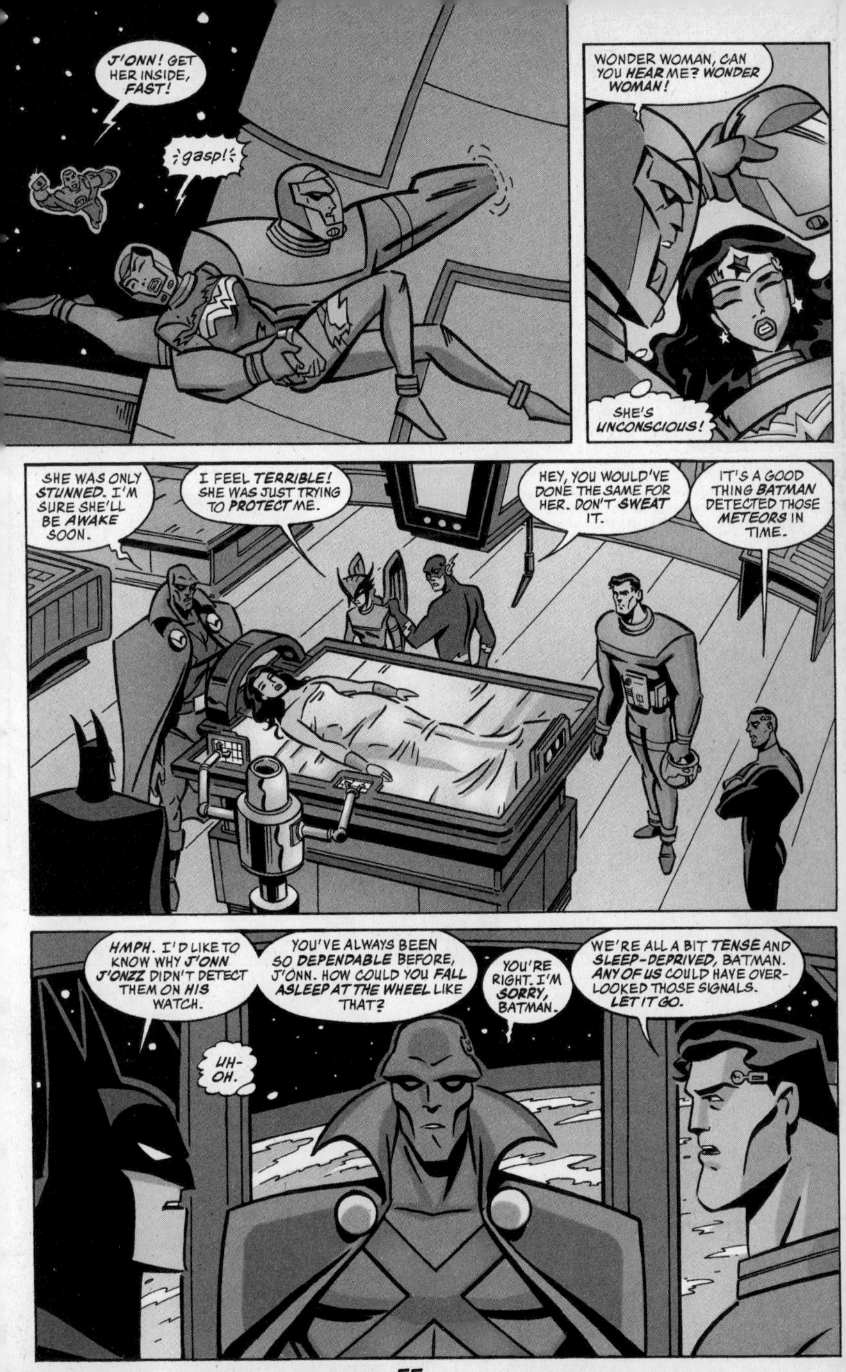
J'ONN! GET HER INSIDE, FAST!
gasp!
WONDER WOMAN, CAN YOU HEAR ME? WONDER WOMAN!
SHE'S UNCONSCIOUS!
SHE WAS ONLY STUNNED. I'M SURE SHE'LL BE AWAKE SOON.
I FEEL TERRIBLE! SHE WAS JUST TRYING TO PROTECT ME.
HEY, YOU WOULD'VE DONE THE SAME FOR HER. DON'T SWEAT IT.
IT'S A GOOD THING BATMAN DETECTED THOSE METEORS IN TIME.
HMPH. I'D LIKE TO KNOW WHY J'ONN J'ONZZ DIDN'T DETECT THEM ON HIS WATCH.
UH-OH.
YOU'VE ALWAYS BEEN SO DEPENDABLE BEFORE, J'ONN. HOW COULD YOU FALL ASLEEP AT THE WHEEL LIKE THAT?
YOU'RE RIGHT. I'M SORRY, BATMAN.
WE'RE ALL A BIT TENSE AND SLEEP-DEPRIVED, BATMAN. ANY OF US COULD HAVE OVER-LOOKED THOSE SIGNALS. LET IT GO.

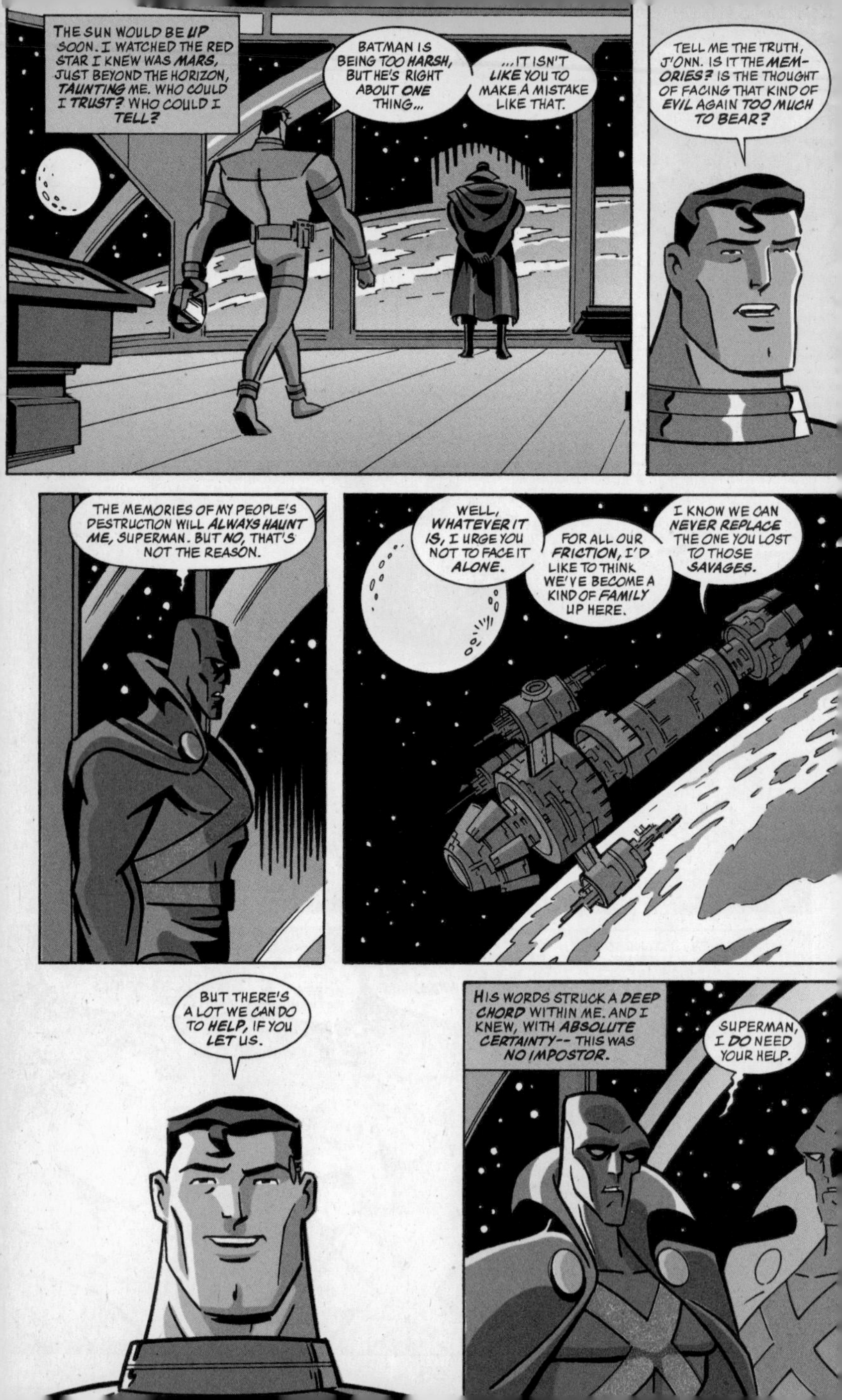
THE SUN WOULD BE UP SOON. I WATCHED THE RED STAR I KNEW WAS MARS, JUST BEYOND THE HORIZON, TAUNTING ME. WHO COULD I TRUST? WHO COULD I TELL?
BATMAN IS BEING TOO HARSH, BUT HE'S RIGHT ABOUT ONE THING...
...IT ISN'T LIKE YOU TO MAKE A MISTAKE LIKE THAT.
TELL ME THE TRUTH, J'ONN. IS IT THE MEMORIES? IS THE THOUGHT OF FACING THAT KIND OF EVIL AGAIN TOO MUCH TO BEAR?
THE MEMORIES OF MY PEOPLE'S DESTRUCTION WILL ALWAYS HAUNT ME, SUPERMAN. BUT NO, THAT'S NOT THE REASON.
WELL, WHATEVER IT IS, I URGE YOU NOT TO FACE IT ALONE.
FOR ALL OUR FRICTION, I'D LIKE TO THINK WE'VE BECOME A KIND OF FAMILY UP HERE.
I KNOW WE CAN NEVER REPLACE THE ONE YOU LOST TO THOSE SAVAGES.
BUT THERE'S A LOT WE CAN DO TO HELP, IF YOU LET US.
HIS WORDS STRUCK A DEEP CHORD WITHIN ME. AND I KNEW, WITH ABSOLUTE CERTAINTY-- THIS WAS NO IMPOSTOR.
SUPERMAN, I DO NEED YOUR HELP.

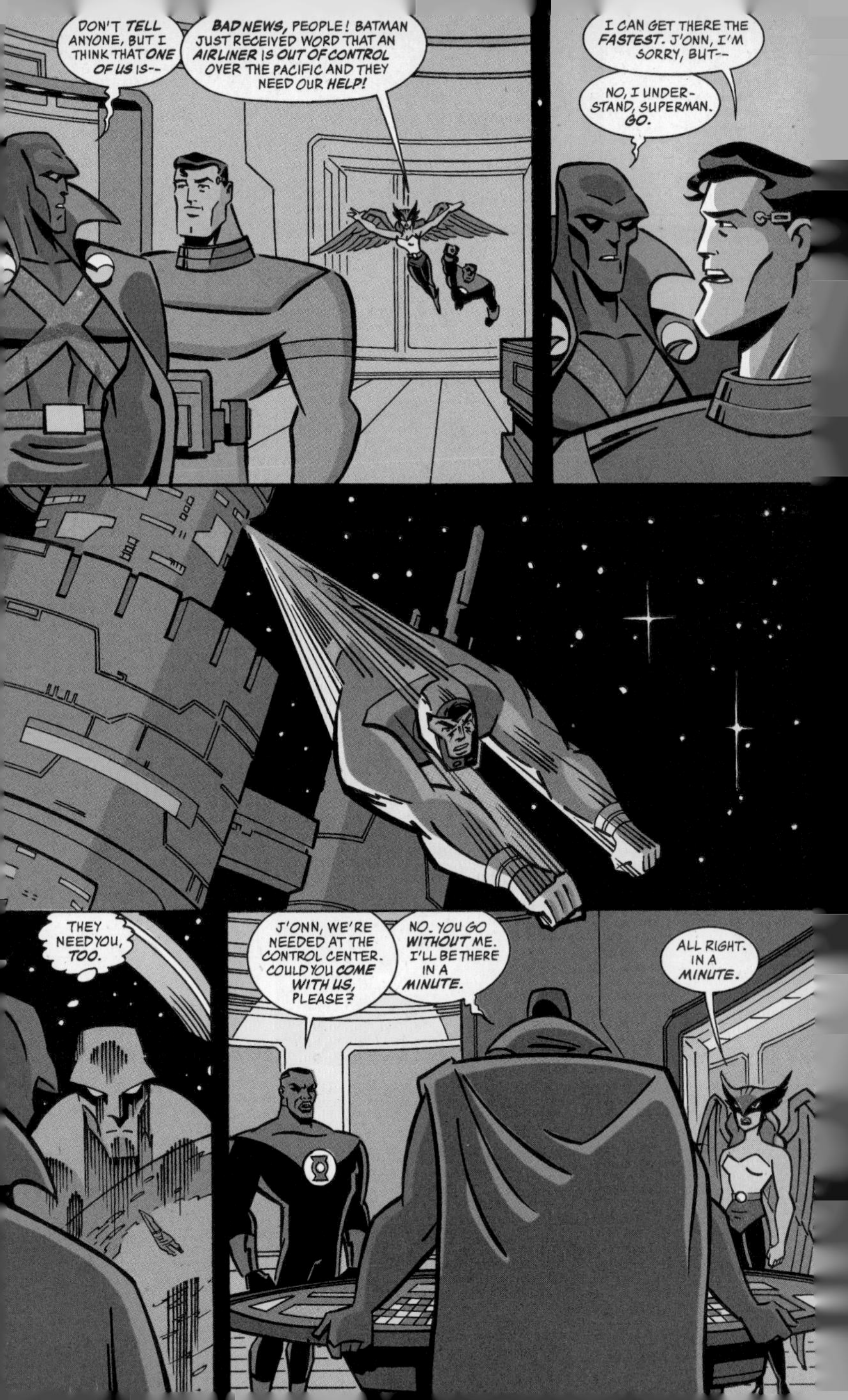
DON'T **TELL** ANYONE, BUT I THINK THAT **ONE OF US** IS--
BAD NEWS, PEOPLE! BATMAN JUST RECEIVED WORD THAT AN **AIRLINER** IS **OUT OF CONTROL** OVER THE PACIFIC AND THEY NEED OUR **HELP!**
I CAN GET THERE THE **FASTEST**. J'ONN, I'M SORRY, BUT--
NO, I UNDER-STAND, SUPERMAN. **GO.**
THEY NEED YOU, **TOO.**
J'ONN, WE'RE NEEDED AT THE CONTROL CENTER. COULD YOU **COME WITH US,** PLEASE?
NO. YOU GO **WITHOUT** ME. I'LL BE THERE IN A **MINUTE.**
ALL RIGHT. IN A **MINUTE.**

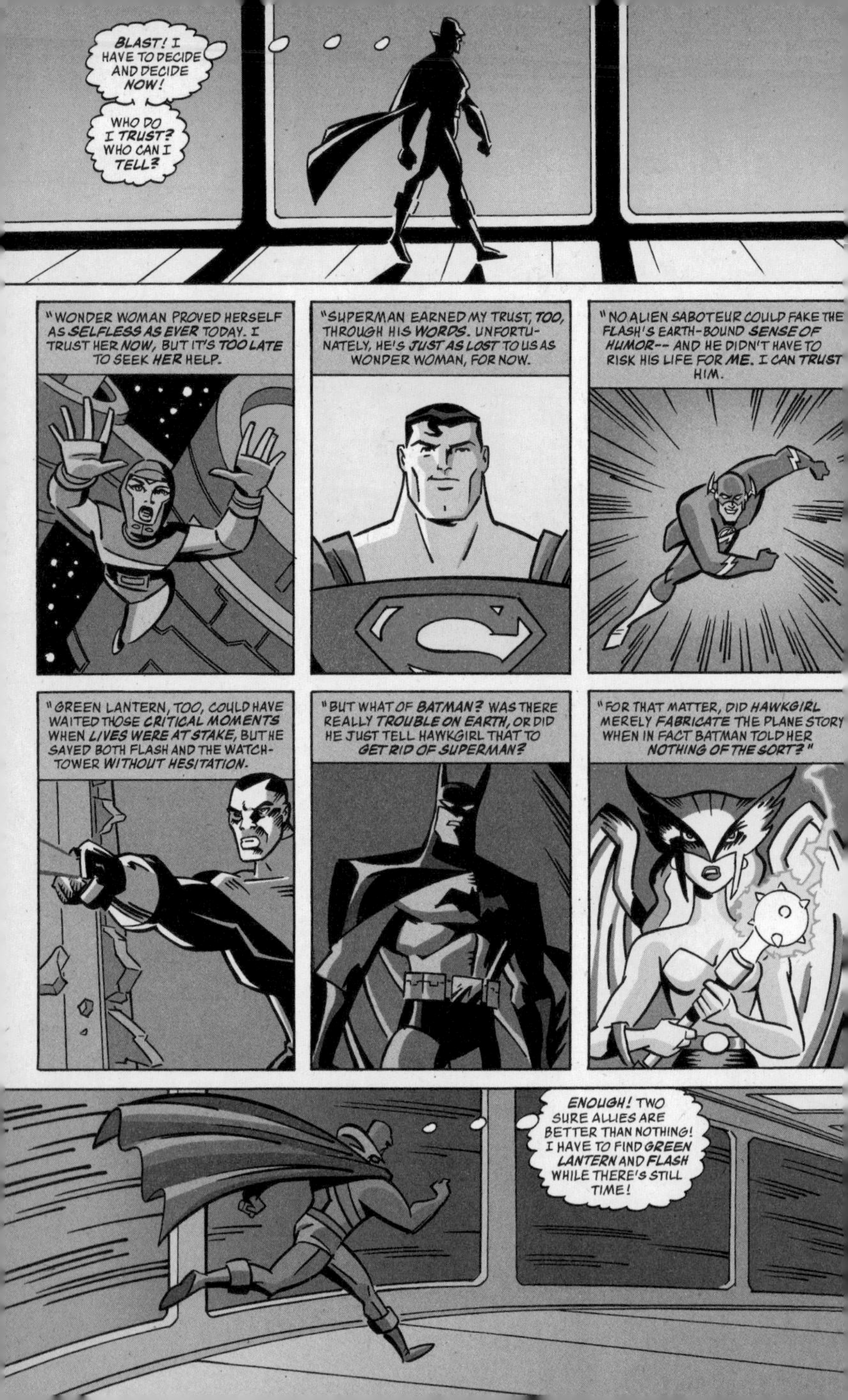

BLAST! I HAVE TO DECIDE AND DECIDE NOW!
WHO DO I TRUST? WHO CAN I TELL?
"WONDER WOMAN PROVED HERSELF AS SELFLESS AS EVER TODAY. I TRUST HER NOW, BUT IT'S TOO LATE TO SEEK HER HELP.
"SUPERMAN EARNED MY TRUST, TOO, THROUGH HIS WORDS. UNFORTUNATELY, HE'S JUST AS LOST TO US AS WONDER WOMAN, FOR NOW.
"NO ALIEN SABOTEUR COULD FAKE THE FLASH'S EARTH-BOUND SENSE OF HUMOR-- AND HE DIDN'T HAVE TO RISK HIS LIFE FOR ME. I CAN TRUST HIM.
"GREEN LANTERN, TOO, COULD HAVE WAITED THOSE CRITICAL MOMENTS WHEN LIVES WERE AT STAKE, BUT HE SAVED BOTH FLASH AND THE WATCHTOWER WITHOUT HESITATION.
"BUT WHAT OF BATMAN? WAS THERE REALLY TROUBLE ON EARTH, OR DID HE JUST TELL HAWKGIRL THAT TO GET RID OF SUPERMAN?
"FOR THAT MATTER, DID HAWKGIRL MERELY FABRICATE THE PLANE STORY WHEN IN FACT BATMAN TOLD HER NOTHING OF THE SORT?"
ENOUGH! TWO SURE ALLIES ARE BETTER THAN NOTHING! I HAVE TO FIND GREEN LANTERN AND FLASH WHILE THERE'S STILL TIME!

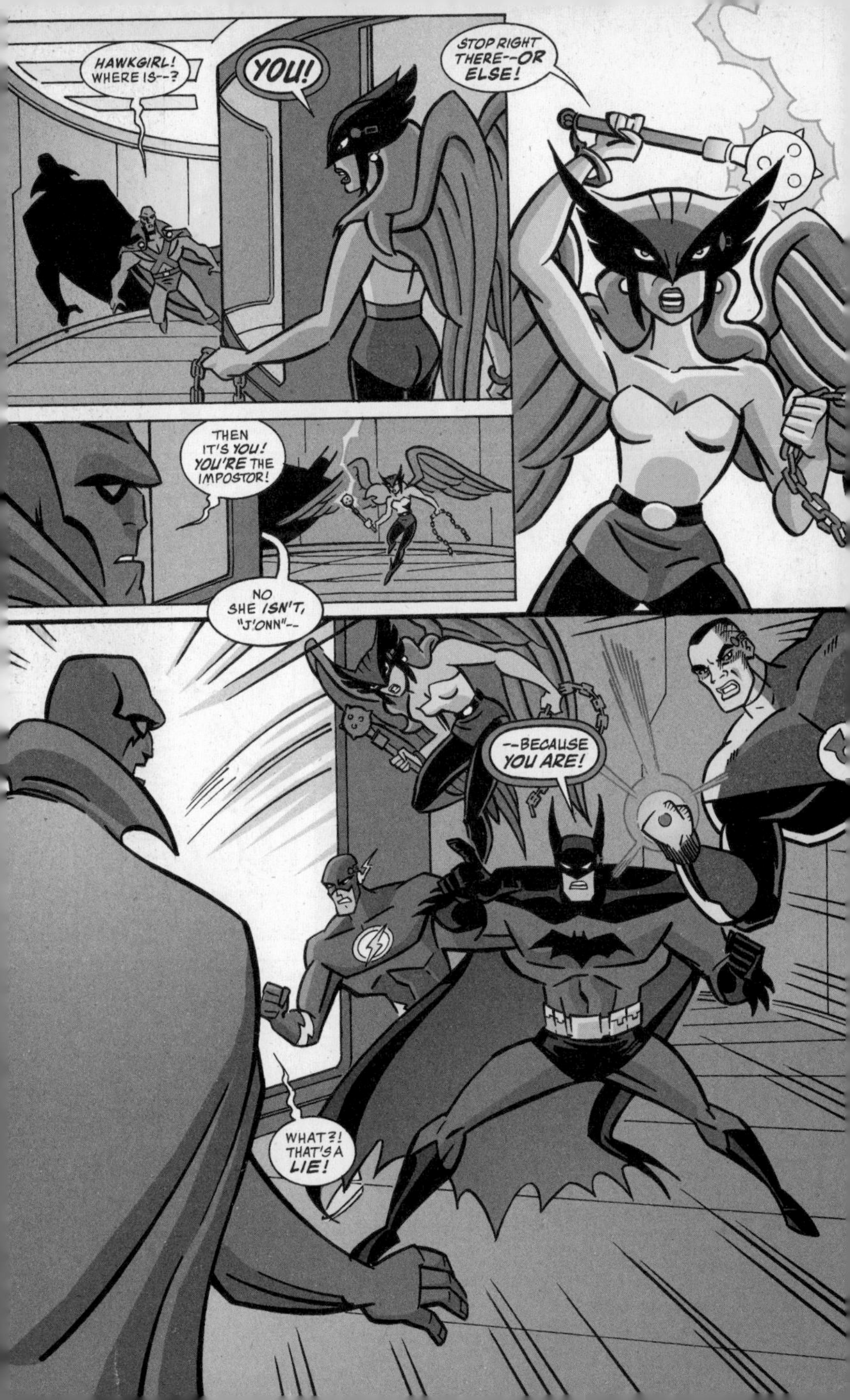
HAWKGIRL! WHERE IS--?
YOU!
STOP RIGHT THERE--OR ELSE!
THEN IT'S YOU! YOU'RE THE IMPOSTOR!
NO SHE ISN'T, "J'ONN"--
--BECAUSE YOU ARE!
WHAT?! THAT'S A LIE!

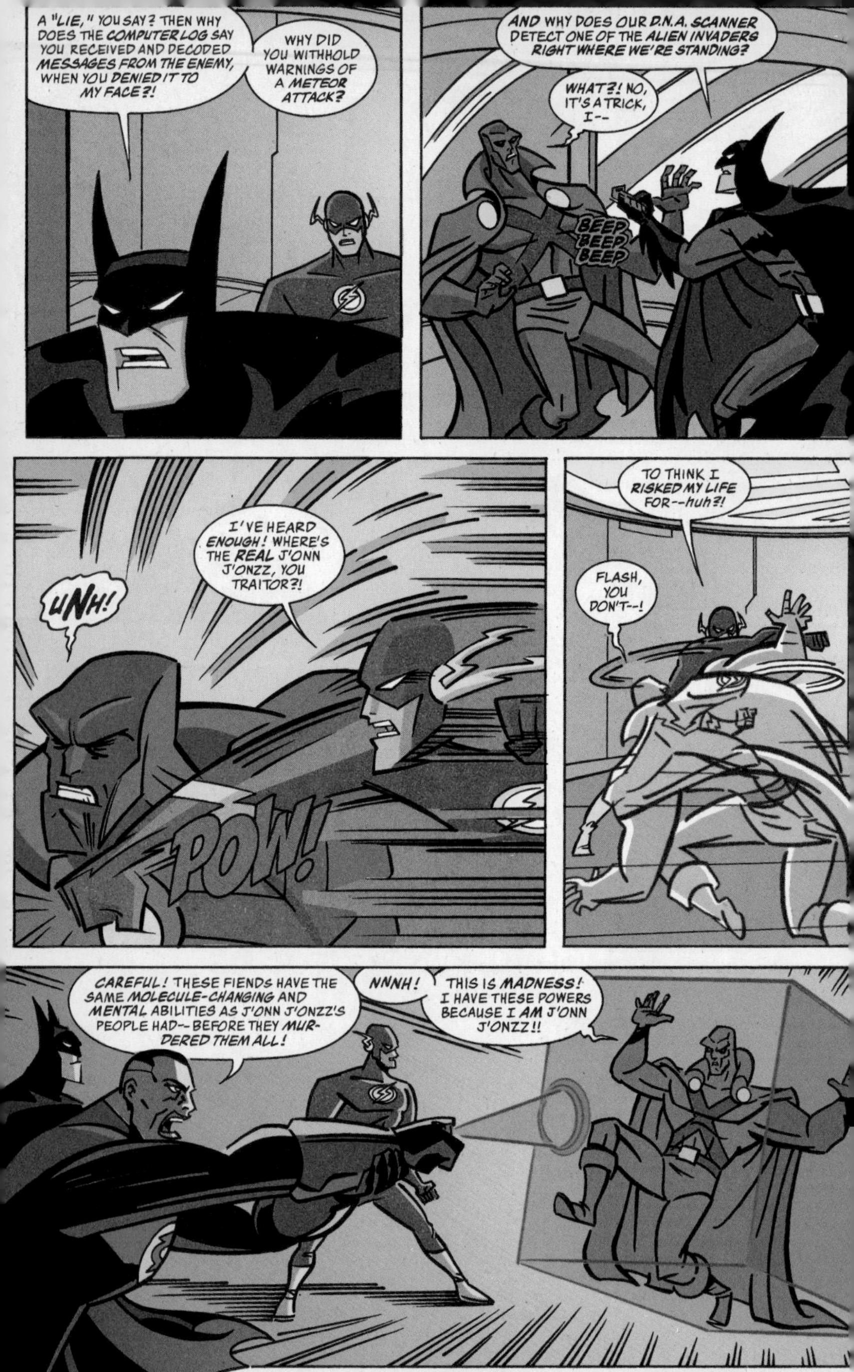
A "LIE," YOU SAY? THEN WHY DOES THE COMPUTER LOG SAY YOU RECEIVED AND DECODED MESSAGES FROM THE ENEMY, WHEN YOU DENIED IT TO MY FACE?!
WHY DID YOU WITHHOLD WARNINGS OF A METEOR ATTACK?
AND WHY DOES OUR D.N.A. SCANNER DETECT ONE OF THE ALIEN INVADERS RIGHT WHERE WE'RE STANDING?
WHAT?! NO, IT'S A TRICK, I--
BEEP BEEP BEEP
I'VE HEARD ENOUGH! WHERE'S THE REAL J'ONN J'ONZZ, YOU TRAITOR?!
UNH!
POW!
TO THINK I RISKED MY LIFE FOR--huh?!
FLASH, YOU DON'T--!
CAREFUL! THESE FIENDS HAVE THE SAME MOLECULE-CHANGING AND MENTAL ABILITIES AS J'ONN J'ONZZ'S PEOPLE HAD--BEFORE THEY MURDERED THEM ALL!
NNNH!
THIS IS MADNESS! I HAVE THESE POWERS BECAUSE I AM J'ONN J'ONZZ!!

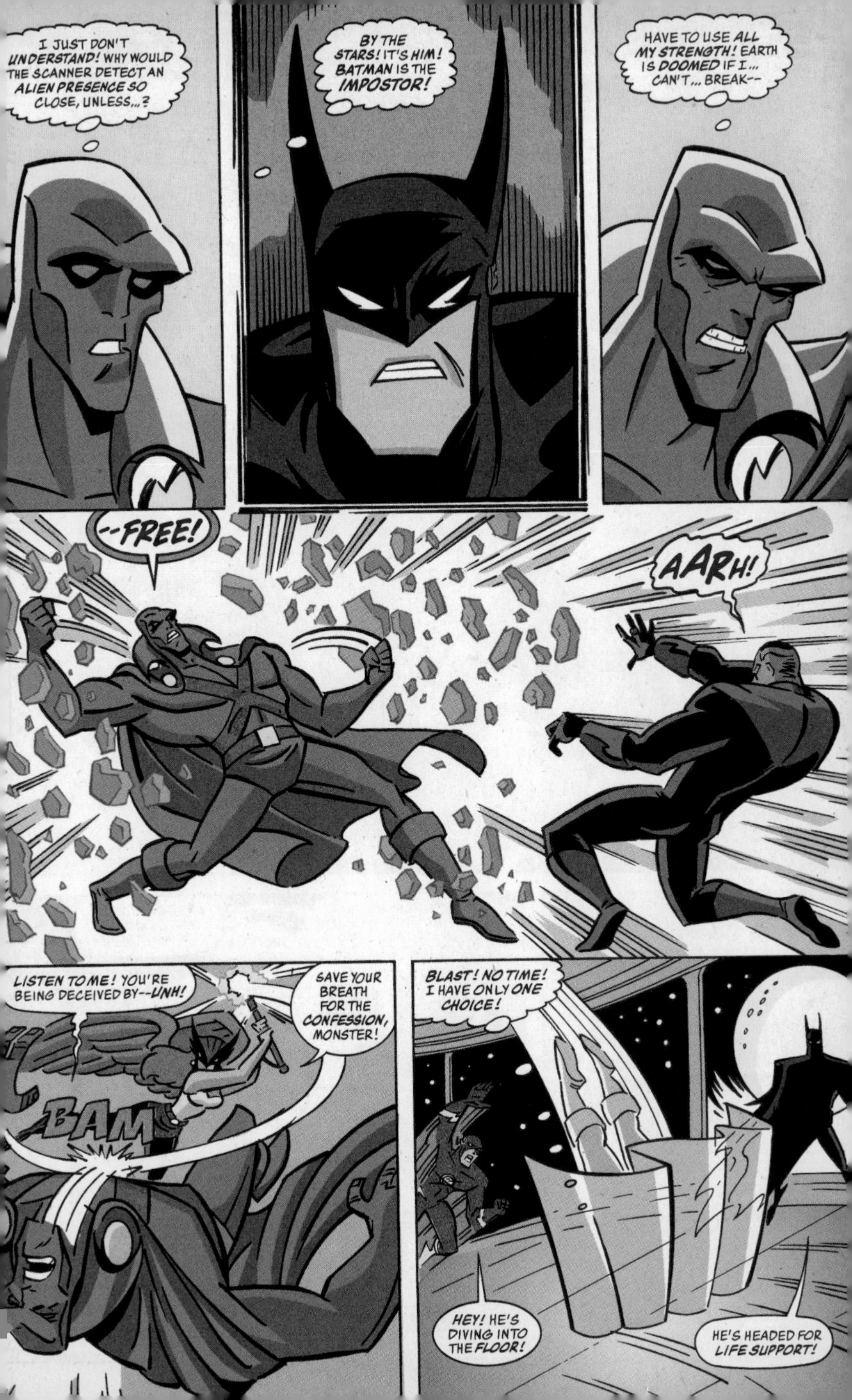
I JUST DON'T UNDERSTAND! WHY WOULD THE SCANNER DETECT AN ALIEN PRESENCE SO CLOSE, UNLESS...?
BY THE STARS! IT'S HIM! BATMAN IS THE IMPOSTOR!
HAVE TO USE ALL MY STRENGTH! EARTH IS DOOMED IF I... CAN'T... BREAK--
--FREE!
AARH!
LISTEN TO ME! YOU'RE BEING DECEIVED BY--UNH!
SAVE YOUR BREATH FOR THE CONFESSION, MONSTER!
BAM
BLAST! NO TIME! I HAVE ONLY ONE CHOICE!
HEY! HE'S DIVING INTO THE FLOOR!
HE'S HEADED FOR LIFE SUPPORT!

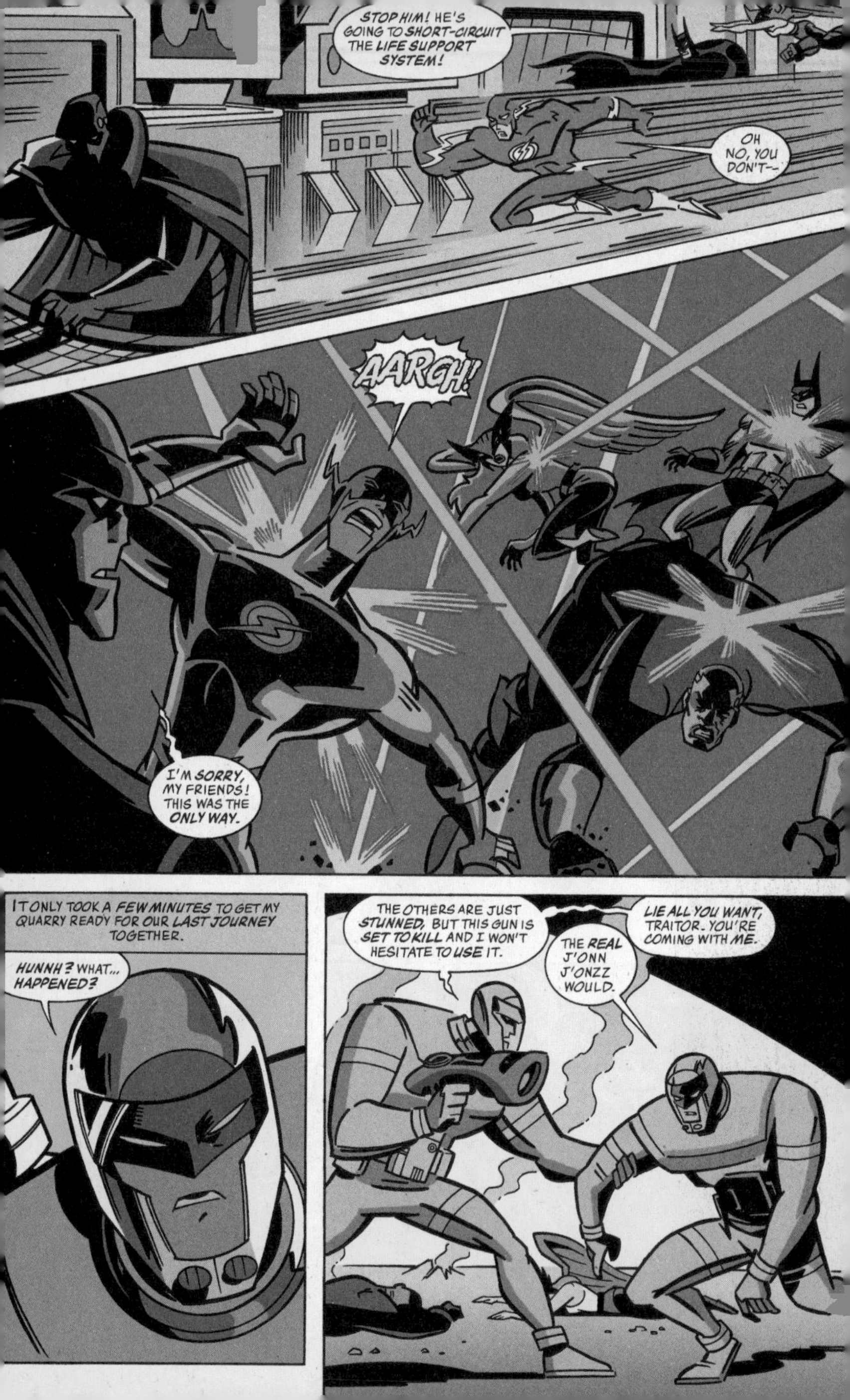
STOP HIM! HE'S GOING TO SHORT-CIRCUIT THE LIFE SUPPORT SYSTEM!
OH NO, YOU DON'T--
AARGH!
I'M SORRY, MY FRIENDS! THIS WAS THE ONLY WAY.
IT ONLY TOOK A FEW MINUTES TO GET MY QUARRY READY FOR OUR LAST JOURNEY TOGETHER.
HUNNH? WHAT... HAPPENED?
THE OTHERS ARE JUST STUNNED, BUT THIS GUN IS SET TO KILL AND I WON'T HESITATE TO USE IT.
THE REAL J'ONN J'ONZZ WOULD.
LIE ALL YOU WANT, TRAITOR. YOU'RE COMING WITH ME.

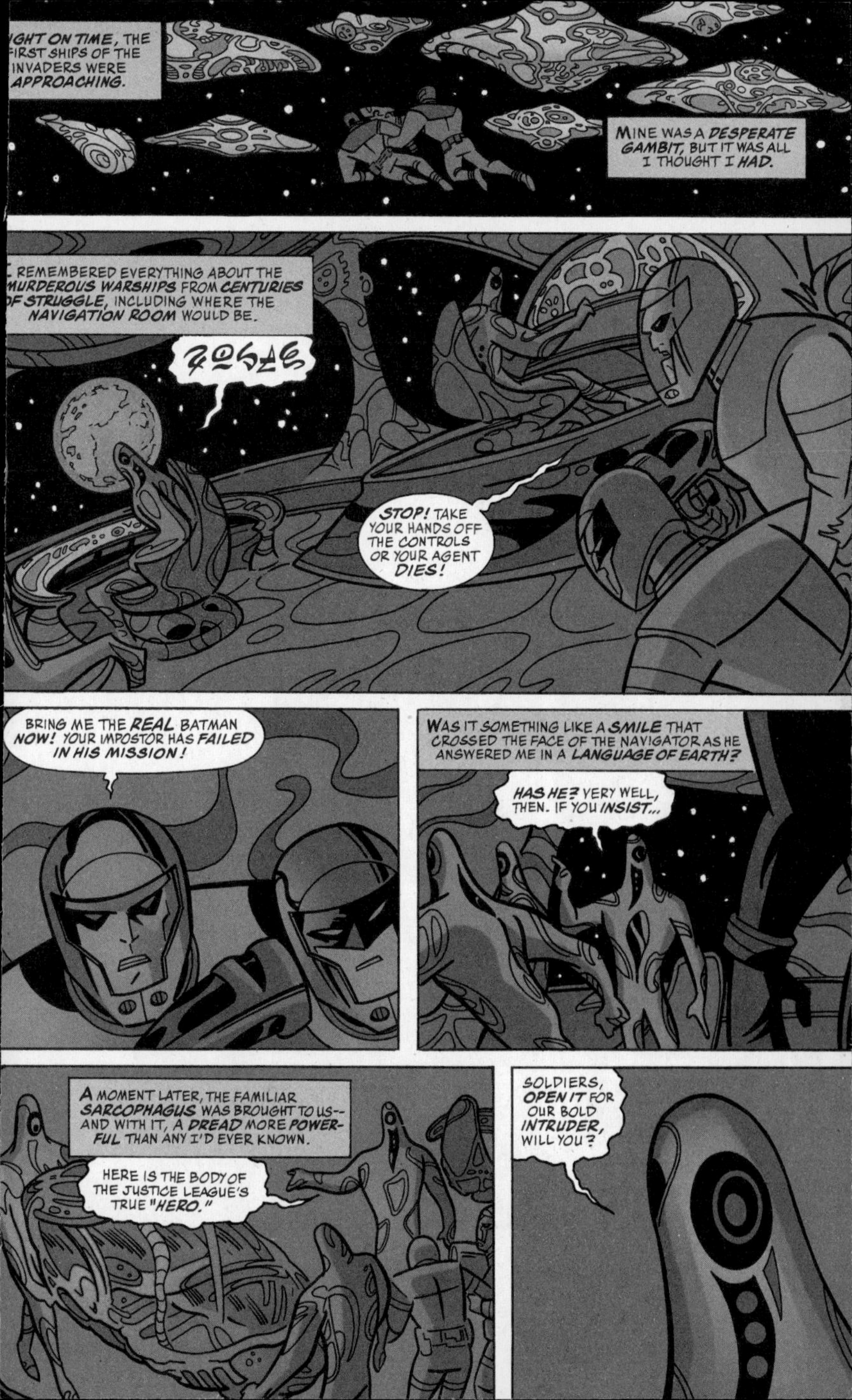
IGHT ON TIME, THE FIRST SHIPS OF THE INVADERS WERE APPROACHING.
MINE WAS A DESPERATE GAMBIT, BUT IT WAS ALL I THOUGHT I HAD.
I REMEMBERED EVERYTHING ABOUT THE MURDEROUS WARSHIPS FROM CENTURIES OF STRUGGLE, INCLUDING WHERE THE NAVIGATION ROOM WOULD BE.
STOP! TAKE YOUR HANDS OFF THE CONTROLS OR YOUR AGENT DIES!
BRING ME THE REAL BATMAN NOW! YOUR IMPOSTOR HAS FAILED IN HIS MISSION!
WAS IT SOMETHING LIKE A SMILE THAT CROSSED THE FACE OF THE NAVIGATOR AS HE ANSWERED ME IN A LANGUAGE OF EARTH?
HAS HE? VERY WELL, THEN. IF YOU INSIST...
A MOMENT LATER, THE FAMILIAR SARCOPHAGUS WAS BROUGHT TO US-- AND WITH IT, A DREAD MORE POWERFUL THAN ANY I'D EVER KNOWN.
HERE IS THE BODY OF THE JUSTICE LEAGUE'S TRUE "HERO."
SOLDIERS, OPEN IT FOR OUR BOLD INTRUDER, WILL YOU?

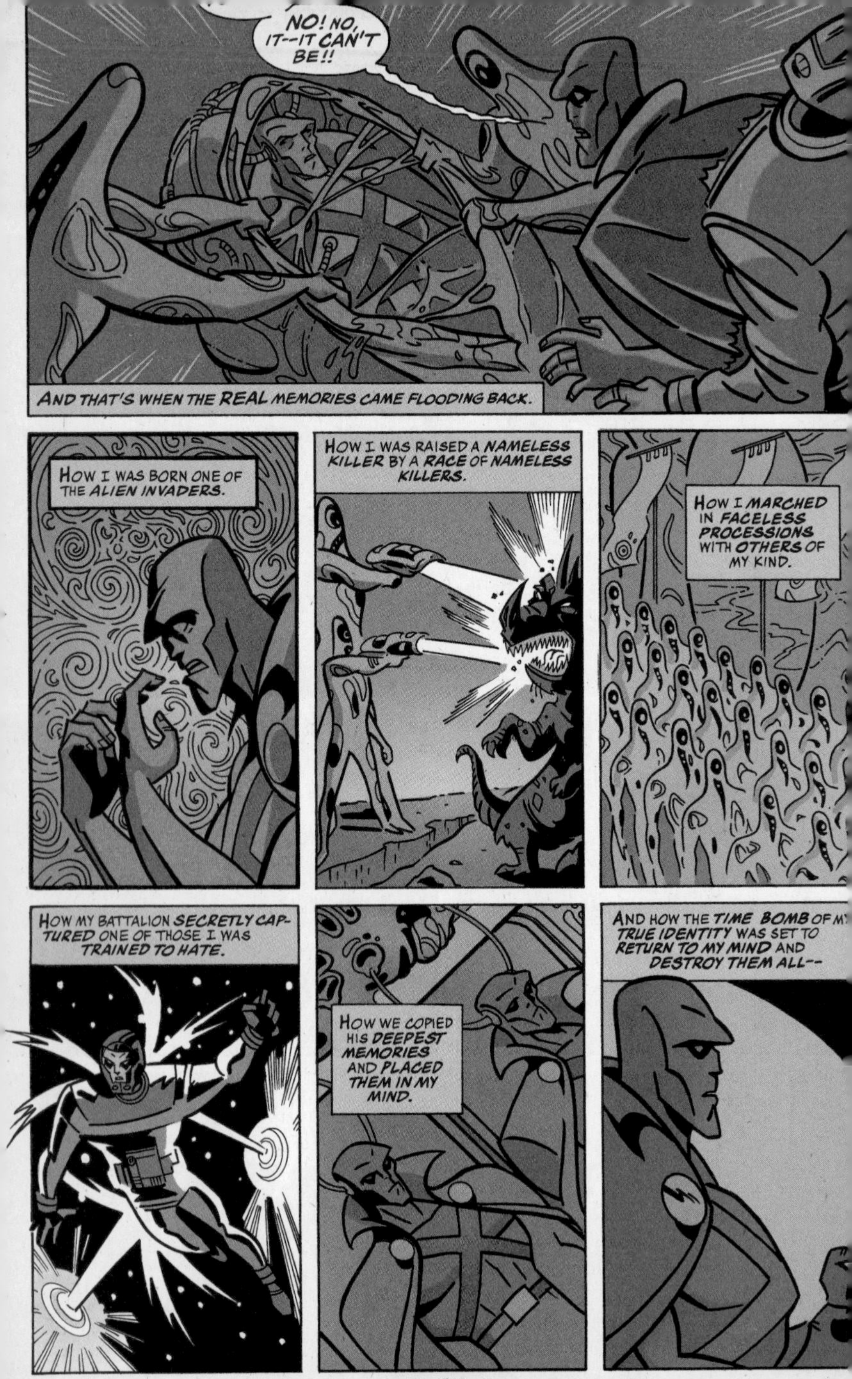
NO! NO, IT--IT CAN'T BE!!
AND THAT'S WHEN THE REAL MEMORIES CAME FLOODING BACK.
HOW I WAS BORN ONE OF THE ALIEN INVADERS.
HOW I WAS RAISED A NAMELESS KILLER BY A RACE OF NAMELESS KILLERS.
HOW I MARCHED IN FACELESS PROCESSIONS WITH OTHERS OF MY KIND.
HOW MY BATTALION SECRETLY CAPTURED ONE OF THOSE I WAS TRAINED TO HATE.
HOW WE COPIED HIS DEEPEST MEMORIES AND PLACED THEM IN MY MIND.
AND HOW THE TIME BOMB OF MY TRUE IDENTITY WAS SET TO RETURN TO MY MIND AND DESTROY THEM ALL--

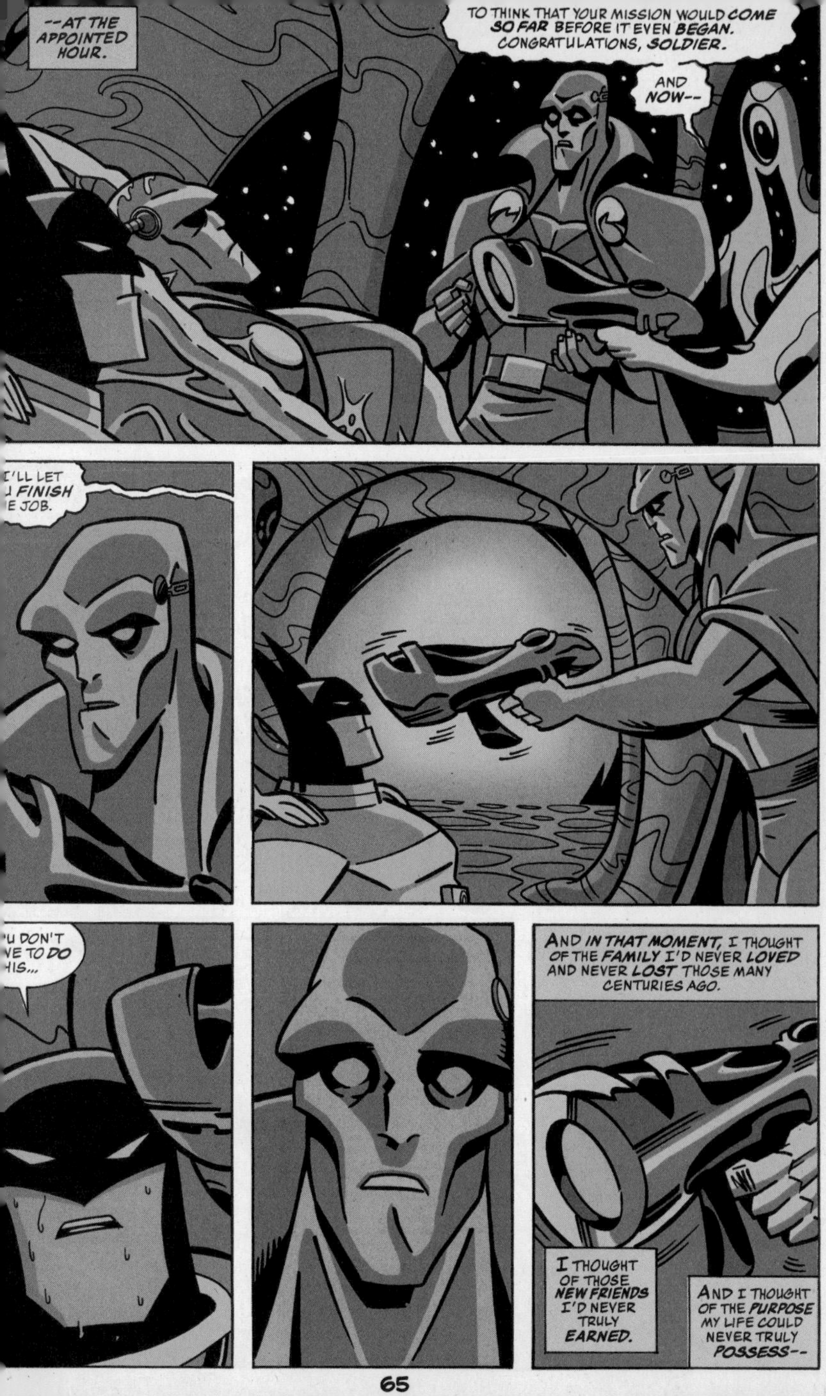
--AT THE APPOINTED HOUR.
TO THINK THAT YOUR MISSION WOULD COME SO FAR BEFORE IT EVEN BEGAN. CONGRATULATIONS, SOLDIER.
AND NOW--
I'LL LET FINISH E JOB.
U DON'T VE TO DO HIS...
AND IN THAT MOMENT, I THOUGHT OF THE FAMILY I'D NEVER LOVED AND NEVER LOST THOSE MANY CENTURIES AGO.
I THOUGHT OF THOSE NEW FRIENDS I'D NEVER TRULY EARNED.
AND I THOUGHT OF THE PURPOSE MY LIFE COULD NEVER TRULY POSSESS--

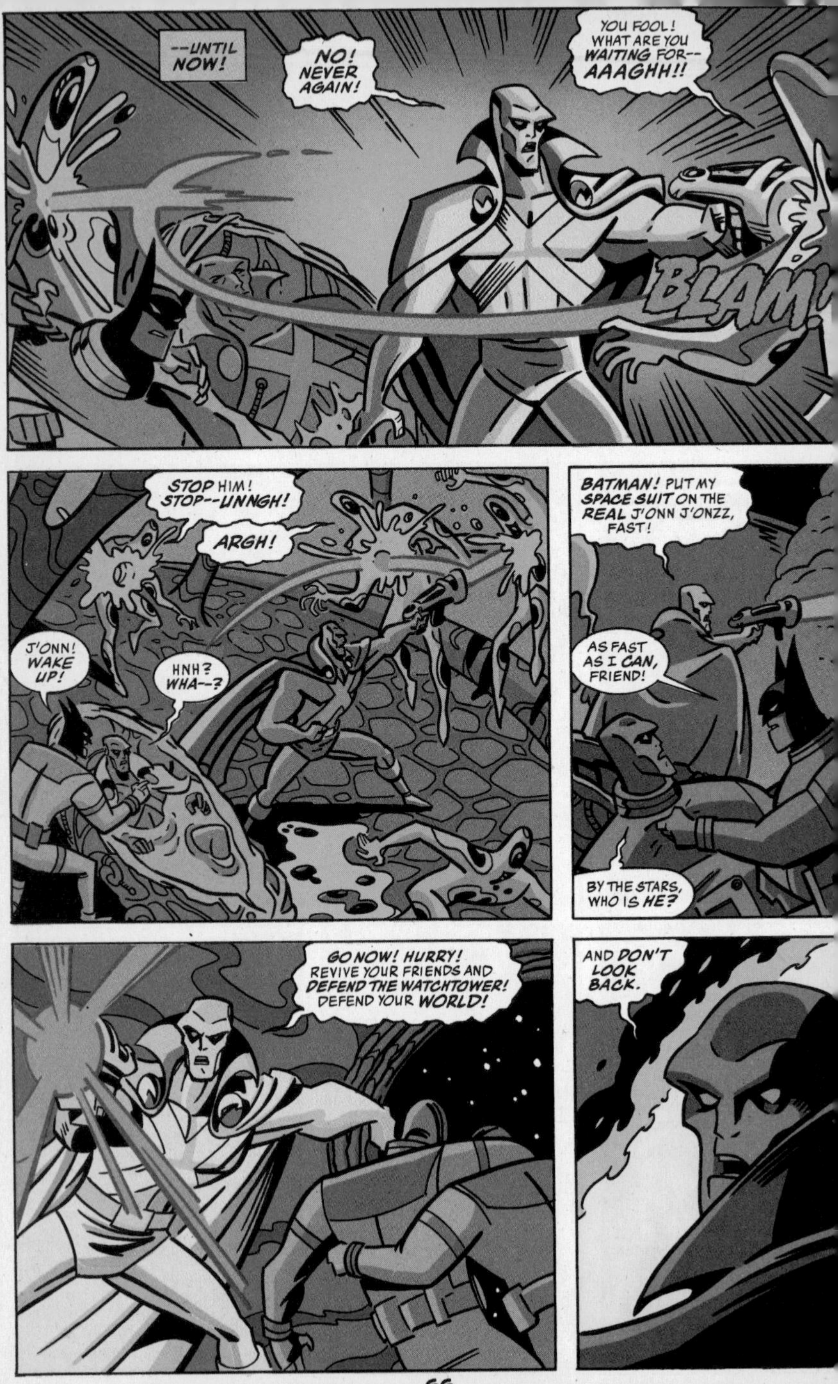
--UNTIL NOW!
NO! NEVER AGAIN!
YOU FOOL! WHAT ARE YOU WAITING FOR-- AAAGHH!!
BLAM!
STOP HIM! STOP--UNNGH!
ARGH!
J'ONN! WAKE UP!
HNH? WHA--?
BATMAN! PUT MY SPACE SUIT ON THE REAL J'ONN J'ONZZ, FAST!
AS FAST AS I CAN, FRIEND!
BY THE STARS, WHO IS HE?
GO NOW! HURRY! REVIVE YOUR FRIENDS AND DEFEND THE WATCHTOWER! DEFEND YOUR WORLD!
AND DON'T LOOK BACK.

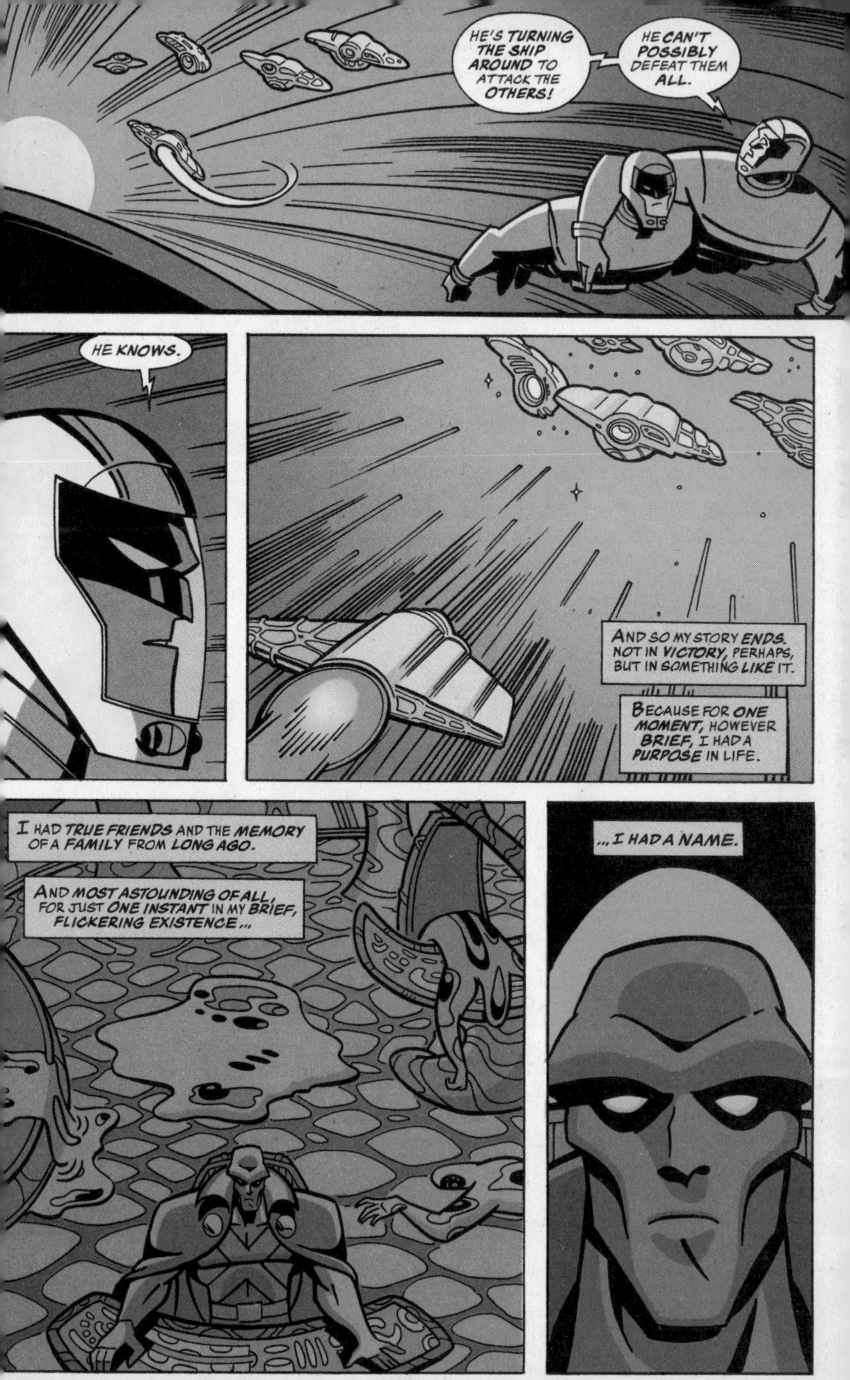
HE'S TURNING THE SHIP AROUND TO ATTACK THE OTHERS!
HE CAN'T POSSIBLY DEFEAT THEM ALL.
HE KNOWS.
AND SO MY STORY ENDS. NOT IN VICTORY, PERHAPS, BUT IN SOMETHING LIKE IT.
BECAUSE FOR ONE MOMENT, HOWEVER BRIEF, I HAD A PURPOSE IN LIFE.
I HAD TRUE FRIENDS AND THE MEMORY OF A FAMILY FROM LONG AGO.
AND MOST ASTOUNDING OF ALL, FOR JUST ONE INSTANT IN MY BRIEF, FLICKERING EXISTENCE...
...I HAD A NAME.

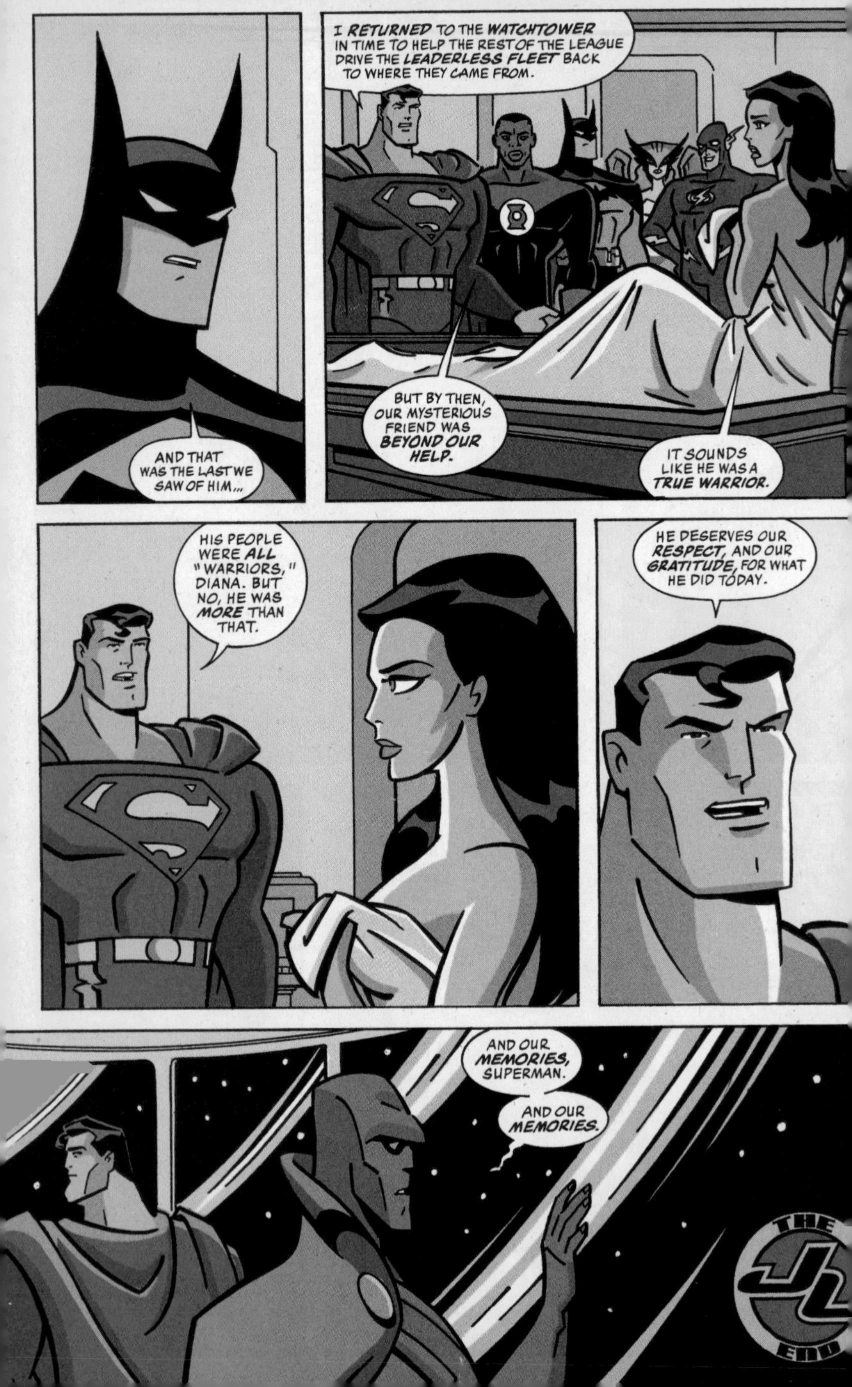
AND THAT WAS THE LAST WE SAW OF HIM...
I RETURNED TO THE WATCHTOWER IN TIME TO HELP THE REST OF THE LEAGUE DRIVE THE LEADERLESS FLEET BACK TO WHERE THEY CAME FROM.
BUT BY THEN, OUR MYSTERIOUS FRIEND WAS BEYOND OUR HELP.
IT SOUNDS LIKE HE WAS A TRUE WARRIOR.
HIS PEOPLE WERE ALL "WARRIORS," DIANA. BUT NO, HE WAS MORE THAN THAT.
HE DESERVES OUR RESPECT, AND OUR GRATITUDE, FOR WHAT HE DID TODAY.
AND OUR MEMORIES, SUPERMAN.
AND OUR MEMORIES.
THE END

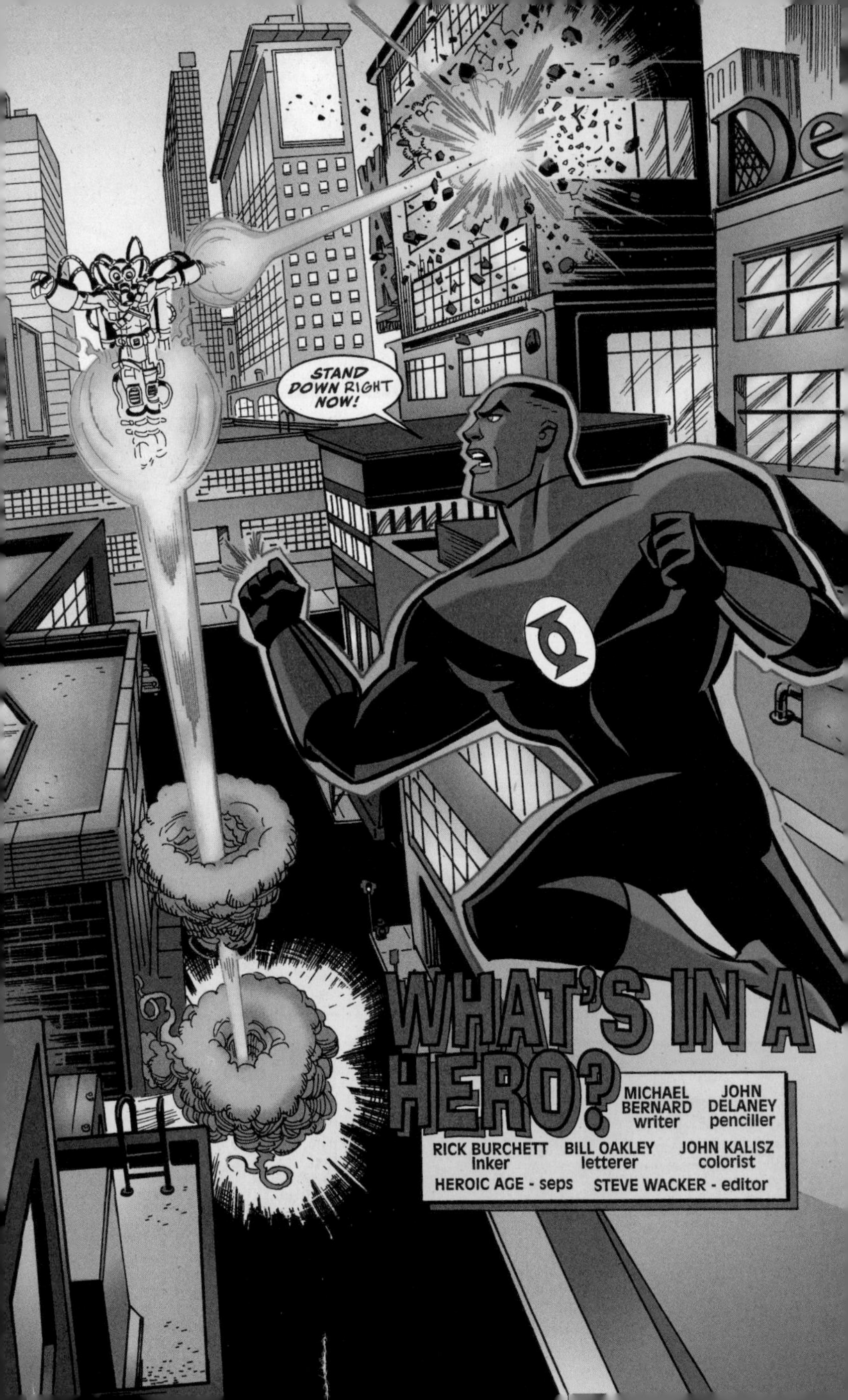
STAND DOWN RIGHT NOW!
WHAT'S IN A HERO?
MICHAEL BERNARD writer
JOHN DELANEY penciller
RICK BURCHETT inker
BILL OAKLEY letterer
JOHN KALISZ colorist
HEROIC AGE - seps
STEVE WACKER - editor

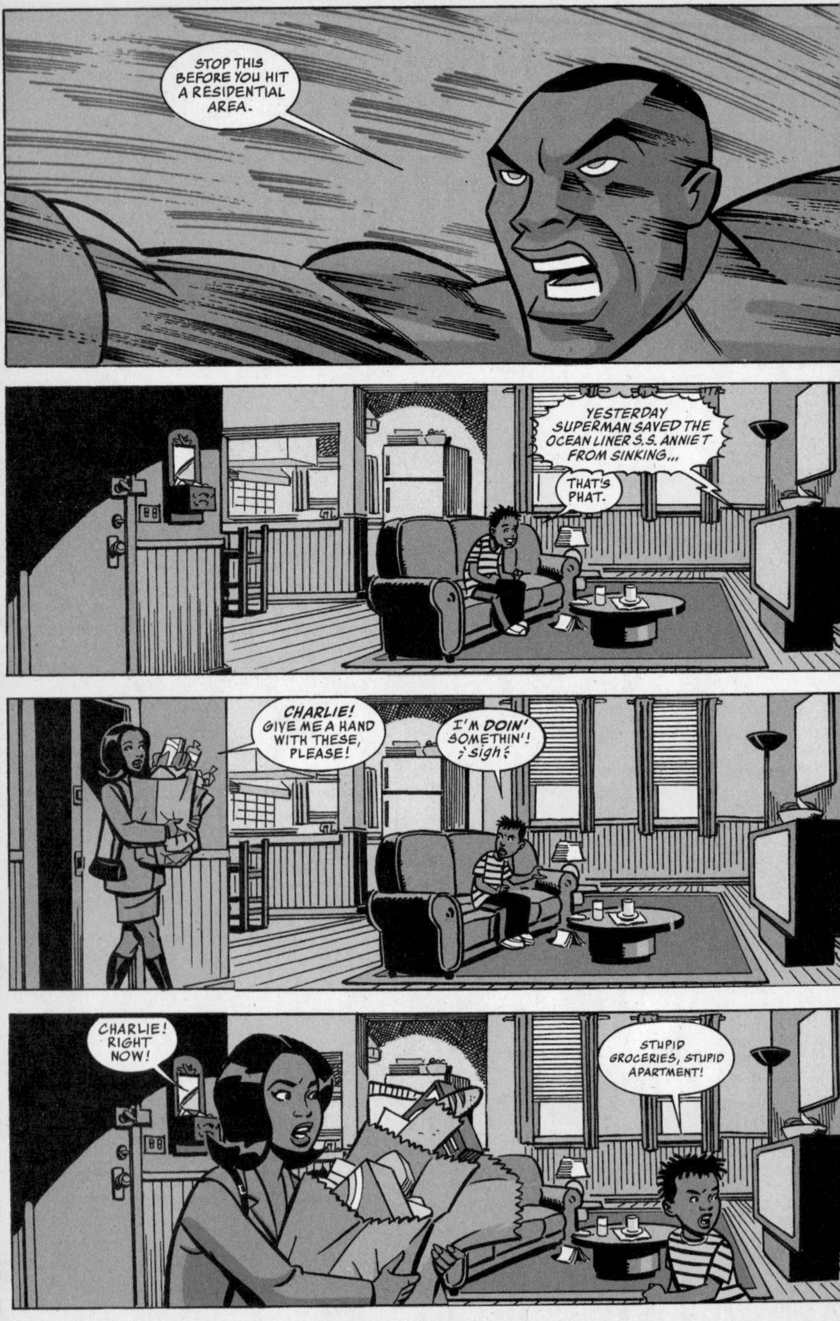
STOP THIS BEFORE YOU HIT A RESIDENTIAL AREA.
YESTERDAY SUPERMAN SAVED THE OCEAN LINER S.S. ANNIE T FROM SINKING...
THAT'S PHAT.
CHARLIE! GIVE ME A HAND WITH THESE, PLEASE!
I'M DOIN' SOMETHIN'! sigh
CHARLIE! RIGHT NOW!
STUPID GROCERIES, STUPID APARTMENT!

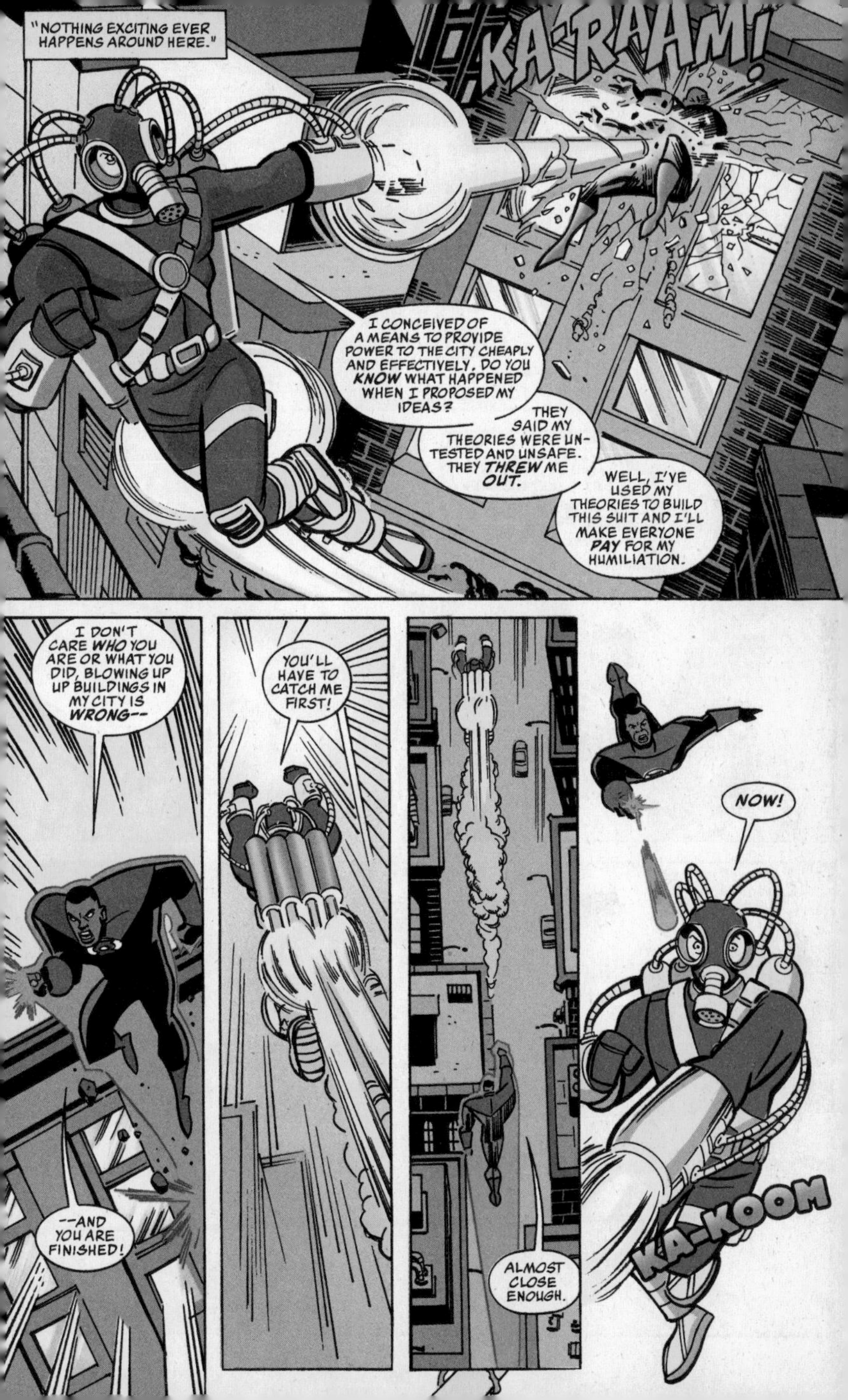
"NOTHING EXCITING EVER HAPPENS AROUND HERE."
KA-RAAM!
I CONCEIVED OF A MEANS TO PROVIDE POWER TO THE CITY CHEAPLY AND EFFECTIVELY. DO YOU KNOW WHAT HAPPENED WHEN I PROPOSED MY IDEAS?
THEY SAID MY THEORIES WERE UNTESTED AND UNSAFE. THEY THREW ME OUT.
WELL, I'VE USED MY THEORIES TO BUILD THIS SUIT AND I'LL MAKE EVERYONE PAY FOR MY HUMILIATION.
I DON'T CARE WHO YOU ARE OR WHAT YOU DID, BLOWING UP UP BUILDINGS IN MY CITY IS WRONG--
--AND YOU ARE FINISHED!
YOU'LL HAVE TO CATCH ME FIRST!
ALMOST CLOSE ENOUGH.
NOW!
KA-KOOM

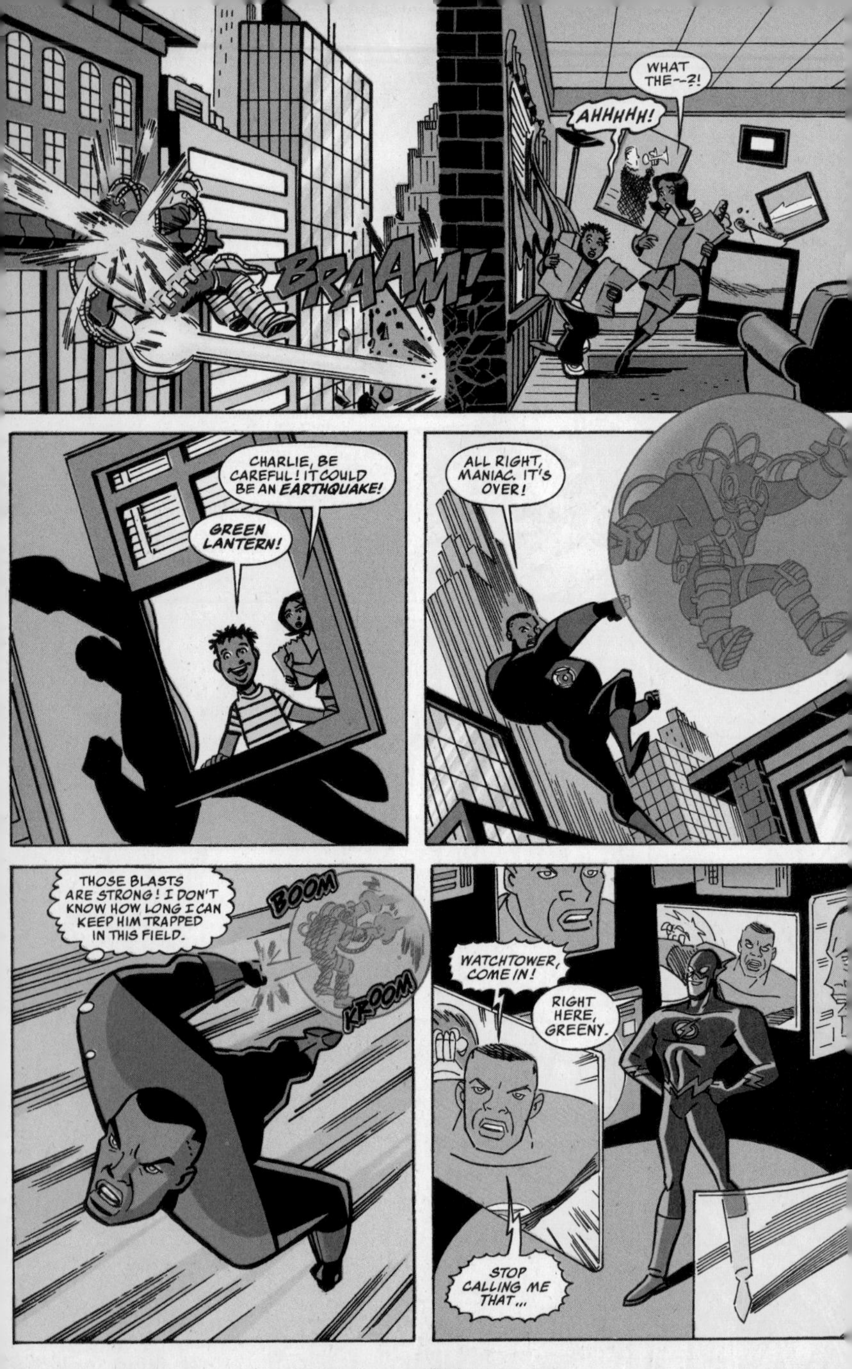
BRAAM!
AHHHHHH!
WHAT THE--?!
CHARLIE, BE CAREFUL! IT COULD BE AN EARTHQUAKE!
GREEN LANTERN!
ALL RIGHT, MANIAC. IT'S OVER!
THOSE BLASTS ARE STRONG! I DON'T KNOW HOW LONG I CAN KEEP HIM TRAPPED IN THIS FIELD.
BOOM
KROOM
WATCHTOWER, COME IN!
RIGHT HERE, GREENY.
STOP CALLING ME THAT...

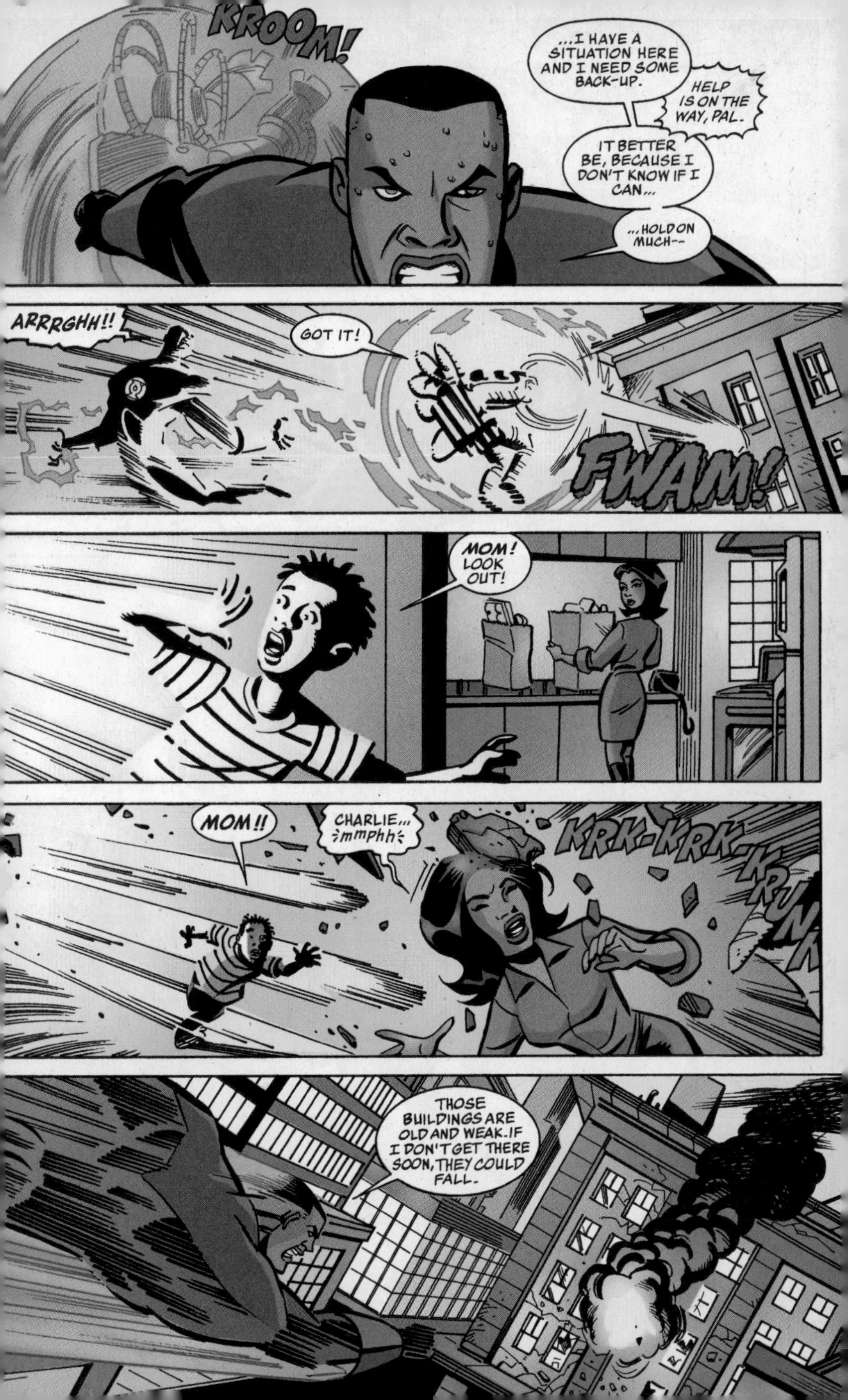
KROOM!
...I HAVE A SITUATION HERE AND I NEED SOME BACK-UP.
HELP IS ON THE WAY, PAL.
IT BETTER BE, BECAUSE I DON'T KNOW IF I CAN...
...HOLD ON MUCH--
ARRRGHH!!
GOT IT!
FWAM!
MOM! LOOK OUT!
MOM!!
CHARLIE... mmphh
KRK-KRK-KRUNK
THOSE BUILDINGS ARE OLD AND WEAK. IF I DON'T GET THERE SOON, THEY COULD FALL.

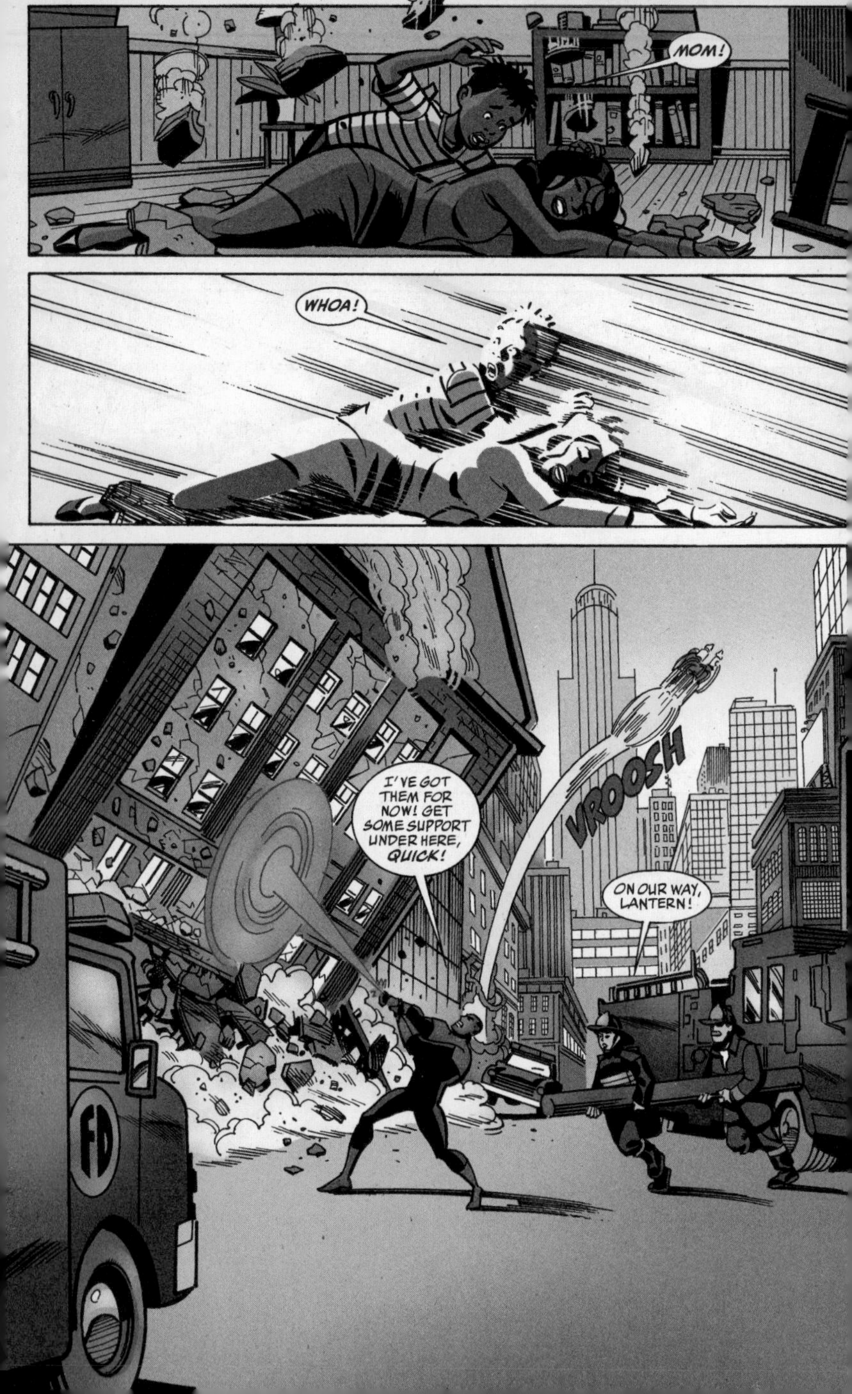
MOM!
WHOA!
I'VE GOT THEM FOR NOW! GET SOME SUPPORT UNDER HERE, QUICK!
VROOSH
ON OUR WAY, LANTERN!

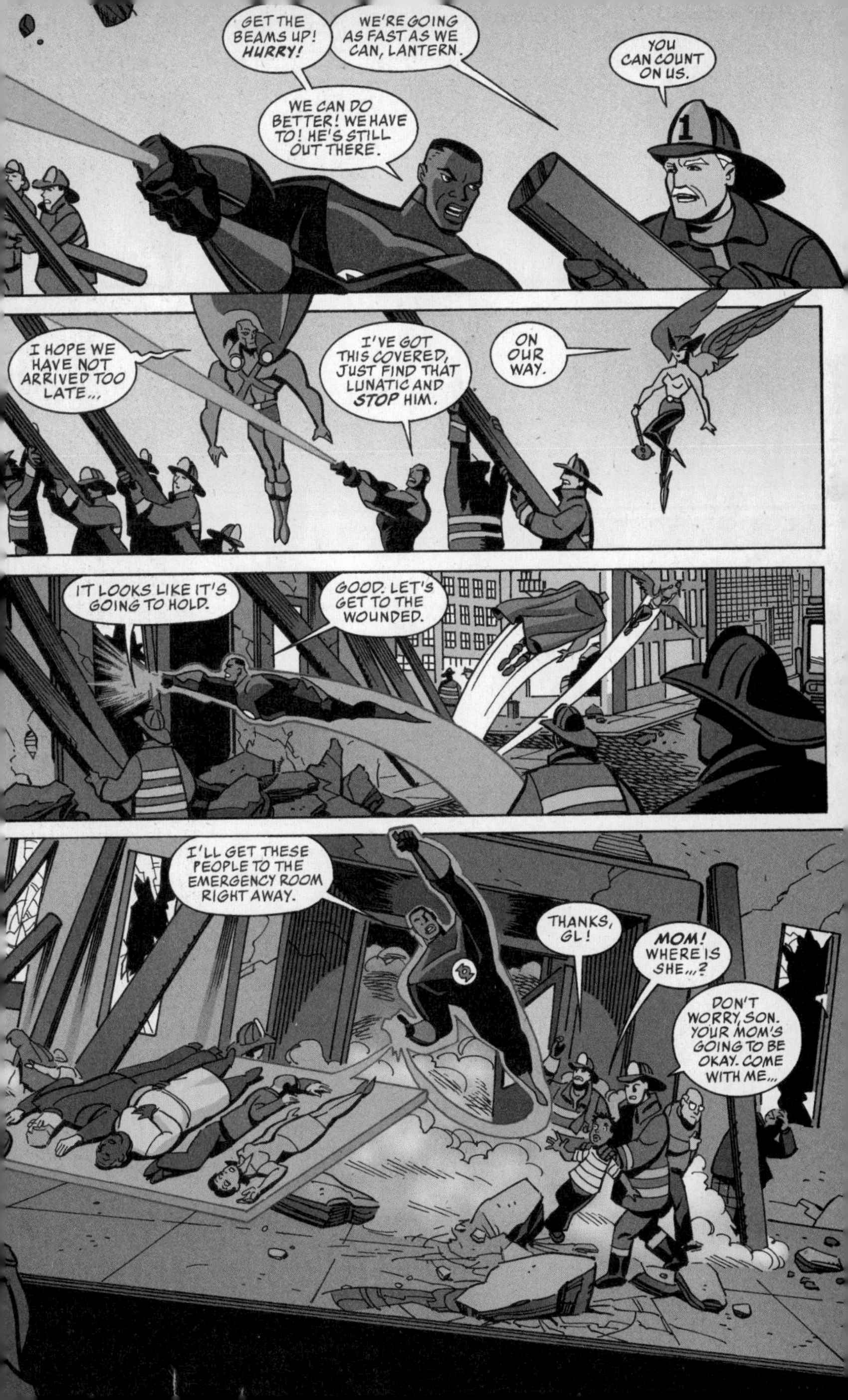
GET THE BEAMS UP! *HURRY!*
WE'RE GOING AS FAST AS WE CAN, LANTERN.
WE CAN DO BETTER! WE HAVE TO! HE'S STILL OUT THERE.
YOU CAN COUNT ON US.
I HOPE WE HAVE NOT ARRIVED TOO LATE...
I'VE GOT THIS COVERED, JUST FIND THAT LUNATIC AND *STOP* HIM.
ON OUR WAY.
IT LOOKS LIKE IT'S GOING TO HOLD.
GOOD. LET'S GET TO THE WOUNDED.
I'LL GET THESE PEOPLE TO THE EMERGENCY ROOM RIGHT AWAY.
THANKS, GL!
MOM! WHERE IS SHE...?
DON'T WORRY, SON. YOUR MOM'S GOING TO BE OKAY. COME WITH ME...

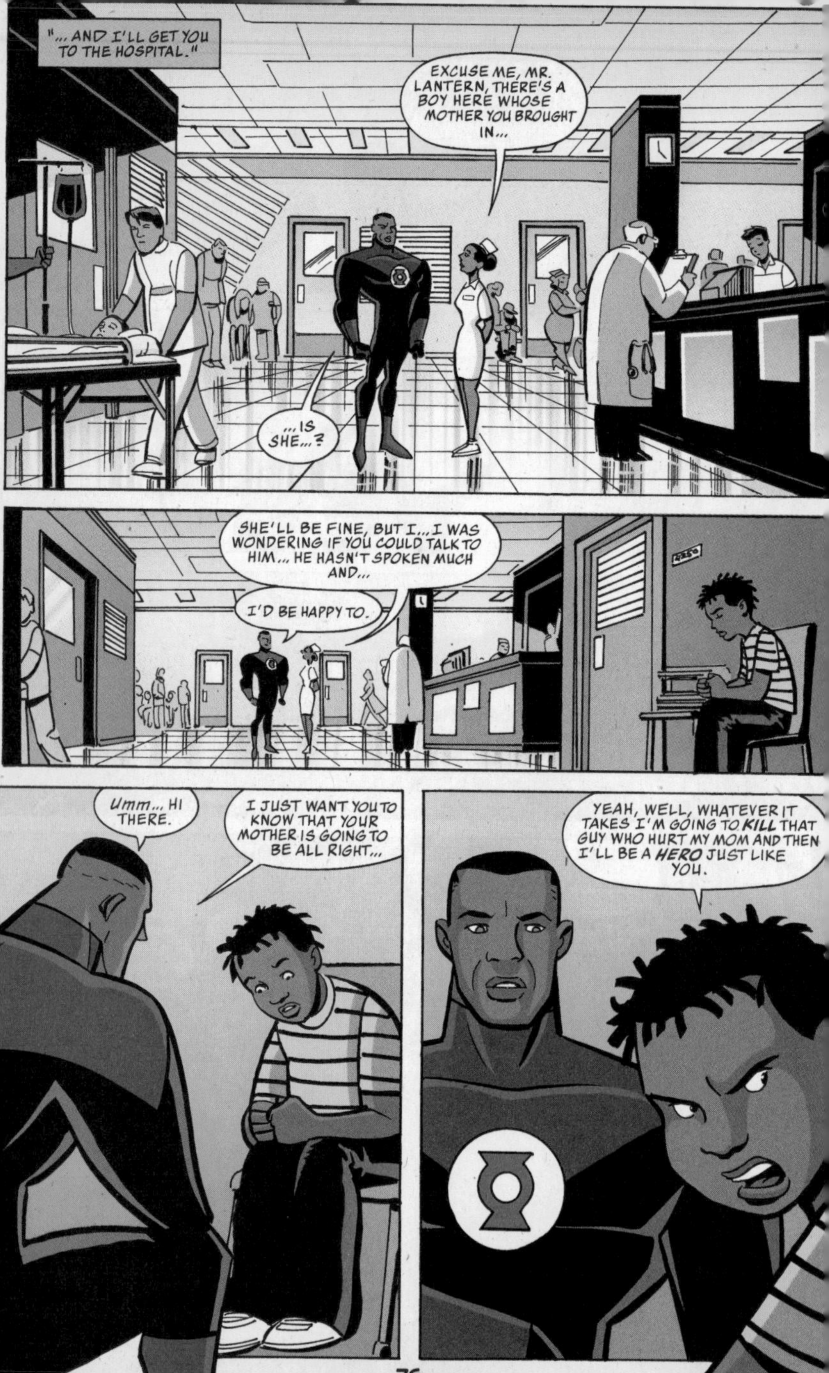
"... AND I'LL GET YOU TO THE HOSPITAL."
EXCUSE ME, MR. LANTERN, THERE'S A BOY HERE WHOSE MOTHER YOU BROUGHT IN...
...IS SHE...?
SHE'LL BE FINE, BUT I... I WAS WONDERING IF YOU COULD TALK TO HIM... HE HASN'T SPOKEN MUCH AND...
I'D BE HAPPY TO.
Umm... HI THERE.
I JUST WANT YOU TO KNOW THAT YOUR MOTHER IS GOING TO BE ALL RIGHT...
YEAH, WELL, WHATEVER IT TAKES I'M GOING TO KILL THAT GUY WHO HURT MY MOM AND THEN I'LL BE A HERO JUST LIKE YOU.

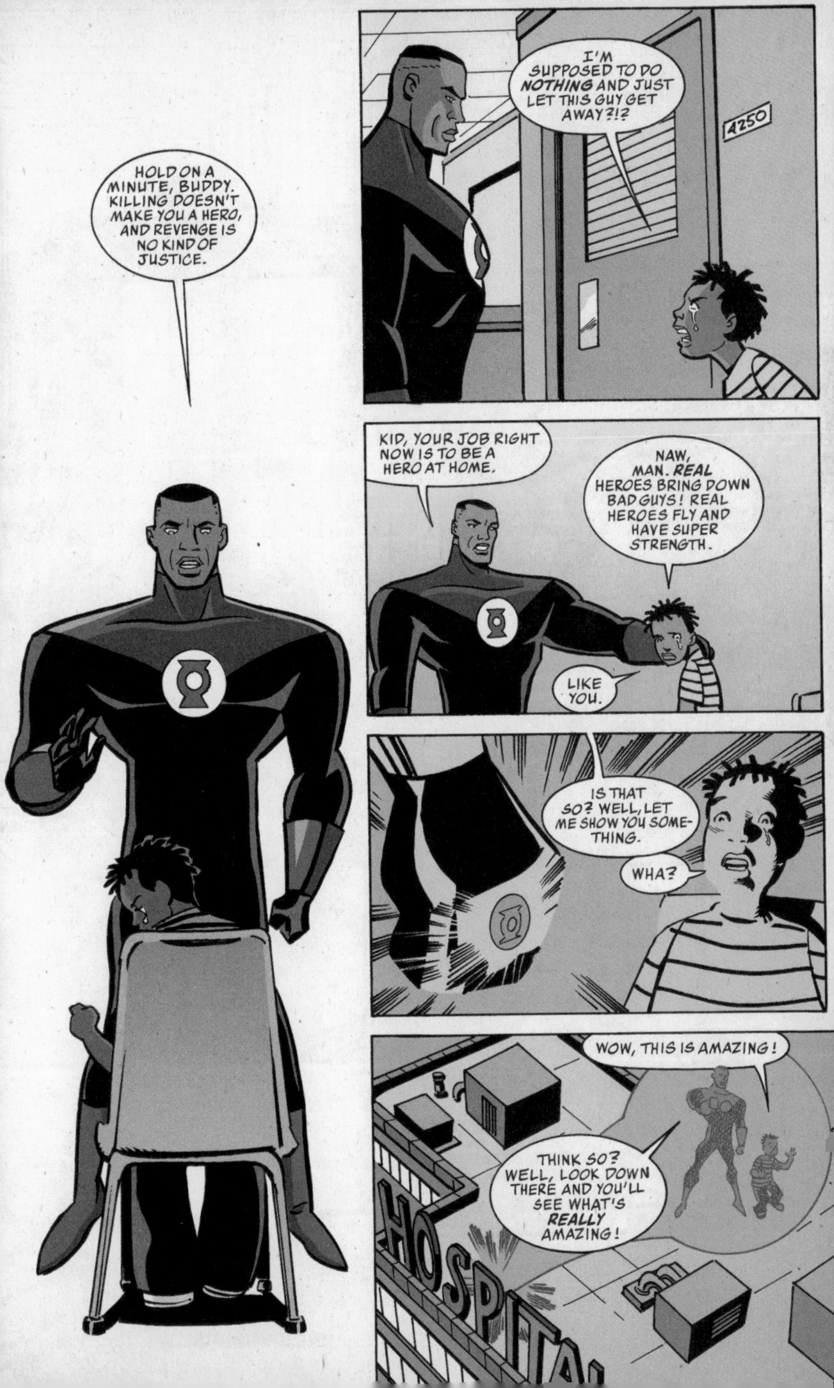

HOLD ON A MINUTE, BUDDY. KILLING DOESN'T MAKE YOU A HERO, AND REVENGE IS NO KIND OF JUSTICE.
I'M SUPPOSED TO DO NOTHING AND JUST LET THIS GUY GET AWAY?!?
4250
KID, YOUR JOB RIGHT NOW IS TO BE A HERO AT HOME.
NAW, MAN. REAL HEROES BRING DOWN BAD GUYS! REAL HEROES FLY AND HAVE SUPER STRENGTH.
LIKE YOU.
IS THAT SO? WELL, LET ME SHOW YOU SOME-THING.
WHA?
WOW, THIS IS AMAZING!
THINK SO? WELL, LOOK DOWN THERE AND YOU'LL SEE WHAT'S REALLY AMAZING!
HOSPITAL

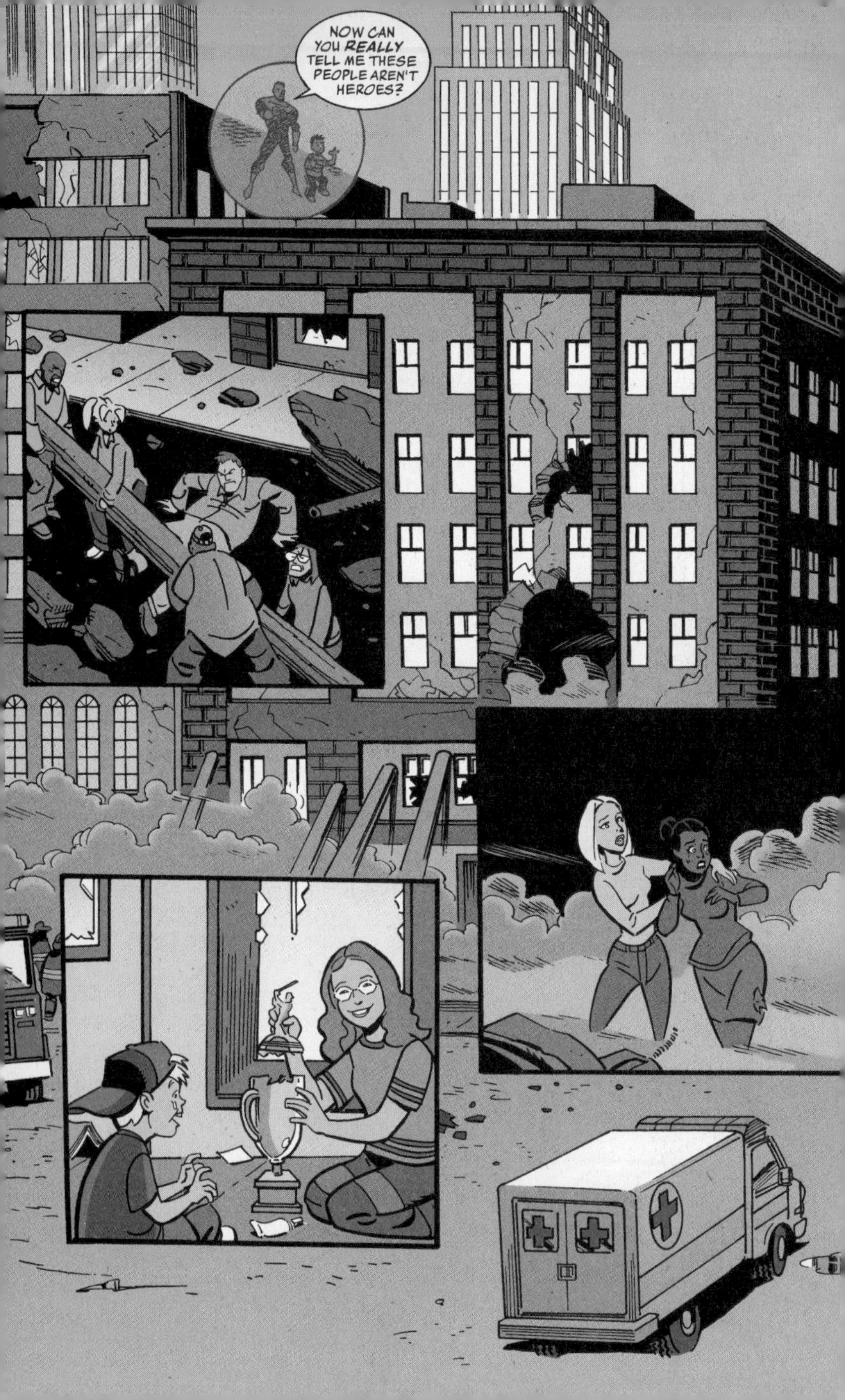
NOW CAN YOU REALLY TELL ME THESE PEOPLE AREN'T HEROES?

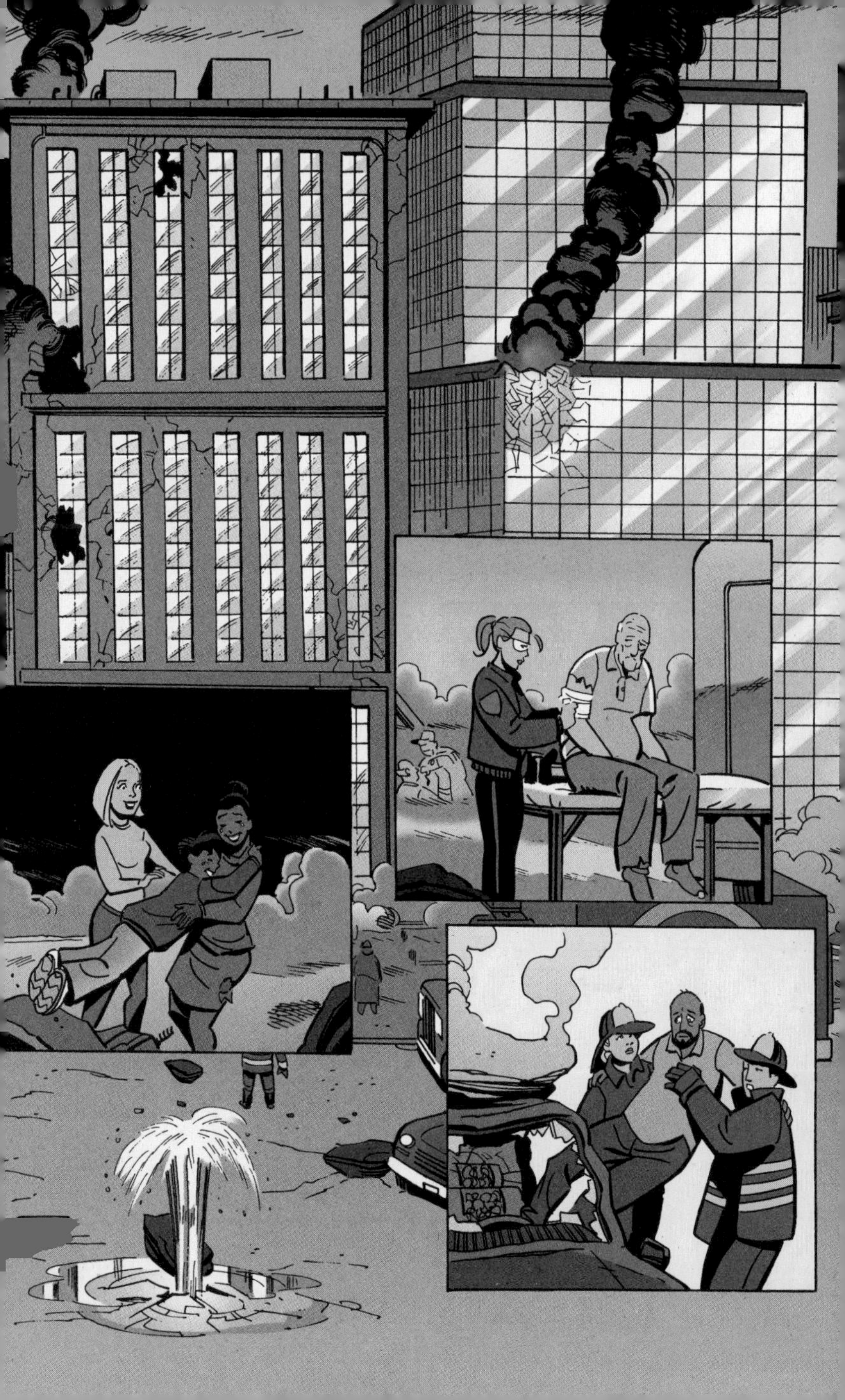

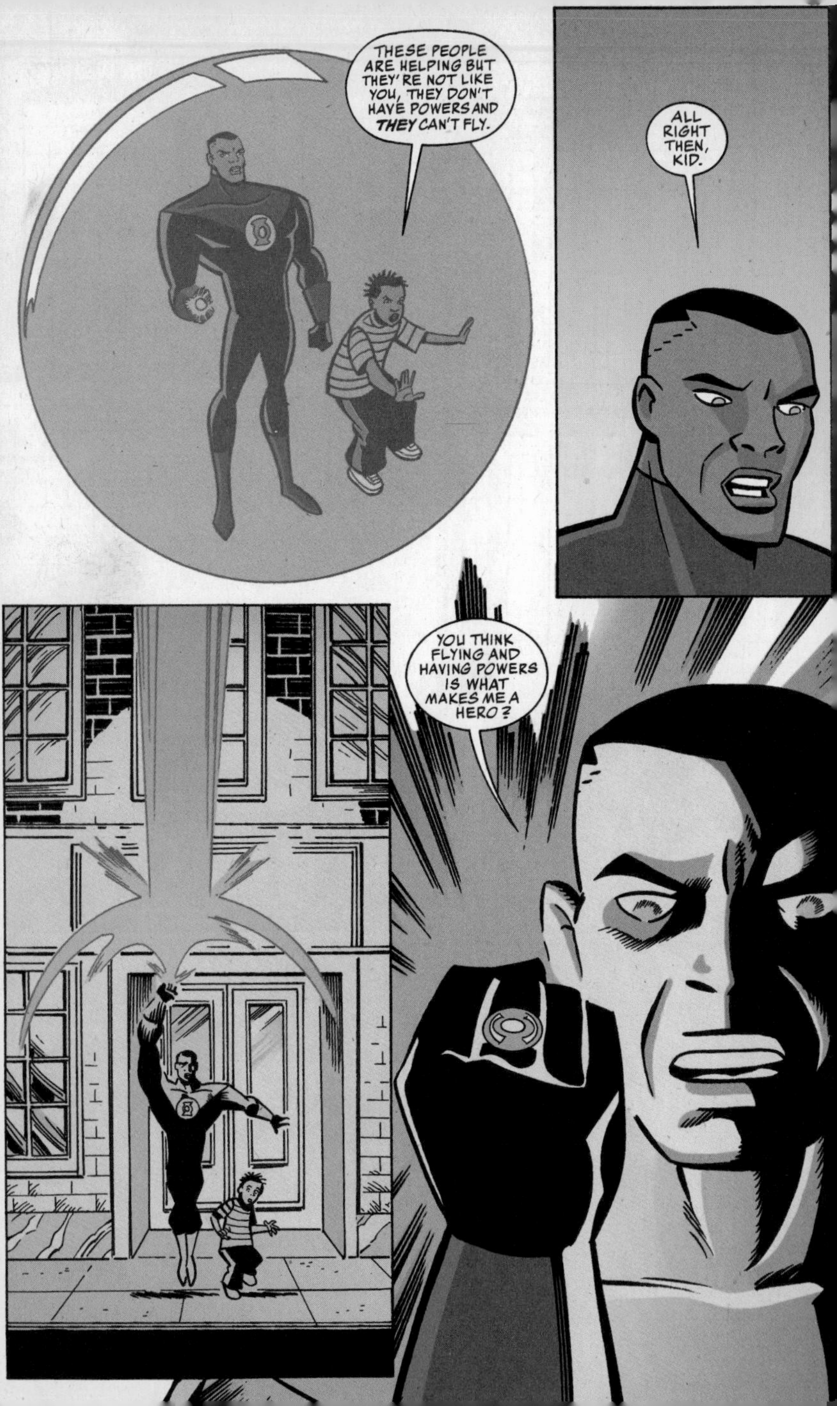
THESE PEOPLE ARE HELPING BUT THEY'RE NOT LIKE YOU, THEY DON'T HAVE POWERS AND *THEY* CAN'T FLY.
ALL RIGHT THEN, KID.
YOU THINK FLYING AND HAVING POWERS IS WHAT MAKES ME A HERO?

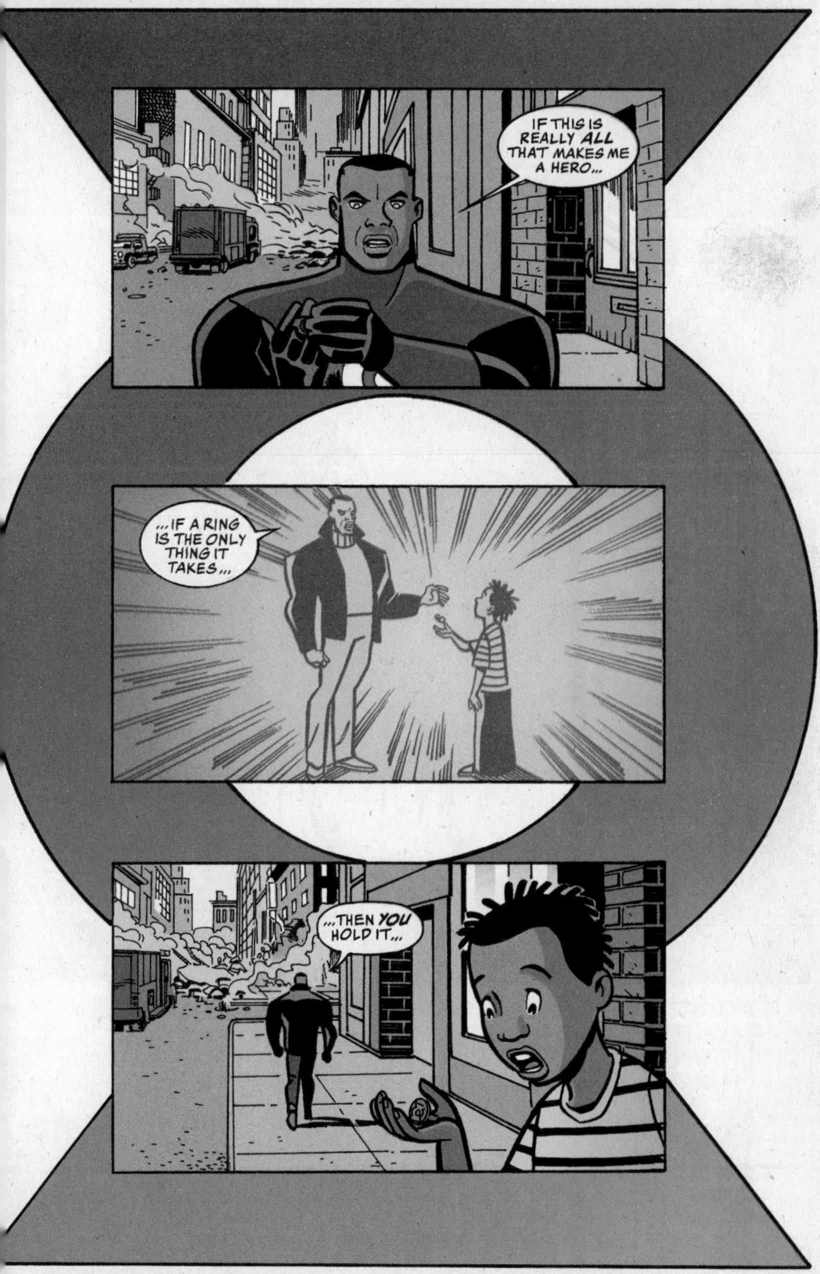
IF THIS IS REALLY ALL THAT MAKES ME A HERO...
...IF A RING IS THE ONLY THING IT TAKES...
...THEN YOU HOLD IT...

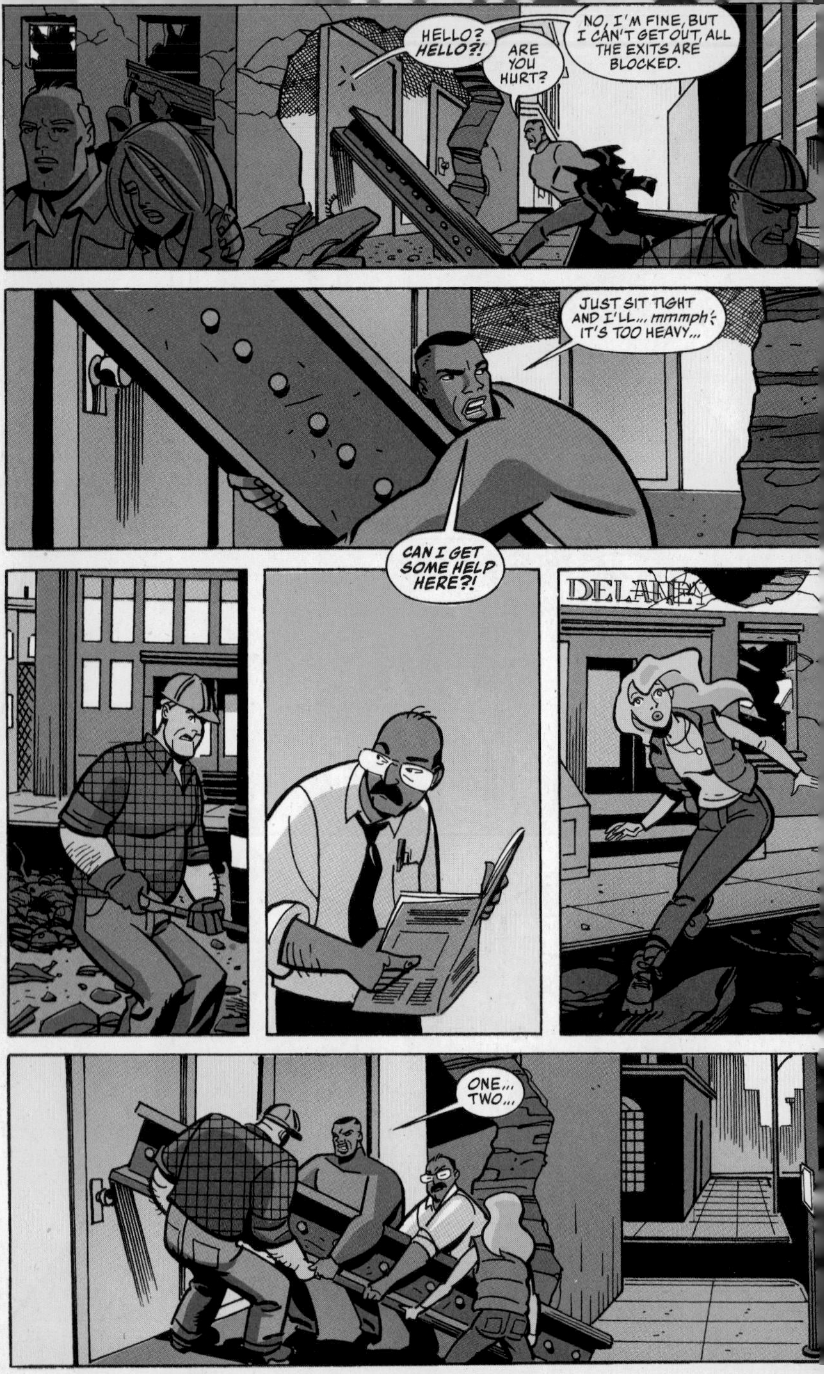
HELLO? HELLO?!
ARE YOU HURT?
NO, I'M FINE, BUT I CAN'T GET OUT, ALL THE EXITS ARE BLOCKED.
JUST SIT TIGHT AND I'LL... mmmph! IT'S TOO HEAVY...
CAN I GET SOME HELP HERE?!
DELANEY
ONE... TWO...

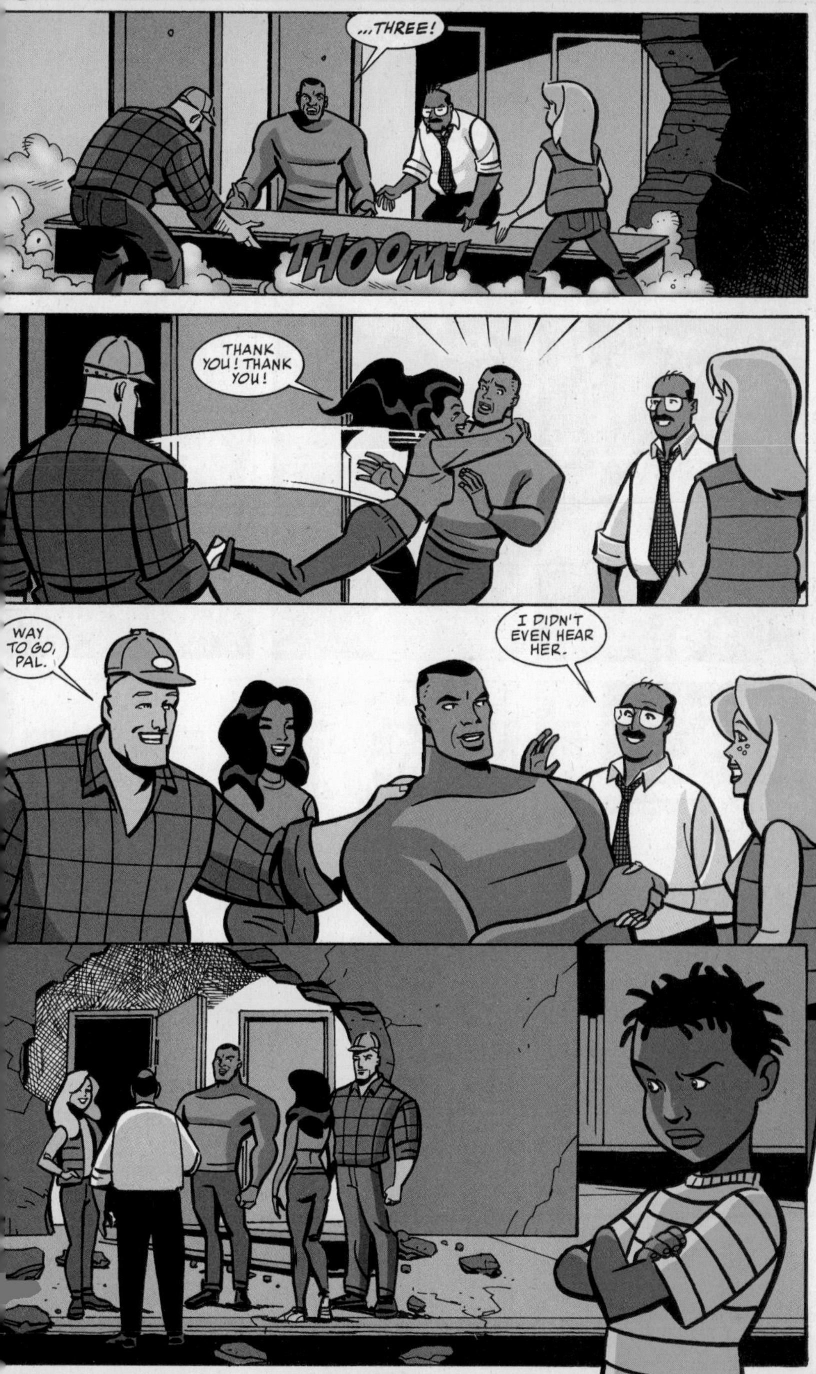
...THREE!
THOOM!
THANK YOU! THANK YOU!
WAY TO GO, PAL.
I DIDN'T EVEN HEAR HER.

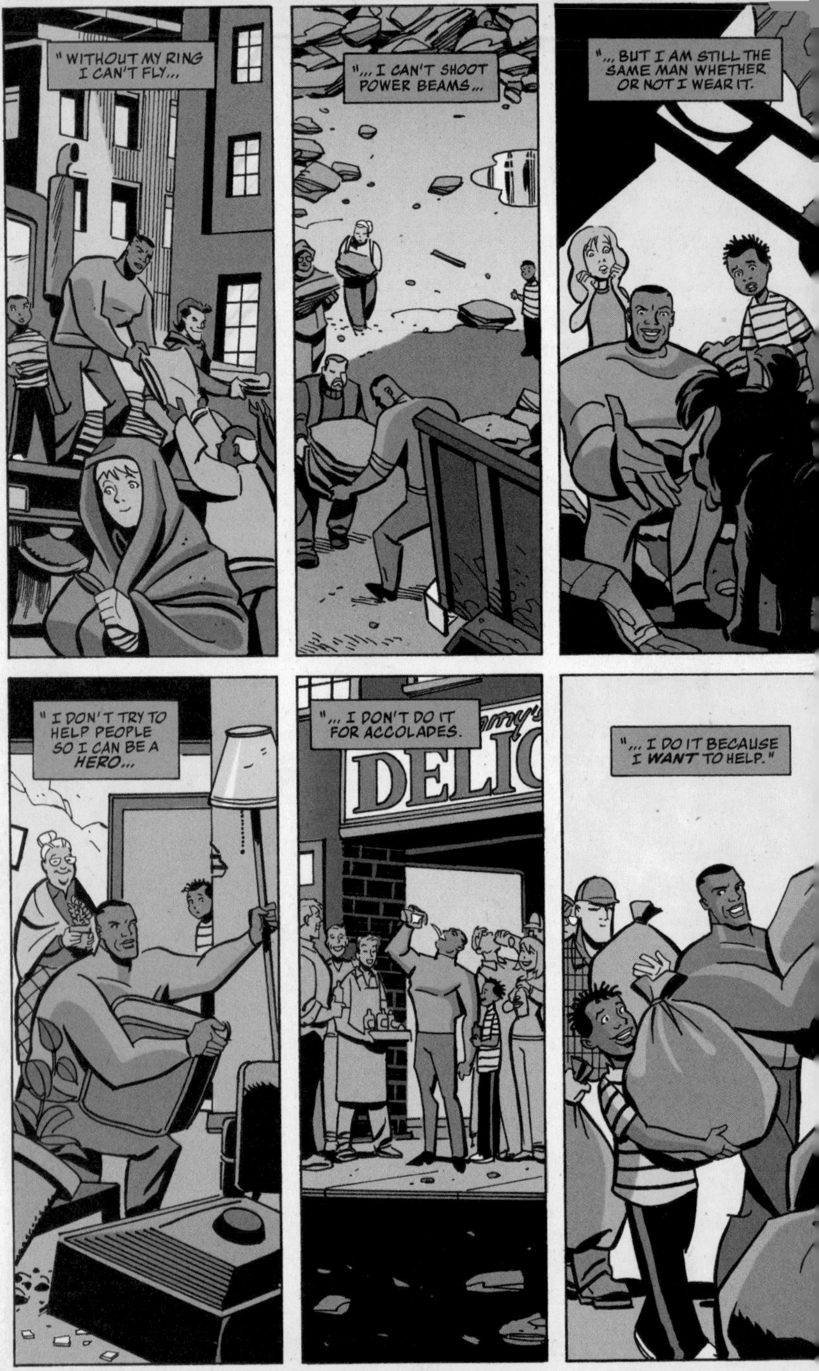
"WITHOUT MY RING I CAN'T FLY...
"... I CAN'T SHOOT POWER BEAMS...
"... BUT I AM STILL THE SAME MAN WHETHER OR NOT I WEAR IT.
"I DON'T TRY TO HELP PEOPLE SO I CAN BE A HERO...
"... I DON'T DO IT FOR ACCOLADES.
DELIC
"... I DO IT BECAUSE I WANT TO HELP."

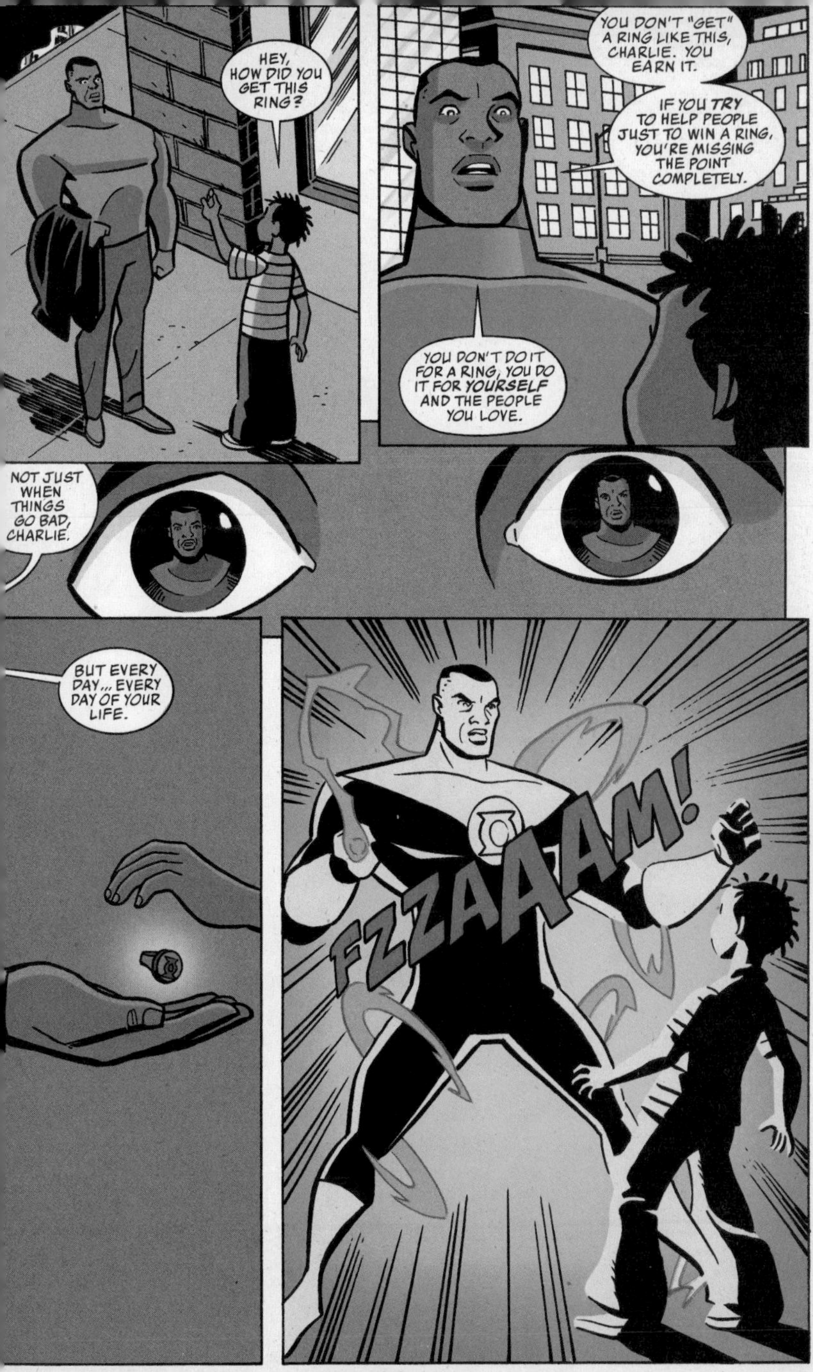
HEY, HOW DID YOU GET THIS RING?
YOU DON'T "GET" A RING LIKE THIS, CHARLIE. YOU EARN IT.
IF YOU TRY TO HELP PEOPLE JUST TO WIN A RING, YOU'RE MISSING THE POINT COMPLETELY.
YOU DON'T DO IT FOR A RING, YOU DO IT FOR YOURSELF AND THE PEOPLE YOU LOVE.
NOT JUST WHEN THINGS GO BAD, CHARLIE.
BUT EVERY DAY... EVERY DAY OF YOUR LIFE.
FZZAAAM!

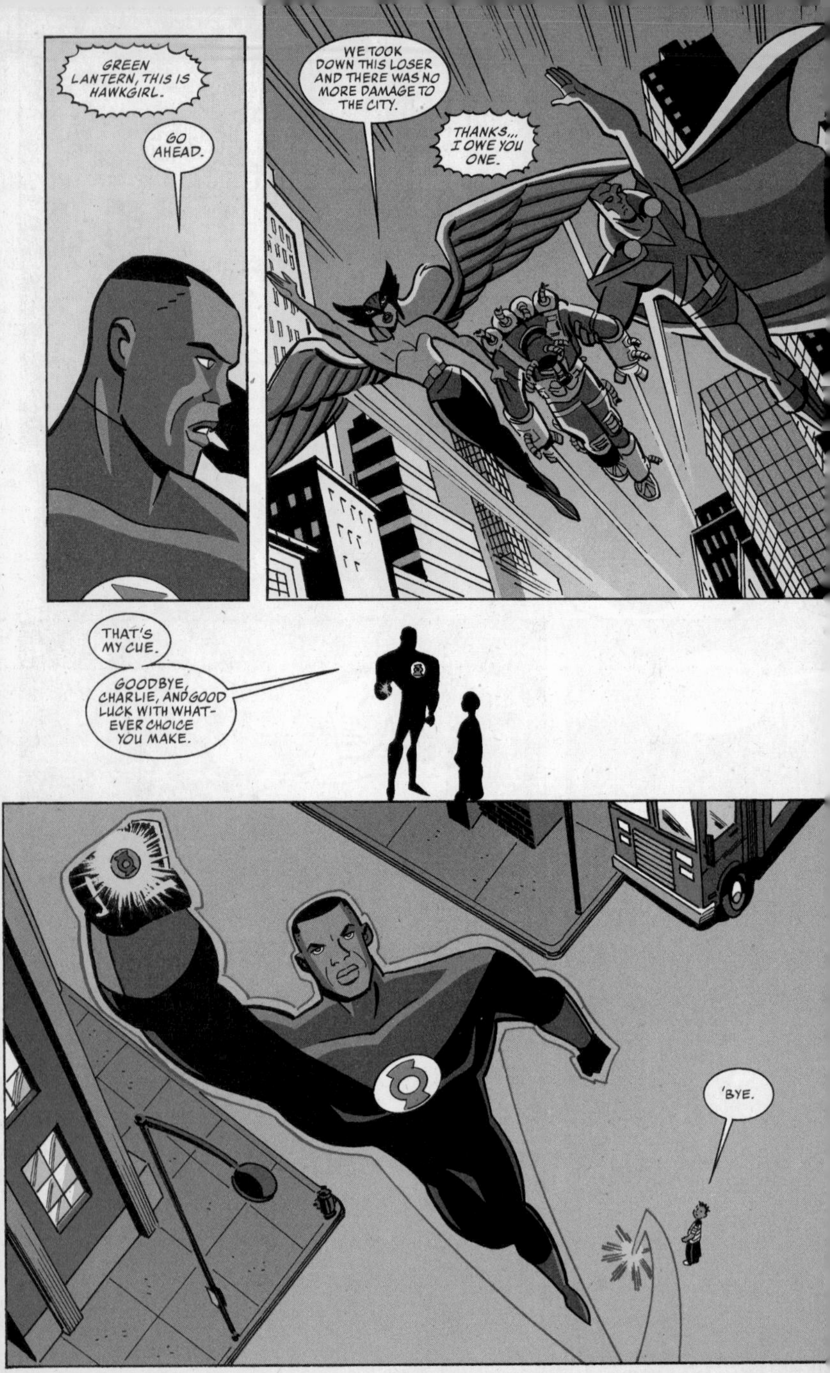
GREEN LANTERN, THIS IS HAWKGIRL.
GO AHEAD.
WE TOOK DOWN THIS LOSER AND THERE WAS NO MORE DAMAGE TO THE CITY.
THANKS... I OWE YOU ONE.
THAT'S MY CUE.
GOODBYE, CHARLIE, AND GOOD LUCK WITH WHAT-EVER CHOICE YOU MAKE.
'BYE.

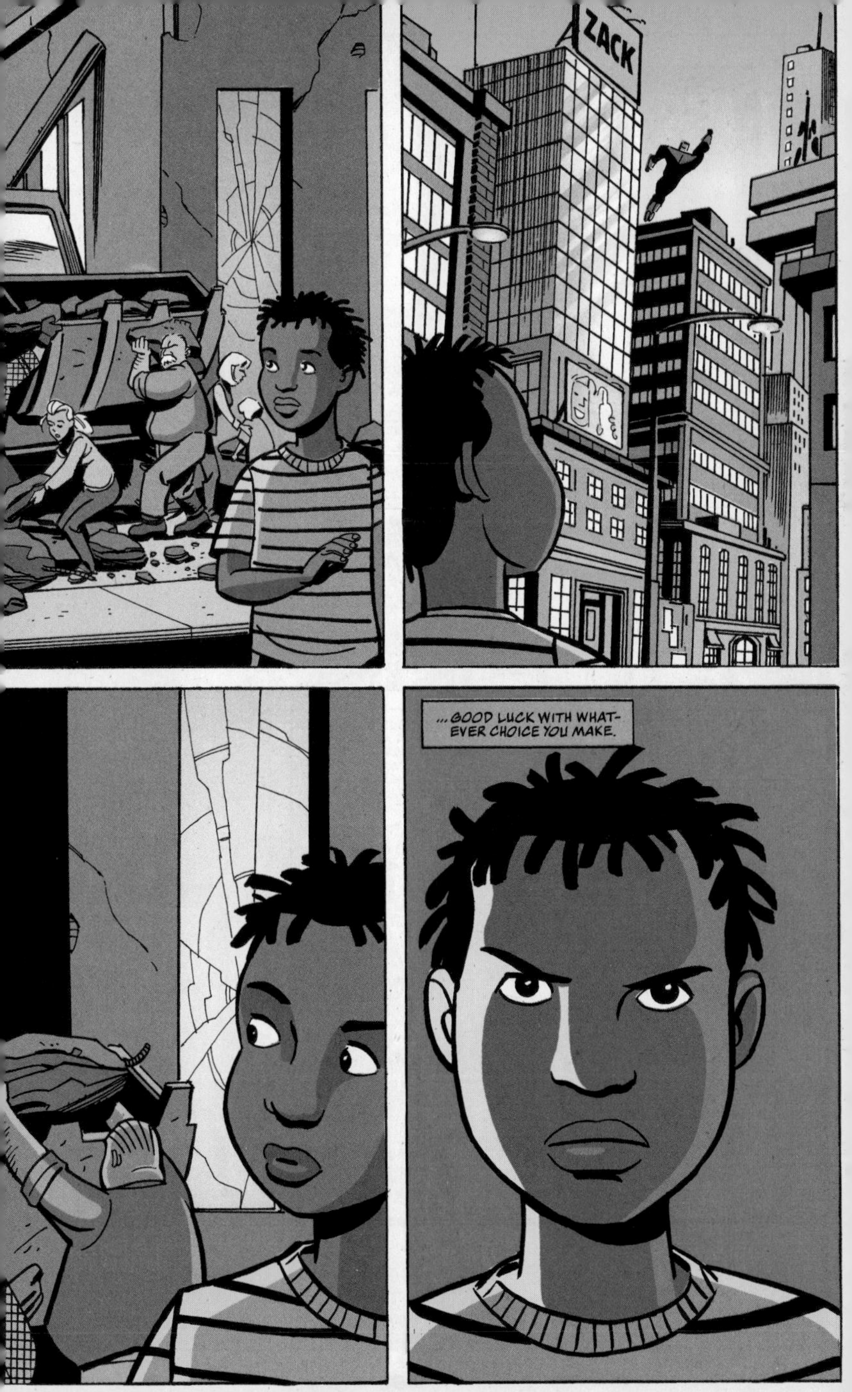
ZACK
...GOOD LUCK WITH WHAT-
EVER CHOICE YOU MAKE.

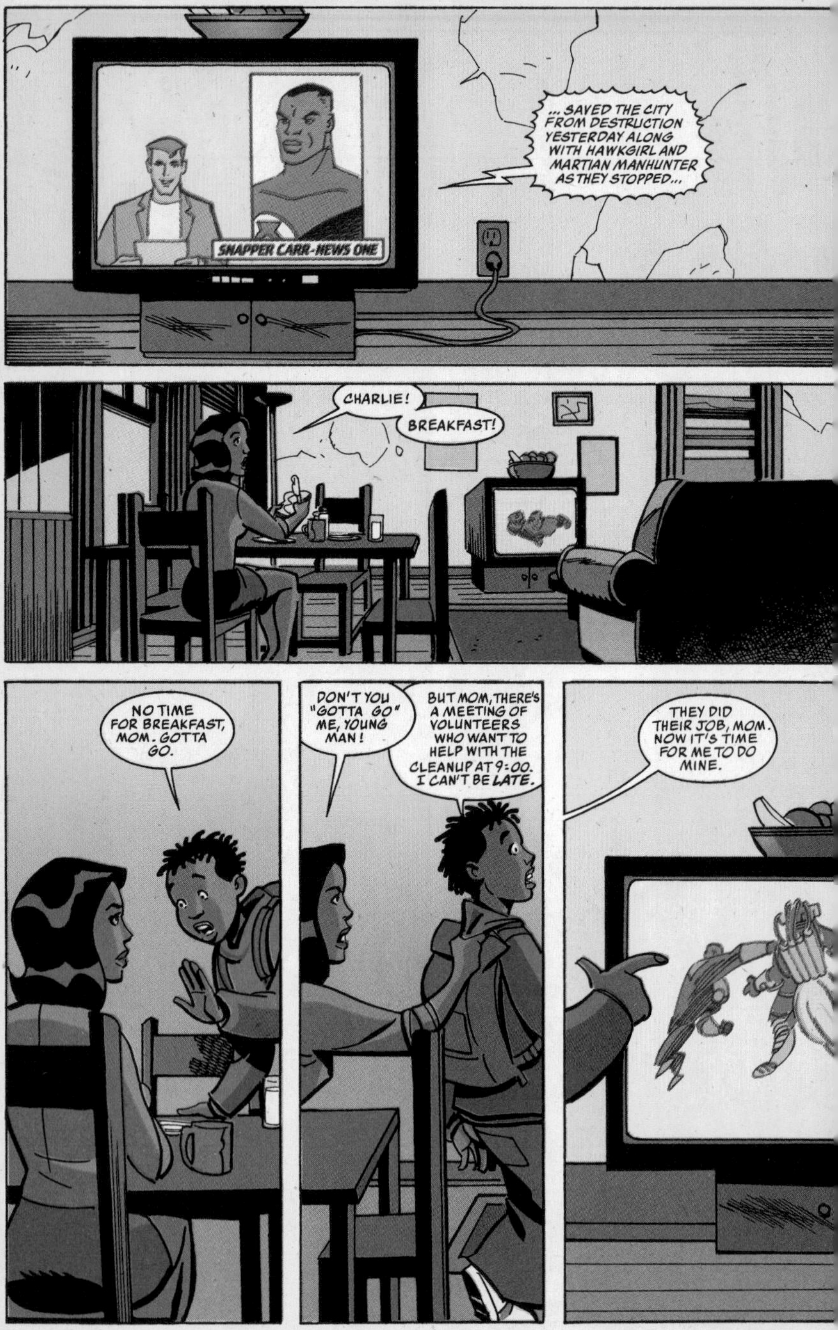
SNAPPER CARR-NEWS ONE
...SAVED THE CITY FROM DESTRUCTION YESTERDAY ALONG WITH HAWKGIRL AND MARTIAN MANHUNTER AS THEY STOPPED...
CHARLIE!
BREAKFAST!
NO TIME FOR BREAKFAST, MOM. GOTTA GO.
DON'T YOU "GOTTA GO" ME, YOUNG MAN!
BUT MOM, THERE'S A MEETING OF VOLUNTEERS WHO WANT TO HELP WITH THE CLEANUP AT 9:00. I CAN'T BE LATE.
THEY DID THEIR JOB, MOM. NOW IT'S TIME FOR ME TO DO MINE.

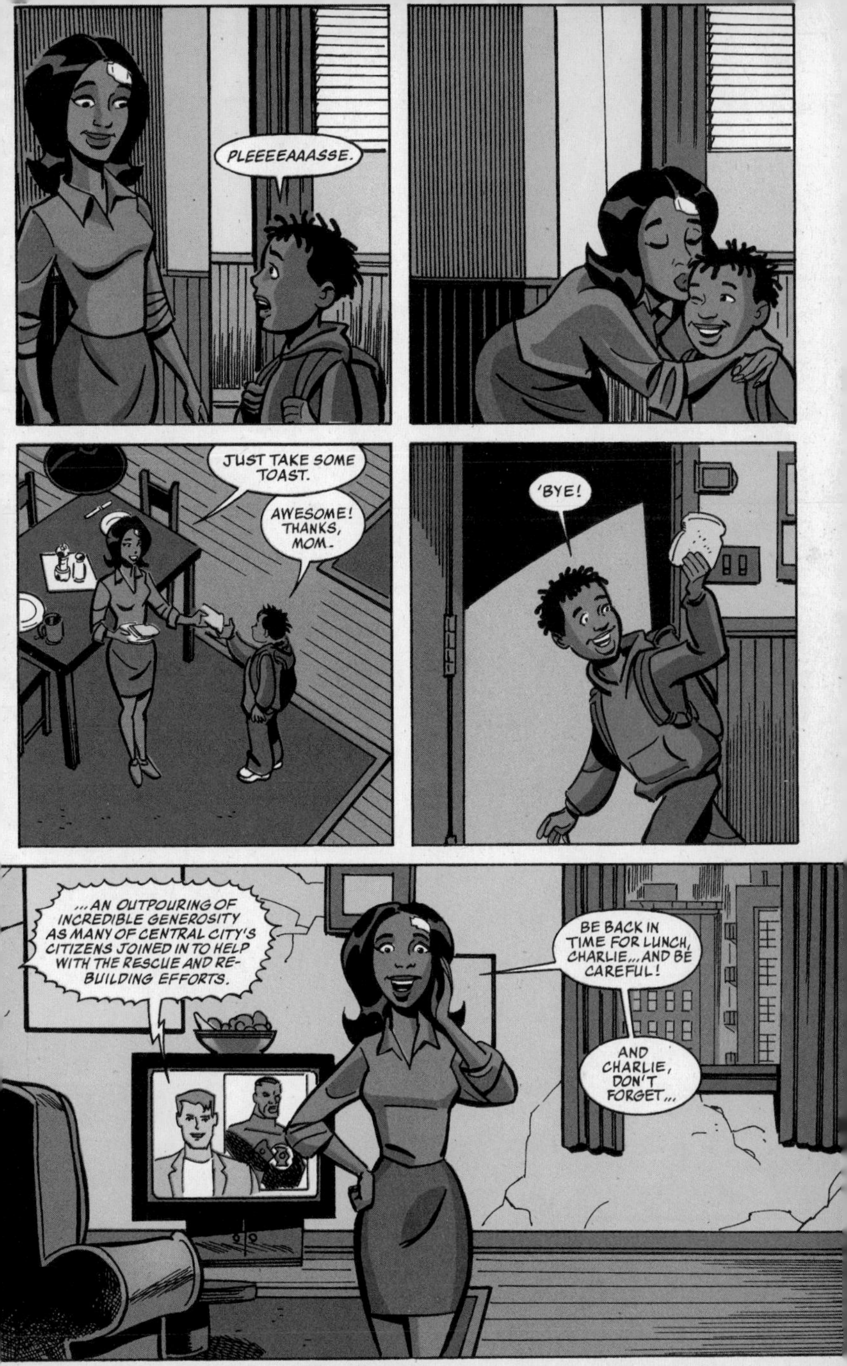
PLEEEEAAASSE.
JUST TAKE SOME TOAST.
AWESOME! THANKS, MOM.
'BYE!
...AN OUTPOURING OF INCREDIBLE GENEROSITY AS MANY OF CENTRAL CITY'S CITIZENS JOINED IN TO HELP WITH THE RESCUE AND RE-BUILDING EFFORTS.
BE BACK IN TIME FOR LUNCH, CHARLIE... AND BE CAREFUL!
AND CHARLIE, DON'T FORGET...

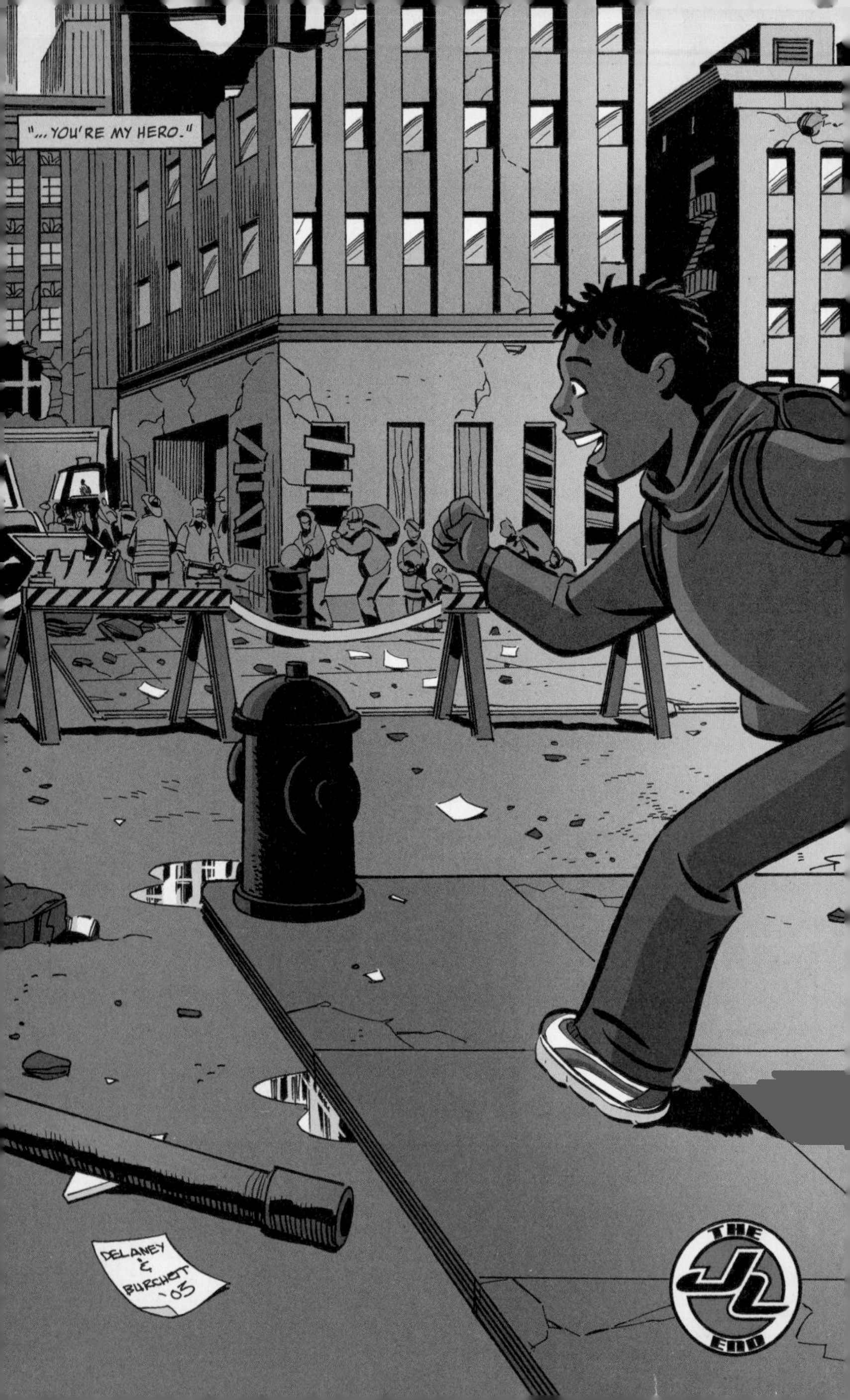
"... YOU'RE MY HERO."
DELANEY & BURCHETT '03
THE END

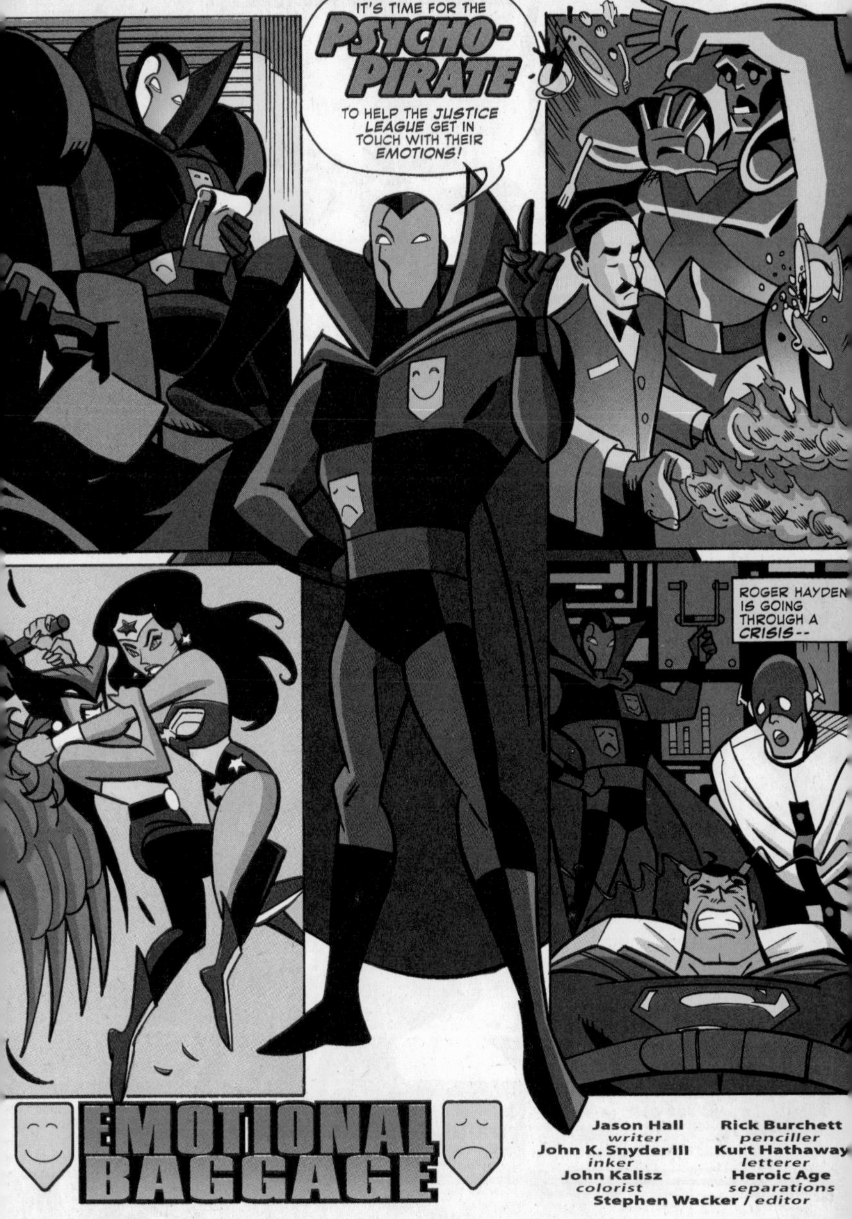
IT'S TIME FOR THE PSYCHO-PIRATE TO HELP THE JUSTICE LEAGUE GET IN TOUCH WITH THEIR EMOTIONS!
ROGER HAYDEN IS GOING THROUGH A CRISIS--

EMOTIONAL BAGGAGE

Jason Hall *writer*
Rick Burchett *penciller*
John K. Snyder III *inker*
Kurt Hathaway *letterer*
John Kalisz *colorist*
Heroic Age *separations*
Stephen Wacker / *editor*

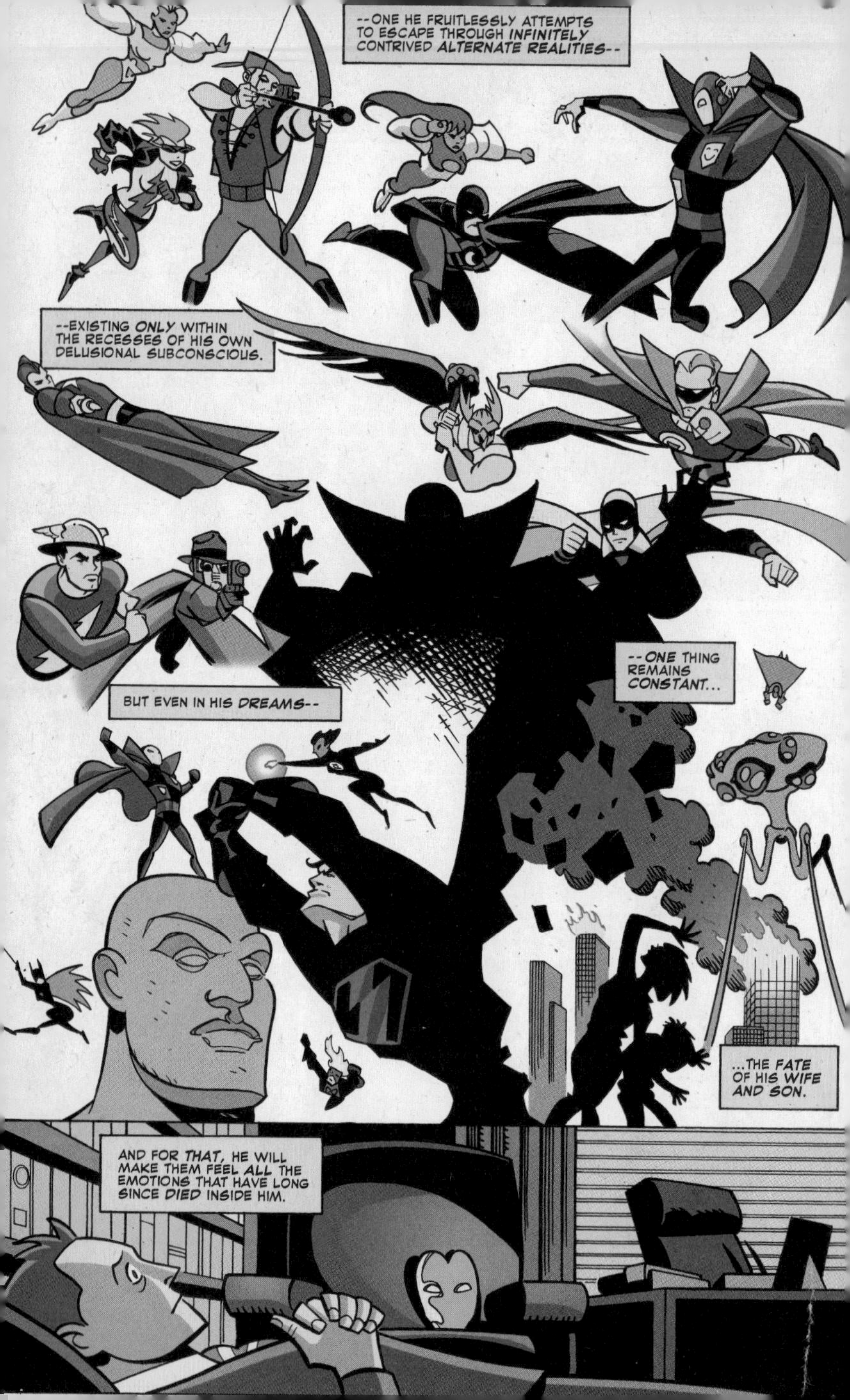
--ONE HE FRUITLESSLY ATTEMPTS TO ESCAPE THROUGH INFINITELY CONTRIVED ALTERNATE REALITIES--
--EXISTING ONLY WITHIN THE RECESSES OF HIS OWN DELUSIONAL SUBCONSCIOUS.
BUT EVEN IN HIS DREAMS--
--ONE THING REMAINS CONSTANT...
...THE FATE OF HIS WIFE AND SON.
AND FOR THAT, HE WILL MAKE THEM FEEL ALL THE EMOTIONS THAT HAVE LONG SINCE DIED INSIDE HIM.

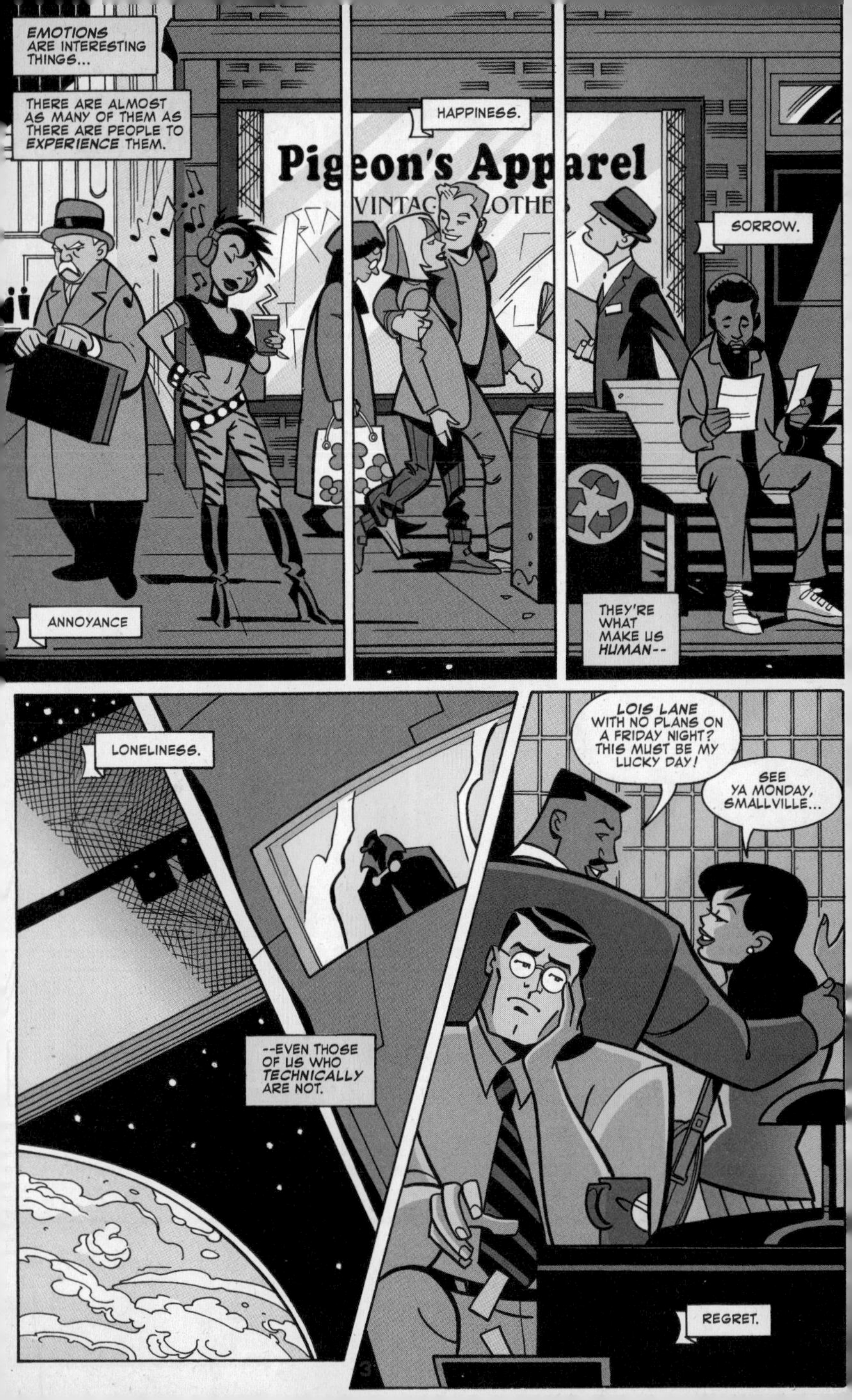
EMOTIONS ARE INTERESTING THINGS...
THERE ARE ALMOST AS MANY OF THEM AS THERE ARE PEOPLE TO EXPERIENCE THEM.
ANNOYANCE
HAPPINESS.
Pigeon's Apparel
VINTAGE CLOTHES
SORROW.
THEY'RE WHAT MAKE US HUMAN--
LONELINESS.
--EVEN THOSE OF US WHO TECHNICALLY ARE NOT.
LOIS LANE WITH NO PLANS ON A FRIDAY NIGHT? THIS MUST BE MY LUCKY DAY!
SEE YA MONDAY, SMALLVILLE...
REGRET.

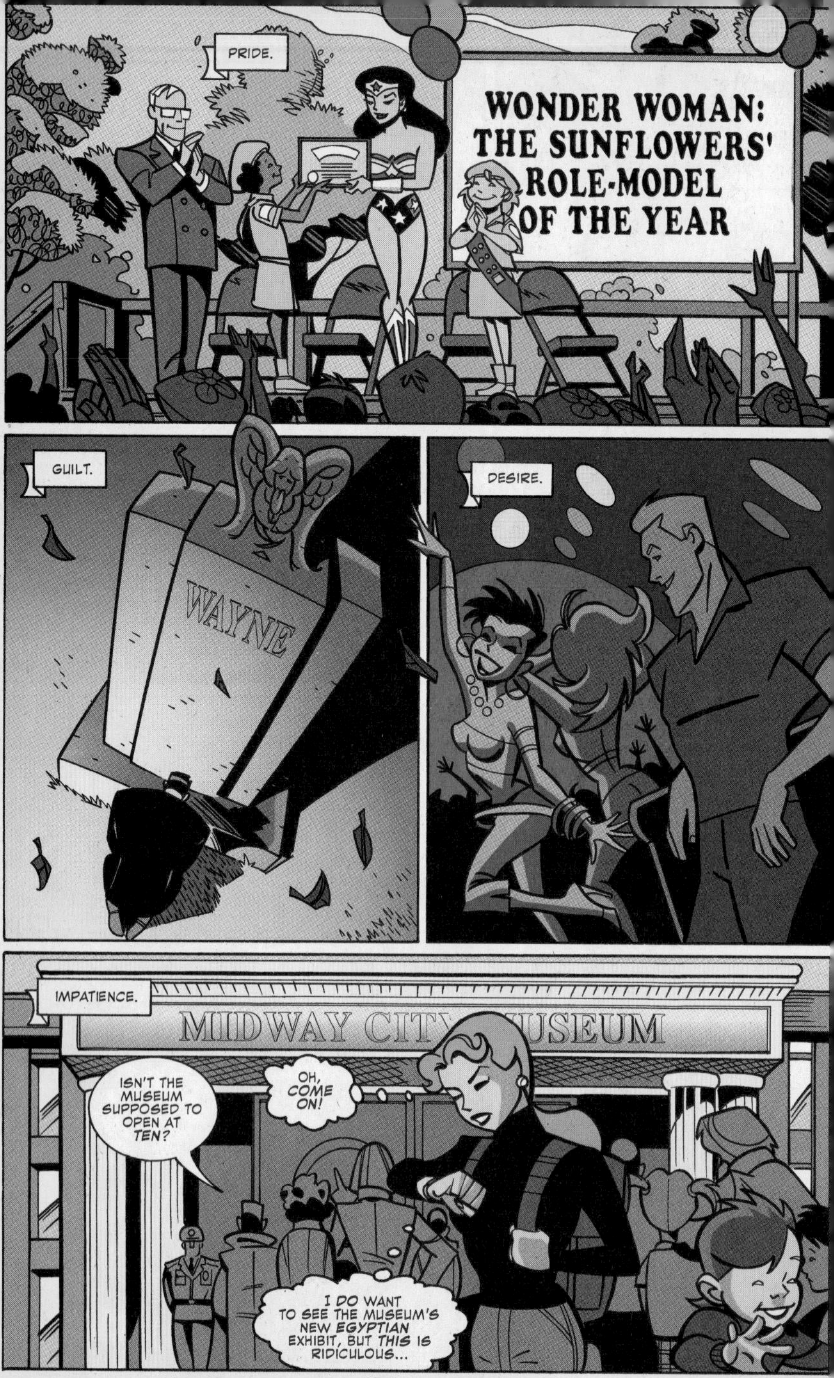
PRIDE.
WONDER WOMAN: THE SUNFLOWERS' ROLE-MODEL OF THE YEAR
GUILT.
WAYNE
DESIRE.
IMPATIENCE.
MIDWAY CITY MUSEUM
ISN'T THE MUSEUM SUPPOSED TO OPEN AT TEN?
OH, COME ON!
I DO WANT TO SEE THE MUSEUM'S NEW EGYPTIAN EXHIBIT, BUT THIS IS RIDICULOUS...

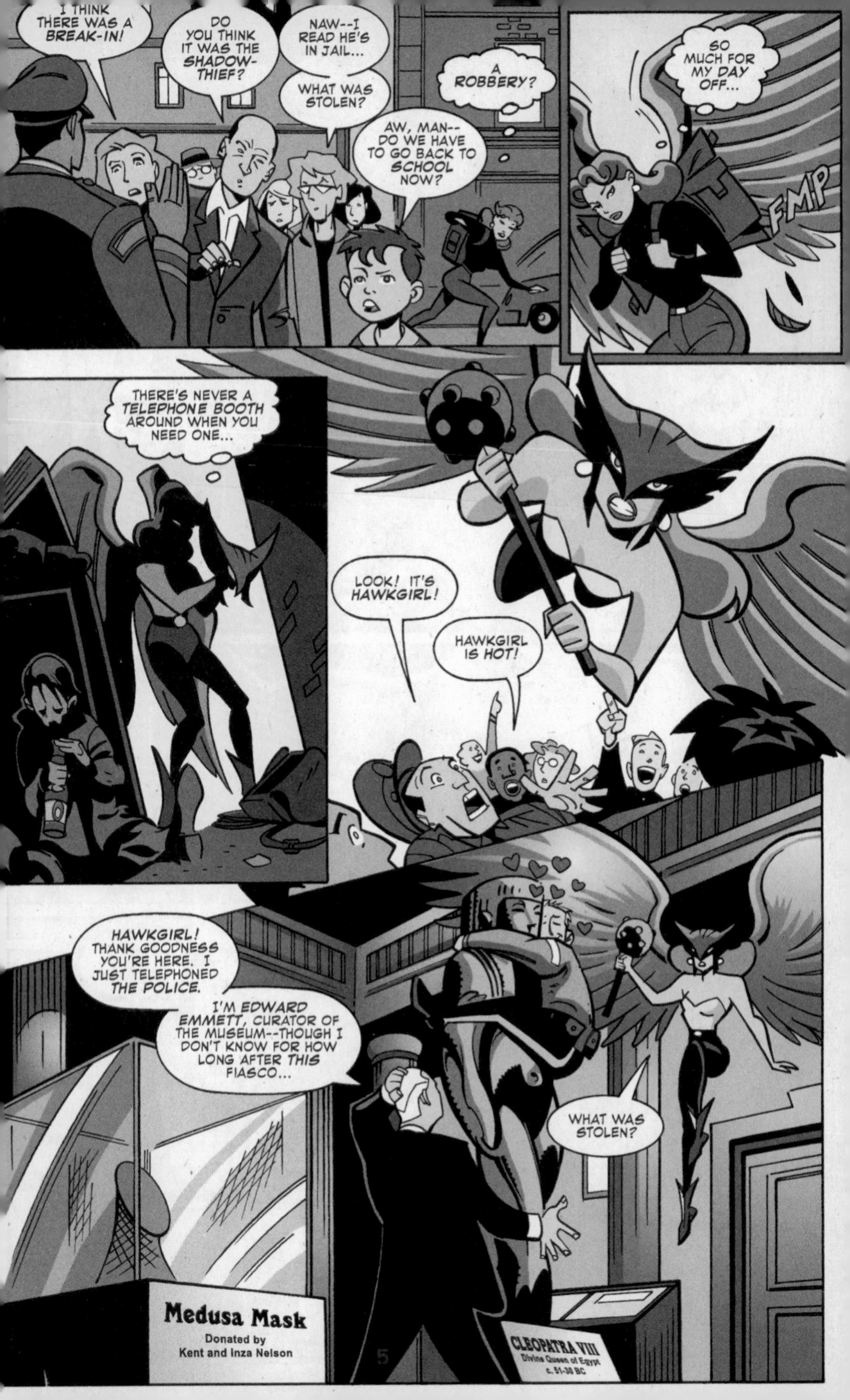
I THINK THERE WAS A BREAK-IN!
DO YOU THINK IT WAS THE SHADOW-THIEF?
NAW--I READ HE'S IN JAIL...
WHAT WAS STOLEN?
A ROBBERY?
AW, MAN--DO WE HAVE TO GO BACK TO SCHOOL NOW?
SO MUCH FOR MY DAY OFF...
FMP
THERE'S NEVER A TELEPHONE BOOTH AROUND WHEN YOU NEED ONE...
LOOK! IT'S HAWKGIRL!
HAWKGIRL IS HOT!
HAWKGIRL! THANK GOODNESS YOU'RE HERE. I JUST TELEPHONED THE POLICE.
I'M EDWARD EMMETT, CURATOR OF THE MUSEUM--THOUGH I DON'T KNOW FOR HOW LONG AFTER THIS FIASCO...
WHAT WAS STOLEN?
Medusa Mask
Donated by
Kent and Inza Nelson
CLEOPATRA VIII
Divine Queen of Egypt
c. 51-30 BC

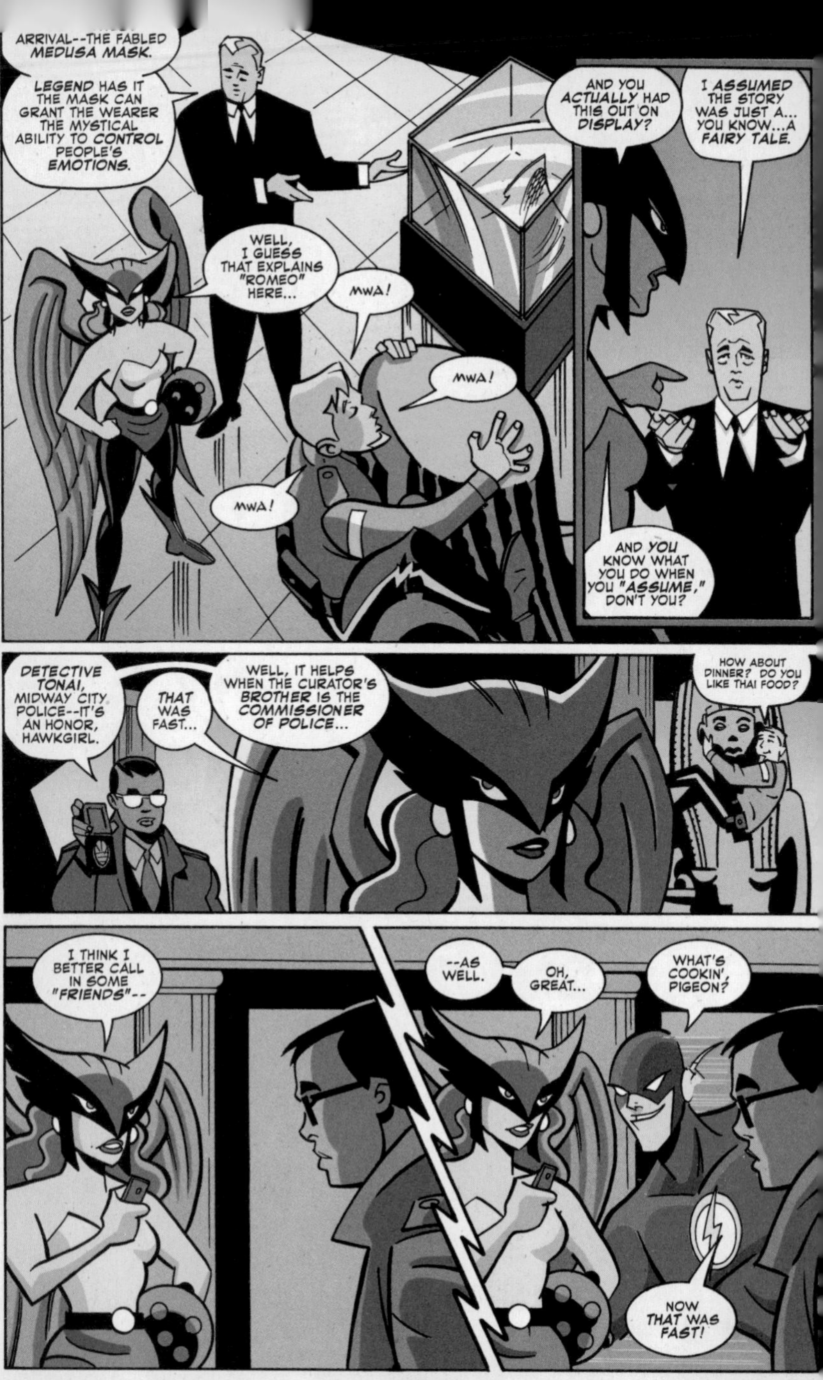

ARRIVAL--THE FABLED MEDUSA MASK.
LEGEND HAS IT THE MASK CAN GRANT THE WEARER THE MYSTICAL ABILITY TO CONTROL PEOPLE'S EMOTIONS.
WELL, I GUESS THAT EXPLAINS "ROMEO" HERE...
MWA!
MWA!
MWA!
AND YOU ACTUALLY HAD THIS OUT ON DISPLAY?
I ASSUMED THE STORY WAS JUST A... YOU KNOW...A FAIRY TALE.
AND YOU KNOW WHAT YOU DO WHEN YOU "ASSUME," DON'T YOU?
DETECTIVE TONAI, MIDWAY CITY POLICE--IT'S AN HONOR, HAWKGIRL.
THAT WAS FAST...
WELL, IT HELPS WHEN THE CURATOR'S BROTHER IS THE COMMISSIONER OF POLICE...
HOW ABOUT DINNER? DO YOU LIKE THAI FOOD?
I THINK I BETTER CALL IN SOME "FRIENDS"--
--AS WELL.
OH, GREAT...
WHAT'S COOKIN', PIGEON?
NOW THAT WAS FAST!

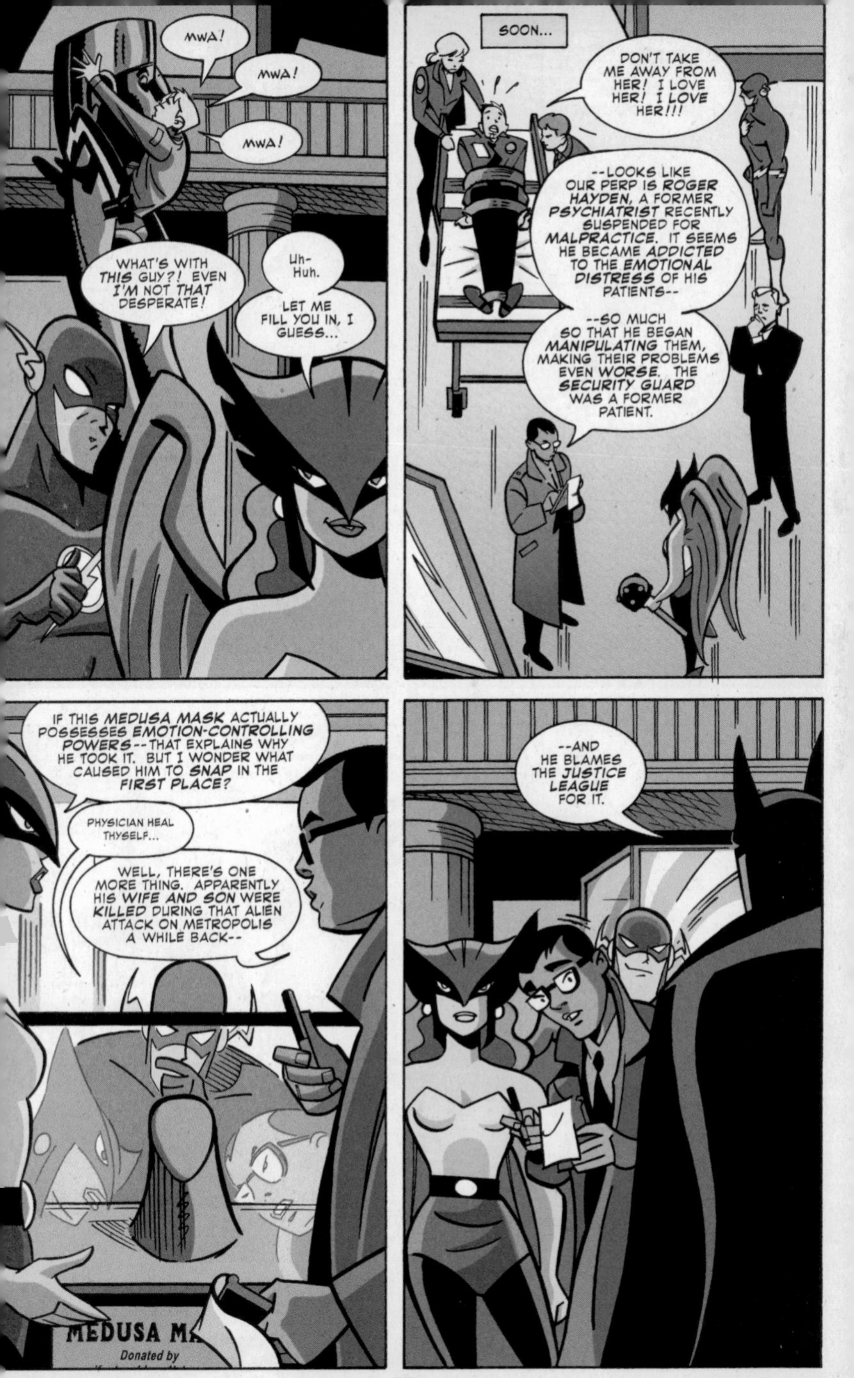
MWA!
MWA!
MWA!
WHAT'S WITH THIS GUY?! EVEN I'M NOT THAT DESPERATE!
Uh-Huh.
LET ME FILL YOU IN, I GUESS...
SOON...
DON'T TAKE ME AWAY FROM HER! I LOVE HER! I LOVE HER!!!
--LOOKS LIKE OUR PERP IS ROGER HAYDEN, A FORMER PSYCHIATRIST RECENTLY SUSPENDED FOR MALPRACTICE. IT SEEMS HE BECAME ADDICTED TO THE EMOTIONAL DISTRESS OF HIS PATIENTS--
--SO MUCH SO THAT HE BEGAN MANIPULATING THEM, MAKING THEIR PROBLEMS EVEN WORSE. THE SECURITY GUARD WAS A FORMER PATIENT.
IF THIS MEDUSA MASK ACTUALLY POSSESSES EMOTION-CONTROLLING POWERS--THAT EXPLAINS WHY HE TOOK IT. BUT I WONDER WHAT CAUSED HIM TO SNAP IN THE FIRST PLACE?
PHYSICIAN HEAL THYSELF...
WELL, THERE'S ONE MORE THING. APPARENTLY HIS WIFE AND SON WERE KILLED DURING THAT ALIEN ATTACK ON METROPOLIS A WHILE BACK--
MEDUSA MA
Donated by
--AND HE BLAMES THE JUSTICE LEAGUE FOR IT.

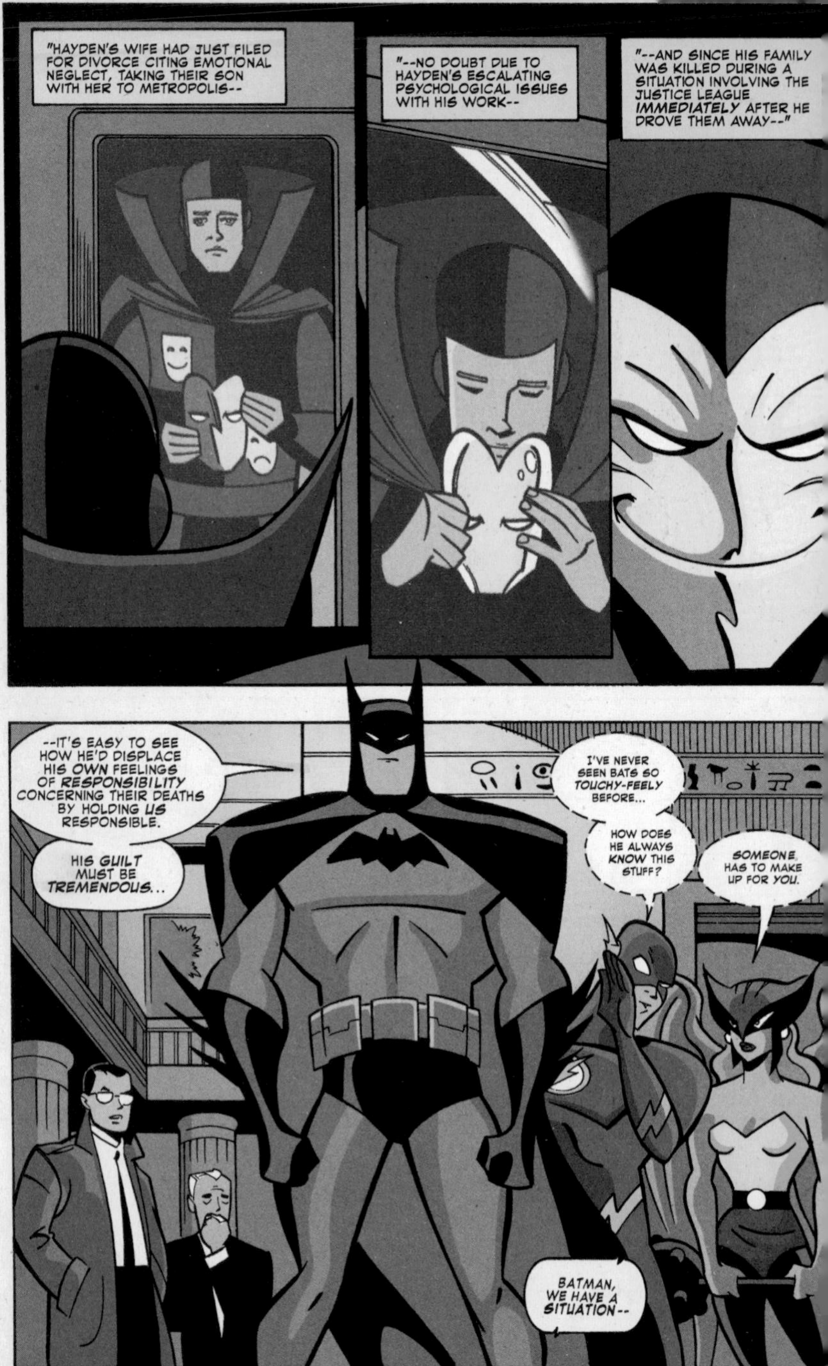
"HAYDEN'S WIFE HAD JUST FILED FOR DIVORCE CITING EMOTIONAL NEGLECT, TAKING THEIR SON WITH HER TO METROPOLIS--
"--NO DOUBT DUE TO HAYDEN'S ESCALATING PSYCHOLOGICAL ISSUES WITH HIS WORK--
"--AND SINCE HIS FAMILY WAS KILLED DURING A SITUATION INVOLVING THE JUSTICE LEAGUE IMMEDIATELY AFTER HE DROVE THEM AWAY--"
--IT'S EASY TO SEE HOW HE'D DISPLACE HIS OWN FEELINGS OF RESPONSIBILITY CONCERNING THEIR DEATHS BY HOLDING US RESPONSIBLE.
HIS GUILT MUST BE TREMENDOUS...
I'VE NEVER SEEN BATS SO TOUCHY-FEELY BEFORE...
HOW DOES HE ALWAYS KNOW THIS STUFF?
SOMEONE HAS TO MAKE UP FOR YOU.
BATMAN, WE HAVE A SITUATION--

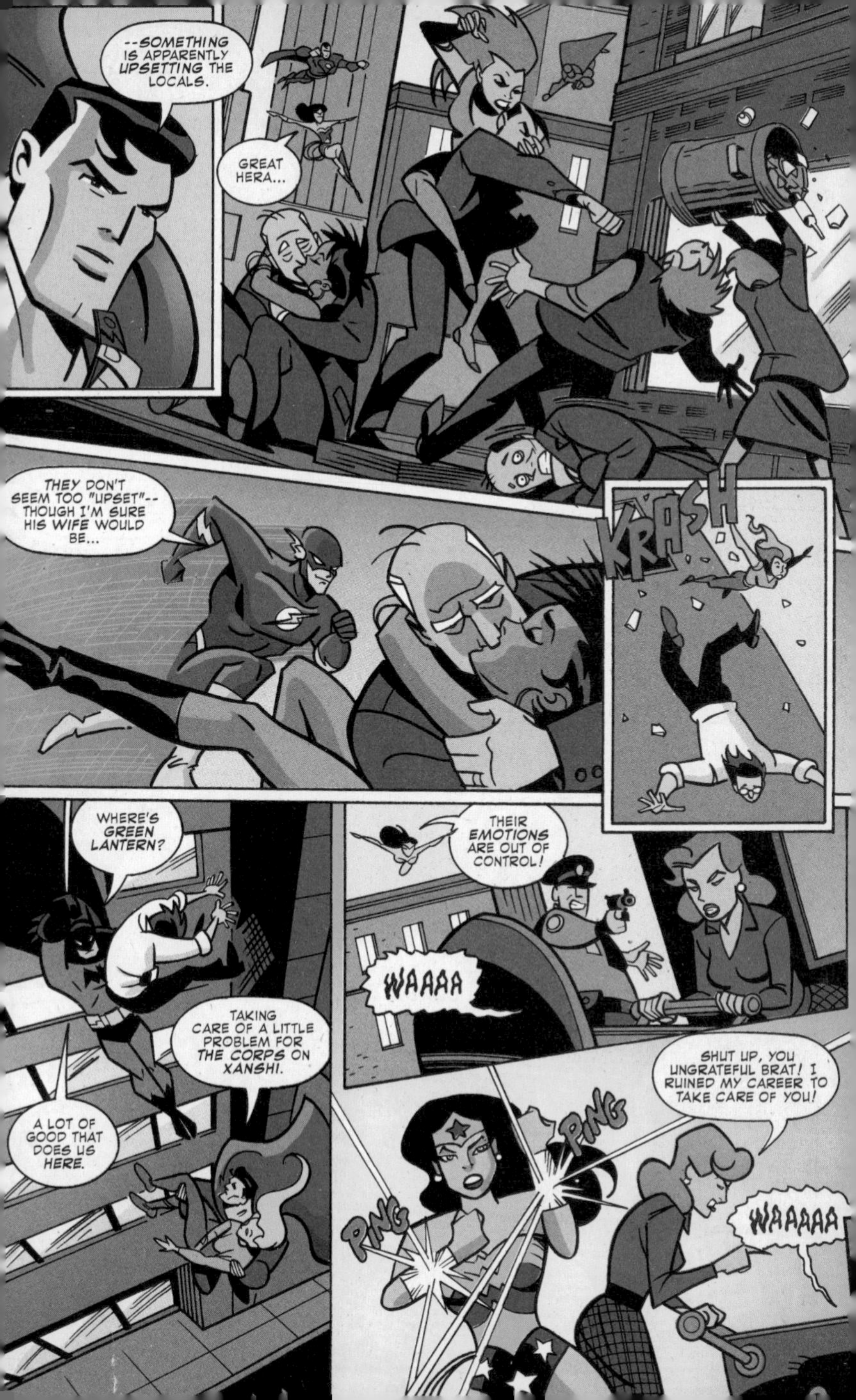
--SOMETHING IS APPARENTLY UPSETTING THE LOCALS.
GREAT HERA...
THEY DON'T SEEM TOO "UPSET"-- THOUGH I'M SURE HIS WIFE WOULD BE...
KRASH
WHERE'S GREEN LANTERN?
TAKING CARE OF A LITTLE PROBLEM FOR THE CORPS ON XANSHI.
A LOT OF GOOD THAT DOES US HERE.
THEIR EMOTIONS ARE OUT OF CONTROL!
WAAAA
SHUT UP, YOU UNGRATEFUL BRAT! I RUINED MY CAREER TO TAKE CARE OF YOU!
PING
PING
WAAAAA

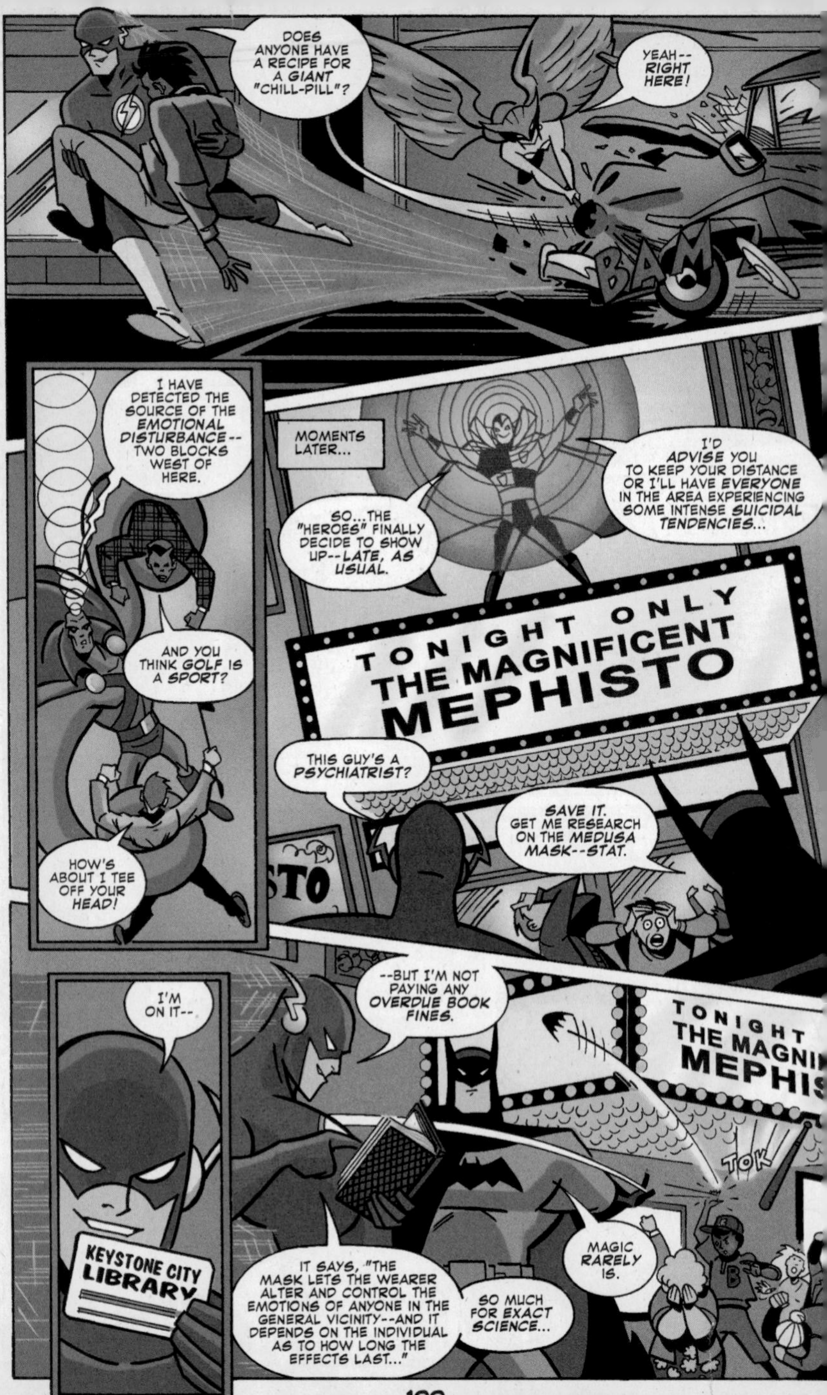

DOES ANYONE HAVE A RECIPE FOR A GIANT "CHILL-PILL"?
YEAH-- RIGHT HERE!
BAM
I HAVE DETECTED THE SOURCE OF THE EMOTIONAL DISTURBANCE-- TWO BLOCKS WEST OF HERE.
AND YOU THINK GOLF IS A SPORT?
HOW'S ABOUT I TEE OFF YOUR HEAD!
MOMENTS LATER...
SO...THE "HEROES" FINALLY DECIDE TO SHOW UP--LATE, AS USUAL.
I'D ADVISE YOU TO KEEP YOUR DISTANCE OR I'LL HAVE EVERYONE IN THE AREA EXPERIENCING SOME INTENSE SUICIDAL TENDENCIES...
TONIGHT ONLY THE MAGNIFICENT MEPHISTO
THIS GUY'S A PSYCHIATRIST?
SAVE IT. GET ME RESEARCH ON THE MEDUSA MASK--STAT.
I'M ON IT--
--BUT I'M NOT PAYING ANY OVERDUE BOOK FINES.
KEYSTONE CITY LIBRARY
IT SAYS, "THE MASK LETS THE WEARER ALTER AND CONTROL THE EMOTIONS OF ANYONE IN THE GENERAL VICINITY--AND IT DEPENDS ON THE INDIVIDUAL AS TO HOW LONG THE EFFECTS LAST..."
SO MUCH FOR EXACT SCIENCE...
MAGIC RARELY IS.
TOK

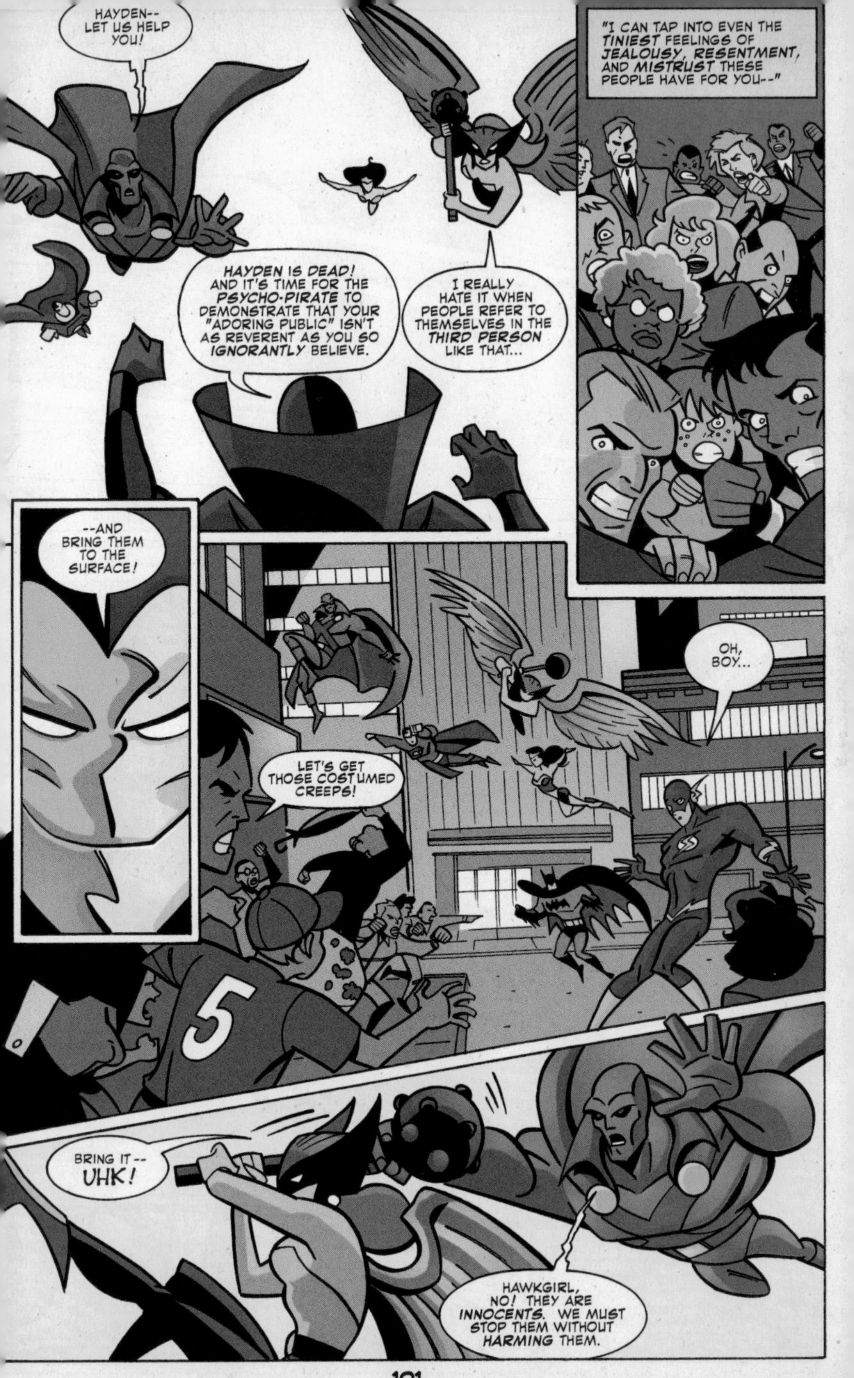
HAYDEN--
LET US HELP YOU!
"I CAN TAP INTO EVEN THE TINIEST FEELINGS OF JEALOUSY, RESENTMENT, AND MISTRUST THESE PEOPLE HAVE FOR YOU--"
HAYDEN IS DEAD! AND IT'S TIME FOR THE PSYCHO-PIRATE TO DEMONSTRATE THAT YOUR "ADORING PUBLIC" ISN'T AS REVERENT AS YOU SO IGNORANTLY BELIEVE.
I REALLY HATE IT WHEN PEOPLE REFER TO THEMSELVES IN THE THIRD PERSON LIKE THAT...
--AND BRING THEM TO THE SURFACE!
OH, BOY...
LET'S GET THOSE COSTUMED CREEPS!
BRING IT -- UHK!
HAWKGIRL, NO! THEY ARE INNOCENTS. WE MUST STOP THEM WITHOUT HARMING THEM.

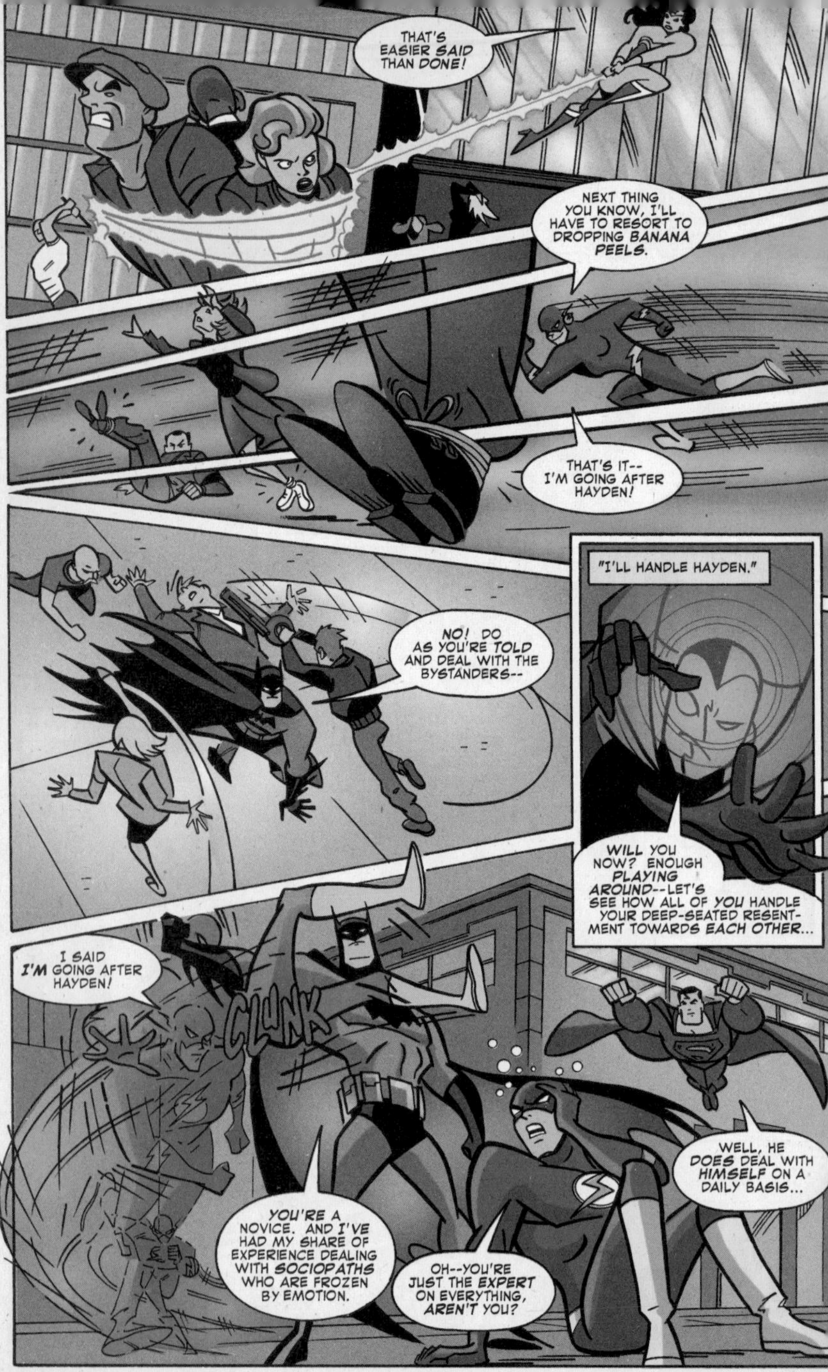
THAT'S EASIER SAID THAN DONE!
NEXT THING YOU KNOW, I'LL HAVE TO RESORT TO DROPPING BANANA PEELS.
THAT'S IT-- I'M GOING AFTER HAYDEN!
NO! DO AS YOU'RE TOLD AND DEAL WITH THE BYSTANDERS--
"I'LL HANDLE HAYDEN."
WILL YOU NOW? ENOUGH PLAYING AROUND--LET'S SEE HOW ALL OF YOU HANDLE YOUR DEEP-SEATED RESENTMENT TOWARDS EACH OTHER...
I SAID I'M GOING AFTER HAYDEN!
CLUNK
YOU'RE A NOVICE. AND I'VE HAD MY SHARE OF EXPERIENCE DEALING WITH SOCIOPATHS WHO ARE FROZEN BY EMOTION.
OH--YOU'RE JUST THE EXPERT ON EVERYTHING, AREN'T YOU?
WELL, HE DOES DEAL WITH HIMSELF ON A DAILY BASIS...

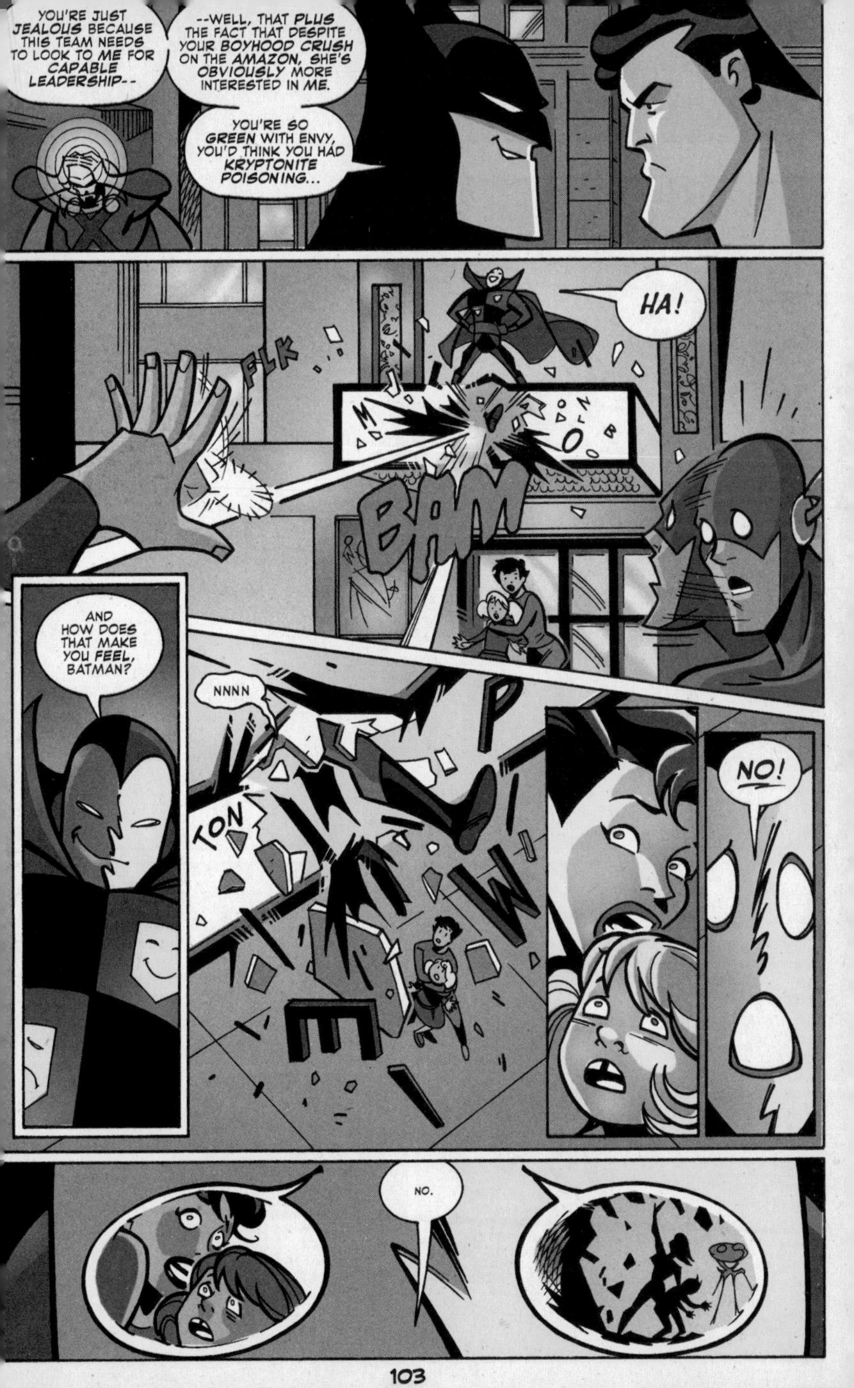

YOU'RE JUST JEALOUS BECAUSE THIS TEAM NEEDS TO LOOK TO ME FOR CAPABLE LEADERSHIP--
--WELL, THAT PLUS THE FACT THAT DESPITE YOUR BOYHOOD CRUSH ON THE AMAZON, SHE'S OBVIOUSLY MORE INTERESTED IN ME.
YOU'RE SO GREEN WITH ENVY, YOU'D THINK YOU HAD KRYPTONITE POISONING...
HA!
FLK
BAM
AND HOW DOES THAT MAKE YOU FEEL, BATMAN?
NNNN
TON
NO!
NO.

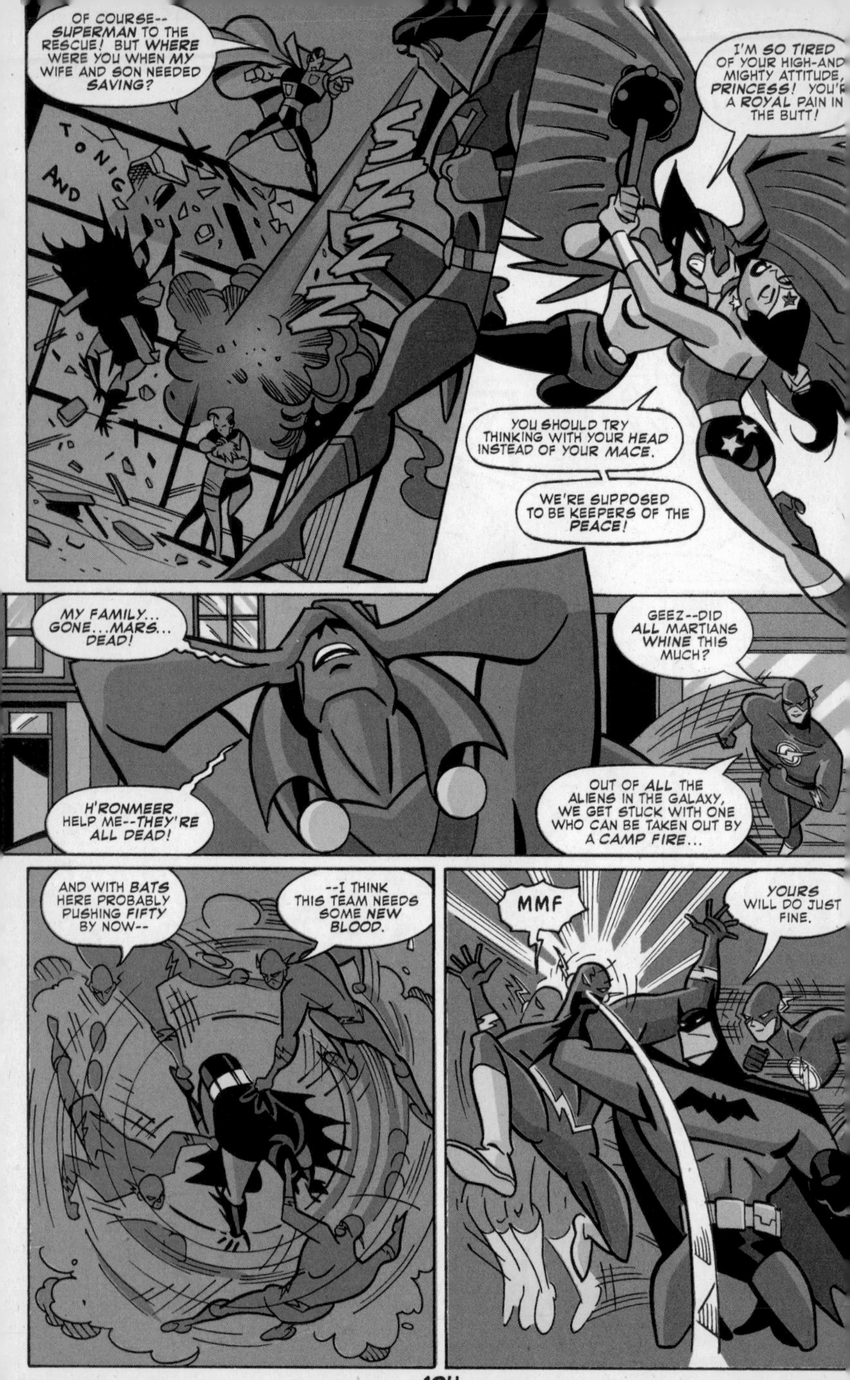
OF COURSE--
SUPERMAN TO THE RESCUE! BUT WHERE WERE YOU WHEN MY WIFE AND SON NEEDED SAVING?
TONIG AND
I'M SO TIRED OF YOUR HIGH-AND MIGHTY ATTITUDE, PRINCESS! YOU'R A ROYAL PAIN IN THE BUTT!
YOU SHOULD TRY THINKING WITH YOUR HEAD INSTEAD OF YOUR MACE.
WE'RE SUPPOSED TO BE KEEPERS OF THE PEACE!
MY FAMILY... GONE...MARS... DEAD!
GEEZ--DID ALL MARTIANS WHINE THIS MUCH?
H'RONMEER HELP ME--THEY'RE ALL DEAD!
OUT OF ALL THE ALIENS IN THE GALAXY, WE GET STUCK WITH ONE WHO CAN BE TAKEN OUT BY A CAMP FIRE...
AND WITH BATS HERE PROBABLY PUSHING FIFTY BY NOW--
--I THINK THIS TEAM NEEDS SOME NEW BLOOD.
MMF
YOURS WILL DO JUST FINE.

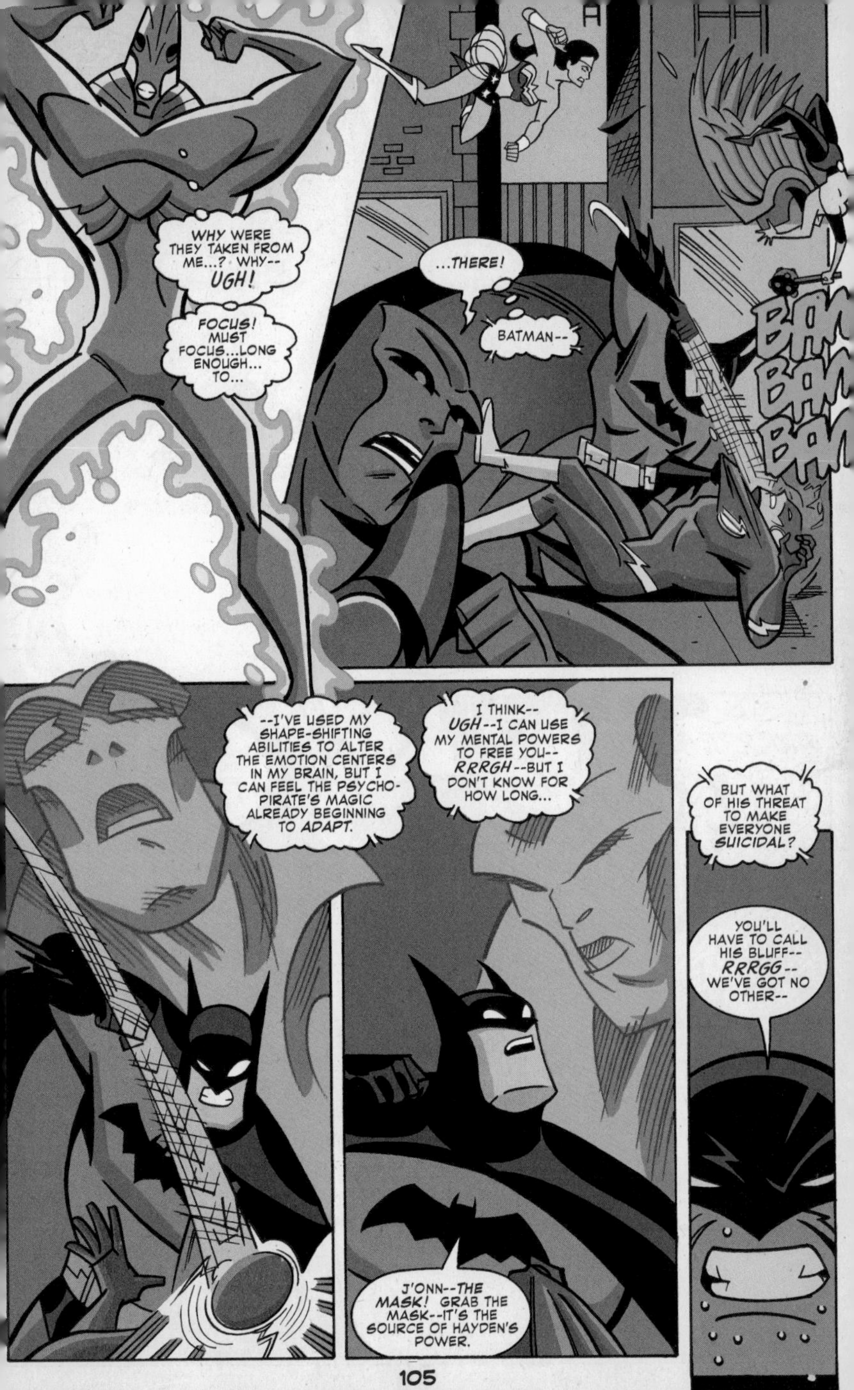
WHY WERE THEY TAKEN FROM ME...? WHY-- UGH!
FOCUS! MUST FOCUS...LONG ENOUGH... TO...
...THERE!
BATMAN--
BAM BAM BAM
--I'VE USED MY SHAPE-SHIFTING ABILITIES TO ALTER THE EMOTION CENTERS IN MY BRAIN, BUT I CAN FEEL THE PSYCHO-PIRATE'S MAGIC ALREADY BEGINNING TO ADAPT.
I THINK-- UGH--I CAN USE MY MENTAL POWERS TO FREE YOU-- RRRGH--BUT I DON'T KNOW FOR HOW LONG...
J'ONN--THE MASK! GRAB THE MASK--IT'S THE SOURCE OF HAYDEN'S POWER.
BUT WHAT OF HIS THREAT TO MAKE EVERYONE SUICIDAL?
YOU'LL HAVE TO CALL HIS BLUFF-- RRRGG-- WE'VE GOT NO OTHER--

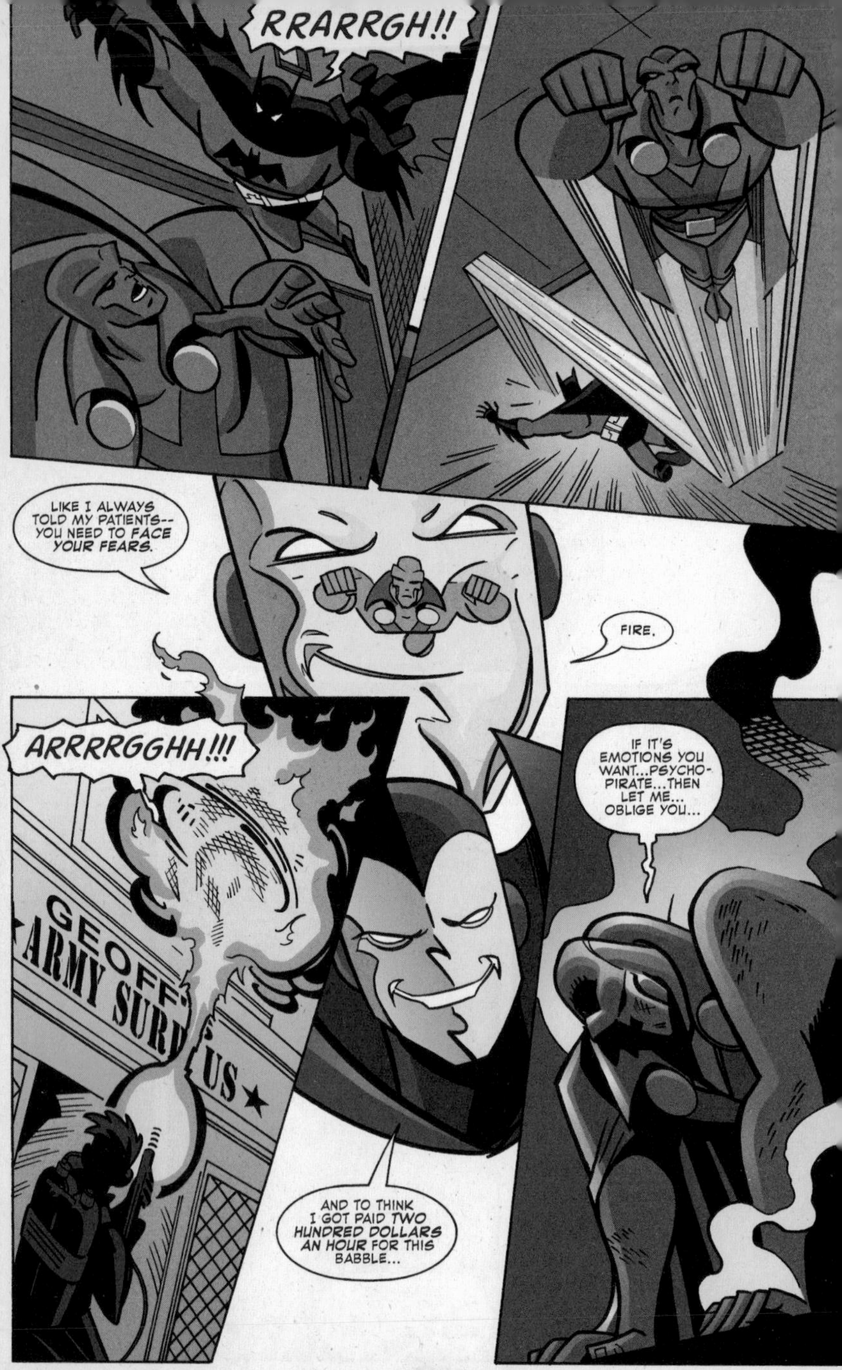

RRARRGH!!
LIKE I ALWAYS TOLD MY PATIENTS-- YOU NEED TO FACE YOUR FEARS.
FIRE.
ARRRRGGHH!!!
GEOFF'
ARMY SURP
US
AND TO THINK I GOT PAID TWO HUNDRED DOLLARS AN HOUR FOR THIS BABBLE...
IF IT'S EMOTIONS YOU WANT...PSYCHO-PIRATE...THEN LET ME... OBLIGE YOU...

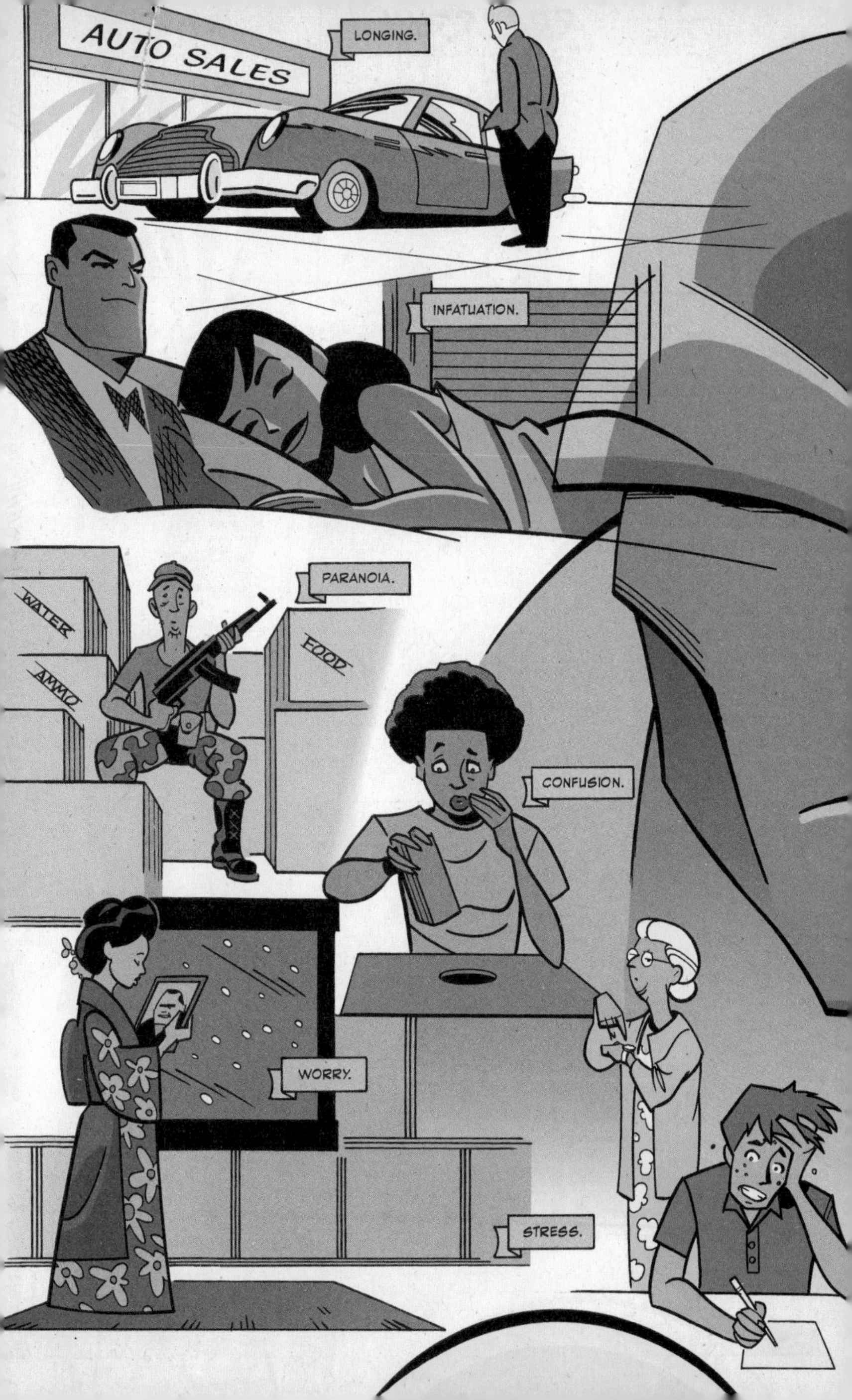

AUTO SALES
LONGING.
INFATUATION.
PARANOIA.
WATER
FOOD
AMMO
CONFUSION.
WORRY.
STRESS.

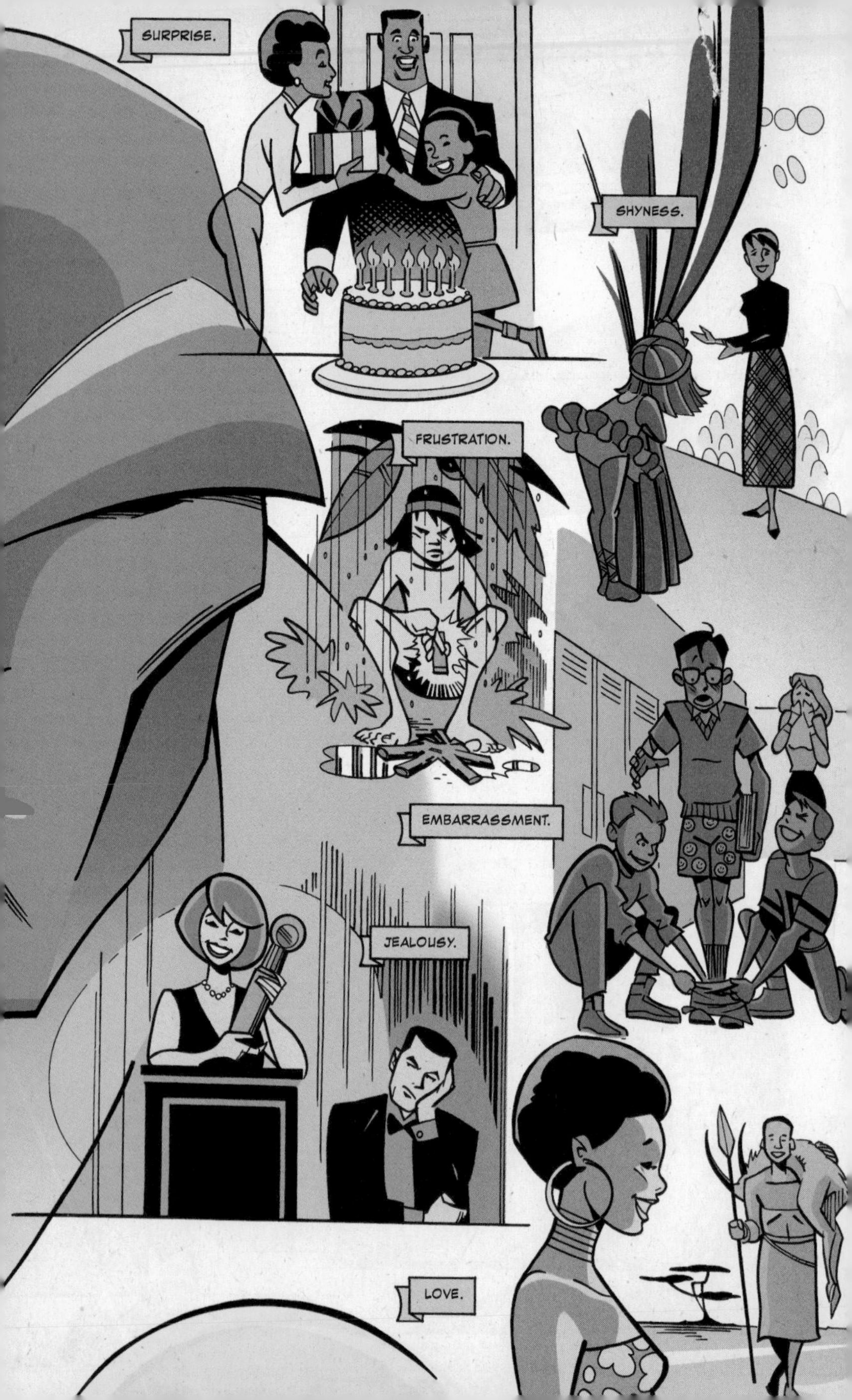
SURPRISE.
SHYNESS.
FRUSTRATION.
EMBARRASSMENT.
JEALOUSY.
LOVE.

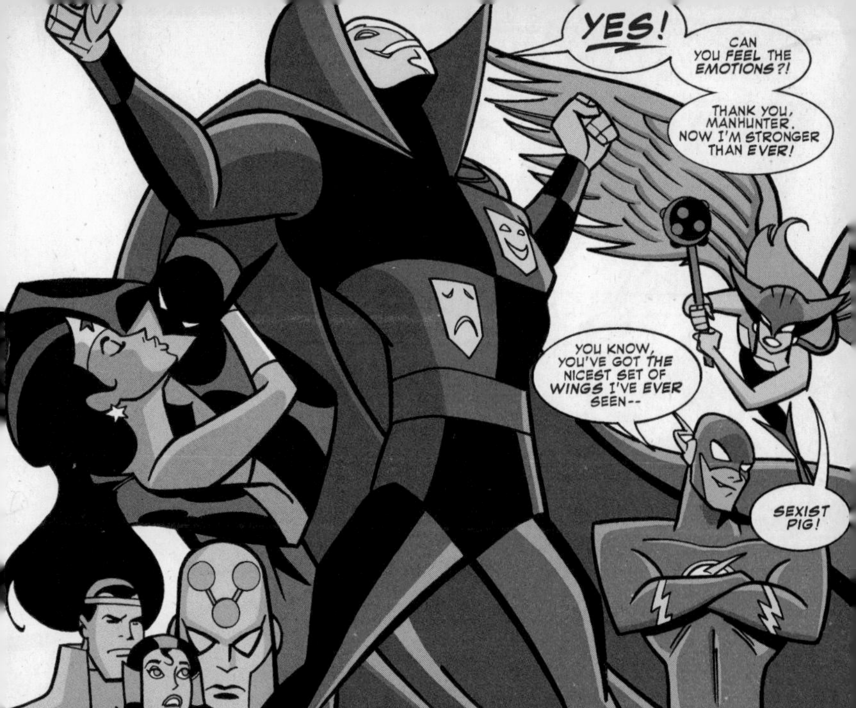
YES!
CAN YOU FEEL THE EMOTIONS?!
THANK YOU, MANHUNTER. NOW I'M STRONGER THAN EVER!
YOU KNOW, YOU'VE GOT THE NICEST SET OF WINGS I'VE EVER SEEN--
SEXIST PIG!
KRYPTON... BRAINIAC... FATHER...
ARRGHH-- NO! NOT AGAIN--

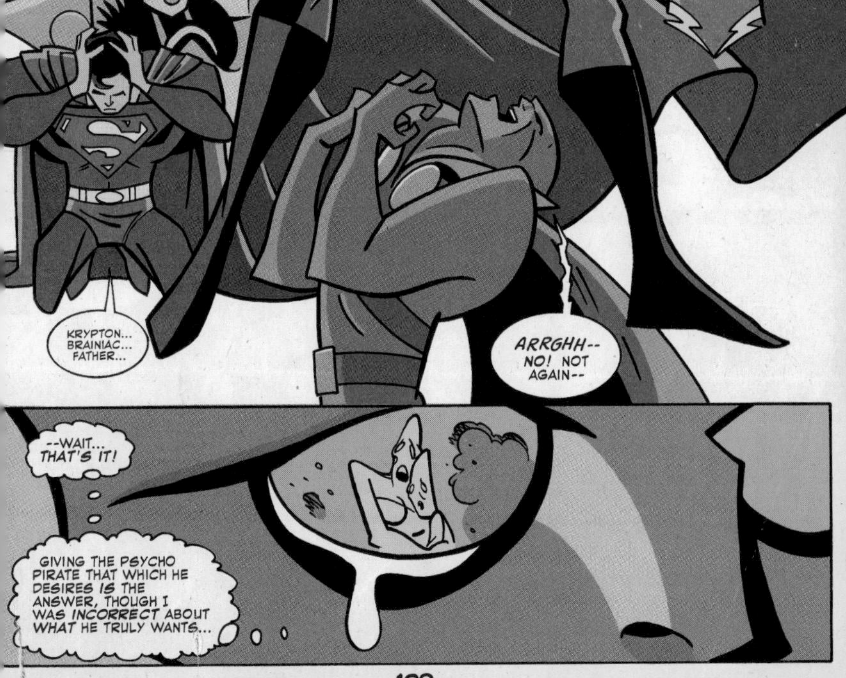
--WAIT... THAT'S IT!
GIVING THE PSYCHO PIRATE THAT WHICH HE DESIRES IS THE ANSWER, THOUGH I WAS INCORRECT ABOUT WHAT HE TRULY WANTS...

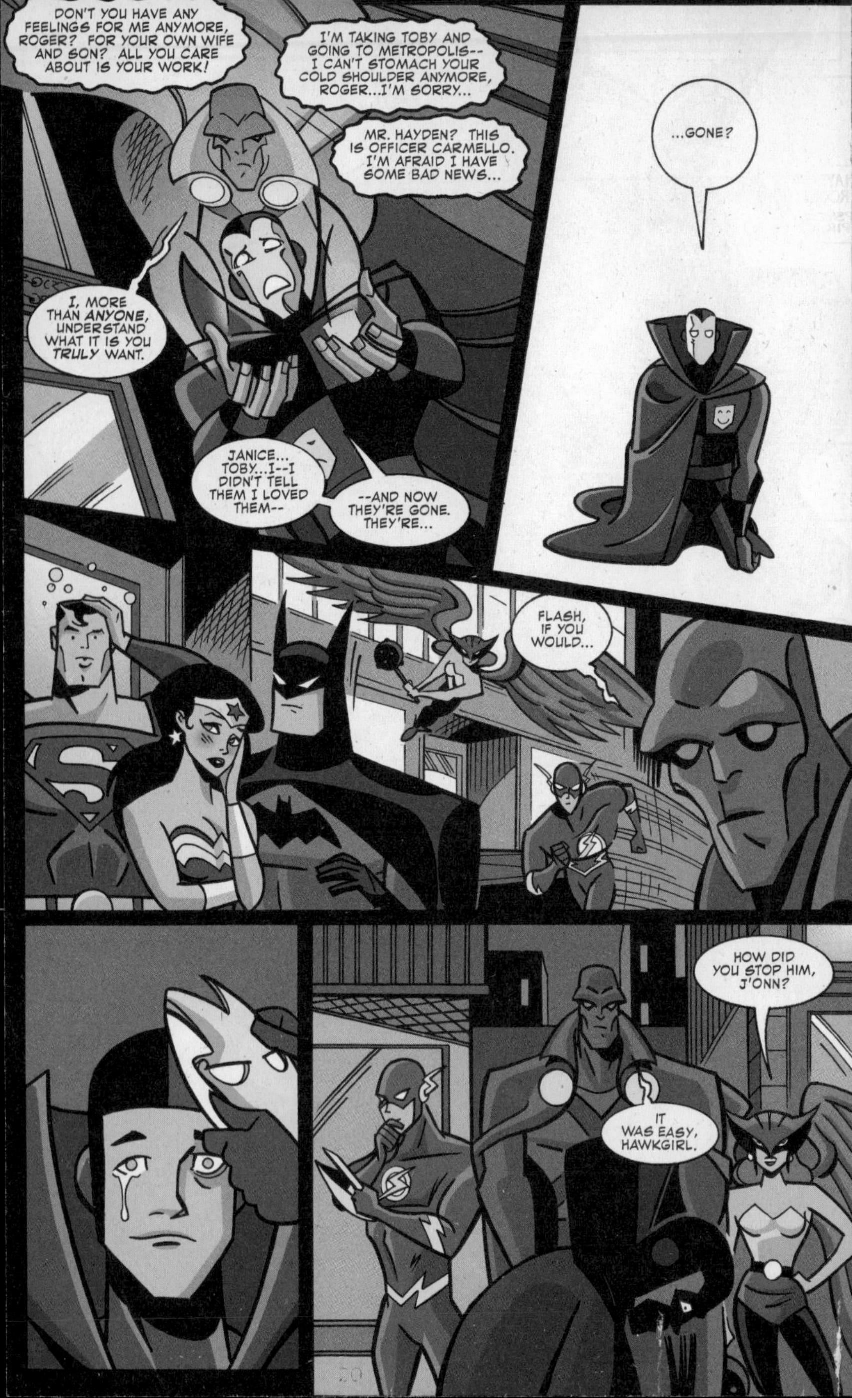
DON'T YOU HAVE ANY FEELINGS FOR ME ANYMORE, ROGER? FOR YOUR OWN WIFE AND SON? ALL YOU CARE ABOUT IS YOUR WORK!
I'M TAKING TOBY AND GOING TO METROPOLIS--I CAN'T STOMACH YOUR COLD SHOULDER ANYMORE, ROGER...I'M SORRY...
MR. HAYDEN? THIS IS OFFICER CARMELLO. I'M AFRAID I HAVE SOME BAD NEWS...
I, MORE THAN ANYONE, UNDERSTAND WHAT IT IS YOU TRULY WANT.
JANICE... TOBY...I--I DIDN'T TELL THEM I LOVED THEM--
--AND NOW THEY'RE GONE. THEY'RE...
...GONE?
FLASH, IF YOU WOULD...
HOW DID YOU STOP HIM, J'ONN?
IT WAS EASY, HAWKGIRL.

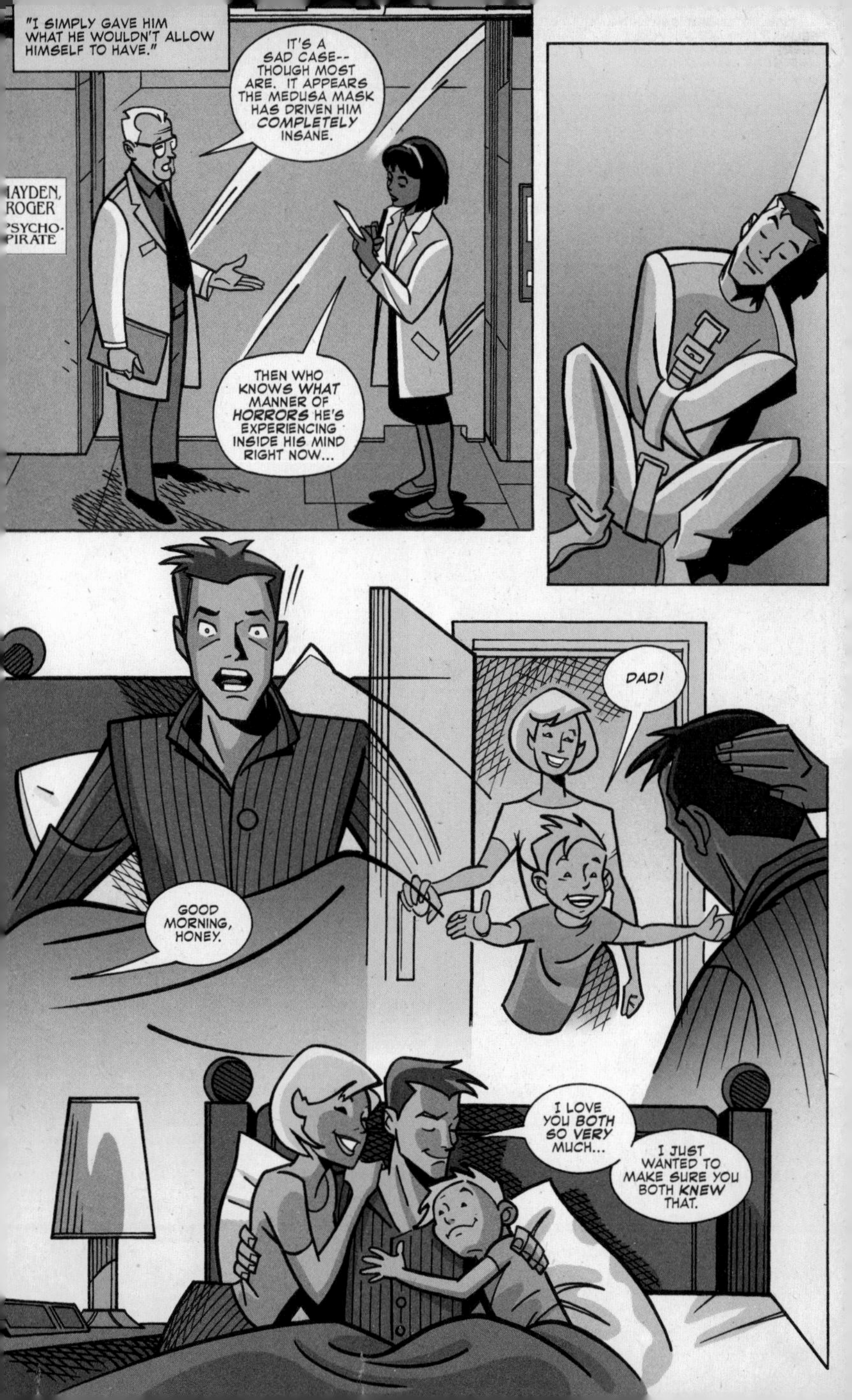
"I SIMPLY GAVE HIM WHAT HE WOULDN'T ALLOW HIMSELF TO HAVE."
IT'S A SAD CASE-- THOUGH MOST ARE. IT APPEARS THE MEDUSA MASK HAS DRIVEN HIM COMPLETELY INSANE.
HAYDEN, ROGER PSYCHO-PIRATE
THEN WHO KNOWS WHAT MANNER OF HORRORS HE'S EXPERIENCING INSIDE HIS MIND RIGHT NOW...
DAD!
GOOD MORNING, HONEY.
I LOVE YOU BOTH SO VERY MUCH...
I JUST WANTED TO MAKE SURE YOU BOTH KNEW THAT.

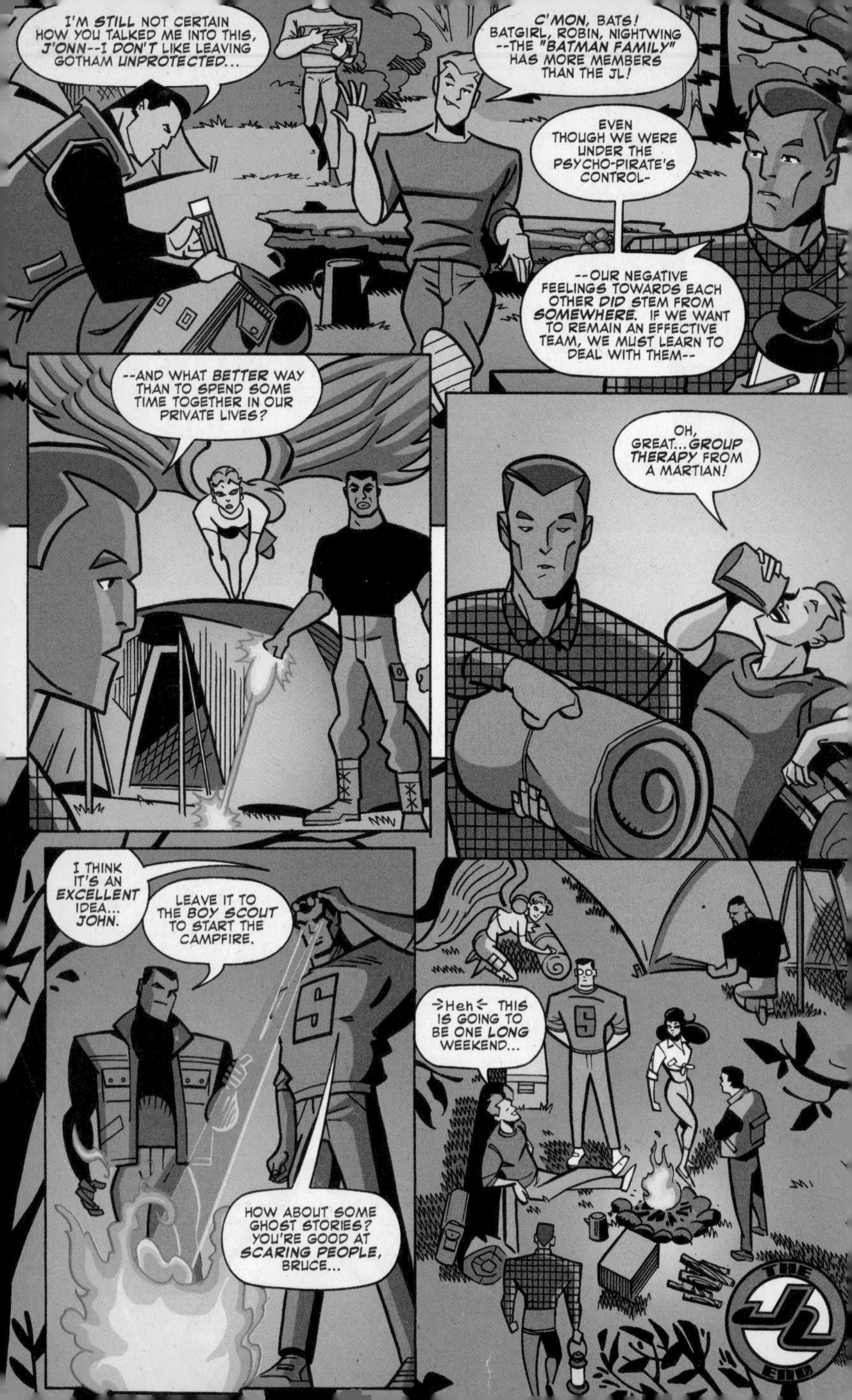

I'M STILL NOT CERTAIN HOW YOU TALKED ME INTO THIS, J'ONN--I DON'T LIKE LEAVING GOTHAM UNPROTECTED...
C'MON, BATS! BATGIRL, ROBIN, NIGHTWING --THE "BATMAN FAMILY" HAS MORE MEMBERS THAN THE JL!
EVEN THOUGH WE WERE UNDER THE PSYCHO-PIRATE'S CONTROL-
--OUR NEGATIVE FEELINGS TOWARDS EACH OTHER DID STEM FROM SOMEWHERE. IF WE WANT TO REMAIN AN EFFECTIVE TEAM, WE MUST LEARN TO DEAL WITH THEM--
--AND WHAT BETTER WAY THAN TO SPEND SOME TIME TOGETHER IN OUR PRIVATE LIVES?
OH, GREAT...GROUP THERAPY FROM A MARTIAN!
I THINK IT'S AN EXCELLENT IDEA... JOHN.
LEAVE IT TO THE BOY SCOUT TO START THE CAMPFIRE.
HOW ABOUT SOME GHOST STORIES? YOU'RE GOOD AT SCARING PEOPLE, BRUCE...
Heh THIS IS GOING TO BE ONE LONG WEEKEND...
THE JL END